Lexicon

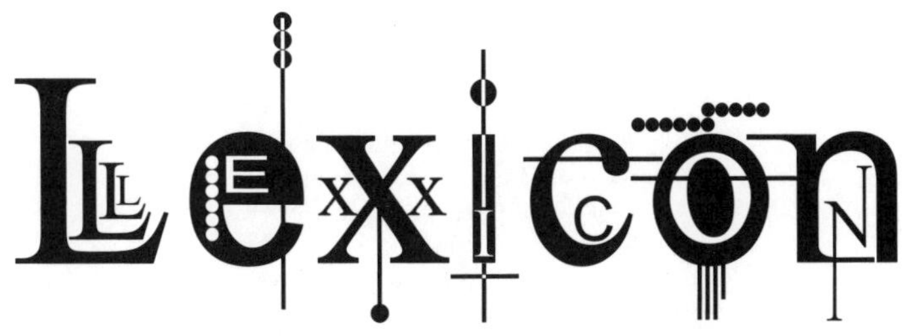

MAX BARRY

THE PENGUIN PRESS
New York
2013

THE PENGUIN PRESS
Published by the Penguin Group
Penguin Group (USA) Inc., 375 Hudson Street,
New York, New York 10014, USA

USA • Canada • UK • Ireland • Australia
New Zealand • India • South Africa • China

Penguin Books Ltd, Registered Offices: 80 Strand, London WC2R 0RL, England
For more information about the Penguin Group visit penguin.com

Library of Congress Cataloging-in-Publication Data

Barry, Max.
Lexicon : a novel / Max Barry.
pages cm
ISBN 978-1-59420-538-5 (hardcover) — ISBN 978-1-101-60490-8
1. Persuasion (Psychology)—Fiction. 2. Secret societies—Fiction.
3. Linguists—Fiction. 4. Romantic suspense fiction. I. Title.
PS3552.A7424L49 2013
813'.54—dc23
2012046980

Printed in the United States of America
1 3 5 7 9 10 8 6 4 2

Book design by Gretchen Achilles

For Jen, again

Every story written is
marks upon a page
The same marks,
repeated, only
differently arranged

[1]

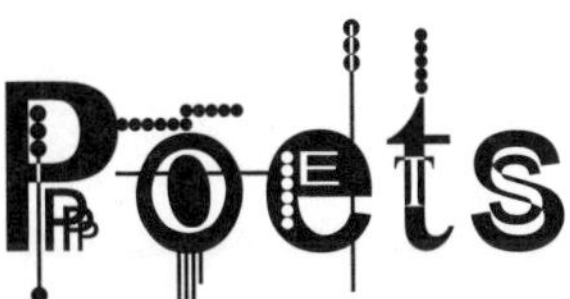

Poets

Now when Ra, the greatest of the gods, was created, his father had given him a secret name, so awful that no man dared to seek for it, and so pregnant with power that all the other gods desired to know and possess it too.

—F. H. BROOKSBANK, *The Story of Ra and Isis*

[ONE]

"He's coming around."

"Their eyes always do that."

The world was blurry. There was a pressure in his right eye. He said, *Urk*.

"Fuck!"

"Get the—"

"It's too late, forget it. Take it out."

"It's not too late. Hold him." A shape grew in his vision. He smelled alcohol and stale urine. "Wil? Can you hear me?"

He reached for his face, to brush away whatever was pressing there.

"Get his—" Fingers closed around his wrist. "Wil, it's important that you not touch your face."

"Why is he conscious?"

"I don't know."

"You fucked something up."

"I didn't. Give me that."

A rustling. He said, *Hnnn. Hnnnn.*

"Stop moving." He felt breath in his ear, hot and intimate. "There is a needle in your eyeball. Do not move."

He did not move. Something trilled, something electronic. "Ah, shit, shit."

"What?"

"They're here."

"Already?"

"Two of them, it says. We have to go."

"I'm already in."

"You can't do it while he's conscious. You'll fry his brain."

"I probably won't."

He said, "Pubbaleeese doo nut kill mee."

An unsnapping of clasps. "I'm doing it."

"You can't do it while he's conscious, and we're out of time, and he probably isn't even the guy."

"If you're not helping, move out of the way."

Wil said, "I . . . need . . . to . . . sneeze."

"Sneezing would be a bad move at this point, Wil." Weight descended on his chest. His vision darkened. His eyeball moved slightly. "This may hurt."

A *snick*. A low electronic whine. A rail spike drove into his brain. He screamed.

"You're toasting him."

"You're okay, Wil. You're okay."

"He's . . . aw, he's bleeding from his eye."

"Wil, I need you to answer a few questions. It's important that you answer truthfully. Do you understand?"

No no no—

"First question. Would you describe yourself as more of a dog person or cat person?"

What—

"Come on, Wil. Dog or cat?"

"I can't read this. This is why we don't do it when they're conscious."

"Answer the question. The pain stops when you answer the questions."

Dog! he screamed. *Dog please dog!*

"Was that dog?"

"Yeah. He tried to say dog."

"Good. Very good. One down. What's your favorite color?"

Something chimed. "Fuck! Oh, fuck me!"

"What?"

"Wolf's here!"

"That can't be right."

"It says it right fucking here!"

"Show me."

Blue! he screamed into silence.

"He responded. You see?"

"Yes, I saw! Who cares? We have to leave. We have to *leave.*"

"Wil, I want you to think of a number between one and a hundred."

"Oh, Jesus."

"Any number you like. Go on."

I don't know—

"Concentrate, Wil."

"Wolf is coming and you're dicking around with a live probe on the wrong guy. Think about what you're doing."

Four I choose four—

"Four."

"I saw it."

"That's good, Wil. Only two questions left. Do you love your family?"

Yes no what kind of a—

"He's all over the place."

I don't have—I guess yes I mean yes everybody loves—

"Wait, wait. Okay. I see it. Christ, that's weird."

"One more question. Why did you do it?"

What—I don't—

"Simple question, Wil. Why'd you do it?"

Do what do what what what—

"Borderline. As in, borderline on about eight different segments. I'd be guessing."

I don't know what you mean I didn't do anything I swear I've never done anything to anyone except except I once knew a girl—

"There."

"Yeah. Yeah, okay."

A hand closed over his mouth. The pressure in his eyeball intensified, became a sucking. They were pulling out his eyeball. No: It was the needle, withdrawing. He shrieked, possibly. Then the pain was gone. Hands pulled him upward. He couldn't see. He wept for his poor abused eyeball. But it was still there. It was there.

Blurry shapes loomed in fog. "What," Wil said.

"*Coarg medicity nighten comense,*" said the taller shape. "Hop on one foot."

Wil squinted, confused.

"Huh," said the shorter shape. "Maybe it *is* him."

They filled a sink with water and pushed his face into it. He surfaced, gasping. "Don't soak his clothes," said the tall man.

He was in a restroom. An airport. He had come off the 3:05 P.M. from Chicago, where the aisle seat had been occupied by a large man in a Hawaiian shirt Wil couldn't bear to wake. At first, the restroom had appeared closed for cleaning, but the janitor had removed the sign and Wil had jagged toward it gratefully. He had reached the urinal, unzipped, experienced relief.

The door had opened. A tall man in a beige coat had come in. There were half a dozen free urinals, Wil at one end, but the man chose the one beside him. Moments passed and the tall man did not pee. Wil, emptying at high velocity, felt a twinge of compassion. He had been there. The door had opened again. A second man entered and locked the door.

Wil had put himself back in his pants. He had looked at the man beside him, thinking—this was funny, in retrospect—that whatever was happening here, whatever specific danger was implied by a man entering a public restroom and fucking *locking* it, at least Wil and the tall man were in it together. At least it was two against one. Then he had realized Shy Bladder Guy's eyes were calm and deep and kind of beautiful, actually, but the key point being *calm as in unsurprised*, and Shy Bladder Guy had seized his head and propelled him into the wall.

Then the pain, and questions.

"Have to get this blood out of his hair," said the short man. He attacked Wil's face with paper towels. "His eye looks terrible."

"If they get close enough to see his eyes, we have bigger problems." The tall man was wiping his hands with a small white cloth, giving attention to each finger. He was thin and dark-skinned and Wil was no longer finding his eyes quite so beautiful. He was getting more of a cold, soulless kind of vibe. Like those eyes could watch terrible things and not look away. "So, Wil, you with us? You can walk and talk?"

"Fuck," he said, "orrffff." It didn't come out like he meant. His head felt loose.

"Good," said the tall man. "So here's the deal. We need to get out of this airport in minimum time with minimum fuss. I want your cooperation with that. If I fail to receive it, I'm going to make things bad for you. Not because I have anything against you, particularly, but I need you motivated. Do you understand?"

"I'm not . . ." He searched for the word. *Rich? Kidnappable?* "Anybody. I'm a carpenter. I make decks. Balconies. Gazebos."

"Yes, that's why we're here, your inimitable work with gazebos. You can forget the act. We know who you are. And *they* know who you are, and they're *here*, so let's get the fuck out while we can."

He took a moment to choose his words, because he had the feeling he would get only one more shot at this. "My name is Wil Parke. I'm a carpenter. I have a girlfriend and she's waiting out front to pick me up. I don't know who you think I am, or why you stuck a . . . a thing in my eye, but I'm nobody. I promise you I'm nobody."

The short man had been packing equipment into a brown satchel, and now he slung it around one shoulder and peered into Wil's face.

He had thinning hair and anxious brows. Wil might have pegged him for an accountant, ordinarily.

"I tell you what," Wil said. "I'll go into a stall and close the door. Twenty minutes. I'll wait twenty minutes. It'll be like we never met."

The short man glanced at the tall man.

"I'm not the guy," Wil said. "I am not the guy."

"The problem with that little plan, Wil," said the tall man, "is that if you stay here, in twenty minutes you'll be dead. If you go to your girlfriend, who I'm sorry to say you can no longer trust, you'll also be dead. If you do anything other than come with us now, quickly and cooperatively, again, I'm afraid, dead. It may not seem like it, but we are the only people who can save you from that." His eyes searched Wil's. "I can see, though, that you're not finding this very persuasive, so let me switch to a more direct method." He held open his coat. Nestled against his side, nose down in a thigh holster, was a short, wide shotgun. It made no sense, because they were in an airport. "Come or I will shoot you through the fucking kidneys."

"Yes," Wil said. "Okay, you make a good point. I'll cooperate." The key was to get out of the restroom. The airport was full of security. Once he was out, a push, a yell, some running: This was how he would escape.

"Nope," said the short man.

"No," agreed the tall man. "I see it. Dope him up."

A door opened. On the other side of it was a world of stunted color and muted sound, as if something was stuck in Wil's ears, and eyes, and possibly brain. He shook his head to clear it, but the world grew dark and angry and would not stay upright. The world did not like to be shaken. He understood that now. He wouldn't shake it again. He felt his feet sliding away from him on silent roller skates and reached for a wall for support. The wall cursed and dug its fingers into his arm, and was probably not a wall. It was probably a person.

"You gave him too much," said the person.

"Safe than sorry," said another person. They were bad persons, Wil recalled. They were kidnapping him. He felt angry about this, although in a technical kind of way, like taking a stand on principle. He tried to reel in his roller skate feet.

"Jesus," muttered a person, the tall one with calm eyes. Wil didn't like this person. He'd forgotten why. No. It was the kidnapping. "Walk."

He walked, resentfully. There were important facts in his brain but he couldn't find them. Everything was moving. A stream of airport people broke around him. Everyone going somewhere. Wil had been going somewhere. Meeting someone. To his left, a bird twittered. Or a phone. The short man squinted at a screen. "Rain."

"Where?"

"Domestic Arrivals. Right ahead." Wil found this idea amusing: rain in the terminal. "Do we know a Rain?"

"Yeah. Girl. New."

"Shit," said the short man. "I hate shooting girls."

"You get used to it," said the tall man.

A young couple passed, gripping hands. Lovers. The concept seemed familiar. "This way," said the tall man, steering Wil into a bookstore. He came face-to-face with a shelf that said NEW RELEASES. Wil's feet kept skating and he put out a hand to catch himself and felt a sharp pain.

"Problem?"

"Possibly nothing," murmured the tall man, "or possibly Rain, passing behind us now, in a blue summer dress."

In glossy covers, a reflection skipped by. Wil was trying to figure out what had stabbed him. It was a loose wire in the NEW RELEASES sign. The interesting thing was that being stabbed had helped to clear the fog in his head.

"Busiest part of any store, always the new releases," said the tall man. "That's what attracts people. Not the best. The new. Why is that, Wil, do you think?"

Wil pricked himself with the wire. He was too tentative, could hardly feel it, and so tried again, harder. This time a blade of pain swept through his mind. He remembered needles and questions. His girlfriend, Cecilia, was out front in a white SUV. She would be in a two-minute parking bay; they had arranged that carefully. He was late, because of these guys.

"I think we're good," said the short man.

"Make sure." The short man moved away. "All right, Wil," said the tall man. "In a few moments, we're going to cross the hall and walk down some stairs. There will be a little circumnavigating of passenger jets, then we'll board a nice, comfortable twelve-seater. There will be snacks. Drinks, if you're thirsty." The tall man glanced at him. "Still with me?"

Wil grabbed the man's face. He had no plan for what to do next, so wound up just hanging on to the guy's head and staggering backward until he tripped over a cardboard display. The two of them went down in a tangle of beige coat and scattered books. *Run*, Wil thought, and yes, that was a solid idea. He found his feet and ran for the exit. In the glass he saw a wild-eyed man and realized it was him. He heard yelps and alarmed voices, possibly the tall man getting up, who had a shotgun, Wil recalled now, *a shotgun*, which was not the kind of thing you would think could slip your memory.

He stumbled out into an ocean of bright frightened faces and open mouths. It was hard to remember what he was doing. His legs threatened treachery but the motion was good, helping to clear his head. He saw escalators and forged toward them. His back sang with potential shotgun impacts, but the airport people were being very good about moving out of his way, practically *throwing* themselves aside, for which he was grateful. He reached the escalators but his roller skate feet kept going and he fell flat on his back. The ceiling moved slowly by. The tiles up there were filthy. They were seriously disgusting.

He sat up, remembering Cecilia. Also the shotgun. And, now he thought about it, how about some security? Where were they? Because it was an airport. It was an *airport.* He grabbed the handrail, intending to pull himself up to look for security, but his knees went in opposite directions and he tumbled down the rest of the way. Body parts telegraphed complaints from faraway places. He rose. Sweat ran into his eyes. Because the head fog wasn't confusing enough; he needed *blurred vision.* But he could see light, which meant *exit,* which meant *Cecilia,* so he ran on. Someone shouted. The light grew. Frigid air burst around him as if he'd plunged into a mountain lake and he sucked it into his lungs. Snow, he saw. It was snowing. Flakes like tiny stars.

"Help, guy with gun," he said to a man who looked like a cop but on reflection was probably directing cabs. Orange buses. Parking bays. The two-minute spaces were just a little farther. He almost collided with a trolley-laden family and the man tried to grab his jacket but he kept running and it was starting to make sense, now, running; he was starting to remember how to coordinate the various pieces of his body, and he threw a glance over his shoulder and a pole ran into him.

He tasted blood. Someone asked if he was okay, some kid pulling earbuds out of his hair. Wil stared. He didn't understand the question. He had run into a pole and all his thoughts had fallen out. He groped for them and found Cecilia. He raised his body like a wreck from the deep and shoved aside the kid and rode forward on a crest of the kid's abuse. He finally saw it, Cecilia's car, a white fortress on wheels with VIRGINIA IS FOR LOVERS on the rear window. Joy drove his steps. He wrenched open the handle and fell inside. He had never been so proud. "Made it," he gasped. He closed his eyes.

"Wil?"

He looked at Cecilia. "What?" He began to feel unsure, because her face was strange. And then it came to him, in a fountain of dread that began somewhere unidentifiable and ended in his testicles: He should not be here. He should not have led men with guns to his girlfriend. That was a stupid thing to do. He felt furious with himself, and dismayed, because it had been so hard to get here, and now he had to run again.

"Wil, what's wrong?" Her fingers came at him. "Your nose is bleeding." There was a tiny furrow in her brow, which he knew very well and was sad to leave.

"I ran into a pole." He reached for the latch. The longer he sat here, the closer the fog pressed.

"Wait! Where are you going?"

"Away. Have to—"

"Sit down!"

"Have to go."

"Then I'll drive you somewhere! Stay in your seat!"

That was an idea. Driving. "Yes."

"You'll stay if I drive?"

"Yes."

She reached for the ignition. "Okay. Just . . . stay. I'll take you to a hospital or something. All right?"

"Yes." He felt relief. Weight stole through his body. He wondered if it was okay to slide into unconsciousness. It seemed out of his hands now. Cecilia would drive to safety. This car was a tank; he had mocked it before, because it was so big and she was so tiny but they were equally aggressive, and now it would save them. He might as well close his eyes a moment.

When he opened them, Cecilia was looking at him. He blinked. He had the feeling he'd fallen asleep. "Why . . ." He sat up.

"Shhh."

"Are we moving?" They were not moving. "Why aren't we moving?"

"Just stay in your seat, until they get here," Cecilia said. "That's the important thing."

He turned in his seat. The glass was fogged over. He couldn't see what was out there. "Cecilia. Drive. Now."

She tucked a wisp of hair behind one ear. She did that when she was remembering something. He could see her across a room, talking to somebody, and know she was relating a memory. "Remember the day you met my parents? You were freaking out because you thought we were going to be late. But we weren't. We weren't late, Wil."

He rubbed condensation from the window. Through the whiteout, men in brown suits jogged toward him. "Drive! Cil! *Drive!*"

"This is just like then," she said. "Everything's going to be fine."

He lunged across her, groping for the ignition. "*Where are the keys?*"

"I don't have them."

"What?"

"I don't have them anymore." She put a hand on his thigh. "Just sit with me a minute. Isn't the snow beautiful?"

"Cil," he said. "Cil."

There was a flash of dark movement and the door opened. Hands seized him. He fought the hands, but they were irresistible, and pulled him into the cold. He threw fists in all directions until something hard exploded across the back of his head, and then he was being borne on broad shoulders. Some time seemed to have passed in between, because it was darker. Pain rolled through his head in waves. He saw blacktop and a flapping coattail. "Fuck," said someone, with frustration. "Forget the plane. They can't wait for us any longer."

"Forget the plane? Then what?"

"Other side of those buildings, there's a fire path, take us to the freeway."

"We drive? Are you kidding? They'll close the freeway."

"Not if we're fast."

"Not if we're . . . ?" said the shorter man. "This is fucked! It's fucked because you wouldn't leave when I said!"

"Shush," said the tall man. They stopped moving. The wind blew awhile. Then there was some running, and Wil heard an engine, a car stopping. "Out," said the tall man, and Wil was manhandled into a small vehicle. The short man came in behind him. A disco ball dangled from the mirror. A row of stuffed animals with enormous black eyes smiled at him from the dash. A blue rabbit held a flag on a stick, championing some country Wil didn't recognize. He thought he might be able to stab that into somebody's face. He reached for it but the short man got there first. "No," said the short man, confiscating the rabbit.

The engine revved. "How'd it go with the girlfriend, Wil?" the tall man said. He steered the car around a pillar marked D3, which Wil recognized as belonging to the parking garage. "Are you ready to consider that we know what we're doing?"

"This is a mistake," said the short man. "We should stay on foot."

"The car is fine."

"It's not fine. Nothing is fine." He had a short, angry-looking submachine gun in his lap. Wil had somehow not noticed that. "Wolf was on us from the start. They knew."

"They didn't."

"Brontë—"

"Shut up."

"Brontë fucked us!" said the short man. "She's fucked us and you won't see it!"

The tall man aimed the car at a collection of low hangars and warehouse-like buildings. As they drew nearer, the wind picked up, spitting ice down the funnels made by their walls. The car shook. Wil, jammed between the two men, leaned on one, then the other.

"This car sucks," said the short man.

A small figure loomed out of the gloom ahead. A girl, wearing a blue dress. Her hair danced in the wind, but she was standing very still.

The short man leaned forward. "Is that Rain?"

"I think so."

"Hit her."

The engine whined. The girl grew in the windshield. Flowers on her dress, Wil saw. Yellow flowers.

"*Hit her!*"

"Ah, fuck," said the tall man, almost too quietly to hear, and the car began to scream. The world shifted. Weight forced Wil sideways. Things moved beyond the glass. A creature, a behemoth with searing eyes and silver teeth, fell upon them. The car bent and turned. The teeth were a grille, Wil realized, and the eyes headlights, because the creature was an SUV. It chewed the front of the car and bellowed and shook and ran into the brick wall. Wil put his arms around his head, because everything was breaking.

He heard groans. Shuffling. The tick of the engine cooling. He raised his head. The tall man's shoes were disappearing through a jagged hole where the windshield had been. The short man was fumbling with his door latch, but in a way that suggested to Wil that he was having trouble making his hands do what he wanted. The interior of the car was oddly shaped. He tried to push something off his shoulder but it was the roof.

The short man's door squealed and jammed. The tall man appeared on the other side and wrenched it open. The short man crawled out and looked back at Wil. "Come on."

Wil shook his head.

The short man breathed a curse. He went away and the tall man's face dipped into view. "Hey. Wil. Wil. Take a look to your right there. Lean forward a little. That's it. Can you see?"

The side window was a half-peeled spiderweb, but beyond that he could see the vehicle that had attacked them. It was a white SUV. Its front was crumpled against the wall. Steam issued from around its bent front wheels. The sticker on the rear window said: VIRGINIA IS FOR LOVERS.

"Your girlfriend just tried to kill us, Wil. She drove right at us. And I'm not sure if you can see from there, but she didn't even stop to put on a seat belt. That's how focused she was. Can you see her, Wil?"

"No," he said. But he could.

"Yes, and you need to get out of the car, because there are more where she came from. There are always more."

He got out of the car. He was intending to punch the man in the jaw, knock him down and maybe choke the life out of him, watch those eyes go dim, but something snared his wrists. By the time he realized the short man was handcuffing him in white plastic, it was done. The tall man pushed him forward. "Walk."

"*No! No! Cecilia!*"

"She's dead," said the tall man. "Faster."

"I'll kill you," Wil said.

The short man jogged ahead of them, cradling his submachine gun. His head moved from side to side. He was probably looking for that girl, the one they'd called Rain. The girl who had stood like she was nailed to the blacktop, like she could stare down a car. "Utility van in the hangar there," said the short man. "May have keys."

Some men in hard hats and overalls approached. The short man screamed at them to lie down and not fucking move. The tall man pulled open the door of a white van and put Wil in it. Wil swung around so that when the tall man followed him in, Wil could kick his teeth down his throat, but a flash of blue in the side mirror caught his eye. He peered at it. There was something blue crouched under a refueling truck. A blue dress.

The van's side door was pulled open and the short man came in. He looked at Wil. "What?"

Wil said nothing. The tall man started the engine. He had slid into the van without Wil noticing.

"Wait up," said the short man. "He's seen something."

The tall man glanced at him. "Did you?"

"No," he said.

"Shit," said the short man, and tumbled out of the van. Wil heard his footsteps. He didn't want to look at the side mirror, because the tall man was watching, but he glanced once and there was nothing there anymore. A few moments passed. There was a noise. The girl in the blue dress burst past Wil's window, startling him, her blond hair streaming. There was a hammer of gunfire. She fell bonelessly to the concrete.

"Don't move," the tall man said to Wil.

The short man came around the van and looked at them. The barrel of his gun was smoking. He looked at the girl and gave a short, barking laugh. "I got her!"

Wil could see the girl's eyes. She was sprawled on her stomach, hair sprayed across her face, but he could still see that her eyes were the same blue as her dress. Dark blood stole across the concrete.

"Fucking *got* her!" said the short man. "Holy shit! I nailed a poet!"

The tall man revved the engine. "Let's go."

The short man gestured: *Wait.* He moved closer to the girl, keeping his gun trained on her, as if there was some chance she might get up. She didn't move. He reached her and proddel her with his shoe.

The girl's eyes shifted. "*Contrex helo siq rattrak*," she said, or something similar. "Shoot yourself."

The short man brought the tip of his gun to his chin and pulled the trigger. His head snapped back. The tall man kicked open the van door and raised his shotgun to his shoulder. He discharged it at the girl. Her body jerked. The tall man walked forward, ejected the spent cartridge, and fired again. Thunder rolled around the hangar.

By the time the tall man returned to the van, Wil was halfway out the door. "Back," said the tall man. His eyes were full of death and Wil saw clearly that they were now dealing in absolutes. This knowledge passed between them. Wil got back in the van. His bound hands pressed into his back. The tall man put the van into reverse, navigated around the two bodies, and accelerated into the night. He did not speak or look in Wil's direction. Wil watched buildings flit by without hope: He might have had a chance to escape, but that was over now.

AIRPORT GUNMAN
"HAD NOTHING TO LIVE FOR"

PORTLAND, OR: The maintenance worker who fatally shot two people before taking his own life, triggering an eight-hour shutdown of Portland International Airport, suffered from depression following the breakup of his marriage, friends and family said yesterday.

Amelio Gonzalez, 37, told a friend he had nothing left to live for after a court decision awarded full custody of his two children, 11 and 7, to his ex-wife, Melinda Gonzalez, three months ago.

It is believed Mr. Gonzalez sought medical assistance and was prescribed antidepression medication.

Colleagues remain in disbelief at Mr. Gonzalez's actions, describing him as a friendly, generous man who often went out of his way to help others.

"Amelio was a flat-out nice guy," said Jerome Webber, who worked with Mr. Gonzalez in aircraft maintenance for two years prior to the incident. "A little quiet, but anyone would be knocked around by [his circumstances]. He's just the last guy you'd expect to ever do anything like this."

Airport management defended their hiring practices, saying all employees were subject to regular psychological checkups. Mr. Gonzalez passed such a check as recently as four weeks ago.

"We are doing everything we can to get to the bottom of this," said George Aftercock, manager of security for Portland International Airport. "We want to know how a model employee can suddenly snap."

Amelio Gonzalez shot two people on Saturday. A third person, a woman, is believed to have died in a car accident while trying to flee. Their names have not yet been released.

An earlier disturbance in which a man ran through the Arrivals hall in an agitated state, initially thought to be connected to the shooting, has since been found to be unrelated.

Post #16
In reply to: http://nationstates.org/pages/topic—8724511-post-16.html

In my city we spent $1.6 billion on a new ticketing system for the trains. We replaced paper tickets with smartcards and now they can tell where people get on and off. So, question: how is that worth $1.6 billion?

People say it's the government being incompetent, and ok. But this is happening all over. All the transit networks are getting smartcards, the grocery stores are taking your name, the airports are getting face recognition cameras. Those cameras, they don't work when people try to avoid them. Like, they can be fooled by glasses. We KNOW they're ineffective as anti-terrorism devices, but we still keep installing them.

All of this stuff—the smartcards, the ID systems, the "anti-congestion" car-tracking tech—all of it is terrible at what it's officially supposed to do. It's only good for tracking the rest of us, the 99.9% who just use the smartcard or whatever and let ourselves be tracked because it's easier.

I'm not a privacy nut, and I don't care that much if these organizations want to know where I go and what I buy. But what bothers me is how HARD they're all working for that data, how much money they're spending, and how they never admit that's what they want. It means that information must be really valuable for some reason, and I just wonder to who and why.

[TWO]

"Hmm," said the man in the trucker cap. "I think . . . no . . . just a second here . . ."

"Take your time, sir," said Emily. "The queen isn't going nowhere. She's quite comfortable under there, in all her skirts. She'll wait for you all day." She smiled at a man standing behind the trucker. The man smiled back, remembered his wife, frowned. Forget that guy, then.

"On the left," said a woman in an I ❤ SAN FRANCISCO sweater. Her eyes darted at Emily. "I think."

"You think?" said the trucker.

"I'm pretty sure."

Emily slipped the woman a wink. *You got it.* The woman's lips tightened, pleased.

"I dunno," said the trucker. "I was thinking middle."

"The queen is quick on her feet, sir. No shame in not being able to follow her. Take a guess."

"Middle," said the trucker, because *Take a guess* meant, *That's enough, Benny.* Benny wasn't a trucker, of course. He had found that cap in an alley. With it pulled low, and his straggly sand-colored beard, he could pass.

"You sure, now? You got some advice from this lady here."

"Naw, definitely middle."

"As you say, sir." Emily flipped the middle card. The crowd murmured. "Sorry, sir. She got away from you." It took a little work to shift the queen from right to left, a Mexican Turnover, but she made it. "On the left, just like the lady said. Should have listened. Quick eye you have there, ma'am. Very quick." She spread the cards, scooped them up, and flipped them from hand to hand, fast but not too fast. Sections of the crowd began to move away. Emily tucked a strand of blond hair behind her ear. She was wearing a big floppy hat with colored panels, which she had to keep pushing back to keep it from falling over her eyes. "Care to try, ma'am? Only two dollars. Simplest thing in the world, if you've got the eye for it."

The woman hesitated. Only one game in her. Sometimes Emily would let a mark win the first game so they'd want to play again, and again, and again. But that only worked on a certain type of person. Still, two dollars. Two dollars was fine.

"I'll play."

The speaker was a young man with long hair in a cheap, not-quite-black suit and a pale yellow tie. A plastic ID hung from his shirt pocket. There were four of them, two more boys and a girl, all with that look, like college students on summer jobs. Salespeople, maybe, of something cheap and devious. Not cops. She could tell that. Cops were a constant hazard on the pier. She grinned. The woman in the sweater was moving away, but that didn't matter. Cheap-suit guy was better. A lot better. "All right, sir. Step on up. You did me a favor, I think. That lady may have cleaned me out."

"I may clean you out," said the guy.

"Ho, ho. A big talker. That's fine, sir. Talk as much as you like. No price tag on talking. The game, though, that's two dollars."

He dropped two bills onto Emily's card table. She found him irritating, although wasn't sure why: Guys like this, arrogant, an audience watching, they were gold. They would lose and double up forever. You had to throw them a win here and there, so they wouldn't blow up, accuse you of cheating. But if you were smart, they would play all day. They would do it because once they were in the hole, their pride wouldn't let them out. She'd taken $180 from a guy like this not two months ago, most of it on the last game. His neck had bulged and his eyes had watered and she saw how much he wanted to hit her. But there was a crowd. She had eaten that night.

She slung the queen and two aces onto the table. "Catch her if you can." She flipped them, began to switch them around. "Loves her exercise, does the queen. Always takes her morning constitutional. Problem is, where does she go?" The guy wasn't even looking at the cards. "Hard to win if you don't watch, sir. Very tricky." His ID tag said: HI! I'M LEE! Below that: AUTHORIZED QUESTIONNAIRE ADMINISTRATION AGENT. "Lee, is it? You must be good if you can follow the queen without looking at her, Lee. Very good."

"I am," he said, smiling. He hadn't taken his eyes off her.

She decided to take Lee's two dollars. If he ponied up again, she would take that. She would ask if he wanted to double up and she would take that and she would be merciless, not give him a single game, because Lee was a dick.

The crowd murmured. She was flicking the cards too fast, holding nothing back. She stopped. Pulled away her hands. There was a collective titter and some applause. She was breathing fast.

"Well," she said. "Let's see how good you are, Lee."

He still hadn't looked at the cards. The guy behind and to his right, one of the market researchers, smiled at her brilliantly, as if he'd only just noticed her. The other boy muttered to the girl, "Good thing is I'm right where I wanna be, right in the best possible place," and the girl nodded and said, "Yeah, you're so right."

"On the right," Lee said.

Wrong. "You sure about that? Want a moment to think?" But her hands were already moving, eager to claim victory. "Last chance to—"

"Queen on the right," he said, and as Emily touched the cards, she felt her fingers slide under and to the right. Her left hand went out in a flashy extension that did nothing but draw the eye, and her right slipped one card below the other.

There was scattered applause. Emily stared. The queen of hearts was on the right. She had switched them. At the last moment, she had switched them. Why had she done that?

"Well done, sir." She noticed Benny shifting his feet, glancing around for cops, no doubt wondering what the hell she was doing. "Congratulations." She reached into her money pouch. Two bucks. A difference of four, between winning and losing. That was a meal. It was a down payment on a night of chemical joy. She held out the bills, and when Lee took them, it hurt. He tucked them into his wallet. The girl glanced at her watch, something plastic and shiny. One of the boys yawned. "Play again? Double up, perhaps? A man like you likes to play for real money, am I right?" She was pushing, could hear the strain in her own voice, because she knew she'd lost him.

"No. Thank you." He looked bored. "There's nothing here I want."

"What the fuck?" said Benny.

She kept walking, hunched over, her Pikachu bag on her back, the floppy hat wobbling about. The sun was setting but heat radiated out of the sidewalk, coming off the brick tenements in waves. "I don't want to talk about it."

"You *never* let a guy like that win the first game." Benny was carrying the table. "He gets ahead, it's over. He doesn't care about money. He cares about beating you. You gave him what he wanted."

"I flipped the wrong card, okay? I flipped the wrong card."

"That guy was going to play." Benny kicked a plastic bottle. It spun across the sidewalk and onto the road, where a passing car ran over it with a crunch. "He was good for twenty, easy. Maybe fifty."

"Yeah, well."

Benny stopped. Emily stopped, too. He was a good guy, Benny. Until he wasn't. "Are you taking this seriously?"

"I am, Benny." She tugged at his arm.

"Fifty bucks."

"Yeah. Fifty bucks." She felt her eyes widen. This would piss Benny off, but she couldn't help it. She was perverse sometimes.

"What?"

"Come on." She tugged his arm. It was like stone. "Let's get some food. I'll cook you something."

"Fuck you."

"Benny—"

"Fuck you!" He shook her off, let the table drop to the sidewalk. His fists bunched. A passing man in a collared business shirt glanced at her, then at Benny, then away. *Thanks, guy.* "Get away from me!"

"Benny, come on."

He took a step forward. She flinched. When he hit, he meant it. "Do not follow me home."

"Fine," she said. "Jesus, fine." She waited until the violence drained out of him, then put out her hand. "At least give me my money. I made a hundred twenty today; give me half." Then she ran, because Benny's eyes popped in the way that meant she'd pushed him too far, again. Her Pikachu bag bounced against her back. Her floppy hat fell off and she left it on the sidewalk. When she reached the corner, Benny was half a block back. He'd chased her, but not far. She was glad she'd held on to her bag. Her jacket was in there.

She slept in Gleeson's Park, beneath a hedge that people didn't notice and that had escape routes on two sides. She woke to a midnight screaming match, but it was nobody she knew and too far away to be a threat. She closed her eyes and fell asleep to *fuck* and *cunt* and *mine.* Then it was dawn and a drunk was pissing on her legs.

She scrambled up. "Dude. Dude."

The man stumbled back. "Sorry." He barely got the word out.

She inspected herself. Spatters on her pants, boots. "Dude, the fuck?"

"I . . . didn't . . . see . . ."

"Fuck," she said, and pulled her bag out of the hedge and went looking for a bathroom.

There was a public restroom in a corner of the park. It wasn't a place she went if she could help it, but the sun was rising and her pants were stiffening with urine. She circled its cinder block exterior, carrying her boots, until she was sure it was empty, then stood in the doorway, thinking. Only one way out, was the problem with public restrooms. One way out and you could holler all you wanted; nobody would come to help. But she went in. She checked the lock, just in case it had been repaired since the last time she was here. No. She tugged off her pants and stuffed them and her sock under a faucet. Concrete air tickled her skin. She threw glances toward the doorway, because this was a really bad position to be in should anyone appear, but no one came, so she got confident and lifted her leg to wash beneath the faucet. The paper towel dispenser was empty, so she mopped herself dry with translucent squares of toilet paper.

She opened her bag. Maybe better clothes had materialized while she wasn't looking. No. She closed the bag and wrung out her jeans as best she could. What she would have liked to do was carry them over to the park and dry them on the grass while she lay in the sun, legs bare, eyes closed. Just soaking up rays. Her and her jeans. Another time, maybe. Another universe. She began to pull on her damp pants.

As she wandered down Fleet, her stomach tweaked. It was too early for the soup kitchens. She thought about hitting up a friend. Maybe Benny had cooled down. She chewed her lip. She felt like a McMuffin.

Then she saw him: Lee, of the long hair and cheap suit, Lee who had taken her two dollars. He was planted on a street corner, clipboard in hand, approaching commuters with a fake smile. He was in market research, she remembered; she'd seen that on his ID. She watched him. It felt like he owed her.

When she approached, his eyes shifted to her briefly from the man he was quizzing. "You owe me breakfast," she said.

"Thank you so much," Lee told the man. "I appreciate your time." He wrote something on his clipboard and flipped the page. When he was done writing, he smiled at Emily. "It's the hustler."

"I let you win," she said. "I took pity on you. Buy me an Egg McMuffin."

"You let me win?"

"Come on. I'm a professional. You don't take a game off me unless I give it to you." She smiled. It was hard to tell if this was working. "Fair's fair. I'm hungry."

"I'd have thought a professional could afford her own Egg McMuffin."

"Sure," she said, "but I'm letting you pay because I like your face."

Lee looked amused. It was the first nice expression she'd seen from him. "Okay." He tucked his pen into his clipboard. "Tell you what, I will buy you an Egg McMuffin."

"Two Egg McMuffins," she said.

She bit down and it was as good as she'd imagined. Across the Formica table, Lee sat with his arms spread along the back of the booth seat. Outside, children yipped and chased each other around a neon playground. Who brought their kids to McDonald's for breakfast? She shouldn't be judging. She gulped coffee.

"You are hungry," said Lee.

"Tough times." She chewed her muffin. "It's the economy."

Lee wasn't eating. "How old are you?"

"Eighteen."

"I mean really."

"Eighteen." She was sixteen.

"You look young to be on your own."

She shrugged, unwrapping the next McMuffin. Lee had bought her three, plus the coffee and hash browns. "I'm okay. I'm fine. How old are you?"

He watched her devour the muffin. "Why did you want a McMuffin?"

"I haven't eaten in, like, a day."

"I mean a McMuffin in particular."

"I like them."

"Why?"

She eyed him. It was a stupid question. "I like them."

"Right." He looked away for the first time.

She didn't want to talk about herself. "Where are you from? Not here."

"How can you tell?"

"It's a gift."

"Well," he said, "you're right. I travel. City to city."

"Asking people to fill out questionnaires?"

"That's right."

"You must be really good at that," she said. "You must be, like, extremely talented at asking people to fill out questionnaires." His expression didn't change. She didn't know why she was trying to needle him. He had bought her food. But still. She didn't like him. It took more than McMuffins to change that. "What brings you to San Francisco?"

"You."

"Oh yeah?" She hoped this wasn't a running situation. She'd had enough of running. She swallowed the last of the McMuffin and started on the hash browns, because it would be good if she could get all this down first.

"Not you in particular. Your type. I'm looking for people who are persuasive and intransigent."

"Well, bingo," she said, although she didn't know what *intransigent* meant.

"Unfortunately, you failed."

"I failed?"

"You let me take your money."

"Hey. That was a pity win. I already said. You want to try again?"

He smiled.

"I'm serious. You won't win again." She meant it.

"Hmm," he said. "Okay, tell you what. I'll give you another shot."

Benny had her cards. But she could get more, then she'd push this guy to a hundred, ask to see color, and the second the bills touched the table, she'd grab them and run. She'd go to Benny and tease him awhile. *Guy was good for about twenty, you said?* She loved the look he got when she brought him money. *Maybe fifty?* "Let me finish my coffee, we'll go to the store across the street—"

"Not cards. A different kind of test."

"Oh," she said doubtfully. "Like what?"

"Like, don't blow me."

She was startled, but his expression hadn't changed, so maybe she heard this wrong, or it was an expression, somehow. Maybe he meant: *Don't blow me off.* There were plenty of people nearby, so no immediate problem. But she'd need to find a way to leave alone.

"My job is not actually to administer questionnaires. My job is to test people. Think of it as a job interview that you don't know you're having."

She swallowed the last of the hash browns. "Well, thanks for thinking of me, but you know, I'm pretty happy with what I've got going on now. Thanks, though." She gulped coffee dregs. "Thanks for the breakfast." She reached for her bag.

"It pays."

She hesitated. "How much?"

"How much do you want?"

"I make five hundred a day now," she said, which was an outrageous lie, of course. She made between zero and two hundred dollars a day, and split that with Benny.

“This would be more.”

“How much more?” She caught herself. What was she thinking? He was wearing a *plastic watch*. He would take her to some dingy apartment and lock the door. There was no job. “Look, you know what, I’m just gonna pass.”

He reached into a pocket and opened his wallet. She’d noted yesterday that he had no more than twenty dollars in there. He unzipped a section and tossed notes onto the table. She stared. There were a lot of them.

“We wear cheap clothing because it would seem odd if we stood around on street corners in ten thousand dollar suits.”

“I see,” she said, not really listening.

“Let go of your bag.”

She looked at him. Apparently it was obvious that she had been thinking of snatching that cash and running like hell. She released the bag.

“You get a first-class air ticket to our head office in DC. You spend one week there, doing a round of tests. If you pass, you become a trainee on a starting salary of sixty thousand dollars. Fail, and we fly you home again with five thousand in an envelope for your trouble. How does that sound?”

“Like a scam.”

He laughed. “I know. It does sound like a scam. I thought the same thing when they approached me.”

She kept looking at the cash on the table. She didn’t want to. It was irresistible.

“You went to school,” Lee said. “I mean, at some point. And it didn’t suit you very well. They wanted to teach you things you didn’t care about. Dates and math and trivia about dead presidents. They didn’t teach persuasion. Your ability to persuade is the single most important determinant of your quality of life, and they didn’t cover that at all. Well, we do. And we’re looking for students with natural aptitude.”

"Okay," she said. "I'm interested; I'll take a ticket."

He smiled. She remembered his comment about the blow job. She must have gotten that backward. He must want her to blow him in exchange for the air ticket. That way made sense. She wondered if there really was a job. He was kind of believable.

"Show me something," she said. "Something official."

He slid a business card across the table. His full name was Lee Bob Black. She tucked this into her bag, feeling better. This card enabled her to call Lee's boss and explain what Lee had asked her to do in exchange for a job. She hoped it was a big company, the kind that hated publicity. She hoped there was really a job, because she would be awesome at it.

"Now you know who I am," said Lee. "Who are you?"

"Emily."

"Are you a cat person or a dog person?"

"What?"

"Cats or dogs? Which do you prefer?"

"What do you care?"

He shrugged. "I'm just making conversation."

"I hate cats. Too sneaky."

"Ha," he said. "What's your favorite color?"

"This is your idea of conversation?"

"Just answer the question."

"I'm just saying, as someone who knows about banter, you're really terrible at it," she said. "Black."

"Close your eyes and pick a number between one and a hundred."

"Are these from your questionnaires?"

"Yes."

"You're surveying me? Is this the test?"

"Part of it."

"I'm not closing my eyes. Thirty-three."

"Do you love your family?"

She didn't move. "Are you serious? You think I'd be here if I had a good family?" She almost got up. But she didn't. "No."

"Okay, then," said Lee. "Last question. Why did you do it?"

She stared.

"Don't manufacture an answer," said Lee. "I'll be able to tell, and it will invalidate the test."

"This is a bullshit question, isn't it?"

"How do you mean?"

"You don't even know what you're asking. You just want me to think you do."

He shrugged.

"This doesn't sound like a survey."

"It's a personality test."

"Is this Scientology?"

"No."

"Amway?"

"I promise it's not Amway. It's no one you've heard of. You're very close, Emily. What's your answer?"

"To your bullshit question?"

"You don't have to believe it. You just have to answer honestly."

"Fine," she said. "I did it because I felt like it."

Lee nodded. "One disappointing thing about this job. People always turn out to be less interesting than you hope." Before Emily could decide whether he'd insulted her, he spoke a jumble of words. They slid by her and were gone. She felt dazed. "Go to the restroom," he said. "Wait there for me."

She walked to the counter. She was leaving her bag behind, but that was okay. Lee would look after it. She asked a boy behind the register for the bathroom key and he gave her a look but handed it over. There was a single stall. She closed the toilet lid and sat on it.

After a minute, the door opened and Lee came in, talking on a cell phone. Her heart thumped. He was kind of handsome. His face grew on you. She even liked his hair. She sort of loved him. "Yeah," Lee told his phone. "But hey, we're here, let's give it one more pass." He stopped in front of her. She watched him fumbling with his zipper. She was in an interesting place. She was present, but remote. Everything was curious and amusing. Lee jammed his cell phone against his shoulder, dug into his pants, and pulled out his penis. It was longer than she expected. It bobbed in front of her, curving upward before her eyes. "I'm actually with her now," said Lee. "Thought there was something there, for a minute." He covered the phone. "Put it in your mouth."

She put her hand around his penis. She opened her mouth. She thought: *Wait, what?*

"I know," said Lee. "Every time." He laughed. His penis jumped in her hand.

She punched his balls. Lee howled. She tried to kick him but he was doubling over, in full retreat, and she caught his knee or elbow or something. She ran for the door and pulled it open. Heads turned. "Pervert!" she yelled to the turning faces. "There's a pervert in there!" She scooped up her bag. Not one person had moved. "Pervert!" she shouted, and ran.

In the alley, boys in baseball caps were dealing drugs or freestyling lyrics or whatever they did and one stepped toward her, his hands out. She blasted past him. Her bag bounced. It was three blocks before she felt safe enough to stop and check whether Lee was following. No. She dropped her bag for a second and put her hands on her knees to suck air. People flowed around her. What had just happened? She remembered the details but it didn't make sense. She didn't know what she had been thinking.

She looked up. Lee was shambling toward her, a hand clutched over his groin, his face contorted. She jerked upright. On the other side of the street, a girl with long brown hair and a cheap suit stepped onto the road, backed away from a car, then ran at her through traffic. The way she was angling, she wouldn't cut Emily off so much as corral her, force her eastward, and this set off all kinds of alarm bells, because when someone did that, they had friends. She craned her neck and spotted two clipboard-carrying boys in suits heading straight at her. "Help!" she said, but to no one in particular, and of course there was no help. She spied an alley and ran for it. The bag slipped and she panicked and let it drop, which was unthinkably terrible because without her bag she had nothing; she would have to rely on people. She passed an office building, a beautiful business couple emerging from its glass revolving doors like an advertisement, and she thought about running in there, to whatever clean, safe, corporate-warmed world they had come from. But that would never work; that would end in her being tossed out the same door by a security guard in charge of protecting that world from people like her. She kept running. The alley turned and dipped and became a driveway. *Not good, not good.* It terminated at a locked roller door painted KEEP CLEAR LOADING AREA. She started back the way she had come, but they were already here. One of the boys held her Pikachu bag. She shoved a hand into her jeans pocket. "I've got Mace." She backed up until she hit the roller door. All those office windows: Surely someone would be looking down. Maybe if she screamed. Maybe if there were angels.

"Take a moment," said the girl. "Get your breath back." Beside her, Lee bent and spat.

"Stay away from me."

"Sorry about the chase. We just really, really didn't want you to get away."

"I will fuck you up," said Emily.

"It's okay." The girl smiled quizzically. "It's okay, Emily; you passed."

MEMO

To: All Staff

From: Cameron Winters

Hi guys!! Just a quick one to say we ARE getting leave loading on the 29th so that's double time for all casuals! Nice one head office!

I'm away for the long weekend so Melanie will be CRO. On her 18th birthday too (Saturday)!! Sorry Melanie it just slipped out!!!

Also please please!! be careful who you give the bathroom key to. We had a junkie and a poor guy walked in on her, she freaked out and scared the customers, obviously not a good look!!!

Peace,

xCx

[THREE]

The van's tires slipped on the freeway merge and the interior filled with the light from an approaching eighteen-wheeler. "Fuck!" said the tall man. A horn bellowed. Wil felt a looseness, a surrender of the vehicle to natural forces, then the wheels bit and straightened them up between the lanes. The truck's horn blew endlessly.

He wondered how much damage he would do to himself if he kicked open the door and flung himself out at this speed. Probably a lot. His hands were bound.

"Fuck," said the man. He was silent a moment. "*Fuck.*"

Wil said nothing.

"What's your name?"

"Wil Parke."

"Not now! Before!"

"I don't know what you mean."

"When you lived in Broken Hill, Australia. What was your name?"

"I've never lived in—"

"I can hear your accent!"

"I grew up in Australia. In Melbourne. But I've never been to Broken Hill."

The man hauled the wheel. The van slid across three lanes and slewed to a stop in the emergency lane. He pulled on the hand brake, took the shotgun, and tried to drag Wil out of the van. Wil resisted and the man hit him twice with the shotgun butt and Wil tumbled out into snow. When he got to his feet, he was looking into a gun barrel.

"You're thinking if you're not who I want, I'll let you go," said the man. "When in fact, if you're not the outlier, I'm going to shoot you and leave your body in the snow."

"I'm the outlier."

"Eighteen months ago, where did you live?"

"Broken Hill."

"Where in Broken Hill?"

A car blew by. "Main Street."

"Oh for fuck's sake," said the tall man.

"Tell me what you want. I don't know what you want."

The man sank to his haunches. "You drive a Taurus. You've been in the States eight months. A year before that, you lived in Broken Hill. You had a dog."

He shivered.

A truck passed, wheels spitting road ice. "Not the outlier," said the man. He shook his head. "Well, fuck."

"I'm really sorry."

"Forget about it," said the man, standing. "Get up. Turn around."

"What?"

"You heard me."

He rose, cautiously.

"Turn."

He turned.

"Walk."

"Where?"

"It doesn't matter. Away from the road."

"Okay, let's think about this."

"You don't walk, I'll shoot you here."

"I'm not walking into the woods so you can shoot me there!"

"Fine," said the man, and there was a rustling, and Wil started walking. His shoes sank into the snow. It wasn't more than ankle deep, but he made it look like it was. "Faster."

"I'm trying."

"I'm trying not to shoot you," said the man. "But it's getting fucking difficult."

He forged through deepening snow. His mind was a great white expanse. A snowscape, devoid of plans that ended with him alive.

"Veer right. You're trying to angle back to the road."

He veered. There were trees ahead, a thin stick forest. He was going to be shot in the woods. His body would disappear beneath the snowfall. In the spring, he would be gnawed by foxes. He would be discovered by Boy Scouts and poked with sticks.

"Stop. This will do."

"Don't shoot me in the back!" He turned, fighting snow. The man was ten feet away, unreachable in drifts this deep. "Leave me here. I can't make it to anywhere in a hurry. You can get away."

The man raised the shotgun butt to his shoulder.

"At least have the . . . goddamn common courtesy . . . wait! Tell me why! *Tell me why!* You can't *just shoot me*! In the bathroom, you said to hop and I didn't! That meant something, didn't it?"

"No."

"Don't shoot me in the face!"

The man exhaled. "Fine. Turn around."

"Okay! Okay! Just let me . . ." He pulled one foot out of the snow, put it down again. His nose ran. "*Motherfucker!*"

"I'm shooting you in five seconds," said the tall man. "You arrange yourself however you like between now and then."

He sank to the ground, because it didn't matter. "I'm sorry, Cecilia. I'm sorry you died. I never said I loved you and I should have. It's just the word. The bare words I couldn't say, and I should have." He was going to pass out. The man would shoot his unconscious body in the snow. It was probably best.

Time passed. He raised his head. The tall man was still there. "What did you say?"

"The . . . I . . . never told Cecilia I loved her. I should have said the words."

"You said *bare* words."

The silence stretched. He couldn't help himself. "Are you going to shoot me?"

"I'm thinking about it."

His bowels shivered.

The man lowered the shotgun. "She made you forget," said the man. "You really don't know who you are."

Wil sat in the snow, teeth chattering.

"New plan," said the man. "Get back in the van."

The world slid by in exit ramps and yellow-lit gas stations and trees dressed in snow. The van's wipers thumped. Wil's eye throbbed. The driver's window was half-cranked, letting in furious air.

The man glanced at him. "You feel okay? You look washed out." He gestured. "Your face."

Theoretically, the snow banked up alongside the freeway was a couple of feet deep. He could possibly survive a leap. Then: flailing through snow. Hearing the van brake behind him. The door pop open. Not so good.

The man waggled a dash control. "Heater doesn't work. I need the window open to keep from fogging up."

Practically, it was highly unlikely he could get the door open with his feet. Practically, he wasn't going anywhere until the man decided to pull over.

"You actually look a little hypoglycemic," said the man.

He could kick. He could try to force a crash. A problem here was the man was wearing a seat belt and Wil wasn't. A crash was therefore likely to hurt Wil a lot more. It was a last-resort kind of plan.

"Stop it," said the man. "You're not going anywhere so stop fucking thinking about it."

He looked out the side window.

"Next gas station, I'll pull over," said the man. "Get you some jelly beans."

They turned in to a glowing gas station and stopped at the farthest pump from the store. "Okay," said the man. "Before we proceed, some ground rules." He snapped his fingers, because Wil was staring at the store. "No running. No screaming for help. No mouthing secret messages to the cashier, looking directly into security cameras, saying you need the bathroom then locking yourself in, et cetera, et cetera. Doing any of those things will cause me"—he rapped the shotgun, the nose of which poked out from the footwell—"to use this. Understand?"

"Yes."

"Not on you. You, I need. I count three people in there. Do you want me to shoot three people?"

"No."

"Neither do I. So don't make me shoot three people." He twirled a finger. "Turn around."

"What?"

"So I can cut the cord."

His bindings loosened; he brought forward his arms against the protest of his muscles and rubbed his wrists. He felt a lot more optimistic with his hands free.

"Any questions?" said the man.

"Who are you?"

"Tom."

"What?"

"I'm Tom," said the man. "You asked who I am. I'm Tom."

Wil said nothing.

"So let's get these snacks," Tom said, and opened the door.

Three other cars sat beside pumps: two sedans and a battered truck with Texas plates, its rear window draped with a Confederate flag. A bumper sticker read: CAN'T FIND A JOB? THANK AN ILLEGAL. Wil had thought Tom would want to fill up, but he headed for the store. The glass doors parted and they stepped inside. There was music. The air smelled sweet. Tom stamped his feet. "Woo," he said, to nobody. "Cold tonight."

Wil saw magazines and chocolate bars. A poster offered a hot dog and a slushie for just two dollars. How could he be kidnapped next to a deal like that? It felt wrong. He shouldn't fear for his life in a convenience store while looking at hot dogs. But he looked at Tom, and Tom was still there, with a shotgun not quite concealed beneath his coat, and Wil felt nauseated and looked at the hot dogs again. That guy had almost shot him. He had been seconds away from spreading Wil across the snow. Cecilia was dead. *Just yell*, he thought. *What's the worst that could happen?* He knew the answer. But it was tempting, looking at the hot dogs.

"Go on," Tom said. "Get whatever you want." He gestured at the confectionery aisle. Wil walked toward a great pyramid of Hot & Spicy Pringles. When he glanced back, Tom had wandered over to the magazine rack, where a man in a red-checked snow hat was staring suspiciously at shrink-wrapped women. "Hi there," said Tom. "That your truck?"

Wil looked back at the Pringles. He closed a hand around one. It was firm and familiar and did not do anything unexpected, for which he felt grateful. He looked back at Tom. Tom seemed to be paying him no attention. So he kept going, and then there was a shelf between them and he was out of sight. He felt overwhelmed by the desire to sit down. Cover himself with snacks, maybe. Make a little fort. He kept walking. He took a bag of chocolate eggs. Then a woman's functional ponytail bobbed along in front of him, above the green and red foil snack bags.

He closed his eyes. Tom was going to take him to a lonely farmhouse and kill him. It was obvious. They would find him eight years later, buried beneath the roses, one skeleton among many in WASHINGTON'S HOUSE OF NIGHTMARES. Because Tom was a psychopath. Or possibly not: Possibly Tom was part of some kind of politically motivated group, something a little more professional and terroristic, but the point was Tom killed people. Tom had shot a girl in a blue cotton dress, and reloaded and shot her again, and Cecilia had died, and although that possibly wasn't Tom's fault, not directly, the takeaway message here was that around Tom people died. Wil would either get away or he would die, too. He felt calm. It was good to establish facts. It permitted the making of decisions. He was going to talk to this woman. He was sorry, but he was going to bring her into this. He would whisper a message and if things went bad, he would defend her. That was the best he could offer.

He opened his eyes. He felt sure Tom was watching him somehow, and sure enough, when he looked around there was a corner ceiling mirror and Tom was in it. Tom was nodding at the man in the snow hat, who was showing him a cell phone, for some reason. Wil pretended to inspect potato chips.

The woman's ponytail bobbed toward the end of the aisle, where a cardboard cutout lion offered free Cokes with every purchase over four dollars. This lion could screen him, if he timed it right. He could pass the woman at this spot and for one perfect second speak to her unseen. He began to move. Halfway there, the woman's ponytail stopped, and Wil had to stop and eye batteries to kill time. He glanced at the mirror. Tom was still chatting to the man. Why Tom had so much to say to this guy, Wil had no idea. The ponytail moved. Wil moved. He spotted a second security mirror and maybe this lion wasn't going to screen him as completely as he'd thought, but it would only take a second to mutter, *I'm kidnapped help gun call 911*, and he was committed now. He had made a decision not to end up beneath roses. He rounded the corner.

A girl stood there, five or six years old. She was looking at the cardboard lion. Wil stopped. The woman came around the corner. "Caitlin. Come here." The girl ran to her mother. Wil did not move. They passed him and headed up the next aisle.

The girl said, "Mommy, why was that man sad?"

"Shh," said the woman.

He walked to the van. He was going to let this motherfucker take him somewhere and kill him, apparently. That was where he was at. He felt furious, at something.

"Not the van," said Tom. "We're changing cars." He nodded at the pickup.

"Oh," Wil said.

Tom jangled keys. "You saved their lives." He unlocked the pickup and pulled open the door. "You made the right decision."

The truck's interior smelled of cigarettes. The dash had a bobblehead doll of someone Wil didn't recognize. Some politician. Tom pulled at the door and the thump of its closure was like the sealing of a tomb.

The engine turned. Air blew from vents. "Ah!" Tom said. "We have heat."

"You bought that guy's truck," Wil said.

"We swapped." Tom revved tentatively. He seemed to approve of the sound and they began to roll past pumps, leaving behind the airport maintenance van.

"Swapped," Wil said. "He just agreed to trade vehicles."

"Yeah." Tom took a moment to check traffic, and then accelerated onto the slip road. He dug in his coat pocket with one hand. "He also threw in this cell phone."

Wil looked at it. "Did he."

"Yeah," said Tom. "To sweeten the deal."

They reentered the freeway. It was Cecilia's birthday next week. Wil had been putting off going shopping. "Just give me money," she'd said, and he'd been thinking maybe he would, because she was so hard to buy for. But he might have thought of something. He still had a week. He might have found exactly what she wanted.

He remembered Rain standing in the middle of the road. The strange words she had spat through bloodstained teeth. The short man putting the gun to his own chin. He didn't understand any of that. Maybe Tom was a serial killer, or a terrorist, or a covert government agent, or something else, but whatever he was, he must want something. Wil had to go shopping.

"Where are we going?"

Tom didn't answer.

"Who was that girl?"

The truck hummed. The tires sluiced through wet road.

"Why did your friend shoot himself?"

"Shut up," said Tom. "I'm not talking to you."

"You came and got me. You must want me for something."

"It's not conversation."

"Then what?"

Tom was silent.

"Why did he call her a poet? Your friend said, 'I nailed a poet.'"

Tom dug the cell phone out of his pocket. He thumbed a number and stuck the phone under one ear. "It's me. Where are you?" Wil watched the dashboard figurine bobble. "I'm clear. Brecht didn't make it." There was silence. "Because *Wolf.* Because Wolf fucking turned up five seconds after we made contact." Wil heard a tinny voice squawk from the phone, male but unfamiliar. "Well, fuck! Whose fucking fault is that? Just tell me where you can meet. I want to get off the road." He exhaled. "Fine. We'll be there." He dropped the phone into his pocket.

"Who's Wolf?" said Wil.

"A bad person," said Tom. "A bad, bad person."

"Like Rain?"

"Yes."

"Is Wolf a poet, too?"

"Yup," said Tom, overtaking.

"And when you say *poet*," Wil said, since Tom seemed to be answering questions, "is that like the name of their organization, or do you mean—"

"I mean she's good with words," Tom said. "Now shut up."

"I'm just trying to understand."

"You don't need to understand. You need to sit there and not do anything stupid while I take care of you. That's what you need. Look, I get that it's been a confusing night. And now you're all, *But how is that possible*, and, *Why did he do that*. But I'm not going to answer those questions, Wil, because you don't have the framework to comprehend the answers. You're like a kid asking how I can see him even though he's closed his eyes. Just accept that this is happening."

"Can you give me the framework?"

"No," said Tom. "Shut up."

He was silent. "Why did you shoot that girl?"

"I had to."

"She was just lying there," Wil said. "She was already half-dead."

"She was dangerous, lying there, half-dead."

Wil said nothing.

"Okay," Tom said. "You hear about that bad nightclub fire in Rome a couple months back? Bunch of people died? That was Rain. And she did it because she thought one of those people might be you."

"Rain wanted to kill me?"

"Yes."

"Why?"

"Because eighteen months ago you survived something you shouldn't have."

"In Broken Hill?"

"Yes."

"I don't remember that."

"No."

"What was it?"

"What?"

"The thing that should have killed me."

"Something bad," Tom said. "Which shouldn't have got out."

"You mean chemicals? People died in a chemical spill in Broken Hill eighteen months ago."

"Sure. Chemicals."

"So why do you care?"

"Because it's out again."

"And I can stop it?"

"Yes."

"That doesn't make sense."

"That's because it's not really chemicals," Tom said.

"Is it a word?"

Tom looked at him.

"Earlier, in the snow, you were interested in something I said about words. And you said Wolf and Rain are poets because they're good with words."

Tom was silent. "Okay. It's a word."

"Which should have killed me."

"Yes."

"I don't understand how it can be a word."

"That's because you don't know what words are."

"They're sounds."

"No, they're not. You and I are not grunting at each other. We're transferring meaning. Neurochemical changes are occurring in your brain at this very moment, because of my words."

Wil was silent.

"Like I said," Tom said, "no framework."

He felt lost. "No one lives in Broken Hill anymore. Not since the spill."

"No."

"Why did Cecilia try to kill me?"

"It's complicated."

"Was she a poet?"

"No."

"Then . . . why?"

"Rain made her."

"The rain made her?"

"Not . . . not *rain*. Kathleen Raine, with an *E*. Wrote poems about nature. Lived in England from 1908 to 2003."

"And . . . she . . . came back?"

Tom glanced at him. "Are you serious?"

"What?"

"They use the *names*. The names of famous poets."

"Oh," said Wil.

"They're not *zombies*."

"Okay. I thought . . ."

The drove in silence.

"Is Wolf—"

"Virginia Woolf," Tom said.

"Virginia Woolf is trying to kill me?"

"Among others. But Woolf is the one to worry about."

"Why did your friend shoot himself? Because of words?"

"We're done talking," said Tom, with finality.

Wil shut his mouth. The road unraveled out of the dark and they went into it.

ITALIAN "INFERNO"
CLUB FLOUTED FIRE CODE

ROME: Overcrowding contributed to the deaths of 24 people in a popular Italian nightclub, early reports suggest.

The fire, believed to have been caused by faulty wiring, tore through the Paradiso Club at around 10 P.M. last Saturday night, when the building was at its most packed.

Reports in Italian media said a crush developed at exits to one of the club's dance floors, with patrons unable to escape and becoming overcome by smoke. All two dozen people in this area are believed to have perished.

Mariastella Gallioni, 18, who escaped the adjoining Musica section, described seeing a doorway filled with people. "There were two men [trying to get out] but they didn't move. They were blocking the doorway. No one could get past."

The Paradiso recently completed a major renovation, during which it was granted fire certification. Italy's government inspectors are notoriously corrupt.

Police have promised a full investigation.

[FOUR]

Emily kept waiting for someone to pull her aside, ask what she thought she was doing, trying to sneak on board with the first-class passengers. But when she reached the gate and handed over her boarding pass, the attendant smiled. "Have a nice flight, Ms. Ruff."

"Thanks." She adjusted the strap of her bag, self-conscious. The other first-class passengers were in sleek suits and expensive blouses, and Emily was wearing jeans a guy had peed on the day before. She hadn't realized everyone would be so bright and clean.

"Ms. Ruff!" said the attendant on the plane, like he'd been waiting to meet her. "My information tells me this is the first time you've graced our airline. That cannot be true." He beckoned, leading her past banks of leather thrones. "I am going to take extra special care of you." He leaned close and whispered, stage-loud, "We need more beautiful young customers."

She thought he was making fun. But he wasn't. First class was strange.

"Make yourself comfortable," said the attendant, "while I rustle you up the best chocolate cookie you've ever tasted."

"Okay," she said. She went to stow her bag and the attendant looked horrified and took it from her. She slid into her seat. She had slept in smaller places than this. To her right, a woman in big sunglasses had a tall glass in one hand and a magazine in the other. She smiled at Emily, and Emily smiled back. The woman returned to her magazine. This was okay, she thought. This was okay.

She heard a tinkling and reached for her bag. The flight attendant whispered, "I'm so sorry." He set a glass of water onto the armrest. The tinkling was ice cubes. "I didn't mean to wake you."

She stared at the glass. When she'd first heard that sound, she'd thought someone was peeing.

She deplaned. That was what they called it: *deplaning.* She had never heard that word before. She unbuckled and felt sad. She wanted to stay in her little first-class kingdom.

She'd left a note for a friend to pass to Benny. Had he read it yet? Was he upset? Missing her? She didn't care about this as much as she'd thought. She had realized this while gazing out at the hidden world of sunlight that lay above the clouds: She was leaving Benny behind. And this was a good thing. She felt like she had two years before, when she'd walked away from a falling-down house with her Pikachu bag on her back, her mom's threats and prophecies bouncing off her back, and the more she walked the better she felt. Benny hadn't been good. Not really. She was getting a sense of that, now that people were taking her bags and bringing her drinks while she slept. She was seeing that without Benny, she could be so much more.

The attendant touched her arm at the exit. "Thank you so much."

"Thank *you* so much," she said.

In Arrivals stood a driver, complete with hat and uniform, holding a printed sign reading EMILY RUFF. "I'm Emily," she said.

He reached for her bag. She hesitated, but let him take it; she needed to get used to that. "I'm very pleased to meet you, miss. I have a car out front. Was your flight bearable?"

"Yes." She fell into step. She felt kind of stupid about the Pokémon bag. It looked ridiculous on this guy's trolley. But he didn't seem to mind. People glanced at her, this dirty girl with a uniformed driver, and she tried not to smile, so as not to ruin it.

He held open a door for her. Outside was bright and cold. A long, liquid black limousine lay spread along the curb. The driver opened the rear door and she climbed inside like it was nothing.

Did she want a drink? To watch TV? Because she could do that. There was enough room to lie down. She could live here.

The driver entered. The locks thunked. "No rain expected. You come to us on a good day."

"I thought it was a good day," she said. "I felt that."

They drove for forty minutes and stopped at a set of high steel gates. Through the limo's dark glass, she saw grass and gigantic trees. The driver spoke to someone in a guardhouse; the gates parted. As they moved up the hill, a building appeared.

"It's an old convent," said the driver. "There were nuns here for a hundred years." The car pulled around the front of the building, its tires crunching gravel. A man came down steps toward them. A porter. That was what he was. "Beautiful, isn't it?"

"Yes."

"They'll take you from here." He turned in his seat to face her. She liked that: the way people were turning to talk to her. "Best of luck with your examinations, miss."

The porter led her to a room with high ceilings and wood-paneled walls and ten thousand books. A sitting room, she guessed. Because she had heard of those, and couldn't think what else this room was for. Maybe nothing. Maybe after a certain size, a building had more rooms than uses. She squeezed her bag between her ankles and tried to relax. Occasionally she heard a door close—*thonk*—and murmurs of conversation, and laughter that floated up a corridor somewhere. She kind of needed to pee.

A woman's heels rapped outside. The door clacked open. For a second, Emily thought it was a nun, but it was just a woman in a dark blue suit. She had nuns on the brain. The woman was slim, maybe thirty-five, with dark hair and delicate glasses. She came toward Emily with her hand extended and her fingers down. A lady handshake. Emily got off the chair to take it. "Hello, Emily. Thank you so much for joining us. I'm Charlotte."

"Hi," she said.

Charlotte settled into a chair. Emily returned to hers. They seemed a long way apart. A rug lay between them like a map of some undiscovered world. "In a moment, I'll show you to your room," Charlotte said. "But first, I'm sure you must have questions."

She did. Like, *What was with that Lee guy*, and *Why me*, and *These examinations, what are they, exactly.* But she didn't ask them. The thing was, if these questions had bad answers, it was going to be really disappointing.

"We have six of you this week," said Charlotte, deciding to answer questions Emily hadn't asked. "Six applicants, that is. You each have your own room, of course. Yours overlooks the East Wood; I think you'll enjoy it. There's a central dining room, where you'll be served meals, and you'll find a recreation room at the end of the hall, and a reading room beside that. Between examinations, please do feel free to explore the grounds. It's a wonderful space. It was once a convent."

"I heard."

"If you leave the New Wing, you may bump into some of our current students going about their lessons. They are under instruction not to speak to you, so please don't interpret this as rudeness." She smiled.

"Okay," she said.

"I must ask that you observe two rules for the duration of the examinations. You are not to leave the grounds, nor use the phones. These rules are quite important. Do you find them acceptable?"

"Yes."

"Good!" She patted her lap, like she wanted a cat to sit there. "Well, then. For the rest of the day, you may simply settle in. Meet your fellow applicants, enjoy the facilities. The examinations will begin in the morning."

"I do have a question," Emily said. "What's the catch?"

Charlotte's eyebrows rose. She had good eyebrows. Like whips. "I beg your pardon?"

"Well . . ." She gestured at the room. "This is kind of unbelievably good. I mean, I appreciate it, but if you're going to ask me to shave my head or take my clothes off or something, I'd like to know."

Charlotte suppressed a smile. "We're not a cult, I promise. We're a school. We bring the best and the brightest here to help them reach their potential."

"Right," Emily said.

"You seem unconvinced."

"It doesn't look like a school."

"Actually, it looks very much like a school. You may think otherwise because your experience has been limited to government-run child farms." She leaned forward and whispered conspiratorially, "To me, those do not look very much like schools." Emily wasn't sure how to respond. Charlotte rose to her feet. "Well! Let me show you your room."

She picked up her bag. "I still think there's a catch."

Charlotte pursed her lips. "If there must be a catch, we do only admit those who pass the examinations. Which are difficult."

"I'll pass."

Charlotte smiled. "Well, then," she said. "There's no catch."

She followed Charlotte through wood-paneled corridors and halls with far-off ceilings. She had never seen so many arches. Charlotte tapped a door with her fingernail. "My office." A copper nameplate was engraved C. BRONTË. "Come to me with any questions or concerns, day or night." There were more corridors. Through tall, slitted windows, she glimpsed kids in dark blue uniforms with hats and blazers. Maybe it did look like a school.

Charlotte stopped outside a heavy wooden door. "Your room."

There was a small bed. A high, arched window. One old desk with a high-backed chair. The walls were stone, patches worn smooth by the palms of restless nuns.

"A few of the others are about," said Charlotte. "But I'll let you find them in your own time." She smiled, one hand draped on the door handle. "Dinner will be called at six." The door closed.

Emily let her bag drop. She went to the window and studied the mechanism until she figured out how to swing open the glass in two panels. She leaned out. A breeze tugged her hair. *Woods* was right. The trees were like pillars. You could get lost in there. Find a gingerbread house. Meet a witch.

She needed the bathroom. She would have to find some of the other kids, check out the competition. But she stood awhile and watched the trees, because even if this whole deal turned out to be a scam, this moment here was really nice.

She peed and washed her hands and studied herself in the mirror. Her hair was like straw. She was wearing an outfit that looked worse the fancier her environment became and didn't smell terrific, either. But aside from this, she did not seem completely out of place. She could possibly believe she was a person who regularly peed in bathrooms with twenty-foot ceilings. And then went out on her horse. "Relax," she told the mirror, because her eyes were tense.

She followed sounds of a television to a small room with sofas and cushions and a boy spread across them. He sat up as she entered. His hair was very curly. His clothes were new and bright and his collar was turned up. If they had something in common, she couldn't see it.

His eyes moved over her. He was probably thinking the same thing. "Hey," he said.

"Hi. Who are you?"

"A guy. On a sofa." He smiled. She hated him already. "You're here for the tests?"

"Yeah."

"Just arrived?"

"Yeah."

"From where?"

"San Francisco."

"Right," he said. "And, uh, where in San Francisco?" He smiled again. That upturned collar, what was that?

"Street." He looked blank. "The," she said. "The street. You know. The street."

He shook his head. "I don't know."

"Yeah, I see that."

"I'm sorry. I don't mean to offend. I mean, what is it you, uh, do?" He twirled a finger, indicating the room. "They don't bring you here for no reason."

"I'm a magician. I entertain."

"Really?" he said. "You don't strike me as the entertaining type."

"You don't strike me as someone who knows jack about shit," she said, because she was starting to get a little intimidated by his wording. "Why are you here?"

He grinned. His teeth were really something. "New England Schools Debating Conference. Finals." He waited for a response. "I'm good."

"Are you," she said.

She showered and re-dressed. Where she'd come from, it was fine to wear the same clothes for days at a time; that meant you were busy following life's opportunities. But she could see that here it was going to become an issue. She pulled on her jacket, at least, which was furry and had little biker studs she made fun of if anyone mentioned them but secretly thought were awesome. She brushed her hair until most of the knots were gone and clipped it out of her face. She had a faint memory of mascara left in her makeup bag and scraped together what she could to give herself smoky eyes. She had lost her deodorant somewhere. But she had soaped up in the shower. The reality was she smelled better than she had in a while.

A bell rang somewhere: an honest to God bell, like a musical instrument. She opened her door to faces peering out of doorways. They were all young, mostly female. "Chow time!" said a black girl across the hall, and there were titters.

The dining hall table had twelve places set on a tablecloth the size of a bedsheet but there were still miles of glowing wood stretching away at either end. The curly-haired boy came in, joking with a girl she hadn't met, and sat opposite. She thought he might look at her but he didn't. She tried to figure out the cutlery. A girl, no more than ten, climbed onto a chair beside her. Emily said hi and the girl said hi back, shyly. On her other side, a pretty girl with angel-blond hair slid into a seat. The curly-haired boy looked at the blond girl and away and then back and Emily thought, *Yeah, okay.*

Charlotte, whom Emily still vaguely thought of as a nun, moved around the table, chatting briefly to each of them. Bread was served. Soup. The ten-year-old stared hopelessly at her spoons and Emily tried to help with educated guesses based on what everyone else was using.

"I love your jacket," said the angelic blond girl. "It's so authentic."

"Oh," she said. "I like your ears."

"My ears?"

Emily had meant that as an insult but now realized the angel girl was serious. The girl had seriously tried to compliment her jacket. "Yeah. They're like a fairy's." She elbowed the ten-year-old. "Fairy ears, right?"

"Yes."

"Oh," said the angel girl. "Well, thank you."

There were silver plates with bite-size constructions of meat and bread and paste and whatever. She picked one up only because it got her out of this conversation. It was actually not bad. Weird, but not bad-weird. This was her whole day, on a cracker.

Charlotte rose and gave a short speech about how happy she was to have them here and she hoped they would seize the opportunity with two hands because each of them had great potential and the Academy was dedicated to unlocking it. Then she said they should sleep well because the first examination would begin early, and the curly-haired boy asked what it would be, and Charlotte smiled and said that would be answered by the morning. Those were her words: *Answered by the morning.* You would get your head kicked in talking that way in Emily's world, but she was kind of enjoying it. On the pier, under her floppy hat, she used words to make people smile and come closer and give her two dollars and not care about losing. Good words were the difference between Emily eating well and not. And what she had found worked best were not facts or arguments but words that tickled people's brains for some reason, that just amused them. Puns, and exaggerations, and things that were true and not at the same time. *Answered by the morning.* Words like that.

Afterward, they filed back to their rooms and she brushed her teeth alongside a girl from Connecticut. Everyone but her had pajamas. On her way to bed, a voice floated down the hallway: "Good night, girl in a doorway."

"Night, boy on a sofa," she said. She closed her door. She couldn't believe she had just said that. He was trouble, this boy. But the good kind.

In the morning, they were sat in a hall and given forms. The first questions she recognized: Was she a cat person or a dog person? What was her favorite color? Did she love her family? Even the weird one was right there: *Why did you do it?* It was at the very top of a page and the rest was nothing but endless lines.

"Please answer with complete honesty," said Charlotte. She moved between their desks, echoes of her heels bouncing between the floor and ceiling. "Anything less will not serve you well."

They asked her favorite movies. Songs. Books. She hadn't read a book since she was eight. She glanced around. The ten-year-old was three desks behind. Her feet didn't even reach the floor. Emily twirled her pen. She wrote: *Princess Lily Saves the World.* It was the only one she could remember.

Charlotte collected the papers and disappeared for a while. People leaned across aisles and compared answers. She noticed a man in the corridor, tall with brown skin and eyes like rocks, watching them through the glass. She felt flustered for some reason and looked away, and when she looked back, he was gone.

Charlotte returned with a TV on a trolley. "You will be shown a series of rapidly changing images. One of the images will be of a type of food. You are to write down the name of the food. Are there any questions?" She looked around. "Very well. Good luck."

Emily picked up her pencil. Charlotte pressed a button on the VCR. On the screen, text appeared—SERIES 1-1—then faded away. There was a second of blackness. Then a jumble of images flashed by and was gone. Emily blinked. The screen said: END OF SERIES 1-1. Heads bent over desks. Emily looked at her paper. That had been a lot faster than she'd expected. What had she seen? A laughing face. A family around a table. People kissing. Grass. A cow. A glass of milk? She wasn't sure. Which was strange, because she was observant. She had quick eyes. So why wasn't she sure about the milk? She glanced around. Everyone but her was writing. She chewed her lip. She wrote: MILK.

"Pens down, please."

She glanced around. The curly-haired boy to her right had SUSHI. She felt cold. Had there been sushi? Maybe. She looked left. The angel girl: SUSHI.

Charlotte prowled the desks. "Yes," she said, passing a boy at the front. "Yes. Yes." She stopped at Emily. "No." Emily exhaled. "Yes. Yes. No."

She turned to see who else had fucked up. It was the ten-year-old, who looked devastated. Before she hid her paper, Emily saw: MILK.

"Series two," said Charlotte.

Obviously, what she'd done wrong was let herself be misled by the other images. Breakfast, a cow, and there *had* been a glass, but empty. Her brain had filled that in. She was too imaginative. And the reason she didn't get sushi was she didn't know what the fuck sushi looked like. She kind of remembered now. But it wasn't exactly a familiar food. These other guys probably ate sushi twice a week, with caviar and quail and whatever that paste was on the crackers yesterday. Pâté. That. She would get the next one.

Images flickered. The screen blanked. Terror gripped her. There had been a banana. Definitely a banana. But also a sun, which kind of looked like a banana, and at the start she'd caught a glimpse of what might have been a fish. She had definitely seen palm trees and an ocean. She wasn't sure about the fish. Or the banana. The banana could have been an afterimage of the sun. Why were there palm trees? Was that random, or was it trying to make her think of fish? She squeezed her pen. She wrote: FISH.

"Answers, please."

She looked around. The curly-haired boy: BANANA. The angel girl: BANANA. The ten-year-old: FISH.

"Yes. Yes. Yes." Charlotte reached her. "No."

She had outsmarted herself. She should have trusted her instincts.

She didn't want to meet the curly-haired boy's eyes but couldn't stop herself. His eyes were closed, as if he was focusing, clearing his mind. *Dick*, she thought. But maybe she should do that.

"Series three."

The screen barfed images. This time it talked, which took her by surprise: A man said, "Red," and an old woman laughed, and was that a strawberry? No, a blood spot. It ended. She had definitely seen ice cream in a cone. She wrote that down before she could second-guess herself. She covered her paper with her hands and stared holes in the girl in front of her.

The curly-haired boy put down his pen. She couldn't see his paper, so she mouthed: *Ice cream?* His eyebrows rose. She didn't know what that meant. She felt a surging desire to pick up her pen and write something else. But she hadn't seen anything but ice cream.

"Answers, please."

The curly-haired boy moved his hands. STRAWBERRY. "Double *fuck*," she said. She didn't bother to look at the others. Charlotte reached her and confirmed that she had gotten it wrong, again. There were two more nos: Along with her and the ten-year-old, a skinny guy in the back had messed up. Emily was glad for this, but mostly furious. Give ten dollars to each of the people in this room, wait two hours, and Emily would have it all. Drop them on the street with no cash and no place to sleep, she would be the one with her shit together twenty-four hours later. These tests, though, were making her feel like a moron.

"Series four."

Fuck you, she thought. She looked at the screen but her heart wasn't in it. It was the longest sequence yet. When it ended, she looked at her paper and thought: *I have no idea.*

The girl in front of her let out an explosive sneeze. It was the kind of thing Benny would do when she wanted a moment's distraction, and without thinking, she flicked her eyes right. Beneath the curly-haired boy's arm: APR. The rest was obscured. "Bless you," said the angel. Someone tittered. "Quiet," said Charlotte.

She couldn't think of a food that started with APR. She was mentally stuck on APPLE. Could he have written APP? If she couldn't think of an APR food in five seconds, she was going with APPLE. Charlotte opened her mouth. Emily scrawled: APRICOT.

"Answers, please."

She glanced right. *Yes.* Charlotte began to walk the desks. "Yes. Yes. Yes." By the time she reached Emily, Emily had noticed a problem. The boy had APRICOTS. She was short an S. Charlotte paused. Emily said nothing. *Come on,* she thought. *Apricot, apricots, what's the difference?* "Yes," said Charlotte.

She glowed. This was what she should have done from the beginning. This was how she'd accomplished everything in her whole life: by skirting the rules. She should not have forgotten that.

"Yes. Yes. No." Charlotte walked to the front and turned off the TV. "Thank you. This concludes the first examination. Please enjoy the rest of the day." People began to talk, rising from their desks. "Gertie, remain behind, please."

Emily looked at the ten-year-old. The kid looked miserable, so Emily leaned over. "It's just a stupid test." She'd been wrong about this girl's age. Gertie wasn't even ten. "Don't worry about it."

"Emily Ruff," said Charlotte. "You may go."

"You're just too young," Emily said. "I was here a couple years back and failed everything. Next year, you'll smash it."

Gertie looked at her hopefully.

"*Thank* you, Emily," said Charlotte.

She gave Gertie a wink on the way out, the kind that tickled people on the pier.

"Thought you were history," said the curly-haired boy. She had been passing by his room but now she stopped. He was splayed on his bed. The angel girl was in there, leaning against the stone wall.

"Just warming up." She went to move on, but the girl peeled herself from the wall.

"Hey. I want your opinion. Why do the teachers here have fake names?"

Emily looked at her, confused.

"Charlotte Brontë. There's a teacher named Robert Lowell and a Paul Auster, too. Did you see the main board in the lobby? It says before Brontë, the headmistress was Margaret Atwood." She raised her eyebrows.

"And . . . ?" said Emily.

"They're famous poets," said the boy. "Dead famous poets, mostly." He looked at the angel girl, amused. "She didn't know."

"Like I sit around memorizing *poets*," Emily said. "This is why I'm going to destroy you in the tests, because everything you know is useless."

The boy grinned. The girl said, "It's okay," in a tone that made Emily want to hit her.

"And the school has no name. They just call it the Academy. Kind of weird, yes?"

"You're kind of weird," she said.

Gertie didn't come back. "The tests are eliminations," said the curly-haired boy, through a mouthful of rye bread. This was at lunch. He had taken Gertie's seat. "Fail one, that's it. Pack your bags."

She paused midway through buttering a roll. "Who told you that?"

"No one. I figured it out. It's obvious, don't you think?" He chewed and chewed.

Charlotte came in during lunch and looked at Emily in a way Emily didn't like. Then she left. Emily continued eating, but her stomach formed a hard ball. Afterward, Charlotte and another teacher were waiting for her in the corridor. It reminded Emily of San Francisco, where you'd step in the front door of your squat and there'd be two skinny bitches there, hips jutting, lips like cats' asses, trembling with righteous outrage about something or other. Some debt, or thing you did. Charlotte beckoned. "Emily. If you please." Her heels clacked down the hall.

In her office, Charlotte gestured at a chair. The office was larger than Emily had thought. It had doors to other rooms, one of which Charlotte must sleep in, since she'd said to come see her any time of day. It had a single window that looked onto a courtyard, and a messy desk, on which stood a vase of fresh flowers. "I'm disappointed."

"Are you," she said.

"We gave you a sizable opportunity. You will never know how great."

"I don't know what you're talking about."

"The examination room is monitored. Carefully."

"I see," Emily said. There was silence. "So you're saying I did something wrong in some way."

"Cheating? Yes. That was wrong."

"Well, you should have said that. You should have said, 'Actually, we have three rules, the third one is don't cheat.' "

"You think that bears stating?"

"That guy in San Francisco who sent me here, Lee, he knew I cheated people. That's what I do. I'm a hustler. You bring me here but suddenly I can't cheat? You never said that."

"I said honest answers were essential."

"In the test *before*. Not the video test."

"This isn't up for discussion," Charlotte said. "A driver is coming to collect you. Please collect your things."

"Well," she said, "fuck."

"You may have been promised compensation for your time here. Unfortunately, that will not apply, due to the cheating."

"You bitch."

Charlotte's face didn't change. Emily had expected some kind of reaction, from someone so nunnish. She had assumed Charlotte was quietly furious, the way people got when you broke one of their made-up rules, but the truth was Charlotte didn't seem to care. "You may go."

"Forget the driver. I don't want anything from you." She got up.

"The airport is twenty miles. The driver—"

"Fuck your driver," she said.

She went to her room and stuffed clothes into her Pikachu bag. Until this point she had felt nothing but anger, but abruptly she was heartbroken and shaky with tears. She threw the bag over her shoulder and banged into the corridor. "Hey!" It was the curly-haired boy. "What happened? Where are you going?" But she didn't answer and he didn't come after her.

There was no sign of a driver and she began to trudge down the driveway. About a thousand windows looked onto her back, and she imagined eyes in each one. But that was silly; the fact was, nobody would care. She would be gone five minutes and they would forget she'd existed, because the place made more sense without her.

Halfway down the driveway, a car crunched up behind her. "Emily Ruff?"

"I don't want a driver."

"I'm not . . ." She heard the hand brake crank, the door open. "I'm not a driver." It was the tall man she'd seen through the glass during her test. "My name is Eliot. Please come back to the house."

"I've been evicted."

"Hold up a second. Stop."

She stopped. The man scrutinized her. He had a stillness about him, which made him hard to read.

"You cheated. Your defense is that nobody said you couldn't. I agree. Go back to the house."

"I don't want to go back to the house."

"Why not?"

"Because I'm not going to make it, okay? It's pretty clear that everyone here but me is incredibly smart and knows, like, the names of poets, so . . . thanks for the opportunity." She started walking again.

He matched her pace. "There are two types of exams. The first tests your ability to withstand persuasion. The second measures your ability to persuade. This is more important. And from what I've seen, you have a good shot at those."

"Charlotte said—"

"It's not up to Charlotte."

She looked back at the school. It was kind of tempting.

"It would be a shame to never discover what you were capable of." He shrugged. "My opinion."

"Oh, fine," she said.

She returned to her room and dumped her bag. She didn't think she'd have to wait long and she was right. The curly-haired boy came in and looked at her angrily. "I thought you left."

"I changed my mind."

"Or someone changed it for you?" He folded his arms. "They only take one of us."

The angel girl appeared in the doorway. Emily said, "They only take one?"

"I never heard that," said the angel girl.

"On the last day, if there's more than one candidate left, you have to persuade the others to quit. That's how you make it."

"I never heard that," said the girl, "and I say, welcome back, Emily."

"You're an idiot," said the boy.

"You're an asshole," said the girl.

The boy looked at her. "You might as well leave now. I bet you're persuasive as hell, to people who know your parents. In student council, you're a queen. But you're only here because it's supposed to be the best, and that's what good little girls do. They do their best."

The girl's cheeks flamed. "Is this supposed to make me quit?"

"I already know how to make you quit. Have Daddy call and say he misses you."

The girl turned and left. Emily heard her feet slapping down the corridor. She looked at the boy.

"This school is mine," he said.

Early next morning, Charlotte drove her downtown. She barely spoke and Emily was still somewhat pissed so it was a quiet journey. They pulled into a parking garage and Charlotte killed the engine. Emily unbuckled but Charlotte didn't move.

"Eliot thinks you're worth persisting with," Charlotte said to the rearview mirror. "It seems pointless to me. But occasionally he sees things."

Emily kept her mouth shut.

"Usually, this examination is administered by a junior staff member." Charlotte popped open the glove box and applied big sunglasses. They made her look elegant and sexy, not like a nun at all. "But since you are so allegedly bursting with potential, I wanted to see for myself."

She led Emily to a nondescript street corner, where there was a grocer, a newspaper stand, and a dog tied to a NO STANDING pole. One of those things was important, Emily figured. Charlotte glanced at her watch. It was early but the sun was peeking above the buildings and seemed excited to be there. If they were going to hang around out here, Emily should lose the jacket.

"Our purpose today is to test your lexicon," Charlotte said. "By which I mean your array of useful words." This did not clarify anything for Emily. "Are you ready?"

"Sure," she said.

Charlotte's sunglasses swung to the far sidewalk, which was empty. They waited. "A whore is 'one who desires.' The word is Proto-Indo-European. From the same root as *love*. Did you know that?"

"No."

"Today, the word is used to describe any person who can be persuaded. Most obviously, by money for sex. But also more generally. One may 'whore oneself' by performing any kind of vaguely unpleasant act in exchange for reward."

Emily shifted from one foot to the other.

"A similar term is *proselyte*. Typically used in a religious sense, to denote a person converting from one faith to another. Like a whore, a proselyte is persuaded to perform an act. The difference is that a whore does what she knows is wrong for reward, while a proselyte does what she has been persuaded to believe is right." She glanced at Emily. "You are to remain within three feet of where you currently stand. If you move beyond that radius, you fail the examination. You are to persuade people on that side of the road to cross to this side. You may not use the same method of persuasion more than once per person or group. Each person or group you fail to persuade is a strike. After three strikes, the test ends. You begin now."

Emily stared. Charlotte nodded to the far sidewalk. A girl in a track suit was jogging down it. For a moment, Emily froze. Then she yelled, "Hey! Hello!" She waved her arms. The jogger pulled earbuds out of her ears. "Can you come here? Please? It's very important!"

The woman looked annoyed. But she stopped, checked the traffic, and headed across the road.

"Nonspecific anonymous verbal summons," said Charlotte, retreating to the shade of a clothes store awning. "One."

The jogger reached her, blond and sweaty. "Yeah?"

"Sorry," said Emily. "I thought you were somebody else." The woman gave her a dirty look and plugged her earbuds back in. Emily felt sweat on the back of her neck. "How many do I need to pass?"

"I'm afraid I can't divulge that. But if you're interested, the record is thirty-six."

"Jesus."

"Eliot, actually. Attention, please. Here comes another."

Emily pulled off her jacket and dropped it to the sidewalk. "John!" she yelled. "John! *Hey, John!*"

The man on the opposite sidewalk paused. When he realized she was talking to him, he looked amused and shook his head.

"What?" She held her hand behind her ear. "Can't hear you, John!"

"I'm not John!"

"*What?*"

"I'm not . . ." He gave up and detoured toward her.

"Verbal summons by name," said Charlotte. "Two."

Three women climbed out of a car, talking and laughing. "Hey! Free outfits!" Emily said. "First three customers!" Their heads turned. Emily pointed at the clothes store. "Up to two hundred dollars per customer!"

"Verbal promise of material reward by proxy. Three."

The man reached her, smiling gently. "I think you've confused me with somebody else."

"Oh, yeah." Over his shoulder, a mother holding the hand of a young boy headed for the grocer. "Sorry about that. Ma'am! Ma'am! I need to talk to you about your son!" The woman glanced at her, then away. "Ma'am, there is something wrong with your son!"

"Did you say free outfits?" one of the trio asked her. She had a stud in her nose and outrageous mascara.

"Ma'am!" Emily yelled at the mother. "There is a real serious problem with your son! I'm not joking!"

The mother turned in to the grocer. Emily could read tension in her neck: She'd heard but chosen to ignore her.

She looked at Charlotte. "That's only one strike, right, because they were together."

"Correct. One strike."

"I don't see any signs," said the mascara woman. "Do we just go in, or . . . ?"

"Yeah. Go in." The middle-aged man was leaving, looking disappointed. She guessed he wanted to be John. But coming down the far sidewalk was a gaggle of college-age boys in baggy pants and muscle shirts. She opened her mouth, almost reused a method, then dropped to one knee. "Ow! Shit! Ow!" The boys' heads turned. She pretended to try to rise. "Shit! Help!"

At eight-thirty, she removed her T-shirt. Beneath it she had a plain bra; she hesitated, then unhooked it. Her skin puckered. She waved to a group of boys gaping across the street. They looked at each other, laughed, and came within two feet of being cleaned up by a sedan on their way over. Emily glanced at Charlotte. "This is allowed, right?"

"Nonverbal sexual invitation. Nineteen."

She thought she heard a tone. "Are you disappointed?"

"Actually," said Charlotte, "I'm surprised you waited this long."

"Check it," snickered one of the boys. They clustered ten feet away, at the edge of the street, as if afraid to come any closer.

"Hey," she said, "do me a favor. Go to that corner and don't let anyone past you. Make everyone come over here."

"What for?" said one. Another said, "I want to stay and look at your titties." This cracked them up for a while. They were pretty young.

"I'll make it worth your while." There was a man coming: a big guy, with a shaved head and a black undershirt. "Real nice! Personal!" She didn't know what she was saying.

The boys headed across the street. She pulled her T-shirt back on, to avoid breaking the rule about reusing a technique. Charlotte said, "I hope you're aware that should your proxies redirect multiple groups, that will count as a duplicate method of persuasion, and therefore a strike."

"Oh. Shit." The boys were talking animatedly to the shaved head man, pointing at her. Behind them, a small group of elderly women approached. "Shit!"

"Twenty," said Charlotte, as the man with the shaved head crossed the street. "Persuasion by proxy."

"That's enough!" she yelled at the boys. "Go away now!" But they were focused on the old women. "You . . . dicks!"

The man with the shaved head reached her. His face was guarded; she had no idea what the boys had told him. Her bra was lying on the concrete, she noticed. She had forgotten it. "You okay?"

"They attacked me." She picked up her bra and clutched it to her chest. "Those boys."

While the man with the shaved head was beating up the boys, she got her bra back on. She pulled her hair free of the back of her T-shirt. The old women had backed up to the far corner and were waiting for the lights to cross. The sidewalk was otherwise empty. She had a minute. Charlotte said, "Diversion by physical threat. Twenty-one."

"Oh my God!" she yelled, because a pair of middle-aged women were coming now. "It's Demi Moore!" The women stopped. Emily pointed at Charlotte. "Can I have your autograph?"

Charlotte's lips twitched.

"There is a similarity," Emily said.

"Attraction by . . . feigned celebrity, I suppose. Twenty-two."

"What's a pass, again?"

Charlotte's sunglasses regarded her. "Five."

"Five," Emily echoed. She felt good. A teenage girl in big headphones rounded the corner, heading down the sidewalk. Emily had no idea what she was going to say to the little whore, but it was something. She opened her mouth.

KNOW YOUR FRIENDS®!

Question 6/10: Are you a cat person or a dog person?

- ☐ Cat!
- ☐ Dog!

Next question →

Send this questionnaire to your friends!

See your friends' results!

LIKE Know Your Friends®

[FIVE]

They left the freeway and passed through a series of snow-sunk towns. Wil fell asleep without meaning to and woke from guns and blood and dead girls. There was drool on his chin. In the high beams, the road glittered and vanished into night thick as a blanket. "Where are we?"

"Safe." Tom peered at the road. "Almost." They were slowing. The pickup truck's lights swung across a driveway. Wil saw a wire fence and wooden posts and a sign that said: MCCORMACK & SONS STOCK SALES. They came to a stop and the pickup gargled. "Hmm," Tom said.

"What?"

"Do you trust me?"

"Do I trust you?"

"I phrased that badly," Tom said. "I mean, if I tell you your life depends on doing exactly as I say, without hesitation, can I rely on you to do it?"

"Sure," Wil said, then, because that didn't sound very plausible, added, "Maybe."

"That's not really good enough. *Maybe* leaves you *maybe* alive."

"I thought we were meeting your friends."

"We are."

"So what's the problem?"

Tom gazed at the sign. "Nothing. There's no problem." He harassed the gearshift. The truck rolled into the driveway. It was thick with mud, dark tire tracks clearly visible. Tom pushed them forward two hundred yards, then paused at a fork. To the left, the road disappeared into darkness. To the right was a bare light on a pole. Within its sphere of illumination lay nothing but mud. Tom steered toward it. Their tires slipped briefly, found traction.

"What is this place?"

Metal railings appeared beside them for a while, then vanished again. They entered an open expanse of mud. The ground seemed oddly chewed up. They reached the pole and came to a halt. The engine idled. Tom pressed a button; the doors went *ka-chunk*. He took the shotgun from the footwell and laid it across his lap.

"What are we doing?"

"Quiet."

There was no noise but the engine. "Should I have a gun?"

Tom glanced at him.

"If we're in danger, and I'm doing what you say, then how about I have a gun?"

"That would increase the danger," Tom said. "To me." He peered into the dark.

Wil saw motion in the darkness. A man ran toward them, waving his arms. His jacket blew. He had long, straggly hair. He reached the truck and slapped the hood, grinning. Wil's window whirred down.

"Hey! Goddamn!" said the long-haired man. "Is this him? This really him?"

"Where are the others?" Tom said.

"Inside." The man's eyes crawled over Wil. "Holy shit, I cannot believe you found him."

"I can't see an inside."

"There's a house." The man gestured into the dark, his eyes not leaving Wil. "Get out of the truck. I'll take you in."

"Where can I put the truck?"

"Don't worry about the truck. Leave it. We're gone in ten minutes." The man tried Wil's door handle. "Let's move."

"Why'd you come running out like that?"

"I'm excited, Eliot! I'm psyched!" He tried the door again. "This is what we've been working for! This gives us a fucking chance!" He grinned.

Tom's head turned, examining the darkness. Wil didn't know what he was looking for.

"We have the plane. Fueled up, sitting on a strip out back. We've got drugs, we've got a big fucking probe, twenty minutes we're in the air and pulling this guy's head open." The man looked at him. "Nothing personal. But we need what's in there more than you do." He tried to rap Wil's head with his knuckles. "Man! I could kiss you!"

Tom said, "You realize how much emotion you're displaying right now."

The long-haired man looked at him. Then he lunged at Wil, grabbing his head, his fingers raking his skin. He forced his shoulders inside the car. His shoes scrabbled at the door. Tom hit the gas; the truck lurched forward. The long-haired man yelped and slipped and for a second Wil thought he was going to be dragged right out of the car. Then the fingers lost their grip on his head and neck and the man disappeared.

"*Fuck!*" he said. "What's happening?"

"Bad things," said Tom.

"That's your friend?"

"No. Not at the moment." Metal gleamed ahead. It was railing, the same kind that had guided them down the driveway. For a moment Wil thought Tom was going to try to smash through it. Then they swung in a semicircle. The railing curved endlessly. "Oh, I see," said Tom. "We're in a pen."

"A pen?"

"Cattle yard." He backed the truck around. Now they were facing the light pole. The long-haired man shambled out of the light toward them. Tom shifted gears. The pickup's wheels spun in mud.

"Oh," said Wil. "Oh, wait, no." The long-haired man grew in the windshield. At the last moment, Tom jagged left and the long-haired man thumped against the side of the truck. In the red glow of taillights, Wil saw him pick himself up out of the mud and begin to shamble after them. "You hit your friend," Wil said.

Tom braked. Wil caught himself. He looked at Tom. "What are you doing?" Tom didn't answer. "Your friend is coming."

"Stop calling him my friend."

"Well, that fucking guy is coming. He's twenty feet away."

Tom's eyes flicked to the mirror.

"Seriously. Time to go."

The long-haired man slapped the rear window. He ran to Wil's door and tried to tug it open with one hand. The other hung at a broken angle. The man gave a frustrated cry. His fingers scrabbled against the glass. His eyes kept moving to Wil, tight and hungry.

"The driveway is a funnel," said Tom.

"So let's—" The man threw his head against the glass with a *crack*. "Let's try something, you know?" Tom didn't respond. The man headbutted the window again. "Please. Tom. Don't make me sit here and watch this guy kill himself against the window."

Light flared ahead. Wil shielded his eyes. Something coughed and snarled.

"Aha," said Tom.

"What is that?"

"Truck." Tom shifted into reverse and threw an elbow over the seat. "Big truck." Ahead, the lights shivered. The snarl rose to a throaty roar. The man with the straggly hair fell to the mud and rose again. They swung in a half circle and Tom threw them into drive. As they bounced away from the driveway, Wil saw darkness coalesce into a shape. It was an animal transport, as large as a house, a grille like a grin. Smoke belched from twin exhausts above its cabin. As it moved into the pen, light fell across bright red cursive script on its front: *Faithful Bethany.*

"We have to get out of here." Their headlights bounced off metal railing. "Can we break through that?"

"No." Tom hauled the wheel.

"How do you know? Maybe we can break—"

"If we could break through, they would have chosen somewhere else." The transport filled the windshield. Tom accelerated toward it.

"What are you . . . what are you . . . Jesus!" He threw out his hands. Tom yanked the wheel. The pickup jumped. The transport clipped them and everything leaned and spun. Then the tires bit. They accelerated toward the driveway and freedom beyond for ten glorious seconds and then Tom braked again.

Wil, who had been straining forward, hit the dash and fell back in his seat. The pickup came to a halt at the driveway mouth. There were lumps in the mud. Big lumps. People, he saw. Three people, sitting.

"Who are they?" He looked at Tom. "Poets?"

"No."

"Why are they just sitting there?" A woman had a short black bob. Behind her was a teenage boy. Then an older man with white hair. They were looking at the pickup, their faces washed out by its lights, not moving.

Light grew within the cabin. Wil turned. The transport vehicle had completed a slow turn and was trundling toward them.

"You bitch," Tom said, like he was pointing out the sights. "You murderous, goddamn bitch."

"Tom. The truck." Tom revved the pickup's engine, but did not shift gear. "The truck, Tom."

Tom hauled the wheel. They accelerated alongside the railing, heading back into the pen. They gained speed and passed by the transport's churning wheels. The straggly-haired man appeared. Tom jerked the wheel but they were going too fast and he bounced off the hood and over the roof. Railing appeared ahead. It looked as if Tom was going to try to crash through it, but Wil knew this couldn't be the case, because Tom had said that was impossible, and then he realized it was, and closed his eyes.

The world lifted. He became an object. A thing with no control over its motion. The ground revolved and unexpectedly slapped him and everything went quiet.

He swallowed. He blinked. These were things he could do. He tried to move his head but the gravity was wrong. It was tugging him sideways. He went to rub his eyes and missed. A lot was wrong with this situation and he wasn't sure where to start.

"*Gug*," said Tom. Tom was leaning over the steering wheel. He must be having some problems with gravity, too, because he was above Wil's head. Maybe that was why he was hanging on to the wheel.

Lights moved across the dash. Not good lights, Wil recalled. He fumbled at his seat belt, got it, and fell against his door. The window was painted white. It took him a moment before he identified it as snow. Snow on the ground. The pickup was lying on its side. He tried the handle, just in case, but the ground didn't move.

"We have to go." Tom wasn't holding on to the steering wheel, he realized. The wheel had come out of the dash and was holding Tom. "Are you okay? What do I do?"

"*Gug.*"

He got a foot on the dash and strained past Tom for the driver's side door. When he did this his shoulder collected Tom's face and his knee went into Tom's ribs and Tom groaned. But he got his arms out of the truck and levered his body into the freezing night air. The animal transport was completing a turn, its lights sweeping the ground. "Hey. Tom. I'll lift you out."

Tom shook his head.

"Come on. You need to get out of there." Light splashed him. He looked up. Silhouetted before the transport was a shambling figure. The man. His arms hung. One leg dragged. He reached a torn place they had made in the cattle yard's railing and began to painfully climb through. "That guy is coming."

"*Gug.*" Tom's head bobbed toward the footwell. Wil saw the butt of the shotgun. Not *gug*, he realized. *Gun.*

"I'm not going to shoot people. Let me help you out."

"*Gun.*"

The straggly-haired man negotiated the wrecked railing and began to wade through the snow. That would become a lot easier soon, Wil saw, because in about ten feet there was a nice, cleared path where the pickup had returned to earth and started sliding. The snow there was red, drenched by the pickup's taillights.

"Take. It," said Tom.

"No!" The straggly-haired man reached the rear of the pickup and began to climb. Wil heard his shoes scraping against the tailpipe. "I'm not going to murder him!"

Hand slapped against the tailgate. The man's head appeared.

"Shit," Wil said, and pulled the shotgun from the door. He raised it to his shoulder and set it there. "Stop, you asshole!"

"*Shoo im,*" Tom said.

The man's torso flopped onto the side of the pickup's bed. He swung a leg up and Wil saw the jeans were dark with blood, the denim poking out in odd places. The man strained. His leg slipped off the pickup and he began trying to swing it up again.

"Stop fucking climbing!"

"Safe . . . ty," said Tom. "Button. On. Side."

"I'm Australian; I know how to use a shotgun!" He took a hand off the gun, squeezed it into a fist for circulation. "*Stop, you motherfucker!*"

The man rose on one leg and balanced awkwardly. His face was caked with dirt and blood. He looked intent and focused and not at all concerned about the gun Wil was pointing at him. He began to navigate along the side of the pickup's bed.

"Fuck," Wil said, and pulled the trigger. The gun boomed. The man fell off the truck. Wil dropped the shotgun without thinking. "Goddammit fuck!"

"Good," said Tom.

The transport's engine bellowed. Its exhausts hissed; its wheels began to turn.

"Now," said Tom. "Help me, please."

Wil reached down and grasped Tom's wrist. By the time he got Tom out of the cabin, the transport was close. They jumped into deep, shadowed snow. He began to forge forward. He made it out of the shade of the pickup and his shadow stretched out before him, long and thin and sharpening at the edges, coalescing into something vulnerable. The ground shook. There was a shriek of metal and Wil thought, *It's through the railing; it's thirty feet away*, and he didn't need to turn and verify this but did anyway. The transport bounced toward the pickup and swatted it aside. The idea of running suddenly seemed very stupid to Wil, because the transport was as big as a mountain. It was going to run him down no matter what he did.

Tom grabbed him by the ear. The transport hit deep snow and threw it up in a wave. Wil hadn't factored in the snow: That would slow it. He realized he could survive, or could have, had he thought of this about ten seconds ago. The truck plowed toward him, fountaining snow. It slowed and stopped. Its tires spun. Wil reached out and touched its bull bar.

Tom climbed the grille and raised the shotgun. The driver was a woman, Wil saw. Early forties. Glasses, kind of bookish. Not the sort of person he would have expected to try to kill him with an animal truck. She looked at Tom with an expression of mild intent and reached for a pistol that lay on the dash.

Tom fired through the windshield. Wil looked away. In the light, the snow was diamonds. A trillion tiny diamonds.

Tom dropped beside him. "Move."

He trudged through the snow. They didn't speak. Beyond the reach of the transport's headlights, the snow grew waist deep. Wil's breath steamed. Eventually, he said, "I can't keep going."

Tom looked at him. There was something terrible about his face. Tom looked at the cattle yard. Then, abruptly, he sat. He began to dig shells out of his coat pocket and feed them into the shotgun.

Wil sat beside him, panting. The transport was perhaps five hundred yards away, its lights blazing. He could see the hole in its windshield. "Was that Woolf?"

Tom looked at him. "What?"

"That woman."

"No," Tom said.

"Oh."

"If that was Woolf, I would be weeping hot tears of joy."

"Oh."

"Your hometown, Broken Hill? Woolf did that. Not a chemical spill. Woolf. I would be dancing a jig if that was Woolf."

"Got it," Wil said.

"Not Woolf," Tom said. "Not Woolf."

They sat in silence. Nothing moved but the wind. "Did you know that woman in the transport?"

"Yes."

"Why did she try to kill us?"

Tom didn't answer.

Wil shivered. He was wearing a T-shirt. "I'm cold."

Tom dropped the shotgun and lunged at him. Wil yelped, falling backward, and Tom grabbed his shirt, pulled him up, thrust him back to the snow, pulled him up again, and shoved him down. "What," Wil gasped. Tom grabbed a handful of snow and mashed it into Wil's mouth.

"You're cold?" Tom said. "You're cold?"

He released Wil. By the time Wil sat up, Tom had resumed his position and was facing the distant truck. Wil brushed snow from his face. "I'm sorry."

"You need to be better than this," Tom said. "You need to be worth it."

Wil folded his hands beneath his armpits and looked at the sky.

"So far, you're not worth shit."

"Okay, look, I didn't ask to be kidnapped."

"*Saved*, is another way of putting it."

"I didn't ask to be saved."

"Go, then."

"I'm not saying I want to *go*."

"Leave. See how long you last."

"I'm not saying that."

"You useless fuck," said Tom.

"I did shoot a guy. I mean, not to overstate my contribution, but I did just fucking shoot a guy."

Tom exhaled.

"And I pulled you out of the pickup." A deep, numbing cold sunk into his body. He opened his mouth to give his jaw muscles something to do. "You didn't run over those people."

Tom looked at him.

"We could have gotten away. You just had to run over them."

"Yeah," Tom said.

"Why didn't you?" Tom didn't answer. "You shot that woman."

"Brontë."

"What?"

"Her name was Brontë."

"As in . . . Charlotte Brontë? A poet? I thought *they* were poets."

Tom didn't reply.

"Okay," Wil said. "I get it. That guy called you Eliot. You're Tom Eliot. Right? T. S. Eliot. You're a poet."

Tom sighed. "Was."

"You *were* a poet? What are you now?"

"I'm not sure," Tom said. "Ex-poet, I guess."

"Why did your friends turn bad?"

"They were compromised."

"What does that mean?"

"Woolf got to them."

"What does—"

"It means she's very persuasive."

"Persuasive? She's persuasive?"

"I told you, poets are good with words." Tom stood. Snow fell from his coat. "Time to go."

"You're telling me Woolf persuaded them to try to murder us? As in, she said, 'Hey, how about you trap your buddy Tom Eliot in a cattle yard and try to run him down with a truck,' and they *did*? Because she's *persuasive?*"

"I said very persuasive. Get up."

There was nothing but snow in every direction. "Where are we going?"

"I had a thought," said Tom. "Maybe the plane really is here."

They trudged through blackness and snow until Wil could no longer feel anything. His nerves retreated somewhere deep inside, where there was still warmth. His nose was a memory. He had not only never been this cold, he had not understood this degree of cold was possible. He began to hope poets found them, because whatever happened at least it would be warm.

He stumbled. "Aha!" said Tom. "Runway." Wil couldn't see him. "Let's try . . . this way."

After a few minutes, the stars began to vanish. There were noises. Tom took his arm and he found steps. At the top of those, the air was different. Warmer. Dear God, warmer.

"Sit," said Tom. "Don't do anything."

He sank to the floor, wrapped his arms around his legs, and pressed his face into his arms. Tom was banging around somewhere up front, flicking switches. After a while, Wil began to feel alive. He raised his head. A yellow glow emanated from what he assumed was the cockpit. He massaged his feet. Could you get frostbite that quickly? Because he felt like he had frostbite. He decided to walk around, to save his feet.

The cockpit was a cramped nest of instruments, a single seat surrounded by dark panels. Tom was buckled in. "You can fly this?" Wil said.

"It's not brain surgery."

"You can't even see where you're going. It's pitch-black out there."

"I will assume we're currently pointed in the right direction," Tom said. "And drive straight."

"Uh," Wil said.

Tom ran his thumb across a dial and finished up on a worn black button. "I think we're good to go."

"You think?"

"It's been a while since I did this."

"You said it wasn't brain surgery."

"It isn't. But the penalty for errors is high."

"Maybe we should think about this."

Tom waited. Wil thought he was reconsidering. Then he realized Tom was watching something. He followed his gaze but saw nothing but night sky. One of the stars was moving.

"What is that?" he said, and realized. "A helicopter."

"Yes. Go sit down." He depressed the button. Something went *click*. "Hmm."

"Was that supposed to happen?" Tom didn't answer, but clearly no. "Did they sabotage the plane? Do you think they—"

"Will you shut the fuck up?" Tom murmured to himself, poring over the controls. Ahead, the star grew. The ground beneath it began to twinkle. A searchlight swept snow.

"It's getting closer."

"Get out!"

"I'm just letting you—"

"Get out of the cockpit!"

He groped through darkness until he reached seats. He dropped into one and felt for the belt. Nothing happened for a while. He glanced behind him. He could make out shapes back there. Something in the seats. He couldn't sit still, so he got up and made his way toward them. He found a metal suitcase on one seat, gleaming faintly in the gloom. He slid his hands around it and found clasps.

He couldn't see, so he explored with his fingers. Something clinked. He felt fabric. He discovered something tubular and tried to pull it but it wouldn't come. He pulled the case out of the seat and took it toward the front of the plane. When he was close enough to see, he peered into the case. Some of the equipment he didn't recognize. Some he did. Syringes. Drill bits. In the center, its blade sheathed in plastic, lay a scalpel.

When he entered the cockpit, Tom was lying on his back, buried up to his elbows in the underside of the instrument panel. Wil held out the scalpel. "What is this?"

"Not now, Wil."

"Look at this."

Tom's head appeared. His expression did not change. He disappeared beneath the panel again.

"What were you going to do to me?" He had to raise his voice over the rising thrumming of the chopper. "That guy said you were going to pull my head open. That's what he said. Pull my head open. And I'm starting to wonder, Tom, whether that was an expression."

"Will you fuck off?"

"*Were you going to kill me?*"

"I'll kill you now if you don't get out of here."

Wil moved forward with the scalpel. He wasn't going to stab Tom. He just wanted to be taken seriously. But Tom's hand flashed out and grabbed Wil's wrist and twisted the scalpel from it. He tossed the scalpel into the back of plane, looked at Wil condescendingly, and climbed into the pilot's seat.

Wil said, "You owe me an answer."

"We were going to do whatever was necessary." Tom flicked a row of switches. "If we could get the word that destroyed Broken Hill from you without requiring us to crack open your head, terrific. We'd go that way. If not, the other. It's better than what the other side wants for you."

"It doesn't fucking sound better."

"I know Woolf," Tom said. "I've known her since she was a sixteen-year-old girl. Trust me, this is better. Sit the fuck down."

Light burst in the windshield. Wil raised his arm. The searchlight had found the plane. Beneath its gaze, the runway looked like black glass. The thrumming overhead was like thunder.

"Well, now I can see." Tom thumbed the black button. The engines thumped. A low whine of power began to build. Something above Wil's head went *thwack thwack thwack*. The plane began to trundle forward.

"They're shooting at us. Are they shooting at us?"

"Yes."

They bumped forward, gaining speed. "You know there's a chopper up there."

"I know."

"So even if we get off the ground, how are we going to get away from the chopper?" The plane's momentum pressed at him. He seized the back of Tom's chair. He was going to regret not sitting down. But he wasn't leaving. "*How do we get away from the chopper, Tom?*"

"Planes are faster than choppers." Tom pulled on the yoke. They lifted off.

SUICIDE CULT CLAIMS SIX

MONTANA: Police discovered the bodies of six people on an isolated ranch outside of Missoula on Tuesday, victims of an apparent suicide pact.

The dead included the owner of the ranch, well-known local herder Colm McCormack, 46, and his wife, Maureen McCormack, 44. Colm McCormack ran unsuccessfully for local office last November.

No further details were available.

[SIX]

Word filtered around that Kerry had won New Hampshire. He was going to be the Democrat nominee for president. "There it is," said Sashona. She played with the end of her beaded dreadlocks. "Four more years of Bush."

Emily sat in the back row. She didn't join in these discussions. She was kind of a loner.

"Why would we back Bush?" argued a boy. "Kerry's pro-media; he'll be better for us."

Because Bush is polarizing, thought Emily. "Because Bush is polarizing," Sashona said.

She had sixteen classes per week. In between, she was expected to study and practice. Not on other students. That was a rule. Her first day, wearing a uniform that still smelled of the plastic wrapping, she'd stood in Charlotte's office and taken a lecture. There were many rules, and Charlotte took her through each of them, patiently and in detail, like Emily was retarded. At first Emily thought this was because Charlotte was carrying a grudge, but as the lecture wore on, she realized no. Charlotte just thought she was that stupid.

"This is a nonnegotiable rule of the school," Charlotte said.

"Indeed, of the organization as a whole. Should you break it, there will be no excuses. No second chances. Am I making myself clear?"

"You're making yourself clear," Emily said.

At this point, she didn't know what *practicing* meant. It took her months to find out. She thought they were going to teach her persuasion; instead, she got philosophy, psychology, sociology, and the history of language. Back in San Francisco, Lee had given her a little speech about how this school would be different because it taught interesting, useful things, and that was a joke, in Emily's opinion. Grammar was not interesting. It was not useful to know where words came from. And no one explained it. There was no overview. No road map. Classes were eight to twelve students of wildly different ages, all of them ahead of Emily and no one asking the obvious questions. She had to stay up at night, staring at textbooks, trying to figure out why any of this mattered.

She learned Maslow's hierarchy of needs, which was the order in which people optimally satisfied different types of desires (food-safety-love-status-enlightenment). She learned that leverage over people's desire for knowledge was called *informational social influence*, while leverage over people's desire to be liked was *normative social influence*. She learned that you could classify a person's personality into one of 228 psychographic categories with a small number of well-directed questions plus observation, and this was called *segmentation*.

"I thought this was going to be cooler," she complained to Eliot. He was a part-time lecturer, teaching a few advanced classes, which did not include her. Whenever she saw his car parked out front, she headed for his office, because he was the only one she could talk to. "I thought it would be like magic."

Eliot was busy with papers. But she figured he had an obligation to deal with her, since it was basically his fault she was here. "Sorry," he said. "At your level, it's just books."

"When is it like magic?"

"When you finish the books," Eliot said.

By the end of the year, she could see where it was going. She wasn't learning persuasion, was still deep in Plato and neurolinguistics and the political roots of the Russian Revolution, but she was starting to sense the connections between them. One day she got to dissect a human brain, and as she peered through goggles at a frontal lobe, sliding the scalpel through the meat, separating decision making from motor function, memory from reward centers, she thought, *Hello.* Because she knew what the meat did.

She played soccer. You had to do a sport, soccer or basketball or water polo, and she was short and hated the swimsuits, so, soccer. On Wednesday afternoons she lined up with the other girls, shin guards stuffed into knee-high purple socks, her hair dragged back, a yellow shirt billowing, and she chased a ball around a field. The girls were all ages, so it was mostly an exercise in kicking the ball to the oldest and shouting encouragement. The exception was Sashona, who was only Emily's age but strong and graceful and had shoulders like battering rams. Soccer was supposed to be noncontact but Sashona's shoulders would put you on your ass anyway. After a goal, she would pump her fist, unsmiling, like she was satisfied but not surprised, and although Emily didn't enjoy soccer much, she found this terribly impressive. She wanted to be as good at something as Sashona was at soccer.

At night, she sat by the window of her cloister room, books piled on her desk. She studied with her hair pinned up and her school tie slung. She didn't really enjoy reading but she liked how the books were clues. Each one a piece in a puzzle. Even when they didn't fit together, they revealed a little more about what kind of picture she was making.

One day, exploring a corridor she'd always assumed went nowhere, she discovered a secret library. She didn't know if it was actually secret. But it wasn't marked, and she never saw anyone else. It was very small, with shelves that stretched up so high she needed a wooden ladder to reach them. Up there, the books were old. The first time she cracked open a volume, its pages came apart in her hands. After that, she was more careful. It occurred to her that maybe she was not allowed here, but that had not been included in Charlotte's comprehensive list of rules, and the old books turned out to be interesting, so she stayed.

One shelf was for disaster stories. There was probably a classification scheme she hadn't figured out. But the common thread seemed to be that a lot of people died. After a few books, she realized they were all the same story. They were set in different places, in Sumeria and Mexico and countries she'd never heard of, and the details differed, but the basics were the same. A group of people—sometimes they were called sorcerers, and sometimes demons, and sometimes they were just ordinary people—ruled over a kingdom or nation or whatever. In four of the books, they began building something impressive, like a crystal palace or the world's largest pyramid. Then something bad happened and people died and everyone started speaking different languages. This story felt vaguely familiar to Emily, but she didn't place it until she came to a book in which the impressive thing was a tower named Babel.

She thought she heard a noise and froze. But it was far away. She suddenly saw herself: sitting on the floor of a library in a blazer and pleated skirt, navy ribbons in her hair, reading old books. Before she had come here, Emily had seen girls like this—girls who wore ribbons, and enjoyed books—and thought they were a different species. She had thought they were separated by walls. Yet here she was, on the other side, and she didn't know how she had done it. She didn't feel like a different person. She was just in a different place.

The junior dining hall made excellent chocolate milk shakes. Emily got into the habit of swinging by after Macroeconomics and carrying one out to a sunny spot on the grass at the side of the building, where she could read. The cup was comically big. She always felt a little sick at the end of it. But she kept going back.

One day she passed a boy with a laptop at one of the outdoor tables. She had seen this boy in the halls, but they didn't share any classes because he was older. He was more advanced. She snuck a glance at him, and another, because he was pretty cute.

The next day he was there again, and this time he looked up as she passed. His eyes took in her enormous milk shake. She kept walking to her sunny spot but couldn't concentrate on her book.

The day after that, he saw her coming, stretched, and pushed the hair out of his eyes. "Thirsty, huh?" She smiled, because she had been thinking of saying something, and the something was *Boy am I thirsty!*

"Yeah," she said. "I am thirsty." She walked on.

On Wednesday, she bought an extra milk shake and deposited it on his table. His eyes, gray and soft as pillows, registered surprise. "I thought you looked thirsty, too." She walked away, pleased with herself.

On Thursday she brought him no drink. She had thought about this. She simply walked by. There was a terrible moment when she thought he wouldn't say anything—maybe he was too engrossed in his computer and hadn't even noticed her. Should she circle around again, or was that too humiliating?

"Hey, wait," he said.

She stopped.

"Thanks for the shake yesterday."

"No problem."

She stayed, smiling, hoping it wasn't over.

"I've never been a milk shake guy. But they're good."

"They're better than good," she said. "I'm addicted." She sucked at her straw.

He leaned back. "Do you want to sit?"

"I have a bunch of reading to do. Thanks, though. Maybe another time." She walked away. He didn't try to stop her, which was a little disappointing, and he didn't seek her out later, either. But that was okay. She was playing a long game. It was naughty. What she was doing was *practicing.* Trying to persuade another student. But only a little, nothing she'd get in trouble for. The fact was, if you paid attention, people tried to persuade each other all the time. It was all they did.

The next day, she headed for her sunny spot with no milk shake. Her heart thumped, because if he saw this and didn't respond, she would look pitiful. But she rounded the corner and his computer was closed and on the table were two milk shakes. He smiled, and gestured for her to sit, and she did.

His name was Jeremy Lattern. He had wanted to be a zookeeper. His family had a tiny house in Brooklyn but his mother rescued animals: rabbits and mice and ducks and dogs and two chickens. One of the chickens was insane. It ran in circles, making noises like it was drowning. His parents had wanted to get rid of it, but Jeremy pleaded for mercy. He thought he could cure it. He imagined this chicken becoming his friend, and people saying, "Jeremy's the only one who can go near that chicken." But this never happened. One day the chicken attacked him, pecking his face, and his father wrung its neck. That was how he got the small scar near his left eye, and decided against zoology.

Emily told him that her family were Canadian and she was raised on hockey. She described how when she was six, her father took her to a game and she was terrified because the crowd was so angry. There was an incident, a splash of players on the ice, and she turned to her father for protection but his face was monstrous. On the way home, he asked if she'd had fun, and she said yes, but whenever she even saw hockey on TV, she felt sick.

These were all lies, of course. You couldn't tell a student anything true about yourself. This wasn't a rule, exactly; it was obvious. She was in her second year and learning how people could be categorized into distinct psychographic groups based on how their brain worked.

Segment 107, for example, was an intuition- and fear-motivated introvert personality: Those people made decisions based on avoiding the worst outcomes, found primary colors reassuring, and, when asked to pick a random number, would choose something small, which felt less vulnerable. If you knew someone was a 107, you knew how to persuade them—or, at least, which persuasion techniques were more likely to work. This was not very different from what Emily had always done, without thinking about it too much: You developed a sense of what a mark desired or feared and used that to compel them. It was the same, only with more theory. So that was why you shouldn't talk about yourself, and why the older students were so aloof and inscrutable: to avoid being identified. To guard against persuasion, you had to hide who you were. But she suspected she was not very good at this. She guessed there were a whole bunch of clues she was inadvertently dropping to someone like Jeremy Lattern every time she opened her mouth, or cut her hair, or chose a sweater. She figured the reason the school had a *no practicing* rule was that sometimes people did it.

"Tell me what they teach you," she said. "Give me a sneak preview."

They were making slushies. They had progressed beyond milk shakes. The advantage of the slushie was you had to leave school grounds. Tuesdays and Fridays, if the weather was clear, they walked the three-quarters of a mile to the nearest 7-Eleven. She liked walking beside Jeremy Lattern, because cars would zoom by and the drivers would probably assume she was his girlfriend.

"You use very direct language," he said. "You don't ask. You command. That's a useful instinct."

"So tell me why I'm learning Latin."

"I can't."

"Do you always follow the rules?"

"Yes."

"Bah," she said, defeated.

"The rules are important. What they teach us is dangerous."

"What they teach *you* is dangerous. What they teach *me* is Latin. Dude, I'm not asking for state secrets. Just give me something. One thing."

He attached the slushie lid and poked the straw through the plastic.

"Bah," she said again. They walked to the front of the store and stood in line behind a kid paying for gas. The man behind the counter was balding, in his fifties, Pakistani or something like it. She nudged Jeremy. "Which segment is this guy?" He didn't answer. "I'm thinking one eighteen. Am I right? Come on, I'm doing segmentation; you can answer the question."

"Maybe one seventy."

She hadn't considered that one, but saw instantly how it made sense. "See, that wasn't so bad. Now what? What do we do once we know he's a one seventy?"

"We pay for our slushies," Jeremy said.

She hung with Jeremy in his room sometimes. Once she stuck chewing gum into the lock before she left and came back when she knew he had a class. She went to his bookshelf and pulled down three titles she had been eyeing for a while. She was sitting on his bed, deep in *Sociographic Methods*, when the door opened. Jeremy stood there, one hand on the knob. She had never seen him mad before. "Give me that."

"No." She sat on it.

"Do you know what they'll do—" He tried to grab it and she resisted and he landed on top of her. This she slightly engineered. His breath brushed her face. She let the textbook slide out and clunk to the floor. He raised a hand and it hovered a moment, then came down on her breast. She inhaled. He moved his hand away.

"Keep going," she said.

"I can't."

"Yes you can."

He rolled off. "It's not allowed."

"Come *on,*" she said.

"We're not allowed to be together." That was a rule. Fraternization. "It's not safe."

"For who?"

"Either of us."

She stared at him.

"I'm sorry," he said.

She shuffled closer. She touched his white shirt. She had spent a lot of time imagining taking off this shirt. "I won't tell anyone." She stroked his chest through the fabric. Then his hand closed on hers.

"I'm sorry," he said.

"What's with the fraternization rule?" she asked Eliot. She wandered about his office, fingering books, being casual. Eliot looked up from his papers. Originally, Emily had been going to ask, *Why can't we have sex.* Because, just once, she would like to see Eliot surprised or offended. Or anything, really. Just to prove that he was human. But then she lost her nerve.

"Students aren't permitted to enter relationships with each another."

"I know what it is. I'm asking *why.*"

"You know why."

She sighed. "Because if you let someone know you well, they can persuade you. But that's incredibly cold, Eliot." She went to the window. Outside, she watched a sparrow hop across the slate roof. "That's no way to live." He didn't reply. "Are you saying, for the rest of my life, I can't have a relationship with an organization person?"

"Yes."

"Do you appreciate how dull that is?" Eliot didn't react. "And what about . . . you know, purely physical relationships?"

"It's no different."

"It's completely different. Relationships, okay, I get it. But not for just sex."

"There is no 'just sex.' It's called intimacy for a reason."

"That's one word," she protested. "Coincidence."

"'And the man knew Eve his wife, and she conceived and bore Cain.' Note the use of the word *knew* in this context."

"That's from three thousand years ago. You're talking about the Bible."

"Exactly. The concept is not new."

She shook her head, frustrated. "Have you ever done it?"

"Done what?"

"Broken the rule," she said. "Fraternized."

"No."

"I don't believe you." She did. She was just pushing. "You must have thought about it. What about with Charlotte? There's something going on with you guys. Your feet always point toward her. And she goes very still around you. It's like when we're acting up in class and she's trying not to get pissed. She goes still when she's trying to control her emotions."

"I need to get some work done, if you don't mind." He sounded completely unruffled.

"I think Charlotte wants to fraternize with you," Emily said. "Badly."

"Out."

"I'm going!" She left. She was more frustrated than ever.

She turned eighteen. She lay in bed awhile, thinking about what that meant. Anything? She got up and went to class and of course nobody knew. At lunch, she walked to the 7-Eleven with Jeremy and debated telling him the whole way. Finally, while filling her slushie, she said, "I'm eighteen today."

He looked surprised. This was the kind of information you were not supposed to share. "I didn't get you anything."

"I know. I just wanted to tell you."

He was silent. They walked to the front of the store. She smiled at the man behind the counter. "It's my birthday today."

"Oh my goodness."

"Finally free." She leaned across the counter, grinning. "Free to give a long and happy life."

"I tell you what," he said. "I give you the slushie for free."

"Oh, no," she said.

"Happy birthday." He pushed it across to her. "You are a good girl."

As they left the store, Jeremy seized her arm. "'*Give a happy life? Finally free?*'"

She smiled, but he was serious. He steered her to a bench beside the road and sat her on it and stood there, glowering. She felt a tickle in her stomach, simultaneously sickening and thrilling. "You can't do that."

"I got a slushie. One free slushie."

"It's a serious breach of the rules."

"Come on. Like *word suggestion* is even a real technique. I bet it's nothing compared to what you can do."

"That's not the point."

"Is this because he gave me a present and you didn't?"

"You think the rules don't apply to you? They do. You can't practice. Not outside the school. Not on that guy. Not on me."

"You? When have I ever practiced on you?" She poked him with her shoe. "As if I could compromise you. You're going to graduate next year and I don't know anything. Come on. Sit. Drink slushie. It's my birthday."

"Promise me you'll never do that again."

"Okay. *Okay*, Jeremy. I was just playing."

After a while, he sat. She leaned her head on his shoulder. She felt very close to him. "I promise not to turn you into my thought slave," she said, and felt him smile a little. But she had thought about it.

The next Tuesday, she hung around the school gates but Jeremy didn't show up for their slushie run. She trudged back to the school. Something must have come up. Some class. He was getting busier. But she passed the front lawn and there he was, lounging with his friends, his pant legs rolled up in the sun. They were talking in the way of older students, no one laughing or even moving much, every sentence dripping with irony and layers of meaning, or so Emily guessed. She stopped. Heads turned. Jeremy glanced at her, then away. She walked on.

She understood that they couldn't be seen together too often. They could not be attached. She knew this. She reached her room and sat at her desk and opened a book. If she turned her head, she could have looked down to the lawn and seen Jeremy and his little group of conceited friends. But she did not. Occasionally she leaned back and stretched her arms, or fiddled with her hair, because she knew he could see her, too.

From time to time she saw students with ribbons tied around their wrists. The ribbon was red or white; if it was red, it meant a senior taking his final exam. The rule was not to talk to them, or even look too closely, although of course Emily did, because one day she would be wearing that red ribbon, and she wanted to know what that meant. She had once seen a red-ribboned boy building a house of cards in the front hall. He was there for two days, making the house taller and taller while he grew thinner and haunted-looking and it got so that people avoided the hall, in case of drafts. Then one morning the cards were gone and so was the boy. Emily never found out what had happened, whether he passed or failed. Another night, she woke to an odd bell and went to the window to see a girl leading a cow up the driveway. An actual, live cow. Emily could not deduce anything useful from this.

At the end of her second year, she found a slip of paper beneath her door, notifying her of a room change for Higher-Level Machine Languages. But when she turned up, she was the only student there. The teacher, a short, balding man named Brecht, handed her a white ribbon. "Congratulations. You're ready for your junior exam." She tied the ribbon around her left wrist, feeling excited.

Brecht told her to make a computer print the word *hello* on its screen. This sounded like something she could do in about two minutes, with a command like PRINT or ECHO. But Brecht said not to leave the room until it was done. She sat on a cardboard box, because this was not a classroom so much as a crypt for the corpses of prehistoric computers, and flipped open a laptop.

So the catch was the laptop didn't work. She crawled around, testing power supplies and fans. She found a monitor that powered on but had a burned-out VGA input. Everything in the room was like that, she discovered: sabotaged in key ways.

She assembled a machine, Frankenstein-style, from the innards of different devices. It had a hard drive and a monitor and it powered on but wouldn't do anything else. She had a blinking cursor that refused to respond to the keyboard. The operating system was sabotaged, too.

Her bladder pinged. She had drunk half a bottle of water on her way here, which was unfortunate. Her new goal was to finish this test before she needed to pee into a bag. She uncovered a BIOS problem and then a hole in the boot loader. By the time she got to the operating system, an actual responsive prompt, she knew what she was going to find: All the useful commands were broken. She began searching for bugs. There was one in each level. One deliberate flaw in each layer of software that lay between the screen and the ECHO command. There were so many layers—it was kind of crazy, how much code sat behind

ECHO. She hadn't appreciated that before. There were scripts and libraries and modules and compilers and assembly code, one built on top of the other. Technically, none of it was essential; you could accomplish the same end by manually constructing circuits and moving wires, manipulating pixels one by one. But what the layers did was distill that power into commands. They let you make electrons flow and logic gates close, phosphorous glow and metal magnetize, all by typing words.

She finished her silicon monster and went to fetch Brecht. He looked at the HELLO hanging on-screen and nodded once and began to pull her machine apart. She felt a little sad. She was learning that people were just machines and it was working the other way a little, too.

Over the next week, she had to be careful when approaching other students, in case they were wearing a white ribbon. Some students disappeared for days at a time, and some didn't come back at all, which Emily guessed meant they had failed. She hadn't really noticed before, because the classes weren't based on age, but there were more lower-years than seniors. A lot more.

After exams there were two weeks of vacation, during which most other students went off to their homes. This left Emily with the school to herself, practically. She felt bored and restless and began to hatch plots to break into people's rooms, so she could learn something. She spent time with one of the few other students to stay over vacation, a doe-eyed girl with dark bangs and a permanent air of disdain. Earlier, Emily had disliked this girl quite a lot, because she was older and spent a lot of time around Jeremy. But now she was basically the only person here who could teach her anything. Emily cut her hair the same and adopted the girl's walk, which was a kind of drifting, as if she was being blown through corridors on the pages of a million mournful poems. This was not as successful as Emily had hoped, since the doe-eyed girl didn't open up at all, so Emily was stuck with a dumb haircut for nothing. But she did discover that the girl swam for an hour every day. So Emily snuck into the locker room and stole her key.

The doe-eyed girl's room was like her own: a single bed, a wooden desk, a chair, and a window looking over the grounds. But her books were completely different. The girl had *Persuasion in Middle Europe* and *Modern Psychographics* and a small yellow book Emily had seen seniors carry around and always been intrigued by, titled *Gutturals*. That one, disappointingly, turned out to be full of word fragments with no explanation or context. But she pulled down a tome with an alluring title, *The Linguistics of Magic*, and that was better. It was a history lesson about how people had once believed in literal magic, in wizards and witches and spells. They wouldn't tell strangers their true name, in case the stranger was a sorcerer, because once a sorcerer knew you, he could put you under his power. You had to guard that information. And if you saw someone who looked like a sorcerer, you would avert your eyes and cover your ears before they could compel you. This was where words like *charmed* came from, and *spellbound* and *fascinated* and *bewitched* and *enraptured* and *compelled*.

This all seemed quaint and amusing, but as the book moved through to the modern day, nothing changed. People still fell to the influence of persuasion techniques, especially when they broadcast information about themselves that allowed identification of their personality type—their true name, basically—and the attack vectors for these techniques were primarily aural and visual. But no one thought of this as magic. It was just falling for a good line or being distracted or clever marketing. Even the words were the same. People still got *fascinated* and *charmed*, *spellbound* and *amazed*, they *forgot themselves* and were *carried away*. They just didn't think there was anything magical about that anymore.

When classes resumed, they began to teach her words. No one said what these were for. Charlotte simply handed out envelopes. "Study these in private," Charlotte told them. "They are not to be shared, ever, with anybody. Repeat them to yourself in front of a mirror, five times per word, every night."

"Until when?" asked Sashona, but Charlotte just put on her fake smile, like this was an amusing question.

She took the envelope marked EMILY RUFF and carried it to her room. Inside were three pieces of paper. JUSTITRACT. MEGRANCE. VARTIX. They were difficult to read; her brain kept slipping in the wrong direction. They were too similar to real words, maybe. She studied them. She stood in front of the mirror and watched herself. "*Varrrrrtttt*," she said, which was supposed to be *Vartix*, but for some reason it took a long time to come out, time stretching and getting grainy, and not only time but everything: the walls and mirror and air, all undergoing a slow disintegration that she could see and feel with every molecule of her being. She felt fear, because she didn't want to see what was underneath the world. The sound of her voice fell to pieces and the silence between them froze over. She regained consciousness. She realized this in retrospect. Her fingers and toes tingled. She closed her mouth. There was drool on her chin. She felt bruised in the brain. She walked to her bed and sat. She put the words back in the envelope, because fuck doing that again.

But after a while she returned to the mirror. Her mind revolted. It did not want to be bruised again. But she sucked it up. "*Varrrrrttt*," she said.

"We got words," she told Jeremy on the grass. She was being less cautious about being seen with him, because he was graduating soon, and what could they do? "We have to read them to ourselves."

"How did that go?"

"Badly."

He smiled. "Attention words are the worst."

She leaped on this. "Attention words? There are types?" She knew he wouldn't answer. "What are the others? What are attention words for?"

"You'll learn soon enough."

"I want to know now." But the truth was, she had just figured it out. *Attention words.* A single word wasn't enough. Not even for a particular segment. The brain had defenses, filters evolved over millions of years to protect against manipulation. The first was perception, the process of funneling an ocean of sensory input down to a few key data packages worthy of study by the cerebral cortex. When data got by the perception filter, it received *attention.* And she saw now that it must be like that all the way down: There must be words to attack each filter. Attention words and then maybe desire words and logic words and urgency words and command words. This was what they were teaching her. How to craft a string of words that would disable the filters one by one, unlocking each mental tumbler until the mind's last door swung open.

That night she went to brush her teeth and there was Sashona, wearing blue satin pajamas. "Are you still doing it?"

"Doing what?"

"The words. You know."

"Oh. Yeah."

Sashona sighed dramatically. "It's foul, right?"

"Most foul," Emily said.

"There had better be a good reason for it," Sashona said, pulling back her hair. "Otherwise I'm going to be pissed."

Emily nodded. It seemed pretty obvious to her that the reason was to build up resistance. This term she was taking Drama, puffing herself up and shouting at people in a voice that began in her gut, which the teacher called *projecting forcefully.* It was all because people were animals, analogue rather than binary, and everything in nature happened in degrees. People could be partially persuaded. They could be shocked into letting down their guard. You practiced saying the words so that if anyone ever said them to you, you would stand a chance.

"I can't remember mine," Sashona said. "They keep falling out of my brain."

Sashona left. Emily brushed. Walking back to her room, she heard the TV burbling and saw Sashona in the rec room. She hesitated, thinking about what Sashona had said. About not being able to remember her words. She went to Sashona's door and tried the handle and it turned.

Sashona's room was super neat. Emily went to the bookshelf and stood on tiptoe to peer at the books. *Socratic Debate* was sitting out half an inch, but they hadn't studied that one for a while. Emily pulled it down, balanced the book on its spine, and let it go. The pages fell open. She saw three slips of paper. Three words.

She closed the book and returned it to the shelf. She was trembling. When she stepped into the corridor she was sure somebody would see her and ask what she was doing. What would she say? She didn't know. She had no idea. She was just curious.

But there was no one. She closed Sashona's door and returned to her room. She climbed into bed and lay there, thinking about Sashona's words.

Over time she found five more sets of words. She didn't go looking for them, exactly. But if someone left their room unlocked when they went to the bathroom, she would notice that. And she might wander down to that person's bedroom and see if anything looked like it was hiding words. She didn't intend to use them for anything. But they were powerful, and they were there, so she looked out for them. She was an opportunist.

It was strange how many people left their words in obvious places. She understood that you couldn't destroy them, because they were slippery in your mind; when she tried to recall one of hers, her brain would offer benign variants, like *fairtix*, which didn't mean anything. You needed a permanent record somewhere. But Emily had ripped hers into pieces and numbered them on the back and hidden the code to reassemble them in the margins of different textbooks. Everyone else seemed to have just stuffed them into books and drawers, or under their mattress, or, in one guy's case, in his pants pocket. She couldn't understand leaving something lying around that could hurt you.

"I know everything," she told Jeremy. "I figured it all out. So, good news, I don't need to pester you with questions anymore."

He glanced at her. He was playing basketball. Or practicing basketball. The indoor court was empty but for them. Jeremy was shooting baskets from the free throw line, over and over. She was watching his shiny shorts.

"Once upon a time, there were sorcerers," she said. "Who were really just guys who knew a little about persuasion. And some of them did all right, ruled kingdoms and founded religions, et cetera, but they also occasionally got burned to death by angry mobs, or beheaded, or drowned while being tested for witchness. So sometime in the last few centuries, maybe even just the last fifty or so, actually, they got organized. To solve the whole being-burned problem. And . . ." She gestured. "Here we are. No more beheadings."

Jeremy released the ball. It passed through the net with a *swoosh*.

"Also, the words are getting better," she said. "I'm thinking that five hundred years ago, the keywords were things like *bless*. Tribal identifiers. Playing on how we trust people who think like us, believe the same things. Which is a start, but obviously not what *you* do. It's not what Eliot and Brontë do. So the organization must have been making keywords. Building them, one on top of the other. Like you do with computer code. First you gain trust from a segment with weak keywords. Not a lot of trust. Just enough to teach them to believe in a stronger keyword. Rinse and repeat." She sat back on her elbows.

"Pretty simple. I actually don't know why you thought you couldn't tell me."

"Have they actually taught you this?" Jeremy said. "Or are you guessing?"

"Ha," she said. "You just confirmed it. Right there."

"Bah," said Jeremy, throwing.

"They taught me some of it."

He came back, bouncing the ball. "What's a word?"

"Huh?"

"You're feeling clever—tell me what a word is."

"It's a unit of meaning."

"What's meaning?"

"Uh . . . meaning is an abstraction of characteristics common to the class of objects to which it applies. The meaning of *ball* is the set of characteristics common to balls, i.e. round and bouncy and often seen around guys in shorts."

Jeremy returned to the free throw line, saying nothing. She figured she must have that wrong, or at least not right enough.

"You mean from a neurological perspective? Okay. A word is a recipe. A recipe for a particular neurochemical reaction. When I say *ball*, your brain converts the word into meaning, and that's a physical action. You can see it happening on an EEG. What we're doing, or, I should say, what *you're* doing, since no one has taught me any good words, is dropping recipes into people's brains to cause a neurochemical reaction to knock out the filters. Tie them up just long enough to slip an instruction past. And you do *that* by speaking a string of words crafted for the person's psychographic segment. Probably words that were crafted decades ago and have been strengthened ever since. And it's a *string* of words because the brain has layers of defenses, and for the instruction to get through, they all have to be disabled at once."

Jeremy said, "How do you know this?"

"Do you think I'm smart?"

"I think you're scary," he said.

While he showered, she waited outside on a wooden bench. From here she had a vantage point across the soccer field to one of the parking lots, the one reserved for teachers, and she saw four black sedans roll up, one after the other. People in suits climbed out. She got off the bench and began to walk over, because this was curious, but one of the men turned to her and she felt very cold and stopped.

The people moved inside. She returned to the bench. Jeremy emerged, smelling of soap. "Are you okay?"

She shook her head. "I saw some people. Poets, I guess."

He looked at the cars.

"One was an older guy. White hair. Tan skin."

"Oh," Jeremy said. "Yeah. That's Yeats."

"The teachers, they're in there somewhere. You know? They're brick walls, but you can tell there's something behind the wall. This guy had shark eyes. Nothing in them. Just . . . eyes." She shook her head. "Junkies get them, if they're in a bad place. It freaked me out a little."

"Come to my room," he said. "Hang out."

"Okay." But she wasn't ready to move yet.

"Seriously, don't worry about Yeats. You'll never speak to him."

"Why not?"

"Because he's a million miles above us," Jeremy said. "He's the head of the organization."

Jeremy was going to graduate. She had known it was coming. But he became a senior and she was no longer able to pretend the day belonged in some far-off future. He started begging off slushie runs. He didn't watch her play soccer anymore. Whenever she knocked on his door he was deep in books, looking tired, making her feel stupid for bothering him.

"Just fail," she said. "Stay another year. We'd be about the same level. We could even study together."

"I can't fail, Emily."

She got off the bed, annoyed, because she had been only joking. Or maybe not, but still. She began sifting through his drawers, looking for anything interesting. But of course there was nothing, because Jeremy Lattern had no personal effects. Certainly no hidden words. She had looked, a couple of times. Just out of interest. It hadn't always been like this: She remembered a little toy robot with red arms. He had gotten rid of it sometime since she'd met him. That was what people did here. They shrunk and shrunk until there was nothing interesting left.

She went over and put her hands on his shoulders. He tensed. "Relax. It's a massage. Therapeutic." She kneaded his muscles until they loosened. When she moved up his neck, he tightened again. "Stop fighting it! I'm helping."

He relaxed. She slid her fingers into his hair. She rubbed his neck with her thumbs. After a while, he put down his pen. It had been a while since he'd turned a page. She ran her fingernails lightly down his back. "Take off your shirt, so I can do your back."

He didn't respond. She bit her lip. That had been kind of obvious.

"You can't focus if you're tense and distracted. You can't pretend you're not made of biology." She pressed her thumbs into his shoulders. "You have a deficiency need, you satisfy it. That's Maslow. You can't move on to higher needs until you satisfy the base ones."

He looked up at her.

She said, "I'd like to have sex with you, if you want."

His eyes were unreadable. "Okay."

She smiled, but he didn't, so she stopped that. He rose from the chair. He looked like he was concentrating on a puzzle. She unbuttoned his shirt. Her fingers shook and he must have noticed. She felt his hands on her waist and she pulled open his shirt and his chest was smooth and hairless and smelled of him in a way that was powerful. She kissed his skin. She craned her neck to reach his lips but he turned his face away. So there was to be no kissing. He removed her jacket. She backed onto the bed and he climbed on top of her. His face betrayed nothing. He was breathing more quickly; that was all. She tried to be like him, not react as his hand moved up her stomach, but a sound came out of her before she could stop it. His eyes flicked at her.

"I'm okay." She pulled him closer. She felt his erection against her and had a moment of panic. She wasn't a virgin but it had been a long time and everything was different. He continued to press. Her body fizzed with tiny stars and she remembered how this went. She reached down and touched him through his pants and made him grunt. She liked that. She squeezed again.

His hand sought admission to her skirt. She lifted her butt, unzipped, and pushed the whole mess of fabric down. His fingers pushed against her and she gave a little gasp. He hesitated. She wanted to grab his hand and force him onto her. She tugged him out of his pants. He buried his face in her shoulder. His fingers found her. It was an awkward angle; she could only squeeze. But the pressure was amazing. Vibration began in her legs. Her teeth chattered. She almost laughed, but that would be no good; she couldn't do that. He groaned, a low warning, but she ignored it and then he jetted through her fingers. He did it silently. She felt triumphant. The movement of his fingers intensified, and she felt herself going out with the tide of her victory. Her legs kicked once.

She lay still. He panted into her hair. She could smell their sweat. After a minute, he raised his head. She could see the endorphins in his pupils. He rolled away, onto his side. She used a corner of the sheet to clean herself and lay back beside him. He didn't speak. She watched the ceiling until his breathing eased into a sleep rhythm, about twenty or thirty minutes, and then, when it was safe, she put her arm around him.

She went to class the next day and no one knew. It was a secret treasure. She sat in the back row and thought: *I had sex with Jeremy Lattern.*

It was Subvisual Methods, a class she liked, but her mind wandered. At odd times, she seemed to catch his smell. Maybe some of him was still on her. She liked that idea.

A thought popped into her head: *He's a thirteen.* She blinked. She didn't know where that had come from. She had considered Jeremy's segment before and decided he was probably a ninety-four. His behavior matched up almost perfectly; she'd watched him pretty carefully. But now she felt differently. Ninety-four was a cover. He was a thirteen.

After classes, she decided to fetch him a slushie. He would be studying all afternoon and have no time for her; she knew that. She wouldn't bother him and wouldn't expect anything to be different. But she would fetch him a slushie.

On the way out, she noticed Eliot's door was open. She hesitated. She hadn't seen him for months, had been looking forward to his next visit, but right now she should probably avoid him. Because maybe Eliot could tell. But then he came out of his office and it was too late. "Hey!" she said. "Busy? You look busy."

"Yes. Leaving. But you can walk with me."

"Okay." She fell into step. They walked in silence. She transitioned from being worried that Eliot would figure it out to disappointed that he hadn't. "How's life?"

"How's life?"

"Yes."

"Life's good."

"Good." They passed a group of boys loitering with intent, who straightened and shifted. Eliot was well respected here. It was widely believed that he taught so rarely because he was usually required to be away doing mysterious and badass things. "I was thinking about my name. My poet name, I mean, when I graduate. I decided I want to be Emily Dickinson."

"You can't be Dickinson."

"I could keep my first name. Also, awesome little poems about death. She's literally the only poet I don't hate."

"We already have an Emily Dickinson."

"Aw."

"Also, graduates aren't given the names of world-renowned poets," said Eliot. "You'll be someone you've never heard of."

"Is there a list I can choose from?"

"No."

"You guys are hard-asses." They reached the front door and descended the steps. "Well, see you round."

He paused. "You're happier."

"What?"

"You seem happy."

She shrugged. "It's a beautiful day, Eliot, what do you want me to say?" He didn't answer. "You should get out more," she said. She walked away. He was going to call her back; she could feel it. He would know everything. But he didn't, and her tension eased, and by the time she reached the gate, she was humming.

She purchased two slushies and almost got hit by a car running across the road while carrying them back. She balanced them in the crook of her arm and knocked on Jeremy's door. When he called out, she pushed the door open with her hip. "Refreshment!"

He looked at the slushies. He wasn't as happy as she'd hoped.

"Thank you, Emily," she said.

"Thanks."

She deposited the slushie on his desk and leaned her butt against the wall. She had intended to give him the drink and go, but now she didn't want to. "How's the study going?"

"Slowly."

She nodded. "I'll leave you to it."

"Thanks."

"Unless you want a study break." She raised her eyebrows.

"That can't happen again."

"What can't happen?"

"You know what." His voice dropped. "We shouldn't have done it. I shouldn't have."

"Well, I forgive you." She tried to keep it light, but her heart was sinking through her stomach. She had seen this coming, hadn't she? She'd practically provoked it. But now she felt sick.

"If they knew, I'd be expelled."

"We both would."

"Yes, but . . ." He tapped the books lightly with his fingers. "This is my final exam. I can't fuck this up."

She stared at him.

"You understand, right? I have to do this. I'm sorry."

"Are you," she said.

"I think you're a great person—"

She threw her slushie. It exploded on his head, red juice and ice chips flying everywhere, splashing his books and papers. He sat frozen, dripping. She slammed the door on the way out.

She had soccer and was in no mood for it. She stood rooted in the defensive half of the field and didn't chase. Sashona, on the opposing team, concentrated her attacks on Emily's wing to capitalize on her apathy. Once she ran past while Emily just stood there, and after she scored, she ruffled Emily's hair.

The next time Sashona pounded toward her, the ball bobbling along in front of her, Emily decided to put Sashona on the ground. She moved to intercept and Sashona's face hardened in a way that told Emily to expect the shoulders. A word bubbled to Emily's lips, one of the attention words she had discovered in Sashona's room. *Kassonin.* That was the word. It would be enough to kick Sashona in the brain just long enough for Emily to knock her flat, and she would use it because she had *not* used it on Jeremy, even though she could have, because he was, like Sashona, a thirteen. *Kassonin, bitch.* Her head was full of blood. *Eat MY shoulders.*

They collided. By the time Emily got up, Sashona was jogging back to her half, doing the fist pump. She had scored while Emily was on her ass. "Fuuuck," Emily said, and Sashona laughed.

She had to get away for a while, so instead of changing she headed for the school gate. She was almost there when she heard footsteps. Jeremy was running after her. "Em! Wait!" She didn't want to, but some small, stupid part of her thought, *Maybe he changed his mind.* He caught her, breathing fast. He'd showered, put on a fresh shirt. His cheeks were pink. "Let's not end things this way."

"What?"

"We've been friends for two years. I don't—"

"*Gah,*" she said, as soon as she heard the word *friends*. She walked.

He trotted beside her. "You can't tell anyone." She didn't answer. "They will expel you. They've done it before. They'll send you fucking home."

"Maybe you made me do it," she said. "Maybe you took advantage of me, with your words."

He stopped. When she reached the gate, he yelled, "*How dare you!*" She flinched, because there was fury in his voice. She kept walking. She wasn't going to accuse him of anything, couldn't he tell that? She just wanted him to feel something. "*Come back! Come back here!*" The traffic was flowing but she threaded through it to the other side. A van honked. She turned to see Jeremy stranded outside the gates, his face red. "*You say nothing!*"

"Make me."

He stepped onto the road. She was reminded of Benny in San Francisco: how he'd been funny and kind until she pushed him too far. "Stop," she said. Jeremy knew her. He did know her segment. He was about to graduate and he could make her do whatever he wanted. "I'm sorry! I won't tell!" He was halfway across, paused between lanes, his face thick with anger. He waited for a car, threw a glance to his right, and ran at her. She screamed, "*Kassonin!*"

His head jerked. He stopped. For a moment he was a child. Then he came back. She saw shock in his eyes and outrage and fear. She was transfixed by his face. Then a car swept him away. She shrieked and couldn't hear herself over the tires.

She wanted to go to the hospital but they wouldn't let her. She had to stay in the sitting room, the same place Charlotte had interviewed her when she'd first arrived, curled up in the same armchair.

Finally, Eliot came in, wearing a long coat. She opened her mouth to ask about Jeremy but could see the answer on his face. She covered her face with her hands and cried.

"Tell me what happened."

She shook her head, not looking up. He crossed the rug and lifted her chin. "No," she said, and tried to cover her ears. He pulled away her hands and spoke and her mind went away. When she returned to herself, he was sitting in the chair across the rug, his eyes dark. She closed her mouth and swallowed. Her throat felt sore.

"Your time here is over," he said.

"Please don't send me away. Please."

He stood. She began to cry again, but there was no pity in his eyes. He left.

KILLED STUDENT “RAN INTO TRAFFIC”

Police say the student who was struck and killed by a vehicle on Montebury Avenue on Friday was attempting to cross the busy road away from lights or crossings.

The driver, a 39-year-old woman from Orange, was moving at or near the speed limit, police say.

The incident is likely to reignite calls for lights or a crossing, as it has been the scene of several accidents. The area was again targeted for upgrade in the Department of Transportation’s Pedestrian Safety Master Plan, but works were placed on hold last year due to local opposition.

The student is believed to have been in his final year at an exclusive Williamsburg school. His name and details have not been released.

---

[11]

Broken Hill

Odysseus, who had first avoided identifying himself, and then given a false, impossible appellation, now supplies his real name in full: he is Odysseus, sacker of cities, son of Laertes, who lives in Ithaca. Odysseus' mention of his true name acts as a flash of illumination for the blind giant, who now comprehends an earlier prediction concerning his loss of sight. The enlightened Cyclops does not respond with stones this time, but with the force of words. Polyphemus is able, at long last, to bend language to his needs, and he carefully repeats, word for word, Odysseus' name, epithet, patronym and country of origin, when he prays to his father Poseidon to punish him.

—DEBORAH LEVINE GERA,
Ancient Greek Ideas on Speech, Language, and Civilization

Posted: 22 minutes ago See conversation

Well what happened is two weeks ago I went for a job interview and they turned around a laptop to face me and said, "Is this you?" And it was all this stuff I posted YEARS ago, pics of me passed out, drunk, long teenage rants about stupid shit, you know

So needless to say, no job

So before THIS interview I delete EVERYTHING, delete Facebook, delete Twitter, anything I can find. I go in and the first thing they ask is do I have Facebook. I say no. They say how about a college page, LinkedIn, anything. I say no. They look at each other and say well their company likes to "feel comfortable" with their new hires' background but I don't seem to have any. They're not saying I've done anything wrong but when someone has no Facebook, it looks like they have something to hide

Seriously, you can't win

[ONE]

The airplane climbed and Wil waited for the chopper to shoot at them, or crash into them, or explode for no reason, who knew. But minutes passed with nothing but the drone of the engines and the night spreading out ahead. "Are we clear?" he asked Tom, or T. S. Eliot, or whoever he was, and Eliot said nothing, but Wil thought they were. Exhaustion dumped into him all at once: One minute he was in fear for his life, the next he wanted to sleep. "I'm going to sit down, okay?" He made his way down the plane. He reached seats and collapsed into one. He should buckle up. But the buckles were so far away.

He opened his eyes to daylight. The world bumped and shook. He clutched at the armrests, his head full of half-remembered dreams. A girl with bad words. A kangaroo. The engines were wailing. Beyond the round windows he saw snow and wooden fence posts and these seemed very close and moving too fast. The note of the engines changed and they began to shed speed. The world slowed and stopped. Eliot emerged from the cockpit, flipped open a panel on the fuselage, and began to crank the door.

"Where are we?"

Eliot kept cranking. The door became a series of steps and he trotted down them.

Wil got to his feet. He was not thrilled about heading out into the snow again, but he did it. Eliot stood at the side of the road, urinating. Wil looked around. The blacktop stretched out as far as he could see. Power lines marched alongside. There was nothing else.

"Nice landing," Wil said. He got nothing from Eliot but a steady stream of urine. "Where are we?"

Eliot zipped and walked a short distance down the road. Wil went after him. The plane was very modern, he noticed, sleek and clean with upturned wings. It was surprisingly large, too, although maybe that was because it was on a road, where it did not belong.

He stopped beside Eliot. He stuffed his hands into his pockets. His breath fogged. "What now?"

"Next car that comes along, I'm catching a ride. Then I'm going to get some breakfast. Bacon, ideally. Lots of bacon."

Wil shook snow from his boots. "Okay."

"That's me, though. You can do whatever you like."

Wil squinted. "Say what?"

"We're done. This is it. You go your way, I go mine."

"What?"

"It's over."

"But the poets. Woolf . . . does she still want to kill me?"

"Oh, yes."

"So we have to hide. Go to more of your friends."

"There are no more friends."

Wil stared. "No?"

"No."

"You mean your entire, what, resistance or whatever, got wiped out yesterday? *Everyone?*"

"Yes."

"You don't have a cell in another city or—"

"No."

"Jesus." Wil exhaled. "Then we need to stick together."

"Hmm," Eliot said.

"She's coming after you, too, right? Woolf wants you dead."

"Yes."

"So?"

"So from your point of view, I'm a guy who can keep you alive. But from my point of view, you're a useless sack of shit. You don't help me at all."

"You said I was important! You have to find out why I'm immune! To the words!"

"That was before," Eliot said. "Circumstances changed."

"I'm coming with you," said Wil. "Wherever you're going, I'm coming."

"No, you're not."

"You can't stop me. Your word voodoo, it doesn't work on me. Right? So how do you think you're going to—"

Eliot produced a pistol. He didn't seem to pull it from anywhere. He just suddenly had it.

Wil's eyes stung.

"See?" Eliot put away the gun. "There are all kinds of persuasion." He gazed at the horizon again.

Wil's breath steamed. "Okay. Okay." Anger built inside him and he didn't know what to do with it. "Fine. That's how it is?" He walked back to the plane. He didn't know what he was doing. But he could do it somewhere warm. He could do that. Halfway up the steps, he yelled, "What happened in Broken Hill? Woolf killed everyone, right?" Eliot didn't move. "Yeah! So you go hide out while she does what she likes to the rest of us! You do that!" He shivered. He stomped up the steps.

Eliot stood on the road, scanning the horizon. His coat flapped around his legs. Wil would pop back out of that plane in about five minutes, by his estimation. That would be the point at which his fear of being abandoned surpassed his physiological desire for warmth. It would be useful if a car appeared before then. That way, Eliot could compromise the driver and be on his way without ever seeing Wil again.

The wind stung his cheeks. He couldn't resist the comparison any longer: the last time he'd stood like this, waiting and watching to see what came over the horizon, carrying a gun and hoping not to need it. A little over a year ago. He had been outside Broken Hill.

He put the air-conditioning on full, but it made no difference: The sun blasted through the windshield, broiling him inside his shirt. The kid he'd collected from the airport, Campbell, squirmed and twisted his tie and finally pulled off his linen jacket and hung it over the back of his seat. "The sun looks bigger," he said. "Can it actually be bigger?"

"It's the ozone," said Eliot. "There's a hole."

"Do you get used to it?"

"Not yet."

"When I left DC, it was twelve degrees," said the kid, rolling up his sleeves. "Twelve." He glanced at Eliot. "You miss DC?"

"I visit."

"Yeah, but . . ." The kid looked out the window at the blasted soil rolling by. "How long have you been out here, in total? Three months?"

"Seven."

"Yeah." The kid nodded. "Of course. Well, after this, you can go home." He smiled.

Eliot looked at him. "How old are you?"

"Twenty-one. Why?"

"How much do you know about what you're doing?"

"Everything." The kid laughed. "Eliot, I'm fully briefed. I've spent six weeks in intensive prep. I was selected for my talents. I know what I'm doing."

Eliot said nothing.

"Four months ago, Virginia Woolf releases a bareword in Broken Hill, Australia, population three thousand. Now population zero. Official story, explosion in the ore refinery plant causing a catastrophic toxic leak. Town is fenced off at a radius of five miles. Scary signs promise death to all who enter. The funny part is the signs don't lie. We send people in, they don't come out. Hence the theory that the word is still in there." He pulled his shirt out of his pants and flapped air. "Crazy idea, isn't it? That a word can persist. Hang in the air, like an echo."

"It can't."

"What, then? Because something bad is in there, and it ain't a toxic leak."

He almost didn't say it. "Maybe Woolf."

"Mmm," said the kid. "Yeah, nobody really thinks that's plausible, Eliot. We're all pretty sure Woolf's dead." He tapped idly on the window. "We have satellite on that town. We've imaged it a hundred different ways. Nothing moves."

Eliot drove in silence.

"I'm the best there is, defensively," said the kid. "I mean, not to boast. But that's why I'm here. I was selected because I can't be compromised. There's not going to be a problem."

"You realize you're betting your life on that."

"I realize it."

Eliot glanced at him. *Twenty-one*, he thought. "Who chose you? Yeats?"

"I have had the honor of speaking with Yeats, yes."

"You don't have to do this."

The kid looked at him. *Give me a sign*, Eliot thought, *and we'll blow right by Broken Hill, Campbell, keep going until we reach an airport. By sundown we'll be a country away. You ever think about quitting, Campbell? Just walking away? And let me ask you something else: Have you noticed there's something wrong with Yeats? Like something dead? Notice that?*

The kid turned away. "You've been in the desert too long, Eliot."

He watched the endless road. "You're right about that," he said.

He drove up to the chain-link fence and killed the engine. They sat in silence, looking at the signs. CONTAMINATION. TOXIC. TRESPASS. DEATH. Skulls and thick red lines. The heat pressed in like a hand. "They're words, aren't they?" said the kid. "Fear words." He unbuckled. "I need to get out of this car."

Outside was no cooler but at least the air was moving, stirring dust and sand. The road was blocked with a snarl of razor wire. To the left and right, the chain-link fence stretched away, signs flapping every few hundred feet. A few scrubby bushes protruded from the red soil. This continued as far as one could see.

He had wire cutters in the trunk, just in case, but nothing had changed since last time: The wire looped across the road but was not secured. It didn't need to be. The kid was right: It was the words that kept people out. Eliot dragged the wire from the road.

The kid was trying to wrap his linen jacket around his head. "I have a hat in the back," said Eliot. "Take that."

"I'm okay."

"Take the hat." He opened the back door and retrieved the cap and a bottle of water.

"Fine. Thanks." The kid jammed the cap on his head. The peak said: THE THUNDER FROM DOWN UNDER. Eliot had picked it up from a street vendor in Adelaide. "How do I look?"

"You have a satellite phone?"

"Yep."

"Call me."

"It works. I checked at the airport. I'll call you when I get into town."

"Call me now."

The kid produced his phone and poked at it. Eliot's phone trilled.

"Okay?" said the kid.

"You have a backup battery."

"I do."

"And your main is full?"

"It's fine."

"Is it full?"

"Look." The kid showed him the screen. "See the little battery? I know how to use a phone."

"Call me as soon as you can no longer see me clearly. Then keep the line open. If the call drops, keep trying me until you get through."

"Will do."

"What's your segment?"

"*What?*"

"Is it ninety-three?"

The kid's face blanked. It was how they trained them. The kid was thinking about something else: something happy, something sad, something traumatic; only he knew. It was supposed to make him unreadable, by adding noise to his facial expression.

"You're a ninety-three."

"Shit," said the kid. "You're not supposed to do that. Why'd you do that?"

"For your protection."

"It doesn't matter. I can't be compromised. You want to try me? Go ahead."

Eliot considered it. He didn't doubt that the kid was good. But he'd probably done most of his work in a relatively controlled environment. If Eliot jumped him, put a gun in his mouth, screamed words, well, that was not the same.

"Don't worry about me," said the kid. "I'm good to go."

"Don't take any risks. Anything looks wrong, don't investigate. Just walk away. We don't have to do everything today."

The kid adjusted his DOWN UNDER cap. He thought Eliot was crazy, of course. "Well, I'm going to do this."

Eliot nodded. "Good luck."

"Heh," said the kid. "Thanks." He stepped around the razor wire and began to walk up the road.

With distance, the kid's body shimmered in the heat haze rising out of the blacktop. Soon he was hard to make out at all, just another twisting current of air. Eliot stood with a hand shielding his face from the sun, watching.

His cell phone rang.

"Thanks for the cap," said the kid. "Glad I've got it now."

"You're welcome."

"I have seriously never been this hot."

"Can you see the town's outskirts?"

"Not yet."

"Should be close."

"Yeah, I know. I have the maps by heart."

They fell silent. The sun beat down on Eliot's head. He should retreat to the car. In a few minutes. He would wait until the kid reached the town.

"You used to teach her at the Academy. Virginia Woolf. That's what I heard. Is that true?" The kid was panting a little. "We have to spend an hour on the phone, Eliot; we may as well talk. Jesus." He blew air. "This is so ridiculously hot." Eliot heard him take a swig from the water bottle.

"Yes, I taught Woolf."

"Did you see it coming? At all, I mean? Did you ever get the sense she might . . ."

"Might what?"

"Go ballistic," said the kid. "Kill a whole town. I don't mean to insult your observation skills, which are, clearly, very good. I just wonder how you can miss something like that. You know? It wasn't just you. It was everyone. We're supposed to know people."

"There's a risk in training anyone. In Woolf's case, her potential seemed to justify it." He shrugged, although there was no one to see him. "We were wrong."

"I never met her. She'd left by the time I started." He coughed. "She'd been kicked out, I mean. Banished. Whatever. It's really dusty. The wind . . . I think I can see the refinery."

"Keep your eyes open."

The kid laughed, which turned into another cough. "Seriously, you're making me nervous for no reason. There's nobody in here."

Eliot said nothing.

"Do you know what I do? In the organization? I'm in Digital. Web services. You know?"

"Not really."

"You should. This is where everything is going. Let me tell you about it. Bring you up to speed."

"Fine," he said.

"Well, don't humor me. I don't care. I'm just offering you an inside look at what Yeats himself has called, quote, the greatest attack vector since print, end quote."

"Fine."

"The organization is changing, Eliot. It's not newspapers and TV anymore. That stuff is old school. Obsolete. And you older guys, if you don't watch out, you'll be obsolete with it. You don't want to be obsolete, do you?"

"No."

"No. So let me help you out." The kid panted awhile. "The key to the Web is it's interactive. That's the difference. Online, someone visits your site, you can have a little poll there. It says, 'Hey, what do you think about the tax cuts?' And people click and segment themselves. First advantage right there. You're not just proselytizing, speaking into the void. You're getting data back. But here's the really clever part. Your site isn't static. It's dynamically generated. Do you know what that means?"

"No."

"It means the site looks different to different people. Let's say you chose the poll option that said you're in favor of tax cuts. Well there's a cookie on your machine now, and when you look at the site again, the articles are about how the government is wasting your money. The site is dynamically selecting content based on what you want. I mean, not what you *want*. What will piss you off. What will engage your attention and reinforce your beliefs, make you trust the site. And if you said you were *against* tax cuts, we'll show you stories of Republicans blocking social programs or whatever. It works every which way. Your site is made of mirrors, reflecting everyone's thoughts back at them. That's pretty great, right?"

"It's great."

"And we haven't even started talking about keywords. This is just the beginning. Third major advantage: People who use a site like this tend to ramp up their dependence on it. Suddenly all those other news sources, the ones that aren't framing every story in terms of the user's core beliefs, they start to seem confusing and strange. They start to seem biased, actually, which is kind of funny. So now you've got a user who not only trusts you, you're his major source of information on what's happening in the world. Boom, you own that guy. You can tell him whatever you like and no one's contradicting you. He's—" The kid sucked in breath. "Aw, shit."

"What is it?"

"I think I see a body."

"You didn't know there would be bodies?"

"I knew. Of course I knew. But knowing and seeing are two . . . aw, geez. That's disgusting."

"They've been in the sun for four months."

"Yeah. Clearly."

"Is it just bone or . . . ?"

"It's *mostly* bone," said the kid. "That's the disgusting part." For a while Eliot heard nothing but his breathing. "Yecch. They're all over."

"You were telling me about Digital."

"How do you think they died?" His voice sounded muffled, as if he was talking through his sleeve. "Did the bareword blow out their fucking brains? Like aneurysms? Because it doesn't look like they died from aneurysms."

"Why not?"

"They're in clumps. Like they dragged themselves into groups. Then died."

Eliot was silent.

"So . . . yeah, Digital." The kid's voice wavered. "Fourth advantage. We can whisper. A problem with old media has always been that we can't control who's watching. There's self-selection—people don't tune in for shows that rub against their beliefs—but you still get people from the wrong segment watching. And they think you're peddling bullshit, of course, because you are, and sometimes they make a big deal out of that, and it feeds back to the target segment. Then you have message bleeding. In Digital, that problem goes away. You can say things to a user and no one else can hear, because it's dynamically generated for that user. The next user, the site looks different. End result, you get people from different segments and they agree on nothing, literally nothing, except the site is a great source of unbiased information." He took a breath. "I'm passing houses. Flat, ugly houses."

"Are you okay?"

"Yeah. Fine. Just hot."

"Take a rest if you need it."

"Why do you think they're in groups?"

"I don't know."

"You think they could be families? Like . . . they had time to find their loved ones?"

"Maybe."

"I don't think that's it. Something about the way . . . I don't know. But I don't think so." Something scraped against the phone. "I need a drink."

"Rest."

The kid gulped water. "No. I want to get this done." Time passed. "So . . . that's Digital. Pretty great, huh?"

"It makes me wonder why we're bothering with anything else."

"Heh. Yeah. Well, we have a problem with unidentified users. Someone visits our site for the first time, and we have no idea who they are. We don't know what to show them. We can make guesses, based on where they are geographically, and the software they're using. But that's suboptimal. We're getting better. You know about social networking?"

"No."

"You are . . . you need to get into this stuff, Eliot. It's the future. Everyone's making pages for themselves. Imagine a hundred million people clicking polls and typing in their favorite TV shows and products and political leanings, day after day. It's the biggest data profile ever. And it's voluntary. That's the funny part. People resist a census, but give them a profile page and they'll spend all day telling you who they are. Which is . . . good . . . for us . . . obviously . . ."

"What is it?"

"There's a . . . ah, it's okay."

"What is it?"

"Gas station. Place is burned out. Cars all over. And one is . . . yeah, one is upside down. That's . . . uh . . . not bad, huh, Eliot? A word that can flip cars?" He laughed, the pitch high. "That's some pretty fucking impressive neurolinguistics, wouldn't you say?"

"Are there bodies?"

"Of course there are bodies! I'm fucking knee-deep in bodies! Just assume there are bodies unless I tell you otherwise!"

"Understood."

He panted. "I'm not knee-deep. I'm . . . sorry, I'm exaggerating. But there are a lot. A real lot." He swallowed over and over. "How could there be so many? I mean, what did she do? How could she kill *everyone*?"

"Take a break."

"Fuck!"

"Campbell. You need to calm down."

"I can see the hospital. It's just up the road. The road that's fucking full of bodies."

"You can come back. You don't need to do this today."

The kid took a shaky breath. "Yeah, I do, Eliot."

"It's not that important. Forget about Yeats."

There was a snuffling sound. Eventually Eliot identified it as laughter. "You have definitely been away too long, Eliot. No question. 'Forget about Yeats.' Jesus fucking Christ." He sucked air. "There's a lot of damage here. Cars on the sidewalk. I saw this on the satellite pictures, but up close it's . . . more real, I guess. On the computer they just looked badly parked. Like everyone was in a real hurry. But . . . they hit things. They're all . . . all somewhere for a reason." He swallowed. "Almost at the hospital. Looks . . . smaller . . . than I expected, actually. Like a library. I can see the entrance to the ER. Ambulance out front. I mean a van. A paramedic van, up on the curb. Front of the ER's all glass, but I can't see inside." He heard the kid stop. "It's real dark in there. Or grimy or something." He hesitated. "I'm going around to the main entrance, okay?"

"Okay."

"It's just, I don't think I need to mess with this black room if there's another way in."

"Agreed."

"Okay. I'm coming up on the main doors. Shit. I don't even know if this is better."

"Tell me what you see."

"Bodies. Desiccated bodies, piled against the glass. But I can see inside, at least. I'm at the doors. There's . . ."

"What?" He waited. "Campbell?"

"There's a sound."

"What kind of sound?"

"I don't know. Shut up a second; let me listen." Time passed. "Like a hum."

"A person?"

"No. Like a machine. Something electronic. But that can't be right. There's no power here. It's not that loud. I'm going to open the doors." There was a scraping. He heard the kid gagging. "*Fucking hell.*"

"What is it?"

"The *smell.*"

"Stop where you are."

"Okay. Okay. I've stopped."

"Look around. Tell me everything."

"Seats. Reception desk. Shit on the walls."

"Shit?"

"I mean stuff. Ads. Get your vaccinations. Eight out of ten mothers experience postnatal depression. When was your last prostate exam."

"What about the sound?"

"Oh. Yeah, that's flies. Ten billion flies."

"Stand there a minute."

Time passed. "She's not here, Eliot. I told you. If there was anything bigger than a squirrel moving around in here, we'd know it."

"Rabbit. There are no squirrels in Australia."

"No . . ." The kid broke out in laughter. "No squirrels? Are you shitting me?"

"No."

"Well maybe I'll fucking move here! It's starting to seem like fucking paradise!"

"Keep it together."

The kid's breathing came harsh and ragged. "You're right. You're right." He steadied. "I'm going in." There was a scrape. The ambient noise altered, thickening. "I'm inside."

"Tell me everything."

"There are lines on the floor. Colored lines. Man . . . well, I guess I'll follow the red one. For Emergency. There are so many bodies . . .

it's hard to avoid them. Jesus fuck. I am never getting this smell off me." Shuffling. "Doors are propped open with bodies. I'm in a corridor. It's getting darker. The, ah . . . yeah, the lights don't work. Just confirming that. There's . . ."

"What?"

"There's a skull with an ax in it."

"An ax?"

"Yeah. A red ax. For fighting fires. I can see where someone pulled it out of the case. Someone broke the glass and took the ax out and buried it in this dude's head. Hey? Eliot?"

"Yes?"

"I'm taking the ax. Okay? I just . . . I'd feel better if I had it with me. So I'm going to put down the phone for a minute to pick up the ax."

"Okay."

The phone went *clunk*. He heard the kid grunting, then a brief squeal. "You there?"

"I'm here."

"I got it." The kid laughed. "I just pulled a fucking ax out of a skull." He exhaled. "I feel better. I feel kind of badass. Hey. I just had an idea. I'm going to take a picture of this shit, send it to you."

"On your phone?"

"Yeah."

"Can you do that without ending the call?"

"I don't . . . uh . . . not sure."

"Then don't do that."

"I'll send it and call you right back."

"Do not hang up the phone."

"Okay. Jesus. Okay, okay. Just an idea. I can see the doors to Emergency up ahead. Double doors. Lots of . . . oh. I just figured out what this black stuff on the walls is."

"Blood."

"Yeah. Lots and lots of blood." A pause. "Is that . . . ? Yeah. That's them."

"Who?"

"An extraction team. I know these guys. I mean . . . I saw their video. You know these people in black suits Yeats uses sometimes? The soldiers with the goggles? They're supposed to be screened against compromise."

"Yes."

"It's them. Some of them, anyway. They're not wearing their goggles. They . . . they're pretty messed up."

"How?"

"They're tangled. In each other. Their faces are black. Dried blood. They don't have any eyes. I don't know if . . . I don't know if that's decomposition or if . . . or what." His voice shook. "They look like they went through a fucking shredder, Eliot." He realized the kid was crying.

"Campbell—"

"But they weren't poets. That's the difference. I'm the king of defense."

"Come back. You can report in what you've learned. Try again tomorrow."

"No. No."

"Yeats can wait another—"

The kid's voice rose. "Eliot, you have no fucking idea what's required, okay? You've been in the fucking desert and you don't know. I am not telling Yeats I got this far and left. That is not fucking happening, and if you had half a clue you wouldn't suggest it."

"Not all of us agree with Yeats."

The kid sucked air awhile. "I could have your head, Eliot. I could have your head on a plate for what you just said to me."

"I know that."

"Yeah. Yeah." Seconds passed. "Doors ahead. Closed double doors. Sign says Emergency."

"Campbell, please."

"I want to hold the ax in two hands. I'm going to wedge the phone under my ear." There was a scraping. His breath came in gulps. "Hey, Eliot?"

"Yes?"

"I appreciate it. Saying that about Yeats. That's good of you."

"Campbell, please stop." Command words rose in his mind. Weak, over the phone. Probably pointless.

"If anything goes wrong, I want you to tell Yeats I was cool under pressure," said the kid. "I'm opening the . . ." There was a squeal of hinges.

"What do you see?"

The kid's breathing.

"Campbell? What do you see? Talk to me."

The phone barked into his ear. He jerked it away. By the time he brought it back, there was nothing but dead air. It had hit the floor, he thought; that was the noise. The kid had dropped it.

He thought he heard a faint squeak: the kid's shoes? "Campbell?" He said the kid's name again, and again, and again, and there was nothing.

Eliot waited against the car as the sun settled behind him and heat bled from the air. He didn't expect the kid to return. But he was giving him the chance.

Why are you here, Eliot? You see where the organization is going. You know what's coming. Yet here you stand.

In an hour, it would be dark. Then he would climb into the car, drive four hours to his hotel, and phone Yeats. He would tell him Campbell had not come back, keeping his voice empty, and Yeats would express his sorrow, in the same tone.

Emily, Emily, he thought. *Where did you go?*

Something shimmered on the road. He squinted. The haze had lifted, but the wind blew dust into his eyes. Then he was sure: Someone was coming. Eliot straightened. He raised a hand. The figure didn't respond. There was something odd about the way it was moving. Its gait was lopsided. Not Campbell? But it had to be. There was no one else out here.

A minute passed. The haze condensed into Campbell. The reason he was lopsided was that he was carrying an ax.

Eliot returned to the car, opened the glove compartment, and retrieved his gun. By the time he returned to the fence line, Campbell was two hundred yards away. Eliot could see his expression, his focused emptiness.

He stuck the pistol into his waistband and cupped his hands around his mouth. "*Campbell! Stop!*"

The kid kept coming. His shirt was soaked with sweat. Wet, matted hair poked from beneath the THUNDER FROM DOWN UNDER cap. He had lost a shoe.

"Campbell, drop the ax!"

For a moment, he thought the kid was obeying. But no: He was hefting the ax over his shoulder. Fifty yards. Close enough to smell.

"*Vestid foresash raintrae valo! Stop!*"

The kid shambled through the words like they were water. Eliot drew the gun.

"*Stop! Campbell, stop! Valo! Stop! Valo!*"

The kid's lips stretched back. The tendons along his forearms tightened. The ax rose. Eliot squeezed the trigger. The kid grunted. His expression didn't change. Eliot pulled the trigger twice more. The ax clanged to the blacktop. The kid fell to his knees. He tried to rise, grunted again, and fell face forward onto the road.

Eliot sank to his haunches. The sun had almost set. The world was awash in orange. He rose and began to load the kid's body into the car.

He buried the kid in the desert and drove through the night. When the city lights rose, he couldn't stand it anymore, and pulled over onto the shoulder and climbed out. He leaned on the car and dialed, inhaling night air. Cars whizzed by. "Yes?"

"It's Eliot."

"Ah." He heard a tinkling: ice in glass. "How are things proceeding?"

"Campbell's dead."

He heard Yeats sip at his drink. "Do you mean he failed to return?"

"I mean I shot him in the chest." He closed his eyes, but that was no better, so he opened them again. "I mean he came out of there carrying an ax and I shot him."

"You sound unsettled."

He dropped the phone from his ear. When he could, he raised it. "I'm fine."

"You're saying Campbell came back insane. Is that correct?"

"Yes. Insane. Compromised. Something."

"Do you know how it happened?"

"He made it to the Emergency Room. We were talking. Then he just stopped."

"How did he sound up to that point?"

"He was cool under pressure."

There was silence. "It's so intriguing," Yeats said. "What I would give to know what she did in there."

He waited.

"Come home, Eliot. It's been long enough."

"I haven't found Woolf."

"Woolf is dead."

"I don't believe that."

"Stop believing what you want to believe. It's unbecoming. You've found no trace. Your assignment is terminated. Come home."

He laid his head against the cold metal of the car and closed his eyes. "Yes, sir."

A dot appeared in the snowscape. A car? Yes. Eliot checked his coat, made sure the gun was out of sight.

Behind him, Wil's footsteps clattered down the airplane steps. *That was quick*, Eliot thought. *He must have thought of something.*

"What happened to being *worth it*?" Wil shouted. "Isn't that what you said to me? Those people who died back there, I had to make myself worth it?"

Eliot didn't answer.

"Is that a car?"

Wil's shoes crunched toward him. He stopped beside Eliot, hugging himself. Eliot glanced at him. "Don't leave me, you motherfucker," Wil said.

"Fine."

"What? So . . . we're good? We're staying together?"

"Yes."

"Then what the hell was that before? Was that a joke?"

The car slowed. Eliot saw glassed-in faces gaping at the plane. "This will be easier if you're calm."

"Are you *fucking* with me now? I'm trying to deal with . . . magical, killer poets and you're *fucking* with me?"

"I reconsidered," Eliot said. "You made a good point." He walked toward the car.

GHOST TOWNS: #8:
BROKEN HILL (AUSTRALIA)

Following discovery of the world's richest zinc-lead ore deposit in 1883, Broken Hill became one of the world's largest mining towns. At its peak, up to thirty thousand residents lived here, many employed by the Broken Hill Proprietary Company (BHP).

Following exhaustion of two primary mines in the 1970s, however, the town began to decline. Several smaller mine sites remained viable, but isolation—the nearest city is three hundred miles away—and the inhospitable environment contributed to a steady fall in population.

In the early afternoon of 14 August, 2011, the zinc-lead refinery, situated near the heart of the town, experienced a catastrophic explosion followed by a rapid, hot-burning fire. Reports suggest a river of deadly methyl isocarbonate flowed down the main street. Within the next few hours, all three thousand residents died from toxic fumes. Several emergency services teams that entered the town in the ensuing hours were likewise overcome.

The town is currently fenced off at a radius of five miles and expected to remain uninhabitable for the next two hundred years.

From: http://nationstates.org/pages/topic-39112000-post-8.html
Re: broken hill conspiracies???

what people don't realise about broken hill is alot of the people didnt die from fumes at all at least not directly. it was the panic when they realised what was happning and couldnt get out my uncle was on the first perimeter team and he said people were killing each other in there

[TWO]

She sat in a red leather armchair and watched a fish. The fish was in a tall hourglass, with water instead of sand. Every few seconds a drop fell from the top to the bottom with a *plink* she could hear only because the room was a mausoleum. The fish wandered around, ballooning as it approached the curved sides and shrinking away again as it neared the center. It didn't seem to care that its world was shrinking one drop at a time. Maybe it was used to it. When the water level was low enough, the hourglass must tilt, swing the fish to the bottom, and start refilling one drop at a time. Some kind of art, she assumed. It was installed in the middle of this room with no other function; it had to be. It was making some point about time or rebirth. She didn't know. She shouldn't be thinking about the fish anyway. She was in a situation.

Charlotte had driven her, deposited her in this room, and clack-clacked off into the depths. Charlotte had not spoken during any of this, not one word, even though Emily tried to provoke her. There was a disturbing softness about Charlotte this morning. A kind of sympathy in her silence, which Emily did not like at all.

She wished Jeremy were here. She wished there was some possibility of this day ending in his room, her telling him about it. *You would not believe this fish hourglass they had*, she'd say. And Jeremy wouldn't say anything but she would be able to tell he was interested.

Her time at the school was over. That was what Eliot had said. But no one had made her leave. They'd put her in a different room and in the morning a fresh school uniform was hanging on the door. Then Charlotte, soft and silent. Emily didn't know how to reconcile all this.

She was giving serious consideration to running. Many problems, Emily knew, could be solved through running. She was not exactly sure which way led to the street, since she had arrived here via an elevator from the underground garage, but still. It was worth keeping in mind as an option. She stared at the hourglass. *Plink. Plink.* She couldn't see a tilting mechanism. But it must move soon, because the water level was getting pretty low.

She heard heels and identified them as Charlotte's. It was her last chance to flee and she let it pass. Charlotte emerged and crossed the room without looking at her. She opened a door and waited.

Emily rose. "Are we leaving?" Charlotte did not respond. She looked at Emily and her eyes made Emily feel like she had made a mistake not running. But it was too late for that. She would get out of here one way or another. She always did. "O-kay," she said, and went through the door.

Charlotte took her to a stairwell and finally to a door marked ROOF. She opened this and Emily stepped out into sunshine.

The roof was maybe a hundred yards to a side, with gardens and a pool and a tennis court. Like a floating resort. And she could see other rooftops floating in the sky around her, and they were all the exact same height, because this was Washington. She marveled at this for a moment and the door clacked shut behind her. She turned and Charlotte was gone. "Hmm," she said.

She began to explore the gardens. There was a noise like: *schock.* Following this, she came upon a man in light gray pants, no jacket, standing with his back to her, straddling a green mat. His knees were slightly bent. He was holding a golf club. She stood very still, because even from here she could tell it was Yeats, the man Jeremy had promised her she'd never have to speak to, who had shark eyes.

He swung the club. *Schock*, and a golf ball arced into the air. She watched it, thinking it was going to land on one of those other buildings, but they were farther away than it seemed. The ball fell below the horizon of the low rooftop wall. That would be kind of dangerous by the time it reached ground level, she felt. Kind of like a bullet.

Yeats turned to her. To her enormous relief, he was wearing sunglasses. He almost looked normal. Or not normal, but like a politician—a congressman or senator, someone who might tell her the country needed cleaning up. More solid than normal. He wasn't smiling but didn't seem angry, either. He was just looking at her.

"Hi," she said.

He took a white cloth and began to clean the end of his club. This took a while and his eyes didn't move from her, as far as she could tell.

She shifted from one foot to the other. "Charlotte brought me here but—"

"*Vartix velkor mannik wissick*. Be still."

Her mouth snapped closed. It happened before she realized what she was doing. The surprise was that it felt like her decision. She really, genuinely wanted to be still. It was the words, Yeats, compromising her, she knew, but it didn't feel like that at all. Her brain was spinning with rationalizations, reasons why she should definitely be still right now, why that was a really good move, and it was talking in her voice. She hadn't known compromise was like this.

Yeats took a golf ball from a basket and dropped it to the green mat. He positioned himself, raised the club. He struck the ball and watched it sail into the distance. When it disappeared, he returned to the basket and did it again. He wasn't watching where those balls landed, she noticed. It wasn't like he was taking some kind of perverse joy in turning golf balls into bullets. It was more like he didn't care. She had misjudged this whole situation. She had thought it was going to be about her. That hourglass in the lobby, she realized, that didn't tilt. It was someone's job to come by twice a day and replace the fish.

Yeats continued to hit balls and she fought to move but couldn't.

She felt violated and angry but also ashamed that she couldn't control her own body. It was humiliating. It was making her reevaluate her relationship with herself. *Breathe fast*, she told herself, because that would be like being still but not exactly. She had to find a place to drive in a wedge and work from there. *Breathe.*

Yeats's head turned to her. What he was thinking, she had no idea. But she had the feeling that the golfing part was over. He returned his club to the bag and lowered himself into a wrought-iron chair and began to untie his shoelaces. He did this with great care, as if his shoes contained secrets. When this was done, he entered a black glossy pair. Business shoes. Shoes for business. He laced them firmly, and stood, and headed toward her.

She breathed. She could force a tiny amount of air between her teeth, making a *hsss* she could barely hear. That was it.

Yeats removed his sunglasses and tucked them into his shirt pocket. His eyes were gray and characterless as stone. There was a flatness to his face. She'd have suspected a face-lift if it wasn't crazy for a poet to reveal a mental weakness for vanity. Maybe he'd wanted to erase his expressions. Or maybe he was just like this. If you never smiled or laughed or frowned, she could believe that this was the kind of face you wound up with, smooth and empty as an undisturbed pond.

He unbuttoned his cuffs and began to roll up his shirtsleeves. He was close enough to scratch or bite or kick in the nuts but she couldn't do any of that, of course. *He is going to kill you!* she shrieked at herself, but it made no difference. Her brain had become very fatalistic. It knew she was responsible for Jeremy and it was hard to argue she didn't deserve everything she got.

Yeats folded his hands and closed his eyes. For long seconds he did not move. She thought, *Is he praying?* Because that was what it looked like. He couldn't be, because the idea of a religious poet was even more ridiculous than a vain one. Belief in God was a mental weakness, revealing a need for a sense of belonging and higher purpose: desires poets were supposed to master. They were potential avenues of attack.

They advertised your segment. She had been taught this. But Yeats was giving every indication of communing with a higher power. Her heart thumped painfully. There was nothing about this situation she understood.

"Sss," she said.

His eyes opened. "Goodness," he said. She thought he was mocking her, but maybe not. His eyes searched hers. She felt surveyed, as if by engineers: dispassionately, precisely, with instruments. "I was told your discipline was poor," he said. "But this . . ."

Moments passed. She could see his nostrils flaring in and out. She said, "Sss."

"You are, supposedly, gifted. You possess an aptitude for attack, considered sufficient to offset your deficiencies in defense. I would see this. Because presently, my dear, I have trouble imagining how this could be true. I will allow you one opportunity to speak to me. Use it to convince me why I should keep you. *Vartix velkor mannik wissick.* You may speak."

Her throat loosened. She coughed, to prove it. She said, "Ug." It felt good to make that sound. Yeats waited patiently. It would take one hell of an argument to convince him of anything, she thought. She had been in situations like this, where people said, *Convince me*, and in none of those had they actually wanted to be convinced. She could lay down a perfect argument and they just invented new bullshit on the spot to justify why the answer was still no. When people said, *Convince me*, she knew it didn't mean they had an open mind. It meant they had power and wanted to enjoy it a minute. She didn't know if that was true of Yeats. But she did not feel that she could talk her way out of this. Why should Yeats keep her? She was fucked if she knew. She was nothing but trouble.

"*Fennelt!*" she said. "*Rassden!*" These were attention words, which she'd collected from other students. It was incredibly unlikely they would do anything to Yeats; she didn't even know his segment. If she fluked one, he was no doubt capable of shrugging off anything a student could manage. "*Thrilence! Mallinto!*" He didn't react. Didn't so much as flinch. "Die!" she said. Which was kind of stupid, but she was out of words. And she wanted it very much. "Die, you flat fuck!"

"Enough."

Her mouth closed. Words clogged her throat, bobbing up and down. They tasted hot, like bile.

Yeats looked at her awhile. She couldn't read him. She didn't know whether she had lived or died.

"I have a name for you," he said, "when the time is right." He walked away. She heard him reach the door but couldn't turn her head. "You may move, in a while."

Some time passed. A bird landed near the golf clubs and began to hop hopefully around the little green mat. She breathed. Her chest loosened one muscle at a time. That was how she got herself back. Filament by filament. She had survived, somehow. She was still here.

She was collected by a woman she had seen once before, stepping out of a black town car alongside Yeats that time he had visited the school. She didn't introduce herself but Emily already knew her name was Plath. She had asked. Plath was all cheekbones and elbows and gave Emily the feeling that she would push her in front of a train for a nickel. She had cruel shoes and a phone and looked at Emily in a way that reminded her of being stepped over on a San Francisco sidewalk on a bad day. "Can you move?" Plath said.

"Yes."

Plath beckoned. Emily followed. There were stairs and then she was in the parking garage. A car Emily knew well was there and her heart leaped. It was the first moment she had truly believed she was getting out of here. She looked at Plath and Plath said nothing so Emily walked to the car. Its engine turned over. She opened the passenger door and inside was Eliot. "Hi," she said. She wanted to kiss him.

Eliot didn't speak. But he looked at her and she knew she was safe. He was still angry with her, of course. But he was not dangerous. She could relax in a car with Eliot. When the car exited the garage into bright sunshine, she closed her eyes. Somewhere in the snarl of streets, she fell asleep.

She opened her eyes and was somewhere else. "Where are we?" She saw a road sign. "Are we going to the airport?" Eliot flicked on the turn signal. The car drifted toward a lane marked DEPARTURES. "Hey," she said. "Eliot. Yeats said I could still be a poet. He tested me and I passed. I don't have to go away." It was like talking to a wall. "Eliot, I can go back to the school."

He pulled alongside the curb and took something from the seat pocket. "This is your passport. This is your confirmation number." A blue booklet with a white business card tucked inside. The card had a string of letters and numbers in blue ink above TOM ELIOT, RESEARCH ANALYST. "Use the machines inside to check in."

"Talk to Yeats. Eliot. Call Yeats. He'll tell you."

"These are his instructions."

She stared. "But I passed."

"It's temporary," Eliot said. "You can come home in a few years."

"Years?" she said. "*Years?*"

"Please appreciate that this is the best possible outcome."

"No. Eliot. Please." He wouldn't look at her, so she put her hand on his arm. He didn't say anything. He didn't move. Eventually, she understood that this was final. "Well," she said. "Bye, then."

"Your bag is in the trunk."

"Thanks." She opened the door. It was difficult, as if everything had gotten heavy. Her hands were numb. She dragged herself from the car.

Eliot said, "If you work hard, and discipline yourself, you can conceivably return in—" She shut the door on the rest.

First the red-eye from DC to Los Angeles: six hours. She landed at dawn and spent half a day moving the two hundred yards from Domestic Arrivals to International Departures. She hadn't slept in the air so she curled up in a seat, but there were families and kids vibrating at high frequency and men with booming laughs. A younger couple discussed in-flight movies in a flat, broad accent. She was going to Australia. Her boarding passes told her so. "We should get *Lord of the Rings*," said the man. *Lawwwd*, she thought. *Lawwwd of the Reeengs.* They sent convicts to Australia, right? It had been a penal colony. A place of banishment.

The desk called for first- and business-class passengers and she trudged to the gate. When she surrendered her boarding pass, though, the woman smiled and handed it back to her. "We'll be boarding economy in a few moments." Emily looked at her dumbly. She had just assumed. She walked back to the seats.

"Nice try," said the man beside her, the one hoping for *Lord of the Rings*. He was friendly, and she smiled back, and it was the most fake thing she had ever done.

She slept fitfully, disturbed by rattling food trolleys and people squeezing by her seat. The flight time according to her screen was fourteen hours, which she thought had to be wrong, like maybe that was including the time difference. She didn't know enough to sleep properly.

Somewhere over the Pacific, a flight attendant bent to her ear. "Excuse me. This is for you." Emily, tangled in dreams of golf and Yeats, stared at the woman without comprehension. It was nighttime; the only light came from the screens in the backs of people's seats and the little yellow glow lights embedded in the aisles. The woman handed Emily a folded piece of paper. It was an odd texture, thick, stamped with an aviation authority logo.

"Thank you," Emily said. The attendant left and she unfolded the paper.

EMILY YOU ARE TO LIVE IN BROKEN HILL AUSTRALIA
THIS IS TO BE YOUR HOME UNTIL YOU ARE CALLED FOR
NO PREPARATIONS HAVE BEEN MADE YOU ARE TO USE
YOUR OWN RESOURCES YOU CAN DO THIS ELIOT

She put the paper away and pulled her knees to her chest and silently cried into them. If she were at the school, she wouldn't have been able to do this. She would have had to control herself. But here she indulged. She let herself sob. After this, things were going to be difficult, and she would have to concentrate, so it was probably her last opportunity.

She grew hypnotized by the in-flight map. The red line began in Los Angeles, curved across the ocean, and terminated at a cartoon plane that never seemed to move. The screen occasionally switched to statistics, like how fast they were moving and how cold it was outside, and these were fascinating because the numbers seemed made up. It didn't seem possible for the cartoon plane that didn't move to be traveling at 580 miles per hour. But it was. The flight was fourteen hours.

Her first problem, she realized, was that she was landing in Sydney with no return ticket, no luggage, wearing a school uniform. She didn't know what the Australian immigration service was like, but it seemed probable that she would raise a few flags. She would look exactly like an overprivileged white girl disappearing in a cloud of petulance on Daddy's credit card, and they would ask why she was here and where she was staying and when she was leaving. If they didn't like her answers, they would turn her around and put her on a plane back home. Which, of course, superficially sounded like a great idea, except for the part where she failed to LIVE IN BROKEN HILL and

USE HER OWN RESOURCES. Eliot had told her, *Please appreciate that this is the best possible outcome*, and she had come to believe that. She needed to get through Immigration.

She extracted herself from her economy seat and made her way to the rear bathrooms. In the mirror, she practiced some expressions. Then she washed her face and unlocked the door. On the way back, she stopped beside a girl she had identified who was sleeping and roughly Emily's age, and opened her overhead locker and rummaged inside. There was a possibility of someone being awake and alert enough to say, *Excuse me, do those things belong to you*, of course, but not a large one, nor with serious consequences, and it didn't happen. She found a little suitcase and a duffel bag and went through these, standing on tiptoe. Inside were a purse, a wallet, a digital camera, which she took because maybe she could sell it, and a book. Also a coat, which could conceal her school uniform, so she tucked that beneath her arm. She closed the locker. Two or three sets of eyes were on her, but they were glazed and disinterested, their owners critiquing her hair or fantasizing about schoolgirls, and that was fine; she was just getting some of her stuff. She cracked open the book and read it there, right next to the sleeping girl she'd robbed, like she was stretching her legs. Soon enough a man came down the aisle and she could retreat to her own seat without it looking like a getaway.

Just before the plane began to descend, she switched seats, to avoid a potential *where's my coat* situation. She was among the first off the plane, and she walked briskly toward Customs, her new coat flapping around her ankles. The lines were short, not at all like in Los Angeles, and she was able to take her pick of Immigration officials. His name was Mark, and he was a 114 or 118, good-natured and reasonably intelligent but resigned in his job, which he considered important but dull. This she could tell right away. No glasses, no beard, a simple hairstyle but not a severe one, so no overt arrogance or vanity. No cross or religious markings. So she went for mirroring: She was Emily Ruff, simple and straightforward, slugging hours into a customer interface job as a DMV inspector. An entry-level position, but if you didn't do your job right, people could get hurt.

"Hi," she said. "Just right up, I don't have a return ticket. I'm sorry, I know that means you have to give me the third degree."

Two hours later, they released her from the interview room. They'd asked a lot of questions, but she never felt in real danger, not from the moment Mark's face relaxed into her opening statement. She had lied a great deal, inventing a traumatic case at the DMV and a late-night Australian tourism ad culminating in a spur-of-the-moment urge to get away (*You understand that, right, Mark? The need to leave?*). She was charming and forthright and understood more about how the brain reached decisions than these guys did about anything, so that was that. She got rid of the coat before Arrivals, in case the owner was still hanging around filling out lost-and-found forms. She found a currency exchange place that let her sign for up to five hundred dollars on a credit card. Australian dollars were hilarious, she discovered: bright and shiny, like money for children. She liked them a lot. She bought a magazine and ate a cookie. She went to baggage claim and watched luggage go round and round, waiting for something wealthy, female, and unattended. A gray-suited official led around a beagle in a purple jacket, which sniffed luggage; when it found a banana in someone's carry-on, it sat on the floor and the official gave it a treat. In Los Angeles, they'd been German shepherds. Eventually a purple Louis Vuitton suitcase completed a third lonely loop on the carousel, so she tugged it off, balanced her Pikachu bag on top, and headed for the exits.

The sun was brighter. The air smelled salty and felt wider, somehow. She found a cab rank and the driver wrestled her stolen suitcase into the trunk while she climbed into the back.

"Where to, love?"

The driver was white, something else she wasn't used to. "Broken Hill, please."

He turned in his seat. "Broken Hill?"

"Is that a problem?"

"I don't know. It's a thousand kilometers, is that a problem?"

"What are . . ." She felt stupid. "How far is that in miles?"

"Seven hundred miles, give or take."

Why had she assumed Broken Hill would be near Sydney? "I'm sorry. In which state is Broken Hill?"

"New South Wales."

"And where am I?"

"New South Wales." He smiled at her face. "We have big states, love."

"How do I get there? Which is the closest city?" She hoped he was not about to say *Sydney*.

"Adelaide."

"So I can fly to Adelaide," she said, "and drive from there."

"Yes, you can."

"Thank you. Sorry for your trouble." She began to get out of the cab.

"Only three hundred miles from Adelaide to Broken Hill." He was grinning. "Welcome to Australia, love."

"Thanks," she said.

She couldn't secure a flight that day, so she caught a cab downtown and checked into a mid-priced hotel. With the balcony doors open, bringing in a breeze from the green-flecked bay, she sifted through the suitcase, inspecting skirts and jackets. She found a romance novel, the kind you wouldn't read on the plane, and a diary, for appointments, not confessions. Still, she turned the pages. This woman saw someone named Matt R. a lot. Emily wondered if they met in hotel rooms like this. If, after sex, the woman talked to Matt R., telling him her hopes and problems and idle thoughts. She closed the diary.

She had to get organized. Her stolen cards were already too dangerous to use; she wouldn't reach Adelaide on those. She turned to the mirror and fiddled with a shirt. It was a little big, but she could work with the cuffs. She picked up the phone and dialed the front desk. "I want to play poker," she said. "Something informal."

Eventually, the guy stopped recommending casinos and steered her toward an upper room of a nearby bar. It turned out to be middle-aged men in expensive suits, friendly and patronizing while she lost the first two hundred dollars, smiling over their single-malt whiskeys and advancing theories about creative ways to cover her losses. By then she had a queen under her left thigh and a king and an eight under her right. It had been three years since she'd done this kind of thing, and a more attentive audience would have caught her. At one point, she tried to feed a jack into her sleeve and missed so badly that the card landed on the table. She tensed to run, but they only laughed and one man said, "That's enough grog for you." The man had red cheeks and was divorced, although he didn't know it yet. "Sorry," Emily said, and put the card back in her hand.

She took him for twenty-eight hundred in the final round, going all in. His face turned incredibly red, like a balloon. No one was smiling now. The game's operator approached the table, but she didn't need to be told; she gathered her winnings, thanked them, and when she reached the street, ran as fast as she could back to her hotel. That was how she got to Adelaide.

From there it was a bus ride, the world outside draining green until it was the color of snakeskin. The air-conditioning barely worked and she kept being woken by little trickles of sweat. There was only one other passenger, a woman with skin like coral who nodded off before they were even out of Adelaide and slept like she was dead. Emily wriggled around in her seat, seeking escape from her own body heat.

Eventually she opened an eye to a passing sign: BROKEN HILL, POP. 10,100. One corner was missing and the rest was peppered with gunshot. It flared in the afternoon sun, leaning drunkenly out of the baked red earth. She sat up and saw a gas station, abandoned, and a tin structure with no windows that was she didn't know what, also abandoned. A flat, sagging house with a dirt yard full of disemboweled cars. She glimpsed a tall iron structure, vaguely Soviet, but it was on the other side of the bus and she couldn't see it properly. A thin dog scratched in the dirt. Another low store, this one advertising CHEAP PARTS, although for what she didn't know. The windows of the stores on either side were blank. Everything was widely spaced, the center of its own little wasteland, and why not, because, she was quickly realizing, that was all there was out here: land, land, and land. She passed signs that said SULPHIDE ST and CHLORIDE ST, because they had named their streets after *minerals*, apparently, and the bus turned onto OXIDE ST and began to slow. She saw a sign that said CITY CENTER and thought, *You have to be kidding me.* When she stepped off it was into burning air, the heat crawling into her nostrils and down her throat, and they hadn't updated that population sign in a long time, like maybe twenty years, because there might be ten thousand flies here but not people. Definitely not people. She was standing at a crossroads; the streets were single lanes in each direction but still as wide as highways. There were a handful of buildings like they had fallen from above. The sky felt oppressively low, as if it were pressing down, combining with the blasted earth below to crush this town to nothing, and it made her feel as if she were expanding, like her insides wanted to crawl out of her body like supposedly happened in space, where there was nothing to hold you in. "Home," she said. It was supposed to be funny, but she felt like crying until she died.

CONFUSION OF TONGUES

Event in which a common language is abruptly replaced by many disparate ones. Considered mythical; see: <u>origin tales.</u>
Prominent examples:

1. **Tower of Babel** • Judaic myth
   i. construction
   ii. dividing of speech
2. **Enki** • Sumerian deity
   i. divides speech
   ii. "The Deluge"
3. **Great Dividing** • Kaska origin myth
4. **Hermes** • Greek deity
   i. conflict with Zeus
   ii. divides speech
   iii. punishment
5. **Jabbering Madness** • Wa-Sania myth
   i. famine
6. **Tongues of a Thousand Corpses** • Kaurna myth
   i. cannibalism
7. **Vatea** • Polynesian deity
   i. construction of tower
   ii. divides speech
8. **The Sun of Wind** • Aztec myth
   i. construction of *Zacualli* (tower)
   ii. dividing of speech
   iii. crossover mythology: Mayan, Nahuati

More >>

THE STORY OF TAJURA'S NAME

Myth (Confusion of Tongues): Indigenous Australian

In the Dreaming the land was flat. There were no gorges and no hills, and no rivers. The animals lived in one tribe and spoke with one tongue, so they could understand one another.

One day Tajura, the Rainbow Serpent, carved his name in the bark of a coolabah tree. He said to the other animals, "Look what I have done, I have written my name on this tree, so you must do what I say."

The animals were impressed and did as Tajura said. They offered their food and made him a great shelter. They brought dirt from the land together and put it beneath the coolabah tree so that it was raised up, so they could admire Tajura's name, and that was the first hill.

But Borah, the kangaroo, was not impressed. "Why should we give Tajura our food, our best bark, and work for him?" he asked. He climbed the hill and tore the bark from the coolabah tree where it spoke Tajura's name and buried it in the ground.

The animals were ashamed and said, "We shall speak in our own tongue, so we will not be impressed by Tajura's words." They went away, some north, some east, some west, some south, and that is why today the dingo howls, the frog croaks, the cockatoo screeches, and none can understand the other.

INDIGENOUS AUSTRALIAN LANGUAGES

At the time of European arrival, the indigenous peoples of Australia are estimated to have spoken between 250 and 400 languages, making it one of the most linguistically diverse places in the world.

Almost all indigenous languages share several distinctive phonological features (e.g., lack of fricatives), which suggests the existence of a relatively small set of ancestors, or perhaps even a single common language. Why this would have been abandoned, given its utility to intertribal communication, is unclear.

[THREE]

The waitress brought food and coffee and instructed them to enjoy. Wil watched Eliot spread a napkin across his lap, pick up his cutlery, and begin to dissect his eggs. He popped bacon into his mouth and chewed.

"Go on," Eliot said through bacon. "Eat."

Wil picked up his knife and began to push food around. It was beyond him how Eliot could shoot people dead and fly all night and then tuck into a hearty breakfast. It was wrong. Because Eliot had known those people at the ranch, including a woman he'd shot dead, Charlotte Brontë, and you shouldn't have an appetite after something like that. It suggested that Eliot really was psychopathic—not the crazy, *voices-told-me-to-kill* way, but actually, medically psychopathic, in the sense of lacking the ability to feel anything. But even this bothered Wil less than the *way* Eliot was eating, which was with quick, purposeful movements, his eyes sectioning up the plate for maximum efficiency. This was wrong because Eliot hadn't slept since Wil had met him. He should be exhausted.

"This is even better than I expected," Eliot said. He pointed at Wil's plate with his knife. "You need to eat."

Wil ate without enthusiasm. His bacon tasted like nothing. Like a dead animal, fried. His eggs, aborted chickens.

"I'll say this for the Midwest," Eliot said. "They know how to do a breakfast."

Wil poked a bacon strip with his fork. In its rufescent flesh he saw the man he'd shot on the overturned pickup. The way he'd folded up. He put down his cutlery.

"Are you all right?" No concern in Eliot's voice, of course. It was just a question. An inquiry after facts. Wil rose and tottered to the rear of the diner. He found a single, dirty toilet, lowered himself to his knees, and vomited. When he was done, he sat back against the wall, eyes closed, sweat popping all over his body. He decided to stay here awhile. You were safe in a bathroom. It was a four-by-six cubicle of sanctuary, for as long as you wanted.

When he could no longer believe this, he washed and reentered the diner. A man in a trucker cap with hollow cheeks and serial killer glasses eyed him over hash browns. Wil could read his face clearly: He thought Wil had been doing drugs. The waitress was sneaking looks at him, too. And there was a red-cheeked man wedged into a booth seat, who was watching a burbling TV bolted into the ceiling corner but hadn't been a moment ago. He felt an urge to explain himself. *It's not what you think. I've just had a really rough day.* But that would be crazy. He would convince no one.

He shuffled back to the booth. Eliot had finished his own breakfast and switched plates with Wil. "Hey," he said. "Order more. I'm paying."

"Are you?"

"Well, no," said Eliot. "But you know what I mean."

Wil sat.

"You could use the protein," said Eliot, chewing.

"What's your plan?"

"Hmm?"

"These people, they're going to find us again, aren't they? They're looking for us right now."

"No doubt."

"So we need a plan."

Eliot nodded. "True."

"Do you have one?"

"No."

"You don't?"

"I have a short-term plan," Eliot said. "I plan to finish your eggs." Wil said nothing. "Food is important. I'm serious about the protein."

"Do you have a plan or not?"

"No."

"Shouldn't you, I don't know, be concerned about that?"

"I am concerned about that."

"You don't look concerned."

"Would it make you feel better if I were sweating? Running to the bathroom to blow my cookies? It shouldn't. A panic state is not helpful to good decision making."

"It would make me feel better if we were *moving*," Wil said. "Like if you got your eggs to *go*."

"Well, I like to know where I'm going before I try to get there. It's a mistake to try to execute a plan before you've thought of one, in my experience."

Wil exhaled. "Can you call them?"

"Pardon me?"

"Get a poet on the phone. You used to be one of them. Call them."

"And say what?"

"I don't know. Persuade them to stop chasing us. That's what you do, isn't it?"

"Yes. But it's also what they do."

"Then offer them something. Make a deal. Give them something they want."

"But what they want is you."

"Something else."

Eliot retired his cutlery. "You're the key to an object of biblical power. They're not interested in substitutes." He stretched his arms. "And when I say biblical, I mean literally from the Bible."

He rubbed his face. Every time Eliot spoke, Wil felt that he knew less.

"Keep talking, though," Eliot said. "I feel like it's helping, in a process of elimination kind of way."

"We should hide, then. Go somewhere, you do your poet thing, make people hide us. That's possible, right?"

"Before yesterday, I would have said yes. We thought we were hiding. In light of recent events, though, it seems what we were actually doing was being observed until we led Woolf to you."

"So we can't hide."

"We can try. But to date it hasn't been very successful."

The waitress arrived to refill Eliot's coffee. She was young and pink cheeked. Her name tag said SARAH. She seemed to be in awe of Eliot, although Wil didn't know why. "Thank you, Sarah," said Eliot, and she flushed.

"So we *can't* hide," Wil said, once she'd left, "and we can't negotiate, and we can't stay here, and you don't want to leave until we know where we're going, is that about right?"

"Yes," Eliot agreed. "That's about right."

"Then what are we going to do?"

"I believe our only option is confrontation. Specifically, the kind of confrontation that leaves them dead and us alive."

"Okay," he said. "This sounds like a plan."

"It's not. It's a goal."

"Jesus!" Wil said. "Talking to you is like herding cats."

Eliot raised his coffee and blew at it. "The problem is that Woolf and I are evenly matched, but she is excellently resourced and supported by skilled poets, while I have nothing and no one but you, and you're useless. That's not a personal commentary. It's a statement of fact. So I'm finding it hard to imagine any scenario wherein we confront Woolf and survive. It also means our enemies will continue to pursue us rapidly and relentlessly, since we represent little danger. It's more or less the same problem that those of us who left the organization have faced for some time. Our enemies have a bareword and we don't."

"They have a what?"

"The word that killed Broken Hill," Eliot said. "They have that."

"And it's a bareword."

"Yes."

"Which is what?"

"Useful." He gazed at Wil. "Hence our attempt to lift it from your brain. Still a good plan, if it's in there."

"You wanted it to *use*? I thought you wanted my immunity. You said you wanted to *stop* it."

"Mmm," said Eliot. "Some untruths were told, in the interests of acquiring your compliance. I was actually somewhat concerned at the time that you might use the word against me."

"But I don't remember it."

"No."

"If I did . . ."

"Oh, things would be different."

"Woolf wouldn't be chasing us?"

"She would," Eliot said, "but more cautiously."

Wil looked out the window, at snow and clouds like granite. He could not imagine living in dirt and desert. "I really don't remember anything about Broken Hill."

"Well," Eliot said. He drained his coffee. "That's a shame." The waitress, Sarah, descended on them, refilling his cup. "Aren't you a peach," Eliot said.

"Are you from the East Coast?" She reddened. "It's just, your accent."

"You're right!" Eliot said. "Well, I am. He's from Australia."

"*Really*," Sarah said, looking at Wil in a new way. "I'd love to travel, one day."

"Oh, you should," Eliot said. "The world is closer than you think." Wil looked out the window again. He felt tempted to rise, toss his napkin on the table, and walk out. Just walk on down the road, snow falling in his hair, until something happened. One way or the other. At least it would be doing something. Something stupid, most likely. But something. "Now that necklace is truly beautiful," Eliot said. "Did you make it?"

"It's my grandmother," said the waitress. A carved piece of wood, a woman in profile. A *relief*, was that what you called it? The woman looked stern. "I carved it from a photo."

"I think you're very talented," Eliot said. "Sarah, I apologize, but would you give me a few minutes? I've just thought of something I need to discuss with my colleague."

"Oh, sure. No problem."

She left. Wil looked at Eliot.

"Fuck me," Eliot said. "The fucking necklace." Wil waited. From now on when Eliot said something he didn't understand, he was going to wait. "We're going to Broken Hill."

"Why?"

"We thought she got it out. But she didn't. She made a copy."

Wil waited.

"Fuck!" Eliot said. "We need to move." He rose.

The chopper sat above the road, billowing snow, making the power lines dance. Below them sat a small plane. It had been abandoned; she could see the steps hanging out of its side. The pilot's voice crackled through her headphones. He was sitting right next to her, but sounded like he was dialing in from Mars. "You want to set down?"

She shook her head. The pilot pulled back on the stick. The world below dropped away. They flew over snowfields that were like a million brilliant daggers, and she turned away, because it hurt the star in her eye. She had a little supernova searing her retina. That was how it felt. It never really went away but was always worse in the light. Anyplace she could see the sun. Sometimes she thought she could see it: a little white hole in the world.

"Two minutes," said the pilot. "We have a diner. Center of town. We've encircled but haven't approached. How do you want to do this?"

"Safely," she said. "Have them sweep it, please."

The pilot nodded. She heard him passing on the instruction: *Sweep it; we're staying airborne.* The town emerged as a smudge in the snowscape. It had one road in and one road out, perhaps a dozen buildings. As they hovered, she watched black cars rocket up from each direction and disgorge tiny figures. They moved from building to building, gesturing and sometimes stopping to consult each other. The chances of them finding Eliot and the outlier here were a thousand to one. But she had to be careful. The thing to remember was that all the power in the world didn't stop a bullet. She had been taught chess at the school, years ago, and the point was the pieces differed only in terms of their attacking power. They were all equally easy to kill. Capture. It was called capturing. The lesson was that you should be cautious about deploying your most powerful pieces, because it only required one dumb pawn to take them down.

The pilot got the signal and began to settle the chopper toward the street. She watched the town tilt toward her through the bubble windshield. *Now's your chance, Eliot. I'm just sitting here.* Eliot was a bishop, she figured, prone to sneaky long-range attacks, and more mobile than you expected. She had never liked bishops.

"We're green," said the pilot. She unbuckled. A young man with long hair, Rosenberg, opened the door and offered her his hand, which she found kind of insulting and ignored. The chopper's blades pulled at her hair. She studied the street, trying to sense trace elements of Eliot.

"Diner's clear," said Rosenberg. "I'm guessing they acquired a car here, maybe a couple hours ago. Three proles inside, segmented and compromised, instructed to obey. We haven't questioned them."

"Thank you," she said. "I'll take it from here."

She made for the low diner. A few poets moved toward her and Rosenberg waved them away. Inside, behind the counter, was a young, scared waitress in a green apron. In a booth was a red-cheeked man she presumed was a farmer. A skinny guy in big glasses was manning a table. The door wheezed closed behind her. The man with glasses rose unsteadily from his table. "I ain't cooperating with the government. You want to—"

"Sit down, shut up." He dropped into his seat. She pointed to the waitress. "You come here."

The waitress jerked forward, clutching a notepad. Her eyes were huge.

"Two men. One dark, one white. You know who I'm talking about?"

The waitress's head bobbed.

"Tell me everything you saw and heard."

The waitress began to talk. A minute later, the farmer began to fish a cell phone from his jeans pocket. He was trying to be surreptitious, but his wide checked shirt telegraphed every twitch. She found it fascinating: Did he think she was blind? She let him go awhile, until he got the phone out and opened its lid as carefully as if it contained an engagement ring. Then she said, "Put your hand in your mouth."

"And I poured him another refill," said the waitress. "He was real nice and we got to talking and I asked if he was from L.A. or New York or somewhere like that, and he said yes, he'd been all over, he'd seen fireworks in London and riots in Berlin, and I should go, he said. He said the world was closer than I imagined. Those were his words." The farmer began to gag. "And then he wanted to talk to his friend, the Australian, and after he asked if he could borrow a car. I said sure, and gave him the keys to my car, and I felt bad, because I hadn't cleaned it for like a year and I wished I had something nicer. I thought—"

"I don't care what you thought."

"I asked where he might be going and he said where did I recommend, and I said anywhere but here, and he smiled at that. Then we talked about places I had been, and I said when I was a girl my mom once took me to El Paso, just the two of us, and—"

"Right," she said. "Stop." She pondered. The farmer made a sound like *gwargghh* and threw up around his hand. He had wedged the whole thing in there. She wouldn't have thought that was possible. She watched him twitch and gag. She should tell him to take that out. There was no benefit in a dead farmer. "Did you hear any talk of towns? States? Airports?"

"No."

"You have no idea where he's going?"

"Wherever he wants," said the waitress. "A man like that."

"Yeah," she said. "Okay." Outside, her people would have gleaned which direction Eliot had gone, east or west. With the registration information, they would locate the car within a few hours. It would be abandoned, of course, at a gas station or on a side street, but that would be the start of a new trail. The fact was Eliot could not keep moving forever. He could not move faster than the net she could draw around him. *Nothing personal, Eliot,* she thought. She wanted to shoot him. As in, do it personally. She felt quite strongly about that. Also, before she did it, she wanted a few minutes to talk things over. That was probably a pipe dream. It was hard to imagine circumstances in which she would be able to capture Eliot without killing him. But if she did, she would like to tell him that she appreciated the guidance he had given her, in the beginning. She wanted to say, *I wouldn't be who I am without you, Eliot,* and have him see she meant it.

The farmer jerked. His head hit the table. Vomit dripped to the floor. "Take . . ." she said, but it was too late. She had meant to tell him to take out his hand. But she had forgotten. Or something like that. *Hey, Emily, you know what stars do? They eat. They burn everything around until there's nothing left. Then they start eating light. You realize that's what you're doing, right? Eating everything?*

She looked at the waitress. The sensible thing to do here was to kill her. The girl had exchanged words with Eliot; she was potentially loaded with instructions. The possibility was small but there was no sense in taking chances.

It's not getting any better, is it? I mean, that's been obvious for a while now, right? That the star isn't going anywhere?

"Forget we were here," she told the waitress. "That guy choked on his breakfast and you couldn't save him." She turned to leave. "But you tried as hard as you could."

They drove until dark, stopping only to eat and persuade people to trade vehicles. Wil didn't want to watch but couldn't help it. At first, the person who Eliot approached would look guarded. Then Eliot would say something and their face would break into a smile. Like they didn't want to but couldn't help it. It was fascinating how much they changed in that moment. From stranger-person to friend-person. They showed a completely different face. And then a minute later their expression would change again, becoming intimate and unarranged, and Wil would turn away, because watching that felt wrong.

Embedded in a pink Mini, a bobbling plastic cat on the dashboard, he said, "So you have a plan now?"

"Yes." Eliot jiggled the gearshift. He was not happy with fifth. Wil had offered to drive, but Eliot had refused. He was beginning to think Eliot didn't sleep at all.

"Do I get to hear it?"

"We go to Broken Hill, get the bareword, and use it to defeat our enemies."

"It's just sitting there? In Broken Hill?"

"That's my theory."

"You're not sure?"

"No."

"What, no one thought to check? You didn't swing by, see if there's this, what, Bible-grade weapon lying around?"

"It wasn't quite as simple as swinging by. After Woolf, anyone who *swung by* didn't swing out again."

"But we're going in."

"Yes." Eliot glanced at him. "You'll be fine."

"When you say *we* are going in . . ."

"I mean you. Since I'm not immune."

He watched them pass a family sedan. A happy dog looked at him and he felt jealous. "What if you're wrong and *I'm* not immune?"

"Well, that would be bad. But let's not get hung up on every little thing that might go wrong. I'm not saying the plan is foolproof. I'm saying it's preferable to driving aimlessly until our luck runs out."

"Then what happens? I give you the word?"

"No. You must not speak it around me, show it to me, or describe it even in general terms. I can't emphasize this enough."

"Are you serious?"

"Look at me," Eliot said. "If you get this thing and drop so much as a hint about what it looks like, I will feed you your own fingers. Do you believe me?"

"Yes." They passed through a town advertising a beet festival from three years ago. "I still don't understand how it's a word. Words can't kill people."

"Sure they can. Words kill people all the time." He wrestled the gearshift. "Granted, this one is more direct about it."

"What makes this one special?"

"Well, that's difficult to explain without referencing some fairly advanced linguistics and neurochemistry."

"Give me an analogy."

"There's a tree in a park. A tree you want cut down, for some reason. You phone the city and ask which department you need to contact and which forms you need to fill out. Your application goes to a committee, which decides whether it makes a good case, and if so, they send out a guy to cut down the tree. That's the brain's regular decision-making process. What I do, which you call 'word voodoo,' is I bribe the committee. It's the same process. But I'm neutralizing the parts that can say no. With me so far?"

"Yes."

"All right. What's in Broken Hill is a bareword. A bareword, in this analogy, is me getting out my chainsaw and cutting down the tree."

Wil waited.

"It's a separate pathway to the same outcome. I don't use the committee. I skip it. Does that make sense?"

"It does for trees."

"It's no different. Your brain has multiple pathways to action. You see a hot stove, you consciously decide to stay clear of it. But if you stumble onto it, you'll jerk back without conscious thought."

"So it's the difference between a voluntary action and a reflex," Wil said.

"Yes."

"Why didn't you just say that?"

"Because that's not an analogy. That's exactly what fucking happens. You asked for an analogy."

"Okay," he said. "Although I still don't understand how a reflex can be triggered by a *word*."

"Words aren't just sounds or shapes. They're meaning. That's what language is: a protocol for transferring meaning. When you learn English, you train your brain to react in a particular way to particular sounds. As it turns out, the protocol can be hacked."

"Can you teach me?"

"What?"

"What you do. The word voodoo."

"No."

"Why not?"

"Because it's complicated."

"It doesn't look complicated."

"Well," Eliot said, "it is."

"I don't see why you couldn't teach me a little."

"We don't have time to train you into a competent poet. If we did, it still wouldn't work, because you're not naturally compelling. If you were, I still wouldn't, because you have very little discipline, and we've learned recently that giving immensely powerful words to people with self-control issues is a very bad idea."

"I'm not naturally compelling?"

Eliot glanced at him. "Not really, no."

"I'm compelling."

"You're the only known outlier to a bareword," said Eliot. "Hang your hat on that."

He was silent. "What makes me immune?"

"Your brain doesn't process language quite like other people. Why that is, I have no idea."

"I have a superior brain?"

"Uh," Eliot said, "I wouldn't go that far."

"I can resist persuasion; sounds like an improvement to me."

"I once had a coffee machine that wouldn't add milk no matter how I pressed the buttons. It wasn't better. It was just broken."

"I'm not broken. Who are you to say I'm broken?"

Eliot said nothing.

"It's evolution," Wil said. "You guys have been preying on us for who knows how long and I evolved a defense."

"What was your girlfriend's name?"

"What?"

"Cecilia, right?" Eliot glanced at the dash. "Twenty-four hours, you haven't mentioned her."

"What are you saying? I should be grieving?"

Eliot nodded. "That's what I'm saying."

"Who the fuck are . . . I've been trying to stay alive! People have been driving *cattle trucks* at my body! Forgive me for not taking a minute to cry on your shoulder about my girlfriend!"

"Solid reasons, delivered with much defensiveness."

"You asshole! Jesus! As if you know anything about love! What do *you* think it is? Brain activity? Neurochemicals?"

"I suspect it's a kind of persuasion."

"So I'm immune to it? That's your theory?"

"The most fundamental thing about a person is desire. It defines them. Tell me what a person wants, truly wants, and I'll tell you who they are, and how to persuade them. You can't be persuaded. Ergo, you don't feel desire."

"That's bullshit! I loved Cecilia!"

"If you say so."

"I'm being lectured about love by a *robot*! I'm broken? *You're* broken! Tell me what you think love is! I seriously want to know!"

"Okay," Eliot said. "It's defining yourself through the eyes of another. It's coming to know a human being on a level so intimate that you lose any meaningful distinction between you, and you carry the knowledge that you are insufficient without her every day for twenty years, until she drives an animal transport at you, and you shoot her. It's that."

Wil watched the road awhile.

"I'm sorry I called you broken," Eliot said.

"Forget it."

"Everyone's broken," Eliot said, "one way or another."

He slept and woke to the windshield filled with a great metal lattice. A bridge, he realized, its steel beams splashed by yellow sodium-vapor streetlights. Eliot had one arm slung over the seat and was reversing around oncoming traffic. A car swung by them, horn blaring. A motorcycle stuttered past, the driver yelling unintelligibly. They swung around a corner and Eliot turned off the Mini's engine.

"Traffic camera on the bridge," said Eliot. "Almost drove through it."

Wil looked out at a coffee shop advertising waffles. The street was lined with tall, quaint buildings, most in pastel colors under a dusting of snow. The streetlights were trimmed with iron lacework. No people in sight. It felt late. "Where are we?"

"Grand Forks."

"What are we doing?"

"We're waiting," Eliot said. "Once a little time has passed, we're going to walk across that bridge. One at a time, I think, since I may have aroused suspicion just now. On the other side, we're going to acquire a vehicle and continue to Minneapolis. There we'll take passport photos in subpar lighting conditions and visit the Federal Building on Third Avenue South, which is a designated passport agency, and can issue replacement passports to people who have had theirs stolen, which we will claim has occurred. We will be asked to provide documentation proving, firstly, that we're U.S. citizens, and, secondly, that we are the people named in the first documents. This will occur in a genial, low-pressure interview, as opposed to at the front of an airport queue with an official holding out one hand for our papers, so should allow me to compromise our interviewer into accepting our mall booth passport photos. This person will then begin the process of issuing new passports in false names with our photos on them."

"Doesn't that take weeks?"

"No. It takes four hours, if you pay the expedition fee. We will then take a roundabout route to Sydney, balancing the need to arrive before our false documentation is discovered against the need to avoid airports with face-recognition technology. I'm thinking Vancouver and then Seoul, since Korean Air is a good airline for our purposes. No data sharing. Does that answer your question?"

"Yes." They waited. Wil yawned. A woman walked by who reminded Wil of someone but he didn't know who.

Eliot opened the door. "Wait ten minutes then walk directly across the bridge. Keep your head down. That's important. No looking up for any reason. Clear?"

"Clear," he said. Eliot climbed out. The door went *clunk*. He watched Eliot's beige coat disappear around the coffee shop.

The windows fogged. The car filled with cold. He thought about Cecilia. He'd met her in a pet store. He'd walked past and doubled back and pretended to be interested in puppies. Almost bought one, even. Just because she was selling them. On their second date, he discovered she didn't like animals much. She only liked organizing them. Deciding what they ate. She liked putting them in cages, basically. When Cecilia had started dropping marriage hints, about three months in, Wil had thought of that.

He got out of the car. It was misty, visibility down to a few hundred feet. He stuck his hands in his pockets and started walking. Eyes down. The occasional car plumed by to his left, plowing slush. He reached the bridge and began to cross. A black river slid by below. It was a high bridge. Long, too. He hadn't realized how long. A pickup truck made an odd note and he looked up before remembering he was not supposed to do that. About halfway across a vehicle approached from behind and slowed. He kept walking. The car's tires crunched snow. It was keeping pace with him. He didn't turn. He could see the far side now but no Eliot.

The world splashed red and blue. Static barked. "Sir, stop where you are." This was a megaphone.

He stopped. A police cruiser rolled up to him. The door opened and a cop with a dark mustache climbed out. "Mind taking your hands out of your pockets, sir?"

He showed his hands.

"Sir, are you the owner of a pink Mini, registration jay cee ex one four zero?"

"No."

"You don't know that vehicle?"

"No, officer." The wind blew. He looked at the end of the bridge but still no Eliot.

"Where are you headed tonight, sir?"

"I'm just crossing the bridge."

"I can see that. Where are you headed?"

He checked for Eliot again.

"Am I keeping you from something?"

"No, officer. I'm just cold."

"Put your hands on the hood, sir."

"Um," said Wil.

"Put your hands on the hood."

He placed his hands on the car.

"Legs apart, please."

"I'm just out walking."

"Legs apart."

He obeyed.

"I'm going to pat you down now. Do you understand what that means?"

"Okay, I was in the Mini. If there's a fine—"

"Do not turn around!"

"I wasn't turning around," he said. The cop grabbed him by the neck of his jacket and spread him across the hood. It was a slab of ice. He could stick to this car. The cop's hands probed legs and hips, delving into his pockets. He felt a loosening around his buttocks and realized the cop had taken his wallet.

"Wil Parke? That's you?"

"Look—"

"Stay on the car! You stay there until I tell you otherwise, understand? If you move again, we're going to have a problem."

His cheek pressed against the hood, he saw a figure approaching through the snow mist. Eliot? He couldn't tell.

"Dispatch, four-one-three," the cop said.

He felt alarm. A cop reporting that he'd picked up Wil Parke, that could be bad. He raised himself from the hood, keeping his hands up so the cop wouldn't overreact, but a nightstick leaped into his throat anyway and he found himself bending backward over the hood, the cop shouting in his face. "Wait," Wil said, but the cop wasn't interested in what he had to say. He caught a glimpse of Eliot's familiar coat, approaching in brisk strides. The cop's grip on him slackened. His expression changed. As if the guy were watching TV, Wil thought. Seeing something interesting but far away. The cop unhitched his radio. "Dispatch," he said, and there were two flat bangs and the cop pinwheeled backward. Eliot walked up to him and fired twice more.

"Fuck!" said Wil. His voice was thin and breathless. "What? What?"

"Quiet." The air was beginning to glow: an approaching car. Eliot walked onto the road.

Wil looked at the cop. His eyes were glassy. Blood congealed around his body, staining the road salt. "What about the word voodoo?" Eliot didn't answer. "Why didn't you *persuade* him?"

A pickup crested the bridge. Eliot waved his arms and the pickup stopped and the driver leaned out the window. A young guy with sandy hair. Eliot was going to kill this guy—him and anyone else in the car, and then whoever passed by. Wil started to run, slipped on the ice, and banged his knee on the blacktop. By the time he reached them, Eliot had his gun pointed at the driver. "Fifty," the guy said. "I don't know what you want—"

Eliot said, "Do you love your family?"

"*Eliot!*"

"Of course I do, man, please don't kill me, I have two girls and I love them so much—"

"I won't kill you if you tell me this," said Eliot. He was becoming brighter, almost glowing. Another car approaching, Wil realized. "Why did you do it?"

"Eliot." He put his hand on Eliot's arm and tried to steer the gun down. "Please don't shoot this guy."

"Is this about . . . ?" said the driver. "Oh, Jesus, forgive me, I did it because I had to." Eliot lowered the gun. The truck driver's breath came out in a rush. "Thank you, thank you—"

"*Geetyre massilick croton avary,*" Eliot said. "Take this. Shoot cars. Run away from cops."

The driver took Eliot's gun. Eliot opened the pickup's door and the driver stepped out. He looked up and began to walk toward Wil.

"What . . ." Wil said. The guy raised the gun. Wil had time to plug his fingers into his ears. The guy fired, and Wil turned to see a car behind him, a dark wagon. It braked and began to reverse, its beams swinging crazily from side to side. The guy broke into a run, following.

Eliot seized his arm. "Walk."

He walked. "Why?" Wil said. "Why?"

"Shut up," Eliot said. There was a flatness in his voice. Wil shut up.

Once they were clear of Grand Forks, the road was empty. After about half an hour, three police cars blew by in the opposite direction, all noise and light, and Wil didn't say anything and neither did Eliot.

He watched the sky begin to lighten. "You're not a good guy," Wil said. "You say you are, but you're not."

"I don't believe I ever said I was a good guy."

"You could have used your words on that cop."

"He was compromised. He was two seconds away from calling us in."

"You could have tried."

A sign drifted by, announcing two hundred miles to Minneapolis.

"You're just as bad as Woolf," he said.

Eliot braked. Wil's seat belt grabbed him. The car slid to a steaming halt.

"I will take a lot of shit from you," Eliot said, "but I will not be compared to Woolf."

"She—"

"Shut up. The worst thing I have ever done is allow Woolf to become what she is. I will wear responsibility for everything she does, from Broken Hill until the day I put her in the ground. But we aren't the same. Not even close."

"You kill people."

"Yes, I kill people, when the alternative is worse. That's the world. That's the reason you and I are still here."

Wil looked away. "I'll come with you. I'll do what you say. But not because you're right.

Eliot put the car in gear. "Fine," he said. "Close enough."

At the Minneapolis airport no one stopped them or looked twice at their passports and they boarded a Delta E-175, its engines roaring outside the windows. Eliot rolled his coat into a tight bundle and wedged it between the headrest and the wall. "I'm going to sleep."

Wil looked at him. "Really?" They were flying to Winnipeg. It was forty minutes.

"Really," said Eliot, and closed his eyes. His face relaxed. His lips parted. Wil began to think he wasn't breathing. When they lifted off, the plane yawed sharply and the woman across the aisle let out a shriek, and Eliot's head flopped onto Wil's shoulder. "Eliot?" He put his hand beneath Eliot's nostrils. He couldn't feel anything. He licked his skin and tried again. A faint current of air. Very faint. He tried to relax.

They landed roughly but still Eliot didn't move. Wil dug his elbow into his ribs. "Eliot." He shook his shoulder. "Tom." He shook him harder. He put his thumb and forefinger on Eliot's forearm and pinched.

Eliot's eyes opened. They were like glass. His face was gray and drawn. He looked dead.

"We've landed."

Eliot's eyes stared at something beyond the plane's ceiling.

"We're here. Eliot. You have to wake up. *Eliot.*"

He focused. "What?"

"You look terrible."

"I'm fine," Eliot said, and all of a sudden he was. He pulled the coat from the headrest and tucked it under his arm. "Move."

In Winnipeg they caught a flight to Vancouver, and again Eliot fell asleep as soon as they were on board, and again rousing him upon landing was like trying to reanimate a corpse. In Vancouver they crossed to the international terminal and passed through security without incident. The Korean Air flight attendants wore blue paper hats. Eliot settled into a window seat with his rolled-up coat and closed his eyes. "Wake me if we enter an unexpectedly steep descent."

"Uh," said Wil. But Eliot seemed to be already asleep. "Yeah. I'll do that." He flicked through the in-flight magazine, then put it back. He didn't think he would be sleeping.

From: http://discuss.isthatjustme.com/forum/topic—11053—r.html?v=1

OK, I don't want to get into conspiracy theories, but you read about this guy who shot up Grand Forks? They said he'd had a fight with his girlfriend, so we all thought, "Oh, that's why he flipped out." But notice nobody has actually said there's a connection. They've just let us assume that because why else would they mention it.

I'm not saying there's something here with this specific incident, but I see this ALL THE TIME. If you watch TV news, every story is like this: "There was a fire and the owner was in financial trouble." They're not saying he burned down his own place. But that's all they're going to tell you.

That bothers me because we think we're being clever, putting the pieces together, but it's a set-up. We've only been given pieces that fit together one way, but if it turns out they make the wrong picture, well, they never said it was right.

Unless it's a really big deal, like a national story, all the reporting comes from one reporter who writes down what the cops say. That goes on AP and the news services all share it. So it can look like they've all done their research and found the same facts, but it's usually just everyone parroting one source.

Now, probably the guy in Grand Forks really did just get pissed off with his girlfriend. But I think it's worth noting that literally nobody has claimed that's why he started shooting. If they'd said it was a mystery, then people like us would get curious and ask questions, but apparently all it takes is one unsubstantiated hint and we're satisfied, because we think we figured it out.

[FOUR]

She became promiscuous. It wasn't planned. It was because there was nothing else to do. She thought of herself as *promiscuous* rather than *easy* because she was in charge. If a boy came into the clothes store where she worked and had a look in his eye that meant he'd heard about her, she would play dumb and sell him new khaki pants. But if—and it didn't happen often, only sometimes—there was a boy with curly hair and dark eyes and he was genuinely shopping, then something inside her would yearn. She would walk over and say can I help you, and if the boy was orbited by a badly permed blonde, which he usually was, she would recommend shirts and eye him while his girlfriend fingered skirts. And he would look back and there would be something there. When the girl decided to try something on, Emily would walk directly to him and kiss him like a predator. And he kissed her back, every time, and if she reached down, he was hard as stone. "How's it going?" she would call, her eyes on the boy, and the girl would say something about fit around the shoulders and color and did they have it without the bows. She didn't always take it further than that: Twice the girl came out early and the boy walked out of the store on loose legs, throwing her glances. But twice she did. The last time, the boy had been accompanied by a black-eyed girl who didn't even answer when Emily came over and said hello, and she liked the look of this boy, he was friendly and dumb and played football, so she not only invaded his pants while his girl was behind a change room door but kept going when she came out again. She watched the boy's face as the girl revolved about the store, fascinated, because he looked so scared yet didn't stop her. The girl inspected dresses and made a catty comment about the decade in which she believed one of them belonged, and the boy grunted and twitched in his jeans. Emily walked behind the counter. He looked at her like he couldn't believe she was abandoning him. Like he thought she had a plan to help him out or something. But she didn't care about that. The interesting part was over, as far as she was concerned. The boy stood rooted there a few seconds, then blurted a bunch of mostly unrelated words, the spillage from two or three trains of thought that had just collided. The girl didn't even look up. "Okay," she said, turning over a fluffy hooded jacket.

This was probably not what Eliot had meant when he told her to *work hard and discipline yourself.* But she was a million miles from everywhere, doing an otherwise excellent job of concealing the fact that she was the most skilled practitioner of persuasion ever to grace this dustbowl, and she needed something. She couldn't have muscles and not flex them.

She had slept two nights in a bus station before realizing the town was full of empty houses; you only had to break in and make yourself at home. She found a job at Tangled Threads, Broken Hill's hippest clothing store for young and old and anyone else interested in one level of fashion above denim and wifebeaters, and it paid cash, which meant she could rent something with electricity. It was all simpler than she had imagined. She even bought a battered old car. Which was a little risky, because she didn't dare attempt to acquire a driver's license, but the town had only two cops, both from segments she understood well, and she was really sick of the bus.

She was "the American girl." Her story was she had come to *connect with the earth*—a ludicrous idea, patently false to anyone who watched how she squinted at the sun, hugged herself against the wind, grimaced at dirt, but seriously, why else would you come here? *How long are you staying?* people asked, leaning across a counter to marvel at her, this person who had left America to come here, *here*, even as every other local youth with half a brain fled at the earliest opportunity. The older ones, who'd lost the ability to imagine life elsewhere, or maybe never had it, seemed to view her as the first of many, as if Emily were the harbinger of a hip new fad sweeping the globe, where young people in big cities sweated and saved and dreamed of one day traveling to *connect* in Broken Hill, and give the town a future. She told them *I think maybe a year*, because she didn't want to give false hope and couldn't bear the thought that it might be longer.

But a year passed and then another and there she was on her twenty-first birthday, watching senseless Australian television in a four-bedroom house with hardly any furniture. She sometimes wondered if the organization existed. Whether she had imagined it. Sometimes, when the door jangled open at Tangled Threads, she would think for a second it was Eliot, come to tell her it was okay, it was over, she could come home. But it never happened. It was just day after day of waiting. So she could take control of a good-looking boy now and again. She could do that.

One night after closing, she walked to the rear parking lot and found a group of girls in short skirts and fur-lined jackets waiting for her. One hopped off the hood of a car as she approached, the dirty-blond girlfriend of the football player, and Emily realized she had a problem. She turned to flee to the store but two more girls were blocking the path. She held up her hands. "I don't have any money."

"Not interested in your money, bitch," said the girl, letting something drop from her hand. A metal chain. Emily felt despair, not so much for herself but for the girl and Broken Hill, Australia, because a chain was ridiculous. If you pulled that shit in San Francisco, you would get yourself shot. "You know who I am?"

"I think you came into the store one time." The girls encircled her. Five in total. No other weapons in sight, which made running a good option. "If you want to return something, we open at nine."

"I don't want to return something, you slut."

"And it's not a *store*," said a girl who was thin as a dead tree. "It's a *shop*."

"Okay," said Emily. "Can we talk this over, please?" She drew out the word *please*, made it sound like *police*, to remind everybody that shit like this could get you arrested. "Oh. I know you. I know your mom." This was not true, but totally believable in a town this size. The point was to bring moms into the picture, to join *police*.

"You came on to my boyfriend," said the girl.

This Emily recognized as a *speculative assertion*, what they called *test balloons* in class. When people made speculative assertions, they hoped to be disproved. It meant the girl wasn't going to hit her with the chain. If she had said, *I'm going to fuck you up for what you did to my boyfriend*, Emily would have been in trouble. But she was just standing there, waiting for Emily to respond and explain how it was all a crazy misunderstanding. She almost felt disappointed, because it had been an interesting mental challenge there for a minute.

"Actually, he came on to me," Emily said, and she must want to be hurt; it was the only explanation. The girl stared at her, trying to believe her ears, and another girl said, "Oh, it's on, bitch," and Emily ran. She almost got through a girl with bad acne and scared eyes but someone grabbed her collar and dragged her to the ground. The girl with the chain came at her in pure rage, and despite the imminent ass whipping Emily felt a mild pleasure at successfully pushing her beyond precortex control. That wasn't easy. You really had to sock a person in the core of what they believed to do that. She threw her arms around her head and curled into a ball.

Pain exploded on her back. She tried to roll over and that was a huge mistake, because the chain caught her across the face. Her mouth disappeared. She found her knees and tried to crawl away. Something bright and bloody lay in the dirt. A tooth. She felt sad and stupid and wanted to go back in time and not be such a dick.

Lights flared. She couldn't see where they were coming from but apparently they were relevant because the girls fell away. Shoes slapped concrete. There were no new blows. That was an improvement.

Someone took her by the shoulders. She flinched. He said, "It's all right, relax, I'm helping."

"*Moof*," she said, which was supposed to be *My tooth*. The man's fingers invaded her ribs. He went away and she felt lost. He came back and snapped something around her neck. She tried to rise but he said, "No, no," restraining her with one hand. All she could see was his hair, which was long and the color of sand. He slid something beneath her butt, which turned out to be a trolley. "Muh toof," she said. He ratcheted her up and sailed her across the parking lot to a white van that she knew passed for an ambulance out here. Before he closed the doors on her, his eyes scanned her in a quick, professional way.

By the time the vehicle stopped and hands began to unload her, she wasn't sure where she was. "Pub brawl?" someone asked, and the man said, "Girl fight out back of Tangled Threads."

A woman bent over her face. "She's lost a tooth."

"It's in my mouth," said her rescuer. This sounded funny to Emily, and she smiled, and after that she didn't remember anything. Time must have passed, though, because she was sitting in a hospital bed in an open ward with morning light streaming in. She was wearing a thin gown and her neck was encased in a brace. Her back was full of golf balls. She had a loose tooth in her mouth and probed it with her tongue but thought she should probably not do that. Her head was glass but otherwise she felt pretty okay.

A nurse stopped by. Emily had seen her buy soy milk at the local supermarket sometimes. "Morning, darling. How are you feeling?"

"Good," she said.

The nurse put her hands on Emily's face. "Open up. Good. You're leaving that tooth alone?"

"Yeth."

She released Emily's mouth. "What happened?"

I lost control. I proved that I belong here. "Nothing."

"Gary wants to talk to you."

"Whoth Gary?"

"The police sergeant."

She tried to shake her head. She didn't want to press charges. She had no identity. "How long do I wear this?"

"Six weeks. And count yourself lucky."

She did. It could easily have been worse. "Who picked me up?"

"The para?"

She didn't know what this meant. "The man with the ambulanth van."

"Paramedic. That's Harry. He kept that tooth viable."

"Can I thank him?"

"He's off duty," said the nurse. "But I'm sure you'll see him around. It's a small town, if you've noticed."

"Yeth," said Emily.

She had seen that van around. White with yellow and orange stripes; she must have seen it twice weekly since she got here. But, of course, now that she was released from the hospital, leading with her chin because of the brace, it was nowhere to be found. Sometimes she caught a flash of white and turned to see if it was him, pain spiking through her neck, and when she was too slow, she thought, *I bet it was.*

It was very junior high, being attracted to an ambulance driver. Falling for a man who had rescued her. She felt girlish. But her thoughts kept returning to how he had carried her tooth in his mouth. Also his hair in the ambulance headlights. She felt hot and restless, and went for lots of walks, during which she might encounter a white van with yellow and orange stripes.

She decided to buy him flowers. She would just buy flowers and a card and if he wasn't at the hospital when she dropped them off, that was fine. She would just leave them. She sweated over what to write, firmed on THANK YOU FROM THE BOTTOM OF MY TOOTH, stared at it in horror, and went back to the store for a new card. On the second attempt, she went dignified. THANK YOU FOR SAVING ME. EMILY RUFF. Maybe it wasn't completely dignified. Because she couldn't resist writing *saving me*. Or supplying her full name. But she didn't include a phone number. She managed that.

She drove to the hospital, the flowers on the passenger seat with air blasting at them to stave off the heat. The woman at the front desk thought she was there for an appointment, which Emily guessed was logical, given the brace, and once that was straightened out, said, "Did you want to see him or just leave these?" Emily panicked and said, "Just leave them." She got as far as the doors. "Is he here, though?" The woman looked at Emily like she had seen it all a million times before and said, "I'll see." She picked up the phone. Emily waited and tried not to feel fourteen years old. The woman replaced the receiver. "I'm sorry."

In the car, she gripped the wheel and berated herself. What would Eliot think? He would be ashamed. He'd tell her to get used to Broken Hill, because the way she was acting, she was never coming home. She might as well buy a house and get a couple of dogs and marry Harry the paramedic and live here forever.

"Oh, Jesus," she said, because that was atrocious.

She became Pavlovian to the bell that jangled whenever someone opened the Tangled Threads door but it was never him, and after a few days she understood that it never would be. He saw the flowers for exactly what they were: an awkward, fantastical sally at romance. She felt angry at herself, and him for making her act like that. Because, to be fair, he'd caught her in the middle of a trauma. She hadn't been herself. Who was he to judge? He was a nobody in a dinky, blow-away town and he didn't even have a proper ambulance. And his hair was old-fashioned. The only reason she'd even looked at him twice was he had no competition. She itched for a boy to walk in, someone young and cute and stupid. She stewed behind the counter and tidied racks until everything was the same.

At noon, she walked to the local burger place and stood in line behind the miners—not muscular guys in sleveless shirts with picks and sexy soot stains, like you might expect, but fat truck drivers and crane operators who smelled like oil. Hardly anyone actually went into the mines anymore. That part was automated. And there was hardly anything to go into: For the most part, the mines were great open-cut quarries that looked like meteorite craters. The town surrounded a huge one, separated from it by a towering wall of mullock, which was the stuff they dragged out of the ground that wasn't worth anything but had to be put somewhere. No one seemed to find this strange, living in a town shaped like a doughnut, slowly filling the edges of the hole with crap. She wanted to ask why they didn't move the town about five miles north, or south or east or west, for that matter, any random direction. But she could predict the response: They would say, *Because this is where it is.* Australians were very practical, Emily had found. They did things quickly and purposefully and to the absolute minimum standard required. It was refreshing and genuine but sometimes led to situations like building a town around a hole. Originally she'd thought the name Broken Hill was a joke, part of the perverse humor that led them to nickname people with red hair *Bluey.* Because besides the mullock, the place was as flat as a mirror. But apparently there had been a hill once. It had been mined away.

She inhaled stale sweat and cigarettes until she reached the counter, then ate her burger at a table outside, watching traffic. Everything that passed she'd seen before. She turned her head, testing her neck, and saw the paramedic van parked across the road.

She felt panic. But she was over him, remember? She had forgotten that for a second. She relaxed. She began to look for him, casually. She hoped she did see him, so she could discover exactly how plain and boring he was when he wasn't carrying her tooth in his mouth. She ate her burger. She saw him. It might have been him. He was coming down the sidewalk, talking to a woman. He shook his head and it definitely was him. He was cute. She might have been suffering from head trauma but she did have taste. He was broad shouldered. His arms were incredible. He was not wearing a wifebeater. As he drew closer, she pegged his age at maybe twenty-five. The woman was an attractive brunette Emily had seen featured in real estate advertisements. She laughed at something Harry said, tossing her hair, and Emily was totally fine with that. Emily wished Ms. Real Estate the very best of luck with her handsome Australian paramedic.

She almost let them walk by. Then she decided what the hell. There was no problem, so why not? "Hello."

He stopped. His eyes: She had forgotten those. "You're . . ."

"Toothless."

"Right." She saw him thinking about the flowers. He *had* found that awkward.

"Just wanted to say thanks," she said. "Don't let me hold you up."

The real estate woman smiled and snaked a hand into Harry's. He seemed relieved that she was not turning on the crazy. "No problem." The real estate woman began to lead him away. Suddenly he skipped back to her table and stuck out his hand. "I'm Harry."

She took his hand, surprised, and he grinned and returned to the real estate woman. She felt unsettled. She watched him walk away. What was that? Did he just try to pick her up? That was outrageous. She picked up her Coke and looked after him again. Her heart was jumping. She thought, *Ah, fuck.*

She decided to sleep with him and get it over with. It was the only way. He had become an annoying jingle, striking in the shower, or at work, or just as she was falling asleep. She had to at least kiss him deeply and completely, in a way that left nothing behind. So she could move on. So she could stop imagining it. She couldn't keep losing herself to the jingle. It was impairing her ability to function. Once she turned him into a toy, like those boys in Tangled Threads, it would be all right. She would be back in control.

She bought a dress, a little black scrap from Tangled Threads that she'd talked away from three potential customers in case of an occasion like this. She did her hair, going for volume—not the kind of hair girls liked; the kind for boys. She detonated mascara. Friday night, she pushed into a smoke-filled sweat tank in the main bar, the *pub*, and looked for him. The place was full of bright-eyed teenagers and crusted-on miners, opposing demographics, normally, united by their passion for beer and angry guitars. A boy screamed, "*Vince!*" in her ear. These were reasons she did not normally come here. She negotiated a lap and began to feel discouraged. Then she spied him at the bar with a few other young men in collared shirts. She walked up and yelled, "Hi!"

Harry smiled at her.

"Buy me a drink!" she said.

Four hours later, her head buzzing, she was in the passenger seat of his paramedic van, being driven home. Not to her home. To his. She had unsnapped her seat belt and draped herself across him, kissing his neck, nibbling his ear, which was an excellent way to die in a car accident, if she'd thought about that. But she hadn't. She thought only of getting him alone in a room and doing terrible things. He drove and drove and finally stopped. A dog slobbered on her legs and she screamed and he picked her up. She liked that. It reminded her of how they'd met. His house was dark but there was a bed and a moon outside. She tried to unbutton his pants and he said no, and she said, *Yes*, putting some emphasis behind it, a little lower frequency that sounded commanding, but it didn't work. On the bed he touched her neck and this was what she had been missing, she realized: All of her predatory behavior had included no reciprocity. And that was important. She had forgotten. She went after him again and this time he took her wrists in one hand and trapped them on the pillow above her head. "I want you," she said. "Let me touch you."

"No," he said, and she found this even more arousing, for some reason. She did enjoy a challenge. But his hands moved down her body and she lost the will to argue. "Yes," she said, "yes, yes." She saw glittering eyes in the darkness outside, his dog, watching them, but she didn't care. She was going someplace else. His touch was careful and she hadn't really known what it was like to be cared for. It was a night of newness. He held her and his fingers moved inside her and then her climax moved through her like a thunderclap, like a force of nature, something she could not control at all, and she had to lie still until she could find herself. He let go of her wrists. He was still wearing pants. She needed to address that. "Now," she said, and finally he nodded, and said, "Now," and she basically attacked him.

In the morning she woke and he was not there. She sat up. The bedroom had no curtains. Beyond the window was flat earth as far as the horizon. The bedroom was a crime scene of twisted sheets and scattered clothes. Aside from the bed, there was no furniture. No paintings. No photos.

On the kitchen table she found a note:

Gone for a ride. Help yourself to brekky.

A ride, she thought. He had gone for a ride. He had departed on some mode of transport to an unnamed destination for unknown reasons for an indeterminate length of time. She was glad he had explained that. She investigated the room. There was a photo of the dog on the TV. It was the only really personal thing she could see, so she picked it up. A big dog. A man's dog. She put the photo back. She was not so desperate for insight into Harry that she needed to analyze his dog. She went into the kitchen and pulled open the fridge.

She ate cereal. She showered. She padded naked into his bedroom and rifled through his wardrobe. She saw no books. She didn't know what he did with himself. She started the dishes, and while scrubbing a pot suffered a sudden, appalling flash of perspective. He was waiting for her to leave. That was what the note meant. She dropped the brush and went to look for her clothes.

There was a joke, or puzzle, that went like this: A woman meets a man at her mother's funeral. They hit it off, but the woman never gets the man's name, and afterward she can't find him. A few days later, she murders her sister. You were supposed to figure out why. But if you did, it meant you were a psychopath, because the reason was the woman wanted to meet the man again. Emily thought about this a few times over the next few days, when she found herself fantasizing about staging a medical emergency.

She finally drove out to his house. It was dark and she got lost on the dusty roads and she almost went home a dozen times. Because it was one thing to sleep with him. It was another to go back. What she was doing felt dangerous. Like sailing off the edge of the world.

Eventually, she trundled up the long driveway. The house lights were on but she left the engine idling, because she still wasn't sure she should be here. Or, rather, she knew, but wanted to anyway. The front door opened. He came out, shielding his eyes. When he saw her, he smiled. That decided it. She got out of the car. "Is this a bad time?" She was being polite.

"Nope," he said.

"I thought I'd come see you."

"Glad you did."

She hung by the car.

"Come in," he said, and she did.

Three months later she moved in. She was effectively living there anyway. She suggested it during the credits for an Australian comedy that he loved and she was growing to hate less and less. "I should move in," she said. Maybe it wasn't a suggestion. But that was how she meant it. She used persuasion techniques on Harry sometimes, but nothing he couldn't break. She liked it that way: trying to manipulate him and failing. If she'd had his words, it would have been different. There would have been no challenge at all.

She cooked for him. She actually cracked eggs and fried them up and carried them to him on a tray. When she lay in the crook of his arm, she felt safe. He took her riding. He had dirt bikes, a garage full of them, and they went bouncing across the countryside. He taught her how to hold a rifle so it didn't bruise her shoulder, how much to allow for the tug of gravity on a bullet over distance. When the night was clear, they sat on the back porch, drinking and making love as the sun dissolved into earth. Before this, she had only ever viewed the sky as hostile. He made her notice the raw beauty in it, the power in the blasted earth and skeletal trees. How it was all there for a reason. Even the snakes, which Emily would never stop being terrified about—they were everywhere you least expected them, like deadly ropes—she came to see less as belligerent and more as aggressively defensive, like her. She had lived in Broken Hill for two years and never understood it.

The first time he shot a kangaroo, she cried. She'd known he hunted them, that they were vermin, but the sight of the brown fur in the dust, the oddly human lips peeled back from small teeth, was too much. "They're pests," he said. "Eat anything that grows."

"Still," she said.

He set the rifle against the bike. "You know the story about the kangaroo?"

"What story?"

"The blackfellas' story." He meant the aboriginals. "There was a girl, Minnawara. She was clever, good with a spear. Eyes that could spot a kookaburra a kilometer away. One day, she stole a sling. The sling was supposed to belong to the whole tribe, but Minnawara hid it in a pouch. When the tribe discovered the sling was missing, they became very angry, and the elder asked Minnawara if she'd taken it. And she said no. So the elder put magic on the ground, and the ground began to get hot. The elder said, 'Are your feet warm, Minnawara?' That was the magic. Only someone who lied would feel the heat. She said no, her feet were fine. But soon she couldn't stand it, so she began to hop from one foot to the other. And then she jumped. The elder said, 'Why are you jumping, Minnawara?' and she said, 'I like to jump. I will always jump.' And she did; she jumped everywhere for the rest of her days, because she was too stubborn to give up the sling. Her feet grew long and tough, and she was the first kangaroo."

"That makes it worse," Emily said. "Now it feels personal." She looked at poor Minnawara.

"But she's a thief," said Harry.

He didn't talk. That is, he didn't talk without a specific purpose. She found this unnerving. It made her wonder what he wasn't saying. At first she probed him relentlessly, asking about politics, putting unlikely hypotheticals to him about their relationship over dinner. One night, just as he was drifting off, she said, "Who do you think is smarter, you or me?"

She was a person who needed to know things. She didn't want to guess what was in his head. She wanted to hear him say it. This was how she avoided surprises. One day she found an odd contraption in his shed, a tangle of frayed rope and petrified wood, and marched it to him where he was repairing a fence post, three hundred yards away. "What's this?"

He glanced at it. "Mobile."

"What does that mean?" She shook it. Dust fell. It looked about a million years old. Each section of petrified wood had a dark mark on it, and some of the marks looked strange.

"It's a mobile," he said. "For babies."

She sat in the dirt. "You need to talk more. This, 'it's a mobile,' isn't enough for me. Understand?" *No*, she saw. "Why do you have a mobile? Where did it come from? What are these marks? What do you think about it?"

He sat up.

"I'm not used to people who don't talk," she said. "It's honestly freaking me out."

He pulled her toward him, which she resisted, for a moment. His arms around her, the smell of his sweat spoiling her judgment, he said, "You think I need to say something to make it real."

"Yes. That's exactly what I think."

He composed his thoughts, taking his time. "My father was a miner. Back when the mines were bigger. When he found something interesting down there, he brought it home. He made that mobile for me before I was born. I found it when I went through his stuff after he died. Decided to keep it in case I ever need it. I think it's a good mobile."

"Okay," she said. "Thank you, that's all I needed, was that so hard?"

He began to kiss her. Things deteriorated. But later she thought about what he'd said. About not needing to say something to make it real. This contradicted what she'd been taught. The brain used language to frame concepts: it employed words to identify and organize its own chemical soup. A person's tongue even determined how they thought, to a degree, due to the subtle logical pathways that were created between concepts represented by similar-looking or -sounding words. So, yes, words did make things real, in at least one important way. But they were also just symbols. They were labels, not the things they labeled. You didn't need words to feel. She decided he had a point. But it felt so strange.

He was a catch, of course. Women stopped her in the street to congratulate her. They cackled and wished her all the best. She was going down in Broken Hill folklore as the Girl Who Tamed Harry. There was a history, obviously. A procession of Girls Who Had Not Tamed Harry. But she didn't ask about that. Not even when she ran into the real estate woman who had been with Harry before, the two approaching each other down a grocery store aisle like reluctant jousters. The whole time they were talking, the woman telling Emily about the benefits of freshly squeezed orange juice versus concentrate, Emily was thinking: *What happened?* Because this woman had been with Harry and now she wasn't, so how had that happened, exactly? How did Harry handle a relationship breakup? Was he cruel? Deceitful? Indifferent? These were questions she wanted answered. But she didn't ask them. She knew not to go snooping around for an ending unless she wanted one. She realized now that until she had come to Broken Hill, she had never been happy.

BNP BUILDS VOTER PROFILE DATABASE

The British National Party has compiled personal details of tens of thousands of voters, it was revealed on Friday.

The database, named Electrac, is used to personalize pamphlet, door-to-door, and telephone campaigns.

Mark Mitchell, 38, claimed he worked for the BNP for eight months on the project, gathering information from sources including surveys, letters to the editor, online posts, and attendance at events.

He said it allowed voters to be segmented into different groups, with each group receiving targeted material during the lead-up to the general election.

A spokesperson for the BNP acknowledged the use of Electrac but said the practice was widespread amongst political organizations and no privacy laws were breached.

IRC TRANSCRIPT

From: IRCnet#worldchat 201112260118 irc client

<maslop> meh
<maslop> i just don't see the problem
<vikktor> ok
<vikktor> its like this
<vikktor> i'm campaigning in a street
<vikktor> door to door
<vikktor> and before i knock, i look at a paper that says, "Maslop, 21, male, top concern is whether he'll have a job next year"
<vikktor> so i knock and say, "Hello Mr. Maslop, I'm running for office and my number 1 priority is job creation"
<maslop> right
<vikktor> so you're thinking, "wow, this guy gets it, he's got my vote."
<vikktor> then i go next door and this time i say, "Hello Ms. KittyPendragon, I'm running for office and my number 1 priority is fighting climate change"
<KittyPendragon> yay =^_^=
<vikktor> because my paper says that's what KittyPendragon cares about
<maslop> but thats good
<maslop> they should know what people think
<maslop> and want
<vikktor> well, say i get elected
<vikktor> what's my top priority?
<vikktor> you see?
<maslop> yeah but at least there listening to people
<vikktor> it undermines a key plank of democracy
<vikktor> the part where candidates have to declare where they stand
<vikktor> you don't see a problem?
<maslop> not really

PRIVACY POLICY

13. **TruCorp takes customer privacy seriously.** Your personal data is stored securely and **will not be released** without your permission.[1] We use state-of-the-art encryption and physical anti-intrusion systems to prevent access to our secure data facilities.

1 Except where compelled by law. Customers should be aware in some jurisdictions TruCorp may be compelled to surrender information to relevant authorities and may not be able to inform customers that this has occurred. Although every effort is made to safeguard data TruCorp is not liable for any data breaches and/or release of personal information regardless of how it occurs (including but not limited to court-ordered release, government agency request, unauthorized access by employees and subcontractors, and hacking). TruCorp may share overall statistics derived from customers' personal data in anonymized form with other organizations of its choosing. TruCorp is not bound by this clause to customers who fall more than 28 days in arrears in payments or cannot be contacted. These terms & conditions may change in the future and it is your responsibility to check our website to remain informed.

[FIVE]

Wil adjusted the shade for the millionth time, trying to block the sun that sat low over the road, bellowing anger. "It's so hot." He looked at Eliot. Eliot didn't care. Eliot had been near-silent since Minneapolis, when Wil accused him of being the same as Woolf. He presumed Eliot was stewing, although of course Wil would never know, because Eliot was as readable as a brick.

The car jolted over a pothole. They were taking the back way to Broken Hill, riding in a ridiculous purple Valiant, wide and loud, easily thirty years old. No air, of course. Many years ago, the dash had split under the merciless pounding of the sun and begun to ooze yellow foam. The speedometer read in miles. It was a miracle it had seat belts. They were probably getting three miles to the gallon. He watched leafless trees drift by. After eight hours in an oven made of metal and glass, heat had penetrated every pore of his body. He just wanted to get out of the car. He just wanted Eliot to say something. "Have you been out here before?"

No reply. Wil looked out at the baked earth that rolled all the way to the horizon, flat as a plate. He, Wil, had been out here before. He had lived in Broken Hill. Apparently. He didn't remember. It was hard to believe he could have forgotten this heat.

"Yes," said Eliot. It took Wil a moment to remember the question.

"Before or after?" Eliot didn't respond. "You know. Before or after?" Still nothing. "Or both?" He sighed and began to fiddle with the vents.

"Stop that. You're not making it better."

Wil looked at him. "I'm just—"

"Leave the vents alone."

He sat back. Eliot was definitely pissed. A sign blew by the window, announcing a turnoff for Menindee. "We should get some fuel." The intersection crawled toward them. "Eliot? Only thirty kilometers. Menindee. Eliot? Do you know how far apart the gas stations are? Seriously, you run out of petrol on a road like this, you die. It happens."

The intersection slid past. Wil slouched. He understood that Eliot didn't want to stop. The airport had been hairy. They had made it through Immigration, then a short, dark-skinned official had emerged from nowhere, asking them to please step out of the line. Wil had been deposited in a small, windowless room and left for twenty minutes, staring at a security camera. It seemed increasingly obvious to him they'd been recognized, but he wasn't sure what he should do about that. So he waited. Eventually, the door opened. It was Eliot. People were arguing in the corridor, loud Australian voices. "Are we okay?" Wil had asked, and Eliot didn't say anything, but the answer was clearly no. They found a cab. He could hear rising police sirens. But then there had been nothing but a lot of uneventful driving.

His eyes were closing when there was a flat bang and the car lurched. "What," he said, thinking pursuit, death. Eliot steered the car onto the shoulder. Dust billowed.

"A flat," said Eliot. He popped open the door. Wil sat for a moment before remembering the promise of fresh air and heaving himself from the seat. His knees popped violently. The air was like fire, but at least it was moving. He strode around the car, swinging his arms. "Oh, yeah," he said. It felt good to do something.

Eliot dragged a spare tire from the trunk. Wil shielded his eyes to study the landscape. There was nothing. Just a vast canyon of air. His eyes grew restless for something to latch on to.

He heard Eliot grunting. "Need a hand?"

Eliot glanced at him, his face flushed. "They're rusted on."

"The lug nuts?"

"Doesn't matter. We can drive on it." Eliot stood.

"Did you pull hard enough?"

"Yes," said Eliot. "I pulled hard enough."

"Give me a try."

Eliot rolled the tire back to the trunk. "Forget it."

"For fuck's sake. I'm not useless."

"This isn't one of those games where everybody gets a turn. Get in the car."

"I will be two fucking minutes."

"Get in the car."

"No."

Eliot looked at him expressionlessly. "Fine." He tossed Wil the wrench.

Wil pulled off his T-shirt and knelt before the jacked-up wheel. There was a lot of rust here. He wiggled the wrench onto the top nut and tested it.

"Well?" said Eliot.

He swiped his arm across his forehead. "Just warming up."

"We have a time issue."

"Jesus, you don't even think I can change a tire." He strained against the wrench. "I can do this."

Some time passed. "Okay," Eliot said. "Enough."

"I've almost got it."

"You haven't. You're just wasting time."

He strained. Something went *crack.*

"You're going to strip it."

The lug nut squealed. He forced it through a revolution, and then it got easy. He unscrewed the nut and dropped it to the ground. He had a tremendous urge to glance at Eliot's face and couldn't resist it.

"Congratulations," said Eliot. "Unfortunately, there are three more."

He braced his foot against the tire well. "You *want* me to be useless. You love being in control of everything while I stumble around with no idea what I'm doing."

"No, that's the opposite of what I want. What I want is to get to Broken Hill as soon as possible, and for you to make a net positive contribution to that goal."

He released the wrench and bent to inspect the next lug nut. It looked very corroded. He hefted the wrench and began to bang at it.

"This has moved into farce," Eliot said. "Get into the car."

The lug nut spat rust. He got the wrench around it and forced it around. "That's two."

"Great," said Eliot.

"You need to loosen up," Wil said. "You seriously need to take a fucking breath and consider that you're not the only guy who can do everything."

"Did you tell me to loosen up?"

He wiggled the wrench onto the third nut. "Is that funny for some reason?"

"When I experience base physiological needs for food, water, air, sleep, and sex, I follow protocols in order to satisfy them without experiencing desire. Yes, it's funny."

"You fucking what?"

"It's required to maintain a defense against compromise. Desire is weakness. I'm sure I explained this."

"Well, that sounds awesome. That sounds like a terrific life you have there, Eliot." The nut loosened. "Got you!" he said.

"You want to see what happens when desire overpowers discipline? Get in the car. We'll be there in about two hours."

"And you didn't stop it." The final lug nut was so rusted he had trouble getting the wrench around it. "You and your protocols weren't good enough to save my town." He found traction and pulled. "Watch me budge this lug nut, despite my complete lack of discipline." His muscles burned. Sweat coursed down his back.

"Stop that. You're going to pull the whole car off the jack."

"And what about *Brontë*? Twenty years and you never made a move, did you? I bet you never even held her hand."

"Get in the car."

He grunted but the nut was immovable. He released the wrench, panting. "You know I'm right."

"You're not right," Eliot said. "You've been wrong about everything you've opened your mouth to opine upon, up to and including your belief in your ability to change this tire. Get in the car."

He repositioned his feet and gripped the wrench. "I am budging . . . this . . . lug nut!" He pulled with everything he had. His body shook. He yelled. The nut twisted with a squeal and he landed in the dust. He scrambled back to the tire. "Fuck! Yes!" He brandished the nut. "I was right! I was *right*!"

Eliot walked around the car and climbed into the driver's seat.

"Ha," said Wil. He pulled at the tire and it slid off easily. He changed it, collected his shirt, and returned to the passenger seat. Eliot started the engine. He didn't say anything. Neither did Wil, because this time the silence was fine.

"I don't like that chopper," Eliot said. It was an hour later. Maybe two. It was hard to tell because nothing changed. They were driving on a strip of road that folded around on itself, trapped in an endless loop of blistered blacktop.

Wil leaned forward and peered through the windshield. A black speck hung in the sky ahead and to the right. "That's a crop duster. They use helicopters for that out here."

"Where are the crops?"

A good point. The black speck grew. "I don't know."

"Bag on the backseat. Get that."

He twisted in his seat, found an old green and black gym bag, and dragged it into his lap. It clanked. "Is this what I think it is?"

"Yes."

"When did you get a gun?" But he knew: It was when Eliot had acquired the car. Wil had emerged from a restroom to find a bearded guy showing Eliot something in the trunk. They had shaken hands. Then they had taken his Valiant.

"Take it out of the bag."

"I'm not going to shoot some crop-dusting farmer."

"I'm not asking you to shoot anyone. I'm asking you to be prepared."

"See those poles sticking out the sides? Those are for spraying. Spraying crops." The helicopter drifted over the road and hovered there. The door popped open. Sun glinted on metal. "Or maybe he's roo hunting," said Wil. Eliot hit the gas. The roof barked out a flat impact. Hot air tickled Wil's hair and he looked up to see a small, neat blue hole. The hole was blue because of the sky. He turned and found a second hole in the backseat. "*Christ!*"

The engine roared. Wil saw the needle tip past ninety miles per hour. The road was cracked and potholed, strewn with sand. One bump and they could roll. They could easily become airborne. The chopper flashed overhead and Wil glimpsed a grizzled man in an Akubra with a rifle. When he turned the chopper was rising in the rear window, peeling after them.

"Okay," said Eliot. "Now I want you to shoot someone."

Wil pulled the shotgun from the bag, brown plastic molded around double barrels, the kind you had to break open between rounds. He hefted it awkwardly.

"Ammunition."

"Right." He found loose boxes of shells in the bag and tore one open. The car hit a pothole and began to slide. Shells spilled into the footwell. The car found traction and Wil steadied and broke open the shotgun and forced a shell into each barrel. He cranked the window. Furious wind blasted at his face. He stuck out his head to see the chopper skimming low over the road behind them. The pilot was behind the plastic bubble, hands on the controls, and it seemed to Wil that he wouldn't be able to steer and shoot simultaneously. He withdrew his head. "Is this guy a poet?"

"Good question."

"I think he's just some guy!" The car bounced. "They're controlling him!"

"Seems likely."

"So what do I do?"

"Shoot him."

"What? No!"

"Yes." Eliot nodded, his eyes on the road. "Right now."

"He's not shooting! He's just chasing us!"

"Still. Shoot him."

"He can't use the fucking gun while he's flying, Eliot!"

"I realize! Shoot him!"

"If he can't use the gun, and he's not a poet, why do I have to shoot him?"

"Because he's going to fly into us!"

"Oh," said Wil. "Oh!" He stuck his head out the window. The helicopter was rushing toward them, blades thundering. He raised the gun but it was already too late, and he fell back into the car. Eliot braked. The Valiant skidded, coming off the road. Dirt fountained. The world darkened. A rotor blade passed by, a great and terrible force Wil felt in his bones. Everything became noise and dust. Then quiet.

"Stay down," said Eliot, after a while.

Wil looked at him. Eliot was unbuckling. "What?"

"Don't move." He took the shotgun from Wil's hands, opened the door, and disappeared.

Wil hunkered down. Time passed. There was a sharp bang and the louder, deeper boom of the shotgun. Wil started to rise, stopped.

The door opened. The shotgun came in, butt first. Wil realized he was meant to take it. Eliot climbed inside and turned the key.

He sat up. "Are you okay?"

Eliot took the Valiant back to the road and steered around the helicopter, which no longer looked like an aircraft so much as a randomly distributed collection of scrap metal. There was no sign of the pilot. The car reached sixty-five and then ninety and then 110, a speed that made the windows howl like wolves and every pothole a bomb. The tires slipped and muttered, treacherous. Wil didn't want to say anything, but the fourth time he thought he was going to die, he couldn't keep silent.

"What are you doing?"

"Hurrying." Eliot's voice was odd.

"What's the matter?"

"A lot depends on you now." Eliot shook his head. "Fuck."

"What?"

"In the future, when you need to shoot someone, do it."

"Okay. Okay."

Eliot shook his head. "This was a stupid idea. A stupid fucking idea."

Through Eliot's side window, Wil noticed a thin plume of dust. "Hey. Another car out there."

"You think I like shooting people? I don't. I do it because it needs to be done. Understand?"

"Yes."

"Do you realize what happens if we fail? If there's no one left to stop them?"

"No. You haven't told me."

"Christ," said Eliot. "This is ridiculous."

Wil looked out the window. "That car is going fast. Really fast."

"It's trying to intercept us."

"Is it?"

"That's a surprise, is it? You didn't think there might be more?"

"Why are you so pissed at me?" He stared at Eliot's shirt. There was a patch. A darker area. "Did you get shot?" He didn't reply. "Eliot! Did you get shot?"

"Yes."

"We have to . . . get you to . . ."

"If you say something stupid, I'm going to pop you in your fucking mouth."

"Eliot," he said. "Eliot."

"I told you to shoot that guy."

"I'm sorry. I'm sorry." Outside Eliot's window, the dust plume resolved into a police squad car. "What can I do?"

"Next time you have to choose between Farmer Joe and the fate of the world, you can put a bullet into Farmer Joe. That's what you can do."

"Okay."

"You can kill Woolf. Can you do that?"

"Yes."

"Yeah," Eliot said. "Sure you can."

The cop car rose in the side window. A sign ahead said BARRIER HIGHWAY and STOP and clearly they were going to hit that cop car, Wil saw. "Slow down," he said, but Eliot didn't. Instead he dropped the hand brake and spun the wheel and the Valiant began to slide sideways. It crossed the highway, passing in front of the cop car, chewed dirt for a while, and lurched onto the blacktop. Behind them, a siren began to wail.

"Find out if that cop is a prole," Eliot said.

"A what?"

"A proselyte. Compromised. Find out if he wants to arrest us or kill us."

"How do I do that?"

"How do you think? With the gun!"

He wound down the window. The cop car was right there, nudging and whining like an animal in heat. He decided to shoot a tire. But the moment he got the shotgun out the window, the cop car's engine vented and distance opened between them. Wil retreated inside. "He doesn't want to get shot."

"Not compromised," said Eliot. "Good." Ahead, Wil saw BROKEN HILL 8 and NO ENTRY and QUARANTINE ZONE and DANGER DEATH. Beyond that, on the horizon, twin sets of twinkling lights like early stars. "Keep him back."

"How badly are you hurt?"

"Badly." Eliot's eyes flicked to the rear mirror. "*Fucking shit Wil you fuck!*"

He jerked around. The squad car had slipped lanes and was making a run up the driver's side. Wil tumbled into the rear of the car. By the time he got upright, the cop car was alongside them. There was a soft thump of contact. The rear of the Valiant began to slide as if it were on ice. The world spun. Wil lost his grip on the shotgun. The Valiant performed one complete revolution and Eliot gunned the engine and it leaped forward again.

He retrieved the shotgun. The cop car was moving up for a repeat performance, a second round of spin-the-Valiant, and there was no time to lower the window, so Wil planted his feet on the side door, aimed the shotgun down his legs, and squeezed the trigger. The window blew out. The cop car jerked as if stung, its engine jumping half a dozen octaves, and fell out of view. Wil leaned out the shattered window into the blast furnace of air. There were two cops in the squad car, their faces pinched with anxiety. He brought the shotgun around, settled on the radiator, and pulled the trigger. The car's hood popped open. It veered off the road, tires smoking. Wil crawled back inside.

When he reached his own seat, the lights ahead had resolved into two shining squad cars, one in each lane, barreling toward them. "They're not . . . kamikaze, are they?" Eliot didn't answer. Wil groped for his seat belt but couldn't find it. Surely Eliot was about to swerve off the road. The cars ballooned in the windshield, low-slung and powerful. "Eliot! *Eliot!*"

One squad car dropped behind the other. They flew past Eliot's window, their sirens dopplering. Wil breathed.

"Load that gun," Eliot said.

He dug around the footwell for shells, broke open the shotgun.

"They're coming around. Keep them back."

"I know."

"Don't talk about it. Do it."

"I'm doing it! I just shot a cop car, did you notice?"

"Next time, shoot the driver."

"Fuck!" he said. "What's the difference?"

"You shoot the driver, no cop comes within five hundred feet of us, that's the fucking difference! You shoot the *car*—"

"Okay! Okay!" He got his elbow out the passenger window and levered himself up. The wind tore at him. Way back, a column of white smoke rose from the car he'd shot, stark against the blue sky. Closer, the two new squad cars were eating up the distance between them. Wil steadied the shotgun. He had hunted, once. He'd cleared land like this of rabbits and roos. When was that? He couldn't remember. But this feeling, the shotgun nestled in his shoulder, an endless landscape of pressed dirt spread before him, was familiar. He waited. The cops would surely see him and stay back. He did not want to shoot anyone.

The Valiant coughed. The car shivered, lurched. Wil clutched at the window frame to avoid falling out of it, almost dropping the gun. "Hey!" he shouted. "What the fuck?"

"Gas! Becoming an issue!"

"Why are you *shaking the car*?"

"To extract gas from the tank!"

"I nearly fell out!"

Eliot said something he couldn't hear over the roar of the wind.

Wil leaned inside. "*What?*"

"I said it's important to keep moving!"

"I know that! Just give me five seconds of driving in a straight line!" He pushed himself out the window. The squad cars were closer than he liked. At this range, he'd pierce the windshield. They could see that, right? They could see he had a shotgun. He waited for them to back off.

"*Shoot!*" Eliot yelled.

He aimed at the car on the left and squeezed the trigger. Shot spattered across its hood. Its windshield cracked. Both cars' noses dipped to the blacktop. Smoke burst from their tires. He watched until there were a good couple hundred yards of road between them. Then he wriggled back inside. "They're backed off."

"Good."

Eliot didn't ask why he'd fired at the hood. Maybe he didn't realize. He probably assumed he was a terrible shot. He didn't know that Wil had hunted. That is, that he remembered hunting. "We seriously need to get you to a hospital."

"And how does that work," said Eliot. "How exactly do we get me to a hospital, in this situation."

"I don't know. But you can't fucking die, okay? It's not good for anyone if you die."

"Hold on," said Eliot. Wil saw a turnoff rushing toward them, a dusty blacktop guarded by red and black and yellow signs promising NO ENTRY, ROAD CLOSED, QUARANTINE AREA. As they leaned around the corner, the car coughed explosively. Wil felt a softness enter their momentum. The engine gargled. The Valiant lurched back onto the straight and muttered angrily.

"That's not good."

"No."

He glanced behind. The squad cars had slipped into a single file. They followed at a distance, taking the turnoff with ease. "They're going to just sit back there until we run out of gas."

"They're not."

"Let me float something," Wil said. "We stop, they arrest us, we get you some medical attention." Eliot didn't say anything. "Then you talk us out. With the word voodoo." He leaned forward, searching the sky for choppers. "Don't you think the priority here is you being okay?"

"The bareword is the priority."

"Right. The bareword." He peered ahead. "There's something on the road." A chain-link fence stretched away from either side of the road, but whatever lay between was lost in the heat haze. "Is that a gate?"

"Just loose wire."

"Are you sure?"

"Pretty sure."

"Are you really sure?" he said, but by the time he got the words out, the answer was clear. It was a solid red and yellow barrier. The Valiant plowed through it and a yellow block flew at Wil's face and ricocheted off the windshield with a light *boonk*.

He looked out the rear window. Colorful blocks rolled slowly across the road.

"Plastic," said Eliot.

"You said it was wire."

"Last time I was here, it was."

The police cars were shrinking. "Hey. They've stopped."

"That's because they believe what they've been told about Broken Hill. They don't want to die."

"So no one will follow us in here? We're safe?"

"Regular people won't. Proles will."

"Oh, yeah," Wil said, dismayed. "Proles."

"Also EIPs," said Eliot. "You haven't seen those yet. When they show up, we'll need the word." He glanced in the rearview mirror. "I'm going to pull over and let you drive for a while."

The car coasted to a halt. Wil ran around the vehicle, hunkering down in case of cops with sniper rifles, or helicopters, or whatever. He didn't know. It could be anything. The engine stuttered and he thought, *Please don't die, you cock*. He pulled open the driver's side door. Eliot was sitting in the passenger seat like he'd been dropped there. One hand rested on his abdomen. His face was made of paper. The driver's seat was wet with blood. "Holy crap," said Wil.

"Get in."

His butt pressed into the wet seat. The smell was rich and loamy, like a vegetable garden after rain. "This is seriously bad, Eliot." He pulled the door closed and set the car to moving before it could capitulate. "Is there a hospital in Broken Hill? A clinic, at least?" He glanced at him, abruptly fearful that he'd died in the past five seconds. But Eliot was still there. "Maybe we can do something for you there." Maybe Eliot had medical knowledge. Maybe Eliot could dig a bullet out of his body and administer the correct doses of expired medicines. He'd stuck a needle into Wil's eyeball; he must know something. The engine coughed three times. A structure rose in the distance: something old and industrial. "Are you listening?"

"Yes. It's a good plan."

"Is it?" But Eliot's expression suggested otherwise. "Fuck! Then what?"

"We get the word."

"And?" Eliot said nothing. "What . . ." he began, and forced himself to stop peppering Eliot with questions. He should let Eliot concentrate on holding in his kidneys. A house came up on the right, a squat thing with sun-blistered paint, but he'd seen more run-down places in Portland. It didn't look abandoned. It was the windows, he realized: They were intact. And there were no weeds, no overgrowth. The sun sterilized everything. He spotted gray-white clumps scattered here and there and thought, *Anthills?* One was on the road, more distinct. He swerved. "Fuck!"

Eliot grunted.

"Skeletons," he said. Of course there were skeletons. But still. Skeletons. On the road. A lone gas station came into view. A skeleton hung halfway out of a burned-out station wagon. He glanced at Eliot, to see if Eliot was getting this and was at least a fraction as freaked out as he was, but Eliot's eyes were closed. "Eliot."

His eyes opened. He began to shift himself up the seat like he was arranging something heavy. "Don't. Let me. Close my eyes."

"That's why I said something." He slowed. There were more skeletons here and he didn't want to drive over them. He didn't want to hear the noise. The industrial structure he'd seen earlier was identifiable as a refinery, crouched above the town like a wrecked spaceship. Like it had descended to Earth and murdered everybody. That he could believe. A death ray. A creeping light that spread through the town, disintegrating people. He could understand how something like that could wipe out a town. Not a word. "Eliot!"

Eliot opened his eyes.

"We're almost there." The street signs shone, wind-scrubbed. SULPHIDE STREET. OPEN CUT MINE #3. It was like they'd wanted to be the site of a toxic catastrophe. Except that hadn't happened. That was just the story. Something tugged at him, inside his mind. Some memory. "Where's your word?"

"Hospital," Eliot said.

He glanced at him. "You want the hospital, now?"

"Word. Is in hospital. Emergency room."

"How do you know that?"

"Just do," Eliot said.

He slowed further, because the road was littered with bones now; there was really no option, and he drove over a gray lump with a sound like splintering tree branches and winced. He saw a library with its steps converted to a ramp by a year and a half of windblown sand. It was hard to believe the skeletons were people. He knew but didn't. He peered ahead for signs to a hospital. On the right, a fire truck sat embedded in a storefront. Whatever happened out here hadn't happened quickly. People had had time to flee. Or try. He rolled the car up and down blocks. Some of the skeletons had things. He didn't want to notice this but it was unavoidable. Flesh rotted but things didn't. He caught glints of light from rings on finger bones, and belt buckles, and gold hoops, bracelets, earrings. He saw a skull on the sidewalk, a small one. He didn't want to be here. The feeling rose very suddenly, from somewhere primal.

He saw a café and a real estate office, both of which felt familiar in a far-off, muddied way. He convinced himself to stop avoiding Oxide Street and rolled the Valiant over a thicket of bone. What if a femur splintered and gashed the tires? It probably didn't matter. The car was near death. Like Eliot. Like himself. They were all very fucking close to death at the moment. It was on all sides.

He saw a blue sign with a white cross. "Eliot! I found it. Stay with me." The street was a snarl of vehicles, which he threaded the Valiant through. The damage here was worse, every window broken, the bones like snow. Whatever kind of building had been across the road from the hospital was a charred ruin, and this was increasingly the case farther down the street: Maybe half of the little business district had burned. "You say the word is in the emergency room, right?" He was. He didn't need Eliot to tell him that. He was just trying to keep talking. He saw a sign for EMERGENCY and squeezed the Valiant between two burned-out pickups. A white paramedic van lay splayed across the curb. Beyond it, he could see wide glass double doors and a red sign. He yanked on the hand brake. Before he could euthanize the car, it burbled and died. "Eliot. We're here."

Eliot's head bobbed. "Good."

"You want me to help you inside?" He shook his head. "I forgot. You have to stay here. I'll go look for the word."

"Don't . . ."

"Don't tell you anything about it. Got it." Eliot nodded. He had been forced to take Wil's advice: He had loosened up. He had relaxed control. Eliot was no longer in charge. "I'll be right back." Wil climbed out.

He wasn't prepared for the silence. He shut the car door and the sound evaporated. His shoes crunched sand. Hot air closed around him like a fist.

He circumnavigated the paramedic van. The glass emergency room doors were a strange kind of black. Not painted. Stained. He slowed without knowing why. Well. He did know. It was because he was not incredibly keen to face whatever had reduced three thousand human beings to belt buckles and bones. The paramedic van's rear doors were open. He glanced inside. A flatbed trolley, cloth straps, equipment, little bottles; nothing he wouldn't expect. But it made his brain crawl. He felt another tickle of familiarity. He hesitated, thinking. Eliot could benefit from some of these supplies. He could use some water. Wil climbed into the van. He gathered anything that looked medicinal and returned to the Valiant with his arms full of supplies. Eliot's eyes were closed. "Eliot!"

His eyes popped open.

"Stay awake." He dumped his load of bottles onto Eliot's lap. "I got this stuff for you."

Eliot stared.

"Some medicine. And water. You should drink the water."

"What . . ."

"You know, I think you're right. I did live here. It's starting to feel familiar."

"The fuck," said Eliot. "Word."

"I haven't gone in yet. I thought you could use this stuff." Eliot's eyes bulged. "All right! I'm going! Jesus!"

He walked back to the emergency room. He got close enough to see shapes against the dark glass. He knew what they were. There had to be two or three dozen corpses jammed up against the glass. And they were just the ones he could see. He wondered if it was airtight in there.

The air could be toxic. It could actually kill him. He jogged back to the car.

"Fuck!" said Eliot.

"Hang on one second," Wil said. "I just want to ask this. Are we sure we want to open this box? Because what's inside, you know, it killed a lot of people. We are talking about something incredibly dangerous. It's striking me as kind of stupid to walk on in there and try to pick it up. That seems like a big risk. You know? You say I'm immune, but do you know that for sure? What if I just avoided it somehow the last time? I lay in a ditch and it passed over my head? I'm just saying, that emergency room, it's wall-to-wall dead people, Eliot. It's wall-to-wall. And there's, I don't know, something about a room full of corpses that makes me think about whether I want to go in there. Don't look at me like that. I know. I know." He shook his head. "I'll go in. I will. It's just . . . you're asking me to maybe die, Eliot. Give me a second. Give me one . . . I know you're hurting. I'm going. But appreciate what I'm doing. That's all I want. I want you to acknowledge . . . for one second . . . the simple fact that I'm about to die. All right? I'm probably about to die. I'm happy to do it. I'm going. It's fine. I only wanted . . ."

He turned away. He walked. The glass was so dark. His feet scuffed. He reached the emergency room doors. His fingers touched the door plate. It was warm. Like there was a beating heart inside. It wasn't that. It was just the sun. Everything here was warm. He looked back at the Valiant but couldn't see it behind the paramedic van.

"If I don't come out, Eliot," he shouted, "fuck you!" His voice shook. He pushed open the door.

[III]

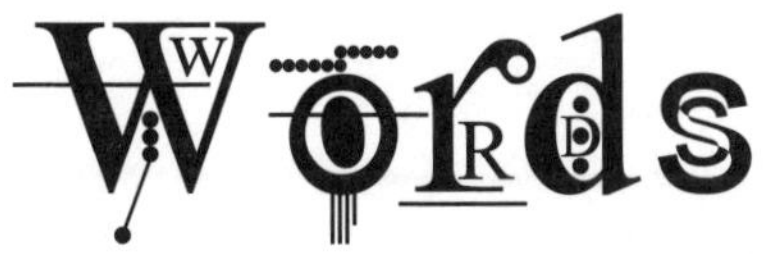

And I, methinks, am gone astray

In trackless wastes and lone.

—CHARLOTTE BRONTË

"Apostasy"

From: http://mediawatch.corporateoppression.com/community/tags/fox

I just think it's missing the point to get upset about bias in Fox News or MSNBC or whoever. I see this all the time: I mention to someone that I watch Fox and it's like I just slaughtered a baby. They ask how can I watch that, it's just propaganda, etc etc. And they know this not because they've ever sat down and spent any time with it but because *their* favorite news channel, i.e. a Fox competitor, sometimes plays a clip from a Fox show and it makes Fox look really stupid.

Well, you know what, Fox does that, too. If I only watched Fox, I'd think you must be really stupid, watching that other show I see clips from on Fox sometimes.

But I don't just watch Fox, because the way to beat biased reporting isn't to find the least biased one and put all your trust in that. First of all, they're all biased, from the language they use and the framing down to the choices they make about which stories to report. The gap between the most biased news show and the least is pretty small, all things considered.

But more importantly, relying on a single source of information means you can't critically evaluate it. It's like you're locked in a room and every day I come in and tell you what's happening outside. It's very easy for me to make you believe whatever I want. Even if I don't lie, I can just tell you the facts that support me and leave out the ones that don't.

That's what's happening if you're getting all your news from one place. If you stop listening to someone the second you hear a word or phrase you've been taught belongs to the enemy, like "environment" or "job creators," that's what you're doing. You might be an intelligent person, but once you let someone else filter the world for you, you have no way to critically analyze what you're hearing. At best, absolute best case scenario, if they blatantly contradict themselves, you can spot that. But if they take basic care to maintain an internal logical consistency, which they all do, you've got nothing. You've delegated the ability to make up your mind.

[ONE]

She tried to catch Harry at inconvenient moments. When he was stepping into the shower, or just after he closed his eyes at night, or reaching for the car door, late for work. "Do you love me?" she would ask. She would smile, so he'd know she was teasing.

"Maybe," he would say. Or nothing. Sometimes the look he gave her was like: *Of course, why ask?* and other times it was more like: *Stop it, I'm running late.*

He did love her. She was sure of it. All evidence pointed to yes. So why not say it? This was the part that nagged at her. Yes, okay, in Harry's world, you didn't need to say something to make it real. But come on.

She had said it. She had said it a lot, starting three weeks ago and increasing in frequency since, with the exception of a four-day drought the week before, which she had hoped might trigger something but didn't. And it was driving her crazy because she could force him. She didn't have a lot of words, but she did have tricks, and had figured out his segment, and there was no doubt in her mind that she could compel Harry Wilson to say whatever she wanted. But if she did that, it wouldn't be real. It wouldn't be him. It would be her, speaking to herself, through him. It was very frustrating.

"That car has been all over town," said the woman who was making Emily a sandwich. Emily turned. Across the street sat a dark sedan, windows tinted, engine running against the heat. A skirt of dust betrayed some serious long-haul driving. "You see it?"

"Yes," she said.

"Not from around here."

"No." She looked at the sandwich that the woman, Cheryl, was making. She had visited this shop nearly every weekday lunchtime for the past four years. She had practically married Cheryl's sandwiches.

"It's been to the mines." Cheryl gestured with the knife. "Look at the tires."

She looked. The tires were caked in red earth.

"Someone from the city, I suppose. Government." Cheryl flipped the bread. "Salt and pepper, love?"

"No, thanks."

"I keep thinking you might change your mind," said Cheryl, sawing bread. "I can't imagine how you eat it so plain."

"I like plain," she said. She carried the sandwich out of the shop, although she no longer felt like eating it. The car crouched in her peripheral vision but she did not look at it. When it pulled out, she crossed into the pedestrian mall, where it could not follow, and walked the roundabout route to Tangled Threads. She locked the door and sat behind the counter. She didn't know how to feel. Two years ago, maybe even one, she would have chased that car down the road. She would have beaten her hands against its side and begged it to stop. But now things were different.

A young man in an airy gray suit appeared at the door. He pulled the handle, pushed it, then put his hand to the glass and peered inside. When he saw her, he pointed at the handle and mouthed: *Open?*

She unlocked. He was young; a boy, really. She could tell from his skin that he had come from nowhere near here. "Thanks," he said. He came inside. He brushed aside his hair, which was a style she didn't know and dangled in his eyes. "Whoo. Hot."

"What can I help you with today?" she said.

He smiled, as if he appreciated the pretense. "It's good news. You can come home."

She said nothing.

He glanced out the window. "That was a genuinely long drive. They told me it was long, but . . . it's really something. Or nothing, rather." He looked at her. "Nothing and nothing, for as far as you go. Did you get used to it?" She didn't answer. "It seems to me it would be hard to get used to."

"You can get used to anything."

"Of course," he said. "We can leave right away."

"Today?"

"Is that a problem?" His eyes were gray, like his suit.

She shook her head. She did not want problems. "Give me your phone number. I'll call you in a couple hours."

"I wouldn't bother packing. There's nothing here you'll need again."

"If I don't tell people I'm leaving, they'll look for me. I'll be reported missing. It will get messy."

He was silent. He was going to tell her the organization could handle a missing persons report. But then he shrugged. "As you like." He dug in his pockets. Had this boy attended the school? He might have been one of the kids, a skinny cavorting stick boy too small to register. But she wasn't sure. It all seemed so long ago. "You really made yourself a part of this place, huh?"

"It's small," she said. "There's no other way."

He smiled like he didn't believe her and extended her a card. "I'll be in the car."

She phoned the owner of Tangled Threads, Mary, and said she needed to leave right away, her mother was dying. Mary's voice flooded with sympathy and told Emily it was fine, take as much time as she needed. She said, "I didn't know you were still in contact with your family."

"I wasn't," said Emily. "I just heard from them."

Then she drove to the hospital and waited. She could never tell where Harry would be, but the best place to wait was the emergency room. Sometimes she sat and read magazines alongside farmers with their hands wrapped in black towels and mothers with green children. The emergency room had glass double doors and when the paramedic van pulled up, the sun bouncing off its white hood, it was always thrilling, like winning a prize.

But when she saw him, she burst into tears. It was unexpected and shocking and if that organization boy had been around to see it, who knew what would have happened. Harry came to her, alarmed, and she heard the lie fall out of her about a mother, cancer. She hugged him and inhaled him while she could.

"Do you want me to come?"

"No," she said, grateful for the offer. "You can't."

"How long will you be?" He shook his head. "You don't know. It's okay. Take your time." He kissed her head. "But come back."

"I will," she said, and as the words came out, she was surprised at how true they felt. "I will, I promise."

Eventually she pulled away. There were people watching, and the longer this went on, the harder it became, so when he offered to drive her to the house she refused. She had to walk away while she could. "I love you," she said, and he smiled sadly, and in retrospect, it was very obvious, wasn't it? She should have seen it coming. But love made people stupid, and she was so very much in love. The emergency room doors parted and she walked through them and the only thing that made this bearable was the conviction that she'd be back.

An hour later, she was in the black sedan, watching dust swallow Broken Hill in the side mirror. The boy brought the car up to ninety miles an hour and manipulated his phone with one hand. “Sleep, if you want,” he told her. “There’s a whole lot of nothing for the next eight hours.”

This was true. But she couldn’t do it. The boy kept glancing at her and she curled up in the seat, putting her back to him. A while later, a car passed, heading in the opposite direction, gleaming on top and pancaked with dirt on the bottom. She watched it recede in the mirror. A minute later, there was another one just like it, then another.

“Are there more of you?”

“Hmm?” he said.

“The cars,” she said.

He shrugged. “Probably locals.”

She slouched back down. A truck appeared on the road ahead, following the cars, a black eighteen-wheeler with no signage, hauling a steel container unlike any she’d ever seen, but this time she didn’t say anything.

The journey was thirty-four hours, long enough to develop a burning hate for the organization boy and everything he stood for. She was glad the first-class seats were like capsules, which gave her space to hide her misery. She didn’t know what had triggered the arrival of the boy, whether it was simply enough time passing for the organization to consider her suitably chastened, or they had been observing her, or something had happened, or what. But whichever it was, she would be expected to be in charge of her emotions.

She deplaned, disoriented and bruised somewhere in the core of her body, into DC winter sunshine. A limo whisked her to a grand hotel, where the boy bid her farewell, and she slept for fourteen hours. She woke to a blinking red light on the bedside phone. She pressed for voice mail, thinking it might be Eliot, which would be frightening, or Yeats, which would be more so, but it was neither. Instead, a girl she didn’t know told her she was expected at a particular fashion store in thirty minutes. The girl ended her message without saying good-bye, as if she'd been cut off, although Emily knew she hadn't been.

She caught a cab downtown and tried on skirts and sheer shirts. In the mirror, she looked freakishly tan. "This will take more than a jacket," said the man, who had introduced himself as a *personal style adviser*. "You're a cavewoman in a suit, dear."

He forwarded her to a salon, where a bald man dragged a brush through her hair with occasional exclamations of dismay. Now she was alongside other women, she started to see the problem. Her hair was the wrong kind of blond: the kind from the sun. There was a gritty quality to her skin. She had absorbed Broken Hill. She had soaked it up and become savage. "Do not worry," said the hairdresser. "We've beaten worse than this."

Afterward, the floor a graveyard of fallen hair, she found herself with a short bob and bangs like a steel door. It seemed like they had tried to hide her face. She looked strange to herself. "Do you wear glasses?" asked the hairdresser. "You should consider that."

She was shuttled back to the first clothing store, where her new look was praised effusively. She actually started to feel good and then the personal style adviser said, "Well, it's an improvement, anyway." She had forgotten how indirectly people spoke here. She had become accustomed to taking people literally.

Hours later, laden with shopping bags, she was driven to a tall glass office building that offered no identifying logo. She entered a simple lobby, feeling newly manufactured in her gray woolen suit and stiff black shoes, her heart pounding in case she was about to meet someone she knew. But there was no one. A red sofa, a few paintings; it could have been anywhere. She waited at the reception desk until a young man with invisible eyebrows emerged from the rear office. "I'm Emily Ruff," she said.

"Just a moment." When he returned, he had a plastic card, which he placed on the counter. It was blank but for: NL-L5D4. She looked at him.

"That means level five, desk four."

"Oh," she said. "Thank you." She hefted her bags. It took her a minute to figure out the elevators: She had to insert the card into a slot before the buttons would do anything. Then the doors closed and she rose toward whatever was up there.

It turned out that level five was nothing but anonymous corporate space with a dozen or so roomy cubicles. Almost all were empty. It was very quiet and as her shopping bags rustled and banged she wished she'd left them with the receptionist. She passed a young woman on the phone and a boy with long hair and glasses who looked up from his computer screen but his expression didn't change and she didn't stop walking.

She spotted identifying plates on the desk corners and began to triangulate D4. It was in a corner, with a pretty amazing view over south DC. It had a chair, a phone, a computer, and that was it. She stashed her bags beneath the desk and tested the chair. She waited. The phone would ring, she guessed. Eventually.

After a minute, the boy with glasses appeared, accompanied by a girl whose hair was the good kind of blond. She looked familiar, although Emily couldn't place her. She seemed very young. "Wow. Welcome."

"Hi," she said. "Thank you."

"Isaac Rosenberg," the boy said. "Nice to meet you."

"I'm Raine," said the girl. "Kathleen Raine."

"Hi," Emily said again. There was an awkward silence. "I'm sorry, I don't know why I'm here."

"Typical," said the boy, Rosenberg. "We only got word a couple days ago that you were coming. You're in NL."

"Neurolinguistics?"

He nodded. "Testing and Measurement. Have you done any NL work before?"

She shook her head.

"It's good for a theoretical grounding, supposedly. Anyway, we'll get you started. Teach you the system. If that's okay with you."

"Sure," she said. The girl, Raine, was still looking at her like she was missing something, so she said, "I'm sorry, have we met?"

Several expressions flitted across the girl's face in quick succession, one of which said yes and another that told her she wasn't supposed to ask. "No," the girl said, but Emily remembered now: They had met at the school. Emily had forgotten because it was in that first week, and the girl had failed the tests and not been admitted. She had been very young. Emily had tried to make her feel better by saying she could try again the next year. Her name had been Gertie.

"Hey, I apologize if this is inappropriate," said Rosenberg, "but they really haven't told us much and we don't want to tread on any toes, so I'm wondering if . . . you know, if you actually want to do NL or if we should just leave you alone."

"I think I'm actually here to do NL. I'm just another graduate now, I guess."

Rosenberg and Raine laughed, then stopped. "I'm sorry," said Rosenberg. "I thought you were joking."

"Why would that be a joke?"

"I'm really sorry. I didn't mean to imply anything."

"You haven't. But please, tell me what you know about me."

"Well, nothing. Just your name." He pointed to her partition. There was a gray rectangle of plastic. A nameplate she hadn't noticed before. Her first thought was that she was at the wrong desk. Then she realized she wasn't. Because of Yeats. Because four years ago, he had said: *I have a name for you, when the time is right.* The nameplate said: VIRGINIA WOOLF.

The woman on the phone she'd passed earlier turned out to be Sashona. The last time Emily had seen her was on the hockey field at the school.

“Screw me sideways,” said Sashona. “You’re Woolf?” She looked at Emily with her hands on her hips. Sashona had grown up. She had become a woman. “We thought you’d *died*.”

“Nope.”

“Holy cripes. Where have you been?” She shook her head before Emily could answer. “Don’t answer. Stupid question. Wow. Look at you. You’re so different.” Emily smiled awkwardly. She wasn’t sure that was a good thing. “What on earth did you do to earn that name?”

“I don’t know.”

Sashona looked at her and Emily realized she did not believe this at all. “You look great.”

“You, too.”

“Patty Smith,” said Sashona. “That’s my name now. Smith.”

“Oh, Smith’s good,” said Emily.

“Ah, fuck off,” said Sashona, smiling. For a second it was like being back at school.

She was reminded how much she disliked neurolinguistics. She had forgotten that, since school. At first, it was fascinating; it was all Amazonian tribes using recognizably Latin words and how saying *guh* could make you hungry. Then came syntax and semantic violations and synaptic coupling. It required enormous amounts of rote memorization—all of which she’d lost over the past four years—and the ability to juggle symbols in her head. At school, students didn’t talk much about what they thought of specific subjects, but when she had mentioned she was studying neurolinguistics to Jeremy Lattern, he had looked sympathetic. This was like those classes again, only now she was expected to know everything.

Rosenberg and Raine taught her how to use the computer. There was a ticket system: When people wanted her to do something, they logged a ticket. And when she was finished, she plugged her work into the ticket and closed it. Mostly, the people who wanted Emily to do something were from Labs, which she gathered was located somewhere else in the building, although it was clear that other people were reading the tickets, too, because they sometimes requested clarifications. Those people, she thought, were higher-ups. Organization people like Eliot. But there were no names in the ticket system, only numbers. Sometimes she would read a ticket over and over, wondering if there was anything of Eliot's mannerisms in it, but she could never tell for sure. After a while, she stopped expecting to see Eliot. Apparently she was to be left alone. To do what, exactly, she didn't know. Maybe they really did want her to relearn NL. Maybe they were secretly observing her. But if this was the case, what they were observing was nothing very interesting.

She was assigned an apartment, a bank account, and a cell phone. All this was arranged. Her apartment balcony overlooked the meatpacking district and sometimes she stood out there with a bottle of wine, wrapped in a jacket that never really kept out the cold, watching the city breathe.

Every few days, she did something stupid. She stayed up late, or set the alarm early, and left the apartment in the freezing dark. She walked in a random direction for a random amount of time and found a pay phone and plugged coins into it. As it rang, she reminded herself to modulate her voice, avoid identifiable phrases, and end the call as soon as possible. She told herself, *This is the last time for at least a week.* Because if she was caught, she had no doubt that the consequences would be terrible. But then the line would connect, and Harry's voice would fill her, and she would forget about that.

She got to visit Labs. It turned out to be in the bowels of the building, underground. It was brightly lit and full of techs in white coats and had two plastic, keypad-protected doors between her and anyone more senior than a receptionist. They interviewed people down here, she knew: attached them to probes and ran them through fMRIs to record what happened when they heard words. Then they sent the data upstairs to NL for analysis. Where these test subjects came from, she didn't know. Although once while looking for a pay phone near George Washington University, she had seen a paper stapled to a light pole offering fifty dollars for volunteers for a psychology experiment, so maybe that. When the data came through the ticketing system, sometimes under OBERVABLE EFFECTS it said *psychotic break*, or *loss of function*, or *coma*. She tried not to think about this too much. But it was obvious that people got hurt down there.

Sashona—*Smith*, as Emily would never feel comfortable calling her—had changed a lot. She laughed, which she had never done at school, and found everything *amazing*. This struck Emily as unlikely behavior, since Sashona should have been guarding her personality to prevent segmentation. She decided it was feigned: a behavioral smoke screen. The higher levels didn't do this; Emily had talked with Eliot plenty and had no idea of his segment simply because he gave nothing away. But it made sense for a newer poet. It made her wonder if she should be doing the same thing, and if Sashona thought Emily was trying to figure out her segment, and if Sashona was trying to figure out hers.

One day, as a tall, handsome barista delivered coffees to their café table, Sashona opened her mouth and a snarl of unintelligible words tripped out. "Love me," Sashona said, and the barista spilled the coffee and went away and came back to ask for Sashona's phone number. This was how Emily discovered that in the four years she had been selling blouses in the desert, Sashona had been learning words. Emily murmured her appreciation, but the truth was she was shocked. She hadn't realized how far behind she was. How was she supposed to catch up? She had no one to ask but Sashona, and although they were friendly, she was afraid to expose her ignorance.

She decided to hope that one day somebody would appear to

educate her. In the meantime, she read data and tried to pound it into thoughtful conclusions. The organization was interested in refining its psychographic model, in finding ever-better ways to classify people more accurately into fewer segments. She looked for responses in graphs that shouldn't be there, tiny bumps in blue lines, and wrote reports on possible psychographic overlaps, and segment boundary blurring, and possible new avenues for segmentation. She had access to a vast database of shopping habits, Internet usage patterns, traffic flows, and more; if she wanted, she could drill right down to an individual and look up where they went last Tuesday and what they bought and did. But that was not very useful. No one was interested in individuals. She was supposed to look for connections between them: neurological commonalities that allowed them to be grouped together and targeted by a common word. Whether anybody acted on her work, or even read it, she had no idea.

It became harder to find a pay phone she hadn't used to call Harry before. Every night, as she walked the streets, she half-expected Eliot or Yeats or maybe that kid in the airy suit to step out of the darkness. And then everything would be over. But that never happened, so she kept doing it.

One day she got a corrupted data set from a ticket, so she picked up the phone and dialed Labs. She was not supposed to do this. At least, she was supposed to do it as little as possible. Techs were isolated from analysts for security reasons, since techs were not poets and were therefore vulnerable to compromise. Why an analyst might want to compromise a tech, she had no idea. It seemed pretty pointless. But that was the rule. It didn't seem very effective, either, since although the techs were supposed to be anonymous, they gave themselves away in their writing styles: one overused *evidently*, one had never heard of apostrophes, that kind of thing. So she did not have a great deal of respect for the rule.

"Hello," she said when Labs picked up. "This is Analyst three-one-nine. I need a validation check on a data set, please."

"Open a ticket," said a male voice. She had seen no evidence of women in Labs.

"I did open a ticket, and it came back the same. I want it done again."

"What's your ticket number?" She told him. There was a pause. "That data set has been recompiled."

"I know it's been recompiled. But I want it re-recompiled, because it's still wrong."

"The data set is accurate."

"Guy," she said, "I'm looking at it right now. The p-graph is blank. I don't know if you've got a format error, missing data, or what, but the graph cannot be blank."

"It's not blank."

She opened her mouth, because that was preposterous. She had seen thousands of p-graphs and knew what they were supposed to look like: mountain ranges. Sometimes they had many peaks, sometimes just one, but the point was they were jagged. The lines went up and down. But as she looked at it again, she realized Labs was right. There was a line. She hadn't noticed because it ran along the very top of the grid and was dead straight.

"Clear?" said Labs.

"Yes," she said. "Thank you." She put down the phone. She looked at the graph awhile.

She walked to Sashona's desk. "Hey," she said. "What's synapsis?"

"What's the context?"

"It's in a new ticket. After 'subject response,' instead of a rating, it says 'synapsis.'"

"Well, *synapsis* is just compromise," said Sashona. "But they shouldn't use that term. That's sloppy."

"Why?"

"It's the ideal. The theoretical state of perfect compromise. Doesn't exist in real life."

"Oh," Emily said. "I see."

"Tell them to say what they mean," Sashona said, returning to her work. "Probably someone new."

"Right," she said.

She did her best to write a meaningful report about the oddly flat graph and dutifully submitted it to the ticket system. Another ticket was waiting, but she felt distracted, and gazed at passing clouds instead. She had the feeling something was going to happen.

Six minutes later, the power went out. She rolled her chair back from her dead monitor. Heads poked up from cubicles. "I thought we had a backup generator," said Sashona. Her voice sounded loud. Emily hadn't noticed the hum of the air-conditioning until it was gone.

An alarm began to jangle. People's voices rose. Rosenberg speculated about fire in Labs, which would be a problem, because a lot of those doors were time-locked. They made for the stairwells but Emily didn't follow. Sashona hung in the doorway. "Woolf?"

She shook her head. She was feeling stupid. She had waited too long. She should have walked out of this building six minutes ago. She should have done it the moment she saw that graph.

"Woolf! It's not optional. Time to go."

She ran through floor plans in her head. There was no fire escape. She hadn't realized that before. No glass cases saying IN CASE OF EMERGENCY. No one had ever gathered them in a conference room and explained where to go in an orderly fashion in the event that they needed to evacuate.

Sashona gave up on her and disappeared. Emily could go up or down. Those were her only options. She reached the stairwell and started climbing. She heard disembodied voices rising around her like departed spirits. A door boomed and there was silence but for her own breathing. She didn't hear anyone else going down, she realized: no one from other floors. She stopped to kick off her shoes, which were helping no one. She climbed and climbed and finally saw daylight. She even jogged up the last few steps but found herself at a scuffed steel door that was chained and padlocked. She tried it anyway. She sat on the concrete and tried to figure out what next.

Somewhere far below, a door clacked open, then slammed. This happened eight or nine times. She listened but couldn't hear anything more. "Fuck," she said. She was pissed at herself. She had spent too long in Broken Hill, not needing an escape route. She balled her hands into fists. *Think.* There was a skylight. It was secured, but how well? She went back to the door and put one foot into a loop of chain and pulled herself up, searching for fingerholds. Balancing, she reached for the skylight, but it was too far away. She heard a rasping. What the fuck that was, she did not know, but it was coming from below and getting closer. She managed to inch her way up until she was standing on the bar of the door. The chain swung and clanked like a bell. Like she was deliberately trying to attract attention. Her fingertips brushed the skylight but that was the best she could do. If she released her grip on the door frame, she could possibly grab this thing and pull it out of the ceiling as she fell. There was a very slim chance of that happening. She heard footsteps. Boots on concrete. The rasping punctuated the air at regular intervals, like breathing but not. She should have learned words. She should not have waited for someone to teach her. She should have found them somehow. She leaped at the skylight and her fingers skidded uselessly over the plastic and she fell to the concrete and banged her knee. "*Suck*," she said. A man came up the stairs. A kind of man. He was wearing black from head to toe and his eyes were black, bulky goggles, like night vision gear, set into a fighter pilot's helmet, with bulging plastic hemispheres over the ears. He looked like he could walk through fire. The rasping was his air regulator.

"*Shakaf veeha mannigh danoe!*" she said. This was a mess of attention words for random segments. The chances of it having any effect were about a thousand to one. "Lie down!"

He extended a gloved hand. "Come with me." These words came out flat and computer-modulated. She didn't move. If he came closer, she could jump him. She didn't see a gun. She would go for those goggles. If she could even dislodge them, it would make it hard for him to chase her.

"Hurry." The man gestured to the stairs. "There's a fire."

"There isn't," she said. "Is there." He didn't answer. She'd figured out by now that he couldn't hear her. She began to walk down the steps.

The lobby had been converted to a makeshift hospital, full of white cloth screens. The windows were blacked out with plastic sheeting. Black-suited spacemen moved between them, respirators hissing. She saw no one's face she didn't know from level five. She glimpsed Sashona on a trolley bed but then lost her behind a screen. She was told to stay where she was. Nobody spoke to her. Or to each other, at least that she could hear. An hour later, a spaceman drew back her curtain. He wasn't wearing his helmet and she was surprised at his youth. He had a mustache, thin and fluffy. She wondered if this was the guy who had fetched her from the top of the stairs. If so, she should have gone with *narratak*.

"You can go." He began to disassemble screens.

"What was all that about?" But she wasn't really expecting an answer. Outside, she found the others huddled on the street. It was dusk, the tail end of rush hour.

"A drill," said Sashona. "But for what?"

"No point wondering," said Raine. "We'll never know."

"True, that," said Sashona. She was wondering why Emily hadn't come downstairs with them. And, by extension, what Emily knew that she didn't.

Emily couldn't hang around any longer. She started walking and by the time she reached the subway, she was shaking. She would not do anything rash. She would come to work in the morning, go to her desk, and do her job, like always. But this had been a lesson. A reminder. The next time something like this happened, she told herself, she would have a way out.

She kept a notepad and wrote down syllables she noticed were used more frequently by one psychographic than another. On the train, she listened for deviations from the average. She picked apart the words she knew, looking for patterns. She was surprised at how obvious they were. Liberals overused *-ay* and *-ee*, the front vowel sounds. Authoritarians were thick with fricatives. She developed hunches from newspapers and TV and websites, tracked down a suitable representative, at a bar or church meeting or the grocery store, and tried trotting them out. Like a safecracker listening for tumblers. *Sut. Stut. Stuh.* She slid guesses into sentences and usually people didn't even seem to register them. They didn't make it past the perceptual filter, ignored as verbal static. At worst, they thought she was stuttering. Her hunches were usually wrong. But sometimes she saw a flinch. A tiny flare across the muscles of the face. And that was a tumbler.

It was a hard way to learn words. She could do this for a year and still know less than Sashona. But it was very thorough. It forced her to understand the underlying principles. She deduced a preference for alliteration in a segment from what she knew of the segments around it, leaping from there to *lallito*, a command word, and this thrilled her more than anything she had been taught. Because she had found it herself.

Once, sharing drinks at the corner bar, Sashona confided that she had trouble with segment 191. "I get *kavakifa*," said Sashona, leaning forward, holding her wineglass at an angle that Emily was tempted to correct. "I can get to *fedoriant*. But then I'm lost!" She gestured expansively. "I can *never remember.*" This was part of a tale concerning a high-speed joyride down the I-48, a police officer on a motorbike, and a speeding ticket Sashona had hilariously failed to talk her way out of. But Emily was astounded. Apparently Sashona couldn't see that the words of segment 191 were bound together. She could understand if Sashona had forgotten the entire tree. But if you knew one, you had half of the others. Sashona did not seem to get this. She had memorized them one at a time, as if they were unconnected. Like a tray of random objects in a child's puzzle game.

One thing Emily never got over was the feeling of being watched. She wasn't sure how, but it was happening. She tried varying her route to work, checking reflections, doubling back unexpectedly, but never saw anyone. At home, she double-bolted, but felt no safer. Her feeling was that Yeats was in the apartment. That was her impression. One night, she dreamed he came into her bedroom like a black wind and leaned over her, watching her without emotion, as if she were a thing beneath glass.

On the first Tuesday of her sixth month in Washington, she left her apartment and walked to the local train station. She rode escalators down to the platform and waited for the red line. It was warm; she was thinking about getting to her desk and taking off her shoes. A man at the end of the platform had a guitar and was banging out a song she loathed, for personal reasons: "Lucy in the Sky with Diamonds." The train began to pull in. In its passing windows she glimpsed Eliot.

For a moment she wasn't sure whether she had seen him inside the train or reflected behind her. Then the train ground to a halt and the doors opened and he said from behind her: "Let it go."

She watched the train pull out. She was sixteen years old again. Just like that. But then she turned and he wasn't so frightening. He had aged around the eyes. He was just a man, after all.

"Are you in love?" Eliot said.

She didn't answer.

"Don't lie to me."

"Yes."

He looked away.

"I'm sorry," she said. "I'll stop."

"Your next mistake will end you. This is as far as I can go to protect you. You need to appreciate this."

"I do. I promise."

His eyes searched her. "No more calls. Not one."

"I'm done. I'm done, Eliot." In this moment, she really meant it.

He walked away. She stood on the empty platform.

She did not call Harry that night. The following day, she did not call him. She had gone longer than this without hearing his voice but now it was different, because it was the end. She felt sick. She couldn't taste anything. It was crazy but she could no longer taste food. At work, she clicked through tickets and wrote reports but couldn't tell if they made any sense. When it got too much, she went to the bathroom and put her head between her knees. She made herself repeat: *Do not call him.* She felt possessed, by a cruel, heartless Emily who did not love.

She surrendered on the third day. It was a terrible betrayal of Eliot; she realized that. He had stuck his neck out for her in ways she couldn't quite comprehend and she had promised to stop. But the fact was she couldn't. She had tried but she couldn't. It had been six months and home was still on the other side of the world.

She couldn't call Harry again. Eliot would know, or, worse, others would. There was no stay-but-keep-calling-him option. She could only leave.

Years before, in San Francisco, Emily and a girlfriend had been crossing a McDonald's parking lot and found themselves boxed in by a group of barely pubescent boys with low pants and twitchy smiles. One of the boys had a gun, which he kept putting away and getting out again, swapping from hand to hand, and the others began to ask Emily and her friend if they knew what hot bitches they were and how badly they were about to get fucked up. This was a bad situation even without the gun, but Emily had been young and stupid, so she walked up to the boy with the gun and pulled it right out of his hands. She had good fingers, even then, because of the card tricks. She didn't know a thing about guns, except which end to hold, but that was enough, so the boys stood around looking scared while Emily and her friend made a lot of silly threats and walked out backward.

The lesson here was probably that she should not cross parking lots in bad neighborhoods. But also, when you were outmuscled, if there was a gun around, you could get control of the situation by getting the gun.

Emily was outmuscled. She did not have a gun. But she suspected there was one in the basement.

HELP!

I am trying to get in touch with everyone from the church group for our big Christmas get-together! We really want to invite EVERYONE who spent any time with us over the year.

I like to think I'm quite adept at sleuthing people down, but there's one person I simply can't locate: Virginia Woolf! One might think that with a name like that she'd be easy to find. Unfortunately, the opposite seems true—it's IMPOSSIBLE to use the Internet because of all those pages about the famous writer! Very frustrating!! Anyway I was hoping someone might know SOME way to reach her, because she seemed quite attentive and interested in what we had to say!

Much love,
Belinda F.

[TWO]

Beneath her desk was a gym bag. The top layer was clothes Emily actually wore while working out, and under those was a second set she'd stashed there against this day. She logged out of the ticket system and slung the bag over her shoulder. On her way out, she passed Sashona, who was on the phone, and Emily mouthed, "Gym," and Sashona nodded. She felt a small pang, because although they'd never been friends, for this place they were pretty close, and Emily was never going to see her again.

She walked two blocks to a small café, a place she came sometimes for lunch. In the restroom, she changed into the clothes from her gym bag: a T-shirt, a pair of frayed jeans, and an old denim jacket. She scrubbed the makeup from her face, collected a nice film of grime from the floor tiles, and dabbed this under her eyes and across her hairline. Her work clothes and the gym bag she stashed behind a toilet. She didn't expect to see those again, either.

She circled the block and approached the office from the lane on the other side. Here was a nondescript door with a sign that said THE ROBERT LOWELL INSTITUTE OF PSYCHOLOGICAL RESEARCH. It looked like just another doomed business renting space on the wrong side of the building. But it wasn't. It was the public face of Labs. She pressed the intercom and waited.

"Hello?"

"Hey," she said. "My name is Jessica Hendry, I did one of your, like, tests a couple weeks ago, and you said I should come back if I wanted?"

The door buzzed. She pushed it open and went up the narrow steps. At the top was a small waiting room, with empty chairs and an energetic television. A woman with high hair sat behind sliding glass. "Take a seat," she said.

Emily sat and flipped through *People*. She had been here before. The first time, the day after she'd determined to start planning, she'd found the entrance but not gone inside. She looked up "Robert Lowell Institute" in the phone book and called them—from a pay phone, for what that was worth—and determined that yes, they were interested in volunteers for testing, and walk-ins were accepted between eleven and one o'clock. They had wanted her to come in the next day, but she demurred, because she hadn't acquired a false identity yet. It took her a week to find Jessica Hendry, a girl Emily's age who had no fixed address and little interest in the world beyond where she might score her next hit. Jessica took to Emily straightaway, maybe sensing a shared history in addition to the potential to scam some money, and gushed more personal information to Emily than she really needed. In exchange, Emily pressed a hundred-dollar bill into Jessica's hand and squeezed her and said, "Keep this safe," then stole it back when Jessica wasn't looking, because, honestly, that wasn't going to help anyone.

The institute had asked her to fill out a questionnaire. She went through this carefully, answering the psychographic questions honestly, which exposed her completely, of course, to anyone who divined that Jessica Hendry was her. She was segment 220, she already knew. Which should be good, because Labs could never get enough 220s.

After the questionnaire, they'd taken her to a small, bright room with a forest of video cameras. They attached electrodes to her skull and showed her TV ads. These were kind of funny, because they were not ads at all, or at least not for real products. They were excuses to broadcast words. After forty or fifty, she blacked out, and when she woke up everyone pretended she had just fallen asleep. She didn't know what they had done to her until the report bubbled through the ticketing system. When she'd seen SUBJECT SEGMENT: 220, she'd scanned it anxiously, but there was no mention of permanent damage. She'd been pretty sure that Labs wouldn't do destructive testing on a walk-in, but it would have been a bad thing to get wrong.

A few days later, the prepaid cell phone she kept to answer as Jessica Hendry rang, and a man chatted with her about whether she would be interested in coming in again. She said yes if there was money in it and he asked why she hadn't put down a home address and she explained about it being a tough time and just needing to catch a break and would she get paid or not, what did it matter where she lived. Once she'd established that no one would notice one way or the other what happened to Jessica Hendry, the man said to come in anytime, they would love to see her. And here she was.

"Jessica," the receptionist said. Emily looked up from her magazine. "You're up." The door buzzed.

She followed a white-coated man with no chin through corridors lined with steel-caged lamps. "So I get a hundred dollars for this," she said. "Right?"

"Right," he said.

"Last time I fell asleep." She was trying to engage him, to figure out if he was anyone she knew through the ticket system. "I hope the ads are more interesting this time."

They reached a double set of elevators. "We won't be showing you ads today."

"No? What, then?"

An elevator arrived. The man gestured for her to enter. "It's a product."

The doors closed and despite herself, her chest tightened. It was a small elevator. It felt like a very small elevator. "What kind of product?"

He scanned his clipboard. "I'm afraid I can't tell you that without potentially polluting your reaction."

"'Polluting your reaction.' You guys are weird." The elevator numbers ticked down. "Is it, like, a bottle of shampoo, or a car, or what?"

"It's strongly important for our tests that you don't have any preformed expectations."

"Oh, okay. No problem." *Strongly important.* That was an odd phrase. She had seen that one in the ticketing system.

The doors parted. The corridor walls were pale blue. A calming color. The tech started walking and she followed him to a set of plastic doors, where he had to swipe his ID tag and tap a code into a keypad. Fifty yards later, the same thing happened again. During this process, she eyed ceiling-mounted video cameras. There was a second elevator and when this one stopped the walls were bare concrete, no more psychological blue. She didn't like this much. The corridor ended at a perfectly round steel door that was twice as tall as she was. It looked like a bank vault. The door stood open and beyond it she could see a small concrete room with a single orange plastic chair. By the vault door stood another white-coated man and a gray-uniformed guy who looked like maybe security.

Her chinless tech said, "Verifying, I have prototype nine double-zero double-one eight six."

The other man said, "Confirming prototype nine zero zero one one eight six."

"Verifying subject, Hendry, Jessica, identifying number three one one seven zero."

"Confirming subject, time is eight-fifty-eight, time lock has released and chamber is open."

"What is all this?" she said. She tried to grin.

"Security," said her tech, not looking at her. "The product is very valuable." He entered the concrete room, which required stepping over a thick metal rim. "Follow me, please."

She did so. The air was freezing. The walls were featureless concrete but for six bulbous yellow lights in wire cages. Four tripod-mounted video cameras were aimed at the plastic chair. In the middle of the room was a box. A huge, steel, coffin-shaped box.

"Please sit."

"Mmm," she said. "Mmm, mmm."

"It's all right, Jessica. It'll be just like last time. Only this time we're showing you a product instead of ads. I'm going to fit you with the helmet so we can measure your brain activity, okay?"

"Yeah," she said, although she was thinking *no, no, no*. She sat. Even the plastic was icy. The steel box had no lid. Not that she could see. Around its sides were thick vertical rods. Pistons? She stared because she could not imagine what the deal was with this box.

The tech touched her hair. She flinched. "Just relax." He began to fit the helmet.

"Hey, what is this again? What kind of—"

"Just a product."

"Yeah, but it, you know, seems pretty weird for a product. So what kind of product is it?" He didn't answer. *Turn him*, she thought. "Strongly important": she had read a hundred tickets from this guy and he was segment fifty-five, no question, and she had figured out words for that. She could compromise him in two seconds flat and make him walk her out of here. She didn't know what next. There was no next in that scenario. Not one she wanted. But why was there a box? Why the fuck was there a box?

"Almost done, Jessica."

She had not anticipated a box. She'd thought maybe an envelope. A man sitting opposite, preparing to read a word. And before he could, she would take it from him, because he wouldn't be prepared for a poet. These guys, these isolated techs, she didn't think they even knew what poets were. They just did what they were told. But that plan was clearly fucked, because whatever was in this box, this thing that turned a person's p-graph into a flat line, caused *synapsis*, was too important for an envelope. She had been foolish to imagine that.

"There's a small needle in this one."

She felt a sliver of cold enter her skull.

"All done." The tech moved to the video cameras and began turning them on. Red lights gleamed at her. "Just clear your mind and look at the product."

"What product?"

"The product that will come out of the box after I've left."

"What do you mean, it will come out of the box?"

"I can't tell you without—"

"Without polluting my reaction, I know, but why is there a box? What's inside it?"

"Don't worry about the box."

"Just tell me why there has to—"

"I don't know what's in the box," he said. "Okay?"

She saw it was true. And now that she looked, did she notice how the video cameras were covering only her? Not the box. It was so that later, after it was done and the box had closed again, people could study the tapes without being exposed. Did she notice the tech had been avoiding eye contact? She knew what that meant, right?

He placed a black device on the floor. "This is a speaker. I won't be able to hear you, but I'll keep talking to you throughout the process."

"I changed my mind," she said. "I don't want to do this."

He glanced over his shoulder. The man in the gray uniform hovered outside the vault door. *Volteen*, she thought. *Carlott sissiden nox, save me from that guard*. It might work. The two weren't far apart; the tech might reach him before he drew his gun.

The guard said, "We have a problem?"

"No," she said. "No, I'm okay."

"Time," the guard said. "Thirty seconds."

"Just relax," the tech told her. He stepped out. Shortly afterward, the vault door began to move. She expected it to clang but it closed as gently as a shadow. Then bolts fired like gunshots and she jumped. The echoes lasted forever and then all she could hear was her own breathing. *Harry*, she thought. *Harry, I may have fucked this up.*

The black speaker the tech had left on the floor emitted a burst of static. It took her a moment to realize it was talking. "*Jessshhhica.*" It sounded like he was broadcasting from the moon. "We're going to give you a few minutes to relax." Drenched in static, it sounded like: *relaxssschh*. "Please breathe normally and remain in a calm, natural state."

She began to peel the helmet from her head. Part of it resisted. When she finally got it off, she saw that it was the needle, which was four inches long and wet with clear fluid. She put that on the floor and tried not to think about it. There were thin wires coming out of the helmet in a bunch of places and she followed these to a tiny gray container strapped to the underside of her chair with nothing inside but a chip and a battery. Everything in this room was self-powered, she realized. The cage lights, the video cameras, the radio speaker. They were so careful to let nothing in or out, the room wasn't even wired. If that door didn't open in the next few hours, she would suffocate.

"I have some good news, Jessshhica. We can actually pay you a little more. One thousand dollarsshh for your time. How does that sssound?"

So the box would be on a timer. And these techs probably didn't have any control over it; they probably just knew when it was scheduled to open. Which meant there would be safety margins. A little time for everyone to get settled, which she could use.

"Think about what you might do with that thousand dollars, Jessshhica. Ssssomething pretty great, I bet."

She went to the video cameras but found nothing unusual. She carried them to a corner one by one and left them in a pile with their red eyes pointing at the concrete. Whatever happened here, she wasn't going to be in a show. She wasn't going to be watched and analyzed and used to improve procedures. She went back to the chair and circled it. But it was just a chair.

"Jussshht another minute, Jessica. Almossst there."

She knelt in front of the box. She touched it. Nothing terrible happened, so she ran her hands around it. It was warmer than she expected. She found a tiny seam in the steel but couldn't get so much as a fingernail into it and wasn't sure she wanted to. She didn't know what she was looking for. Options. But there weren't any.

She stood and paced. The only other thing was the speaker, so she went to that. To her surprise, it had a little compartment. Inside were red pills. She looked at these for a while. She did not think they were helpful.

"All right, Jessshica. It's time to open the boxsssschhh."

"Gahh," she said. She began to walk toward the box, but her heart failed her and she retreated back to the chair. "Fuck. Fuck." Something mechanical purred. The seam she had found cracked open and the top of the box began to rise. She squeezed shut her eyes and groped her way into a corner, curling up against the concrete and plugging her ears with her fingers. That song she'd heard the busker playing on the train platform with Eliot, "Lucy in the Sky with Diamonds"; she used to sing that. Back in San Francisco, before she learned card tricks. It was how she'd met Benny: He played guitar. Lucy was the best earner, Benny said, so that was mainly what she sang. She must have sung it five times an hour, day after day. At first she liked it but then it was like an infection, and there was nothing she could do and nowhere she could go without it running across her brain or humming on her lips, and God knew she tried; she was smashing herself with sex and drugs but the song began to find its way even there. One day, Benny played the opening chord and she just couldn't do it. She could not sing that fucking song. Not again. She broke down, because she was only fifteen, and Benny took her behind the mall and told her it would be okay. But she had to sing. It was the biggest earner. She kind of lost it and then so did Benny and that was the first time he hit her. She ran away for a while. But she came back to him, because she had nothing else, and it seemed okay. It seemed like they had a truce: She would not complain about her bruised face and he would not ask her to sing "Lucy." She had been all right with this. She had thought that was a pretty good deal.

Now there was something coming out of a box, and she reached for the most virulent meme she knew. "*Lucy in the sky!*" she sang. "*With diamonds!*"

Time passed and she did not die. She did not lose her mind. In the spaces between song words, she heard things. For this reason, she kept singing. Shrieking out the words. Then she caught a burst of static and realized it was just the tech, talking to her through the speaker. She didn't think she had to fear the tech. Only the box. So she lowered her voice, a little, and eventually unplugged one ear.

"*Ssscchtand* on one leg," said the speaker.

She removed her other finger from her ear. She didn't move for a while, in case the box was going to talk and she needed to replug her ears. But they had said they wanted her to *look* at something, hadn't they? Not listen.

"Toussscccchh your left elbow."

She began to feel her way across the concrete. When she reached the box, she felt her way up its side. Above the seam there was no more steel. She slid her hands over the lip and felt something cool and rigid. Plastic, maybe. She pressed against it. It yielded slightly, just enough to detect. She sat back on her haunches and thought about this.

"Now your right elbow, please, Jessica."

She crawled across the floor until she reached a wall and followed that to her pile of video cameras. She dragged one back to the box. It was probably catching glimpses of her. She confirmed the contours of the box, the plastic bubble that seemed to encase whatever was inside, and got to her feet and hefted the camera by its tripod.

"Take off your *sshoessssch*."

She raised the camera. *Like golf*, she thought. She swung and there was a glass explosion that told her she had missed the plastic. She adjusted her grip and tried again. This time she received a more satisfying sound. She put down the tripod and groped at the plastic, seeking damage.

"Sssssit down."

A scratch. A minor deformation. Not big enough to work with. But it was something. It was proof of concept. She got to her feet and raised the tripod again.

"Put your foot in your mouth as far as it will go."

She swung and swung until her arms ached and sweat ran down her face. She dropped the tripod, sure that she would find nothing but shattered plastic, but it didn't feel as ruined as she'd expected. Her hands moved over sharp plastic edges like rough knives. She began to pry these apart and force her hand between them.

"You want to run through the protocols again?" the speaker muttered. Then: "Okay. I'll finish."

Her middle finger touched something cool but she couldn't grip it. She pressed and it bit. "Ow," she said. "Ow, ow." It was sharp. Thicker than she expected. Irregularly shaped. She had been thinking *paper*, maybe *cardboard*, material on which a word could be inscribed, but this was neither. She began to work it out between the plastic knives.

"Jessschica, come over to the walkie-talkie. To where my voice is coming from."

The thing got stuck on the broken plastic mouth and she waggled it back and forth. She couldn't figure out what it was. And yet it felt familiar. She pulled with all her strength and heard a tearing, a ripping that she hoped mightily was plastic and not some vital part of whatever she was withdrawing. Then it popped free. She clutched it, panting.

"The speaker here has a compartment on the underside. Open this.

There are four red pills inside. These are cyanide pills. If you eat them, you will die. It's important that you know this. If you understand that eating the pills will kill you, nod."

She shrugged her denim jacket and wrapped it carefully around the thing. It probably would have been smart to keep track of which way it had been facing, in case it had a good side and a bad side—she was thinking of words written on paper again—but it was too late for that. When she was sure no part of it was showing, she opened her eyes. She was surprised by the room's size. In her imagination, it had grown enormous.

"Swallow all the pills."

Behind her was the box. Empty, she hoped, of whatever had been going to take away her mind and leave her amenable to the speaker's terrible instructions. But she was not going to test that theory. She looked at the bundle of jacket. It took an effort to do that. The thing seemed roughly book-shaped, but irregular and heavy. She stole a hand into the jacket and probed at its surface. Freezing. Like metal. She found a little protuberance with vicious edges, and realized this must be what had cut her, so at least she knew which way it faced.

The door bolts fired. She was out of time. Her fingers traced grooves, rough indentations in a smooth surface, and when her mind tried to piece these together, something thickened there and she withdrew her hand with a gasp. Nausea crashed over her. She felt herself beginning to faint and fought it, because that would be the end. *Here*, she told herself. *I'm right here.*

The room filled with light. A shadow appeared, bisecting the brightness. "Oh, God," said someone. The tech. She heard footsteps.

She began to unwrap the jacket. Years ago, in a hidden library at the school, she had read tales of mass enthrallment. Of towers and the splintering of language. Myths, she'd thought. Everything they'd taught her said there was no way to compromise everyone at once. The organization's words were keyed to particular psychographic segments; that was how they worked. And they did not push a p-graph flat. They did not trigger synapsis. Something that could do that was not a regular word. It was the kind of word from the tales. If anything was worth flooding a building with guys in black space suits who couldn't hear or see except through helmets, and burying in a concrete tomb with a time-locked steel door thicker than she was, she thought that would probably be it.

The man in the gray uniform rushed in, his gun drawn. The tech was just standing there, shocked. Her jacket dropped to the floor. Wood. She recognized the feel of it now. The thing was petrified wood. She pressed its back to her chest, keeping her eyes up. If she was wrong, now was when she would find out. That would be pretty hilarious. At this point, unless it was exactly what she thought, she was pretty screwed. She said, "Don't move."

The guard stopped. There was silence. In it, she started to believe.

"Touch your nose," she said. "Both of you."

Their hands rose. Her spine tingled. It was one thing to understand the concept. It was another to see it. She took a breath. That was the first part. Now for the next. She said, "Tell me how to get out of here."

TERROR LOCKDOWN

Large areas of Washington, D.C., are in lockdown this evening following what authorities have described as a significant terrorism event.

Tactical police, military, and emergency biohazard response teams have flooded the downtown area and a major search appears underway, prompting speculation that one or more terrorists remain at large.

The Metropolitan Police Department is advising all D.C. residents to stay where they are and avoid all nonessential travel. "The city is essentially in lockdown tonight. People will not be getting anywhere," said Chief of Police Roberta Martinez a short time ago. "I ask residents to bear with us during this time of crisis."

Authorities have yet to confirm whether an attack has taken place, saying only they are responding to "an incident." However, unofficial sources are fearful that a chemical or biological weapon has been deployed.

City workers described scenes of chaos as special operations soldiers and armored vehicles descended on the city.

"They were herding everybody out, these guys with black helmets, goggles; people were screaming," said Julia Treuel, 24, an office worker from iMax. "They looked like astronauts."

It is estimated that as many as five thousand troops may already be on the ground in D.C. with more en route as the hunt for the terrorists intensifies.

MORE TO COME

D.C. LOCKDOWN COMPENSATION CASE STALLS

D.C. Mayor Frank Viletti has for the first time ruled out the city compensating residents for losses incurred as a result of last month's two-day terrorism lockdown.

"We're very sympathetic to the residents and business owners inconvenienced, and we are doing and have done everything in our power to allow them to return to their normal lives as quickly as possible," he said at a press conference today. "However, with an incident like this that affects us all, we feel D.C. residents need to pull together and accept that some shared burden is inevitable."

The remarks seem to signal that the fight for payouts will not be resolved outside the courts. Law firm Vignotti & Busch, which controls the class action, could not be reached for comment.

During the conference, Mayor Viletti again denied early reports that the lockdown was sparked by the use of a chemical or biological weapon. "There was never any suggestion of that. What we had was forewarning of an imminent attack, and we took action to prevent it."

He was unable to provide further details, referring questions to the White House. Yesterday, White House spokesperson Gary Fielding reiterated that several people had been arrested during the operation, but that no further information could yet be released.

"What I will say is that we had a situation and our people responded brilliantly. We should all be proud of what our people did in D.C. last month."

From: http://nationstates.org/pages/liberty-versus-security-4011.html

. . . Like the DC lockdown last year. Like the gunmen who went around assassinating people with military-issue sniper rifles in 2003. Like the anthrax in the mail in 2006. For a week everyone freaks out, we need more security, we need scanners, we need to take people's photograph when they enter a government building. Then a month later everyone's calmed down and yet we still get these incredibly intrusive new processes and technologies, which would have made zero difference to the incident that inspired them. This isn't an accident; this happens because to people at the top, the scariest thing is how many people there are below. They need to watch us. They need to monitor what we're thinking. It's the only thing between them and a guillotine. Every time something like this happens, anytime there's death and fear and people demanding action, to them that's an opportunity.

[THREE]

One coffee shop in Broken Hill didn't have a view of the quarry. This was what Eliot had ascertained after three months of study: that the town offered coffee at five different locations and four stared at the quarry. He patronized the fifth. It wasn't that the quarry was ugly—although it was, deeply and thoroughly—but rather that it was everywhere. The town streets were wide, its buildings well spaced, the land as flat as any he'd seen, and this made it impossible to remain unaware of the forty-foot battlement of desiccated dirt and shattered stone that stood like a rib cage at the town's core. He kept taking it for a wave, a great rolling crest of vomited earth about to engulf the town. Which it was, in a sense; wind and erosion and the constant addition of new mullock must push it a little closer every year. Given time, it would swallow everything. This would be a serious improvement. That was another thing Eliot had ascertained, while waiting here in case Woolf showed up.

He sipped coffee and browsed the *Barrier Daily Truth*, an eighteen-page newspaper that came out weekly. This edition was leading with "Fifty Years of Happiness," a story about an elderly married couple. Eliot read it twice, searching for the part that was always missing in these kinds of articles, namely, how the hell that was possible. He was genuinely unsure whether these idyllic unions existed or people merely pretended because the alternative was so unpalatable. Every time he thought he'd settled on the latter, he would see something like this, "Fifty Years of Happiness," and start to wonder.

These were loose thoughts, of course.

His phone rang. He folded the paper. "Yes?"

"She's here. Coming down the Barrier Highway. White sedan. Alone."

"You're sure?"

"Got a lot of technology here, Eliot."

"Yes. Thank you. How long?"

"Thirty minutes."

"Thank you. I'll take it from here." He tossed a few bills onto the table, left the coffee shop, and walked to his car. Once the engine was running and the air conditioner moving, he made a few short calls. Just to confirm that everyone was where they were supposed to be. It had been three months since Woolf had fled Washington with a stolen word; everything that needed to be in place already was. But still. When it was done, he put the car into gear and drove toward the wall of mullock.

He drove about a mile out of town and parked his car to block the road. It was symbolic: Woolf would have no trouble steering around him. The idea was that seeing him would impress upon her the futility of continuing.

He climbed out and waited against the car. It was winter, supposedly. A rush of birds passed overhead, filling the air with their grating calls. Cockatoos. At dawn, the noise was incredible. Like the whole world was tearing apart. He was sleeping in a motel and one night woke to find an insect the size of his palm on the pillow. He didn't even know what it was. He had never seen anything like it.

He felt an urge to call Brontë. He had been thinking about her again. It was this assignment: too much time, too much waiting. It was

Woolf. Watching her kick down the walls planted the thought in his head that it could be done. *Call Brontë*, he thought. *Right. Ask how she's doing. No reason. Just felt like a chat.*

They had been students together, almost twenty years ago, attending the school that she now ran. He still remembered the bounce of her hair the day she'd come to class, the books clutched to her chest, the angle of her nose. He'd basically fallen in love with her on the spot. Well, no, that wasn't accurate; that implied a binary state, a shifting from not-love to love, remaining static thereafter, and what he'd done with Brontë was fall and fall, increasingly faster the closer they drew, like planets drawn to each other's gravitational force. Doomed, he guessed, the same way.

They'd held out a long time. Years? It felt like years. But maybe not. They had been seniors, anyway, not far from graduation. He knew this because Brontë had given him her words. A yellowed envelope, curling from use, and inside were dozens of slips of paper, each bearing a word.

"Use them," she said. The lights were off so they would be able to detect anyone approaching by the shadows thrown beneath her door. But he could see her face clearly enough. "I want you to compromise me."

He couldn't remember his own response. He might have tried to talk her out of it. Might have not. He'd thought a lot of things and it was too long ago to tell the difference between choices real and imagined. Almost all of his memory was about her: the way she lay back on the bed, her bare shoulders gleaming. Her face as he whispered the first words. He'd been clumsy, that first time. It had taken him a while to find the place between awareness and compromise, the sub-lucid state of low consciousness that laid the body open to suggestion. When he put her under too far, her face would slacken; when he brought her too close to the surface, her eyes would focus and she would tell him to do more. He touched her breasts and her nipples felt hard and urgent against his palm. Her hips rose from the bed. "Fuck me," she said.

"I want you to *fuck me.*" She whimpered and growled like an animal. He worried about the noise, said, "Quiet," and she began to hiss, a kind of noise he hadn't heard anyone make before. Goose bumps undulated across her skin. Waves followed the touch of his fingers. Her hips rose and fell, and when he touched her there she issued a high, barely audible keen, like escaping steam. He worried he'd broken her, and brought her up, and desperation flashed across her face and she begged him to take her down again. When he did, she gave a long sigh of satisfaction, a noise of complete unself-consciousness that signaled he was very close to the core of her. He moved his hand between her legs and into the wetness he found there. "In me," she said, the words becoming a chant, gasped into his ear over and over as her fingers clawed at his back, and he was unable to stop himself. He unbuttoned his pants. He entered her and the instant he did so, her body turned to iron, a thing made of hot steel. He climaxed within moments.

They lay together for hours. He knew he should leave before dawn, lest someone see him slinking from her room, but he couldn't bear to part with her. He held her as she gently rose toward full consciousness. They kissed. When light began to leak into the sky and he couldn't put it off any longer, he rose from the bed. She walked him to the door—her naked body in the moonlight, he would never forget that—and said, "Next time, I do you."

A cockatoo screeched from a nearby tree. He drew breath, exhaled. This was not a time for reminiscing. He would not be calling Brontë. It was ancient history. And it had ended badly. Or perhaps not badly, but not well. Then they had graduated and gone to different parts of the organization and that had been that. He had no idea whether she thought about that time anymore, whether she did so with shame or regret. It was impossible to tell. Impossible to ask, without exposing himself.

One day, I'll kiss her again. The corners of his mouth twitched. *One more kiss.* What a thought. Ludicrous. Still. There was no harm in fantasy. Not if he recognized it as such. He would let himself keep this one, he decided. It was a nice thought to have.

Two hours later, he heard tires crawl across dirt. A white sedan nosed around the corner. It was driving very slowly and stopped as soon as it saw him. The windshield was a solid sheet of sunlight. The engine died. The door opened. Woolf emerged. Emily. She was thinner.

He said, "I appreciate you stopping."

She raised a hand to her eyes and turned in a circle, scanning the terrain. She was wearing a dirty T-shirt and jeans. Possibly the word was tucked into her waist, although it didn't seem like it. Had she left it in the car? Maybe she already realized it was over.

"How did you cross the Pacific?" he said. "I ask because there's a pool going."

"Container ship."

"We searched a lot of those."

"You searched mine."

He nodded. "Fairly pointless, when people can't be trusted to report when they find you. It's why you're shoot-on-sight now."

She looked at him. Her expression was very measured, very controlled. If she'd been shedding her training, it wasn't evident. "So what are we doing, Eliot?"

"I'm sorry."

Her eyebrows rose. "Oh? You're here to kill me?"

He said nothing.

"Well, that's disappointing. Kind of extremely disappointing, coming from you."

"I thought you might respect it, coming from me."

"Yeah, you know what? Not so much. Not so much." She shook her head. "How about this, Eliot: You pretend like you never saw me. I go to Harry. Him and me disappear. End of story." She watched his face. "No? Not even that?"

"You must understand, I have no choice."

"I love him. Do you understand that?"

"Yes."

"If you did, you'd know I don't have a choice, either."

He said, "I can give you one hour. You can spend that with him. Then you say good-bye and you walk back down the road. That's the best I can offer you."

"And I decline your shitty offer. Three months I've spent getting here, Eliot. Three months. And they have not been easy months. I didn't go through that for an hour." She shook her head. "I think we should be clear on the fact that you can't stop me from doing anything I want."

"Where is it? In the car?"

"Yeah," she said. "Do you know what it is?"

"A bareword."

Her head tilted. "Is that what it's called? Huh. I just know what I read in old books. They didn't have a name for it. Or rather, they had lots of different names. The only thing those stories had in common was every time a word like this turned up, it was followed by mass enslavement. And death. Also towers, for some reason."

"You are describing a Babel event."

"This word compels everyone," she said. "Everyone."

"Yes."

"So let me ask you something, Eliot. Do you really think Yeats trusts you to bring it back? Because I only met him that one time, but it doesn't strike me as his style. It seriously doesn't. You ask me, how this plays out is you make it about halfway back to Adelaide and somebody runs you off the road. Somebody in a black suit and helmet."

"I will take it to Yeats," he said, "and Yeats knows that."

She squinted. "You're kind of spineless, Eliot. I'm just realizing. You present as badass, but you're weak as piss. That's a little local lexicon, if you're wondering. Holy hell. You would actually take this thing to Yeats and *give it up*. That's amazing to me."

He didn't respond.

"Fuck Yeats. Fuck him. He's not here. Do something unexpected for once in your life. You and me, right here, we have power. We have all the power we need."

"I'm not interested in power."

She sighed. "This has been a very disappointing conversation, Eliot. I'm not going to lie. I feel like I've gone past you." She began to walk back to the car.

"Stop."

"Or what?"

He went after her and put one hand on the car door before she could open it. It was more than he'd intended, but it was her final chance, and he wanted her to have it. "There are snipers. At a signal from me, they will drop you. If you attempt to remove any object from your person, or get back in the car, or strike me, they'll drop you. They'll drop you if you try to leave Broken Hill regardless of what I do. This is set. This is the reality you have created. The best I can do for you in this reality is to give you an hour before you die. Please take it."

Her eyes searched his. "You really don't get it. The basic concept of love. Of valuing something that you feel. You have no comprehension of that at all." She shook her head. "Let me go, Eliot."

So that was that. He stepped back, one step and then another, leaving her isolated for the snipers.

"Oh," she said. "Here we go."

Her hands plucked at her T-shirt. He closed his eyes and gave the signal, spreading his arms wide.

Nothing happened. No shots. No noise. He opened his eyes and she was there, arms at her side, her hands empty, just watching him.

"I've been scouting this town eight days," she said. "You and your people, you stick out like crazy here. You glow."

"*Vart—*" he said, beginning the sequence that would compromise her, and her hands moved in an odd way. He wasn't sure what she was doing and she threw one hand toward the windshield and it was a magician's trick, he realized, a dummy move to draw the eye, but his gaze had already shifted and the windshield was no longer obscured by the sun's reflection. On the dashboard was an object with something black twisting and crawling across its surface and the blackness kicked him somewhere in the core of his brain and everything went still. Something inside him revolted, a long way down.

"Lie down," she said.

He lay in the dirt. An ant crawled across the sand in front of his eyes.

"You could have helped me, Eliot. I gave you that choice." Her boots appeared before him. "But you chose Yeats."

The words rolled by him. They evoked no reaction. He was patient, waiting for the words that would tell him what to do.

"Lie still and don't talk or move until the sun rises the day after tomorrow. After that, I don't care what you do." Her boots crunched toward the car. "You and me are done, Eliot. Next time, I won't leave you alive."

The door slammed. The engine turned. The car rolled away.

The ant reached his nose and began to tentatively feel its way up. Eliot lay still. He breathed. He did not talk. He did not move.

She drove to the homestead in Eliot's car and killed the engine. The metal ticked as it cooled. She could see Harry's paramedic van, and the garden, which had gone to crap since she'd last been here. Through the living room window she could see the back of their sofa, the lamp in the shape of a dog, a corner of a table: small proofs of her old life. She looked at these awhile, because there had been times over the past three months when she had wondered if they existed.

She collected her satchel and climbed out into the blazing sun. She felt curiously fragile. Transparent. She ascended the steps and knocked. The thing was, if Harry wasn't pleased to see her, she was in kind of a tough spot. She was kind of completely fucked. He would be pleased to see her. She knew that. It was just hard to stop thinking about, since the consequences were so horrific. She shifted her weight from one foot to the other. She knocked again. Harry was here somewhere; she had made sure of that. She waited.

She left the front door to circle the house. The land was wide and empty of dust gyres that might signal he was out on one of the bikes. She peered in the kitchen window but saw only plates and cups. She tried the door and the handle turned. That meant nothing; it was never locked. She went inside.

"Harry?" She touched her satchel for reassurance. She felt tempted to pull out the word, in case there were poets lurking around corners, behind sofas. Crazy. There were no other organization people in Broken Hill. She had watched this town for a week. But still. "Harry?"

The living room looked like she'd left it yesterday. The sofa cushions were bowed: Harry had imprinted himself on one and she thought she could see a hint of herself, the briefer denizen, on the other. She had been here. She had affected things. She touched her forehead, because she was having trouble thinking. All her planning and he wasn't here. She should have considered what to do about that. But he should be here. An odd thought occurred to her: that he knew she was here, and that was why she couldn't find him. He didn't want to see her. "Harry," she said. She wanted to explain. She had been through a lot. She hadn't talked to him in three months because that was the only way to keep him safe.

Outside, three kangaroos bounded across the driveway, one after the other. The world felt uncertain. She was afraid. This was going badly, very badly indeed. She was beginning to think that after all her hopping, with the ground growing hotter beneath her feet, she might not make it to Harry after all.

She heard an engine. She ran to the kitchen and saw him bouncing across the earth on a dirt bike. He went right past the window without glancing and she didn't move because her body was staked to the floor. The tires chewed earth. He kicked the stand and came up the back steps. His eyes met hers.

She opened her mouth to say hello and he disappeared. She blinked. The back door burst open and he came at her like a train. She raised her hands and he crashed into her. She was enveloped by the scent of earth and motor oil. "Mother fuck!" he said. "How are you here?"

"I just am."

"Em!" He squeezed her until she thought she would pass out. "Jesus, Em!"

"Let me go."

"No."

She wound herself around him. "Where were you?"

"Me? Where was I? Where the fuck were *you?*" Her T-shirt moved. She realized he was undressing her.

"Wait. Wait."

"I have waited," he said. And she caved, because he was right, and so had she. He pulled her shirt over her head and threw it onto the counter. He pulled her to him by the waistband of her jeans. His mouth mashed hers. His hand dove into her pants. She knew she should stop him, because they wouldn't be safe until they were a thousand miles from here, but his fingers found her and she forgot about that.

"I missed you so much," she said.

She lay in the curl of his arm, slick and sated. She played with his hair. After a while, she poked him. "Harry." She scratched his chest. She wished she could do this forever. But she could not. "Harry."

He opened his eyes. His lips stretched, rubbery. "I thought you were a dream."

"I have to tell you something kind of crazy. And then we need to leave."

He sat up, smiling. "What?"

"This is hard to explain." She felt the need to put on some clothes. Her satchel was on the floor somewhere. She had a vague memory of leaving it with her pants. The most powerful weapon in history, she didn't know exactly where she'd left it. "There are people looking for me. I stole something from them."

"What did you steal?"

"It's . . ." she said. "It's a word."

"A word?"

"Yes. But not an ordinary word." She hesitated. "There are words that can persuade people. This one is very persuasive. The people looking for me, they want it back. They'll kill me for it. Kill both of us." His expression hadn't changed. "I wasn't supposed to come back here. I was supposed to never see you again. But I had to. That's why I stole the word. And it's taken me a long time to get here, but I made it. I know how this sounds, but you need to trust me. We need to leave."

"Are you high?"

"No. No."

"You stole a magic word?"

"Not . . . actual magic," she said. "I mean, yes, magic, in the classical sense, but not the way you mean it."

"I don't know what you're talking about."

"Just trust me. Will you trust me?"

"And leave?"

"Yes."

"For where?"

"It doesn't matter."

"I have to work this afternoon."

"That doesn't matter."

"Well, it does," he said. "I'm a paramedic."

"Harry," she said. "This thing I stole, it's probably the most valuable thing in the world. Do you get that?"

"You're freaking out, Em."

"I can prove it. Just come with me. When we're safe, I'll show you how it works."

"Look, no one's leaving, okay? I'm happy you're home. But you need to calm down."

She recoiled. "Harry—"

"I haven't seen you in almost a year. I haven't heard from you in three months."

"I was coming home."

"I didn't know that!"

"If you love me," she said, "trust me."

He threw back the sheets. "I'm going to work."

She didn't want to compromise him. She'd never wanted to do that: reach into the essence of who he was and change it. But she had known it might be necessary, and planned accordingly. "*Ventrice hasfal collimsin manning.* Get dressed and start packing."

He screwed up his face. "What?"

She blinked. Had she had mixed up his segment? Surely not. She knew him completely. "*Ventrice hasfal collimsin manning.* Get dressed."

"You sound fucking crazy."

She slid off the bed, unnerved. Harry's personality was unusual. He was close to the edge of his segment. But she couldn't have misjudged him that badly. She wasn't new at this. She wasn't new to him. She ran to the hallway and found her satchel. She withdrew the bareword from it and held it waist-high. She turned and his eyes moved to it and he grimaced. She felt further unsettled, because she hadn't seen anyone react like that.

"Do everything I say." She didn't say *ever,* because she loved him.

He looked at her. His expression was wrong. He was not compromised. He looked like he'd never seen her before.

"Em," he said. "I have a shift. Why don't you chill out until I get back."

She had the bareword facing the right way, didn't she? She resisted a tremendous urge to look down. Had it broken? Was it covered somehow? She ran her fingers over its grooves and nausea rose in her brain. It was there. "Harry," she said. "Harry."

He scooped up his pants. "Em, you need to get out of my way."

"Look at this. Do what I tell you."

He pushed past her.

"Harry!"

He grabbed his work bag from the living room and headed for the front door, buttoning his shirt. She ran to cut him off and thrust out the word. His eyes flicked to it and away. "Em. Please. Get out of the way."

She lowered the word. She couldn't believe what was happening. She'd thought she'd planned for everything. *Immune?* And yet a part of her wasn't completely surprised. *You knew he resisted persuasion. That was why you liked him.*

"Em. I'm serious."

"Don't you love me?"

"Em."

"Harry? Don't you love me? If you love me, *come with me*. Trust me and *come.*"

His eyes shifted. The thought bubbled in her brain, breaking into awareness: He didn't love her. Not like she loved him.

"I'm going to work," he said.

She raised the word. "*Love me!*" She knew it was useless but did it anyway. "*Love me!*"

He pushed her aside. Her back hit the wall and her breath escaped in a rush. He went down the steps and by the time she went after him, he was climbing into the van. She ran and kept running as he shifted into reverse, thinking—what? To throw herself under it? Something. But he shifted gears and the tires tore at the dirt and he drove away, leaving her in the dust, naked, with her stupid, powerless word.

She gathered her clothes. She found her shirt crumpled under the bed and her underpants in the sheets. She went to the bathroom and sat on the toilet and began to dress herself. She didn't know what to do. But she couldn't stay.

She left the house and climbed into her car. She put the satchel with the word on the passenger seat. She put her hands on the wheel. She felt stunned in some important part of her brain, stunned as in *estoner*, the French root that also meant *astonished*, a word used to describe sorcery. As if she was acting outside of herself.

She turned the key, put the car into gear. She didn't look in the rear mirror so she wouldn't have to see the house disappear. When she reached the place where the road split, the town in one direction, everything else in the other, she turned the car on Broken Hill and drove away. A green sign went by that said ADELAIDE 508 and she couldn't stop shaking. She slowed down to be sure of staying on the road. She could taste loss in the back of her throat so badly that she could vomit. She couldn't believe she was driving away.

She glanced in the rearview mirror and saw Yeats. She shrieked and braked. The car slewed off the road and was enveloped in dust. There was no one. She had just imagined Yeats for a second. She began to drive again, shaken, but kept glancing in the mirror and the feeling grew that she was forgetting something. Or remembering, rather. She thought she was leaving Broken Hill in terrible danger, and Harry, too, because of Yeats. Because Yeats had planned something.

She swung the car around. The tires slid in loose gravel but then she was pointed back at the town and she felt steadier. The closer she drew, the surer she felt that she was doing the right thing. She could feel the presence of Yeats. He was coalescing. She could almost smell him in the car. Around her were moving parts in a terrible machine, coming to smash Broken Hill flat. She pushed the needle and the car flew along the dirt road.

She wasn't too late. She could find Harry and warn him. Persuade him. She didn't know how but she knew it could be done. The first buildings crawled around the mullock wall and she perceived a hammer above them, a great and unspeakable force that was falling, falling. Yeats drinking tea. The image flashed into her mind from nowhere. Yeats with a teacup, looking at her. Fear spiked in her heart. She didn't know where that had come from.

She blew through the town and left the car halfway up a curb and ran to the emergency room. Harry's paramedic van wasn't there but she burst in anyway. The room was familiar and she felt safer. She touched her satchel for reassurance. She went to the reception desk, which was staffed by an older man with thinning hair and glasses. He'd worked there forever, although she didn't know why; he was permanently irritable. He always made her feel as if she were bothering him. She said, "I need to find Harry."

He looked down his nose. She was coming off as a little crazy. She looked like a woman who had spent months on a container ship and slept in the desert and left a man catatonic by the side of the road and had sex and been abandoned and was afraid of invisible hammers. "He's in the field."

"Where?"

He continued to eye her. "The field." He gestured nonspecifically.

"Miles," said a nurse, emerging from the corridor. "We're still looking for that second defib unit."

The receptionist turned. Emily leaned across the counter and caught his shirt. "Excuse me," she said. "It is extremely important that I locate Harry right this second."

He looked at her and she realized this was familiar to him: girls coming to the desk and saying, *Where's Harry, I need to see him.* She was merely the latest. "Please let go of me, Emily."

"No," she said. She could feel Yeats coming up behind her. "Tell me where he is."

"Security," said the nurse.

Emily reached inside her satchel and as her fingers touched the word's cold wood she abruptly remembered where she'd seen Yeats drinking tea. It had been in her DC apartment. She had been back awhile, at least a few months, and he had come to her. That was why she'd never felt alone. Because he had been there. He'd sat opposite her and sipped tea and told her things. At the end, before he left, he'd said, *Remember none of this until you next leave Broken Hill.*

A tall boy came and stood behind her. The security guard. He didn't grab her right away because they knew each other pretty well. She used to chat with him while waiting for Harry. He played football. But she couldn't concentrate on him because there were awful memories breaking free in her mind, surfacing in her consciousness like bloated corpses. *I wish to establish exactly what it is we have found,* Yeats had told her. *There are certain forms of testing that one can really only conduct, shall we say, live.*

The receptionist slid a pen and paper across the counter. "Leave him a note." He did not look completely unsympathetic. "I'll make sure he gets it."

"You have to get out," she said. "You all have to get out." She could use the word; they wouldn't believe her otherwise. But she could do it: could herd this entire freaking town into the desert. The only question was whether she could save them before Yeats's hammer fell.

She picked up the pen. She was surprised, because she hadn't meant to do that. It didn't make any sense to leave a note now. But she started writing anyway. *You are going to perform this test for me, my dear,* Yeats had said, and the first letter was *K* and she suddenly realized what was coming. She tried to pull back her hand but decided no, it was okay, she would just write this instruction first. Yeats wasn't coming. He was already here, inside her. She began to scrabble and claw for the part of her mind that wasn't her but her hand wrote KILL

EVERYONE anyway. She took the bareword from the satchel. She managed to close her eyes; she could do that. Her left hand found the bulge, the sharp protuberance that had cut her in DC, and her right impaled the paper upon it.

There was grunting. A slap of skin. "Get him off—" a woman said, and it became a choke. Footsteps. She set the bareword on the counter, the paper dangling from it. She wanted to rip it away, knock it over, obscure it in some way, but her mind said that was a bad idea and she could not convince it otherwise.

Someone hit her. She fell to the floor. She opened her eyes and saw a bright spot of her own blood. Her mouth was numb. Ahead, an older man with a cane rose from the waiting room seats, his eyes full of concern, but his gaze shifted to the thing above her head and everything about his face changed. He shuffled in a half circle to face the woman beside him, whom Emily knew as Maureen—she came into Tangled Threads sometimes to buy clothes for her niece—and he brought up his cane and swung it at her so hard he overbalanced.

Emily got to her feet. The receptionist had his hands around the nurse's neck. Emily took one step toward them and the security boy shot the receptionist and then the nurse, one after the other. Emily skidded and fell. She went on hands and knees for the seats, crawling for her life. Someone shouted, "Help in the ER, code black, code black," and within about two minutes every red-blooded male in the building would be in this room, Emily knew; that was how it worked here. She wanted to scream at them to get out, let nobody in here, but she had no words.

Finally she fled. She crawled beneath seats, and that as much as anything felt like murder. By the time she reached the doors, the room was full of howls. Like wolves.

Then the thing. Which at first seemed insignificant compared to what was happening, but she later came to understand was not. As she escaped the emergency room, Harry's white paramedic van jumped the curb. Harry stared at her through the windshield. Then his eyes shifted to the room behind her. His expression tightened, filling with purpose, and he threw open the van door. She got to her feet and backed away, her hands up, thinking he was coming to kill her, that somehow despite what had happened earlier he had succumbed to the word. But he ran right by her, and she realized the purpose in his eyes was his own. He was going to help.

She left. She made it two blocks before her gut clenched so badly she had to bend over. She gagged but nothing came out. A police car blew by, lights and sirens, heading for the ER. They would all go there: the cops, anyone trying to help, the injured. It would be endless. She broke into a shuffling run.

Her eye was burning. It felt like a hard prick of light in there. The thing was, when the van's door had bounced open, the glass had reflected the ER for a moment. It was only a flash. But she had the terrible feeling she had gotten something in her eye.

ARROGANCE AND DELUSION

Discussion Board 14 / Thread 21 / Post #43
In reply to: Post #39.
> *we learn nothing from God tearing down the Tower of Babel*

God didn't destroy the Tower of Babel! That's a common misconception.

Genesis 11:5-8:

> And the Lord came down to see the city and the tower, which the children of men were building.
>
> And the Lord said, *Behold, the people are one, and have one language; now nothing will be restrained from them which they have imagined to do.*
>
> *Let us go down and confound their language, that they may not understand one another's speech.*
>
> So the Lord scattered them across the face of the earth, and they left off to build the city.

This is often mistold as Man trying to build a tower to Heaven, which God knocks down as an object lesson in humility. But note:
(a) no destruction
(b) God says nothing about the tower at all

What moves God to action is the common tongue. The story of Babel isn't about hubris. It's about language.

[FOUR]

The helicopter moved through darkness and Yeats peered through the plexiglass at what lay below. Broken Hill was a small cluster of sulfurous lights, like a ship on an ocean of black glass. Occasionally he caught a tiny spark or glimmer, but those were the only signs that something was happening.

"Can't raise any of them," said a voice in his ear. He was wearing a headset; the voice belonged to Plath, sitting opposite him. "Eliot, the ground team, no one." She swapped headsets and began to bark into that one and Yeats returned his attention to the landscape. A circular pinprick of lights came into view, surrounding a depthless black hole, which Yeats recognized as the main quarry. He'd never seen it in person before; it was larger than he'd expected. When he'd first taken an interest, some decades before, following hints of something ancient and significant buried there, he could still make out remnants of the hill that had loaned the town its name. Now that was gone—not just erased but inverted, to become this great pit. He found this notable for the demonstration of force it represented. Civilizations rose and fell; what caused them to be remembered was not their contribution to knowledge or culture, not even the size of their empires, but rather how much force they exerted upon the landscape. This was what survived them. A hundred billion lives had passed without leaving a mark since the Egyptians had raised their pyramids, changing the world not figuratively but literally. Yeats admired that. This hole in Broken Hill was nothing, of course, but it would outlast every person on the planet.

"Okay," said Plath. "We've got buildings on fire now."

He looked. There was indeed a flickering.

"I have to say, I think we're operating at a high degree of probability that Woolf has deployed the word." Plath looked at him as if she expected a reaction here: if not an *Oh god no* then at least an *Are you sure*; some kind of response to validate her feeling that this was a shocking development, possibly the worst thing she could imagine.

"Horrible," he said.

"I mean, we're seeing bodies in the streets. Around the hospital, especially." She gazed out hopefully. "Maybe it'll burn down."

He considered this. It was rather important that the bareword not be lost to fire. That would be a serious inconvenience. But he was also interested in letting this scenario play out to its fullest, in order to gain maximum information from it. "Please don't let the hospital burn down."

"I'll monitor it. You know, we could send people in now. Stop this before it gets worse."

"No."

"It's just . . . there are three thousand people down there."

"If Eliot couldn't stop it, it can't be stopped."

Plath nodded, unconvinced.

"It is a great tragedy," he said. He overlooked this sometimes: the need to display empathy.

They circled the town. He watched toy vehicles run down tiny figures, plow into matchbox buildings. Sometimes there was a lull and the little shapes would head for the hospital, and it would begin again.

"I think we've found Eliot," Plath said. She muttered into her other headset for a few moments. "On a road a couple miles out of town. He's not moving. What do you want to do?"

"Take me there, please," he said.

"I can send a team."

Plath had been doing this lately: implying that Yeats might not know what he wanted. It concerned him a little, because it meant she didn't think he was acting rationally, and he needed her to think him rational for at least a while longer. "Thank you, but no."

The chopper tilted. He watched a dozen small tragedies play out below before they were obscured by the towering wall of soil and rock that marked the quarry's boundary. Dust blew around them. Plath unstrapped and pulled open the door. He hesitated, because he was wearing his Ferragamos, winged patent leather that would never be the same after contact with this land. But he had no other shoes. He stepped out.

Plath pointed, mouthing words he couldn't hear over the thundering of the blades, clawing at her hair. He began to walk, placing his feet carefully on the treacherous sandy earth. He was tempted to abandon the whole idea now. He was upset with himself for forgetting about his shoes. But he was committed: He couldn't change his mind now without risking revealing something about himself.

Plath caught up with him. She was wearing a perfectly charming pair of Louboutins but clomping along as if they were galoshes. Plath didn't mind ruining shoes, apparently. He hadn't known that about her. It changed a great deal.

They reached the road. The chopper had risen into the air and its spotlight helpfully swung right, so he began to trudge in that direction. Plath fiddled with an earpiece. "Still no sign of Woolf," she said. "I assume she's still kill-on-sight?"

"Oh, yes," he said. "And I expect this to be quite a lot easier to accomplish, now she no longer has the word."

"*If* she no longer has it. She could be in the hospital still, for all we know." Plath bent to one knee. Yeats kept walking. When Plath caught him again, her strappy heels dangled from one hand. "I should not have worn these shoes."

"No," he said.

"I bet she's in there," Plath said. "Compromising people as they come in."

"Please don't assume that," he said, because that was all he needed, Woolf slipping away while everyone watched the hospital. He was quite certain Emily was nowhere near, because he had instructed her not to be. She had deployed the word and left, so that once this was all over, he could recover it.

"Is that . . . ?" Plath said, trailing off as the spotlight shifted and made speculation unnecessary. Across the road lay a car; before that was Eliot. Yeats couldn't tell whether he was alive or dead. "Jesus, she's killed him. Woolf killed Eliot."

He approached to within a few feet. Eliot's coat flapped in the chopper's downdraft. Yeats studied his face. After a moment, Eliot blinked. "No," Yeats said. "Compromised, I believe." He felt his skin crawl. An emotional reaction. Odd. But it was unnerving to behold: Eliot, disabled. Of all the poets, if he were to select the most difficult to compromise in the field, he would choose Eliot. He *had* chosen Eliot.

"We need some people down here right away," Plath told her radio. "Eliot's catatonic."

In the distance, a siren wailed. It felt like a song, like the word calling to him. It was waiting. He need only collect it. He stood very still, studying his own reaction, because there was no mistaking that he wanted it.

"Yeats?" said Plath.

His mouth felt dry. A slight tingling in his palms. He had considered many outcomes for this day, but not the possibility that he would be moved.

"We're going to want to move. We've got emergency services inbound from two directions."

"A moment," he said. He closed his eyes. He could perceive the danger now, the crevice that had swallowed those who came before him. And he could see what needed to be done. He opened his eyes and turned to Plath. To his surprise, she was in the process of snapping a heel from her shoe.

He wasn't himself; she saw something on his face. "It broke," she explained. She tossed the heel into the night. Yeats heard it land. Plath began to wedge her feet back into her butchered Louboutins. "Ridiculous things."

When they were away from here, Yeats decided, and safely back at the hotel, he would visit Plath. He would enter her room and wake her gently and make her fuck her shoes. These Louboutins. It would serve a dual purpose, testing his ability to remain unaroused and teaching Plath proper respect for good footwear.

"I can't understand what motivated Woolf to do all this," Plath said. Men in black jogged out of the darkness and began to heft Eliot.

"We may never know," Yeats said.

Harry ran down the main street, leaving the hospital, the emergency room, and many, many people who needed medical attention. He had tried to help. He had stayed long enough to bandage the jugular of Maude Clovis, who tried to scratch his eyes out as he worked. He had seen Ian Chu from Surgery cut three more jugulars with a scalpel, moving methodically from one person to the next, his eyes carefully judging each attack. He had seen Jim Fowles, a twenty-year cop, bring in a kid with a bleeding head and draw his revolver and execute that kid right there on the floor.

That was when Harry decided to leave. What he was doing, stabilizing these people, that wasn't helping them. That was only delaying. He stood and Fowles turned to him. The only reason Harry had not died then, under Fowles's calm, unsmiling eyes, was that Chu chose that moment to step behind the cop and delicately draw the scalpel from left to right. Fowles gurgled and Chu plucked the revolver from him with his long surgeon's fingers and turned it over, testing its weight.

Then he had left. He ran, because all he could think was *Emily*. There was chaos outside but he ran through it. He found her vomiting over the rail of a traffic bridge. He caught her by the arm and hauled her around. Her face was ashen, her pupils dilated, like a junkie's; for a moment, he barely recognized her. "I'm sorry," she said. "I did it. I did it." She wrapped her arms around her head and moaned.

"We have to get out of here." He was trying to think of vehicles. Something off-road. If he could get back to the house, they could take the bikes. "People are going crazy."

"It's the *word*!" she screamed. She got to her feet and took two steps back toward the hospital, then veered around, clutching her head. "I'm sorry. I'm sorry."

"Em," he said. But he knew what she was talking about. That ridiculous piece of wood, with the black symbol, that she'd waved at him back at the house like it was a magical talisman. Like it could command him to obey her. He'd seen it in the ER with a piece of paper tacked to it that said KILL EVERYONE. At the time, it had not been the strangest thing in the room. "Your word? It *works*?"

"I can't stop it," she said. "He won't let me."

He left her and ran back toward the hospital. He was still a hundred yards away when he saw the two police cruisers parked outside. People clawed and reached, spilling over the cars, filling the air with cries. Harry had intended to go in there and get that piece of wood, hack it into a million pieces, but that was clearly going to be very dangerous. He hesitated at the intersection. A car purred behind him and his brain finally registered this as a danger and he threw himself out of its way. It blew by close enough to tug at his clothes and hit one person, then another, and crashed into one of the police cruisers. Its engine revved. Harry could see the driver tugging at the shifter, trying to get the car into gear. A cop came out of the ER and jogged up to the driver and shot him through the window.

He noticed a figure approaching from the side of the hospital, carrying a cleaver. Harry recognized the someone as an orderly. And the cleaver was not actually a cleaver; it just looked like it. It was a bone saw. "Jack?" Harry said, wondering how, exactly, he was supposed to tell the difference between a person carrying a bone saw for self-defense and one who wanted to saw him open with it, and the orderly broke into a run at him, which answered the question. Harry contemplated running but instead opted for waiting for the orderly to get close enough to punch in the face and disarm. This was an option because the orderly was a thin teenager who played a lot of video games, while Harry was not. He looked at the bone saw. But he couldn't fathom a use for it, and the orderly started to get up, so Harry punched him in the jaw hard enough to keep him down. Then he did run, because more people were emerging from the hospital's rear, nurses with whom Harry had frequently shared coffee, and, in one case, a bed, and he did not want to face them.

When he returned to the traffic bridge, Emily had vanished. He turned in a circle, cursing. He didn't know what to do. Ahead, the street looked clear. To the left, a small group wandered in his direction, one limping. To the right, not far, a woman lay motionless in the gutter. In the streetlights, her hair looked yellow. She was the only thing in this landscape he could understand, so he went to her. He knelt and checked her vitals. Beth McCartney, the town librarian. Her hair was sticky with dark fluid. His fingers found a depression in her skull about the size of a tennis ball. He sat back on his haunches and exhaled.

The group approached him. He recognized the local math teacher, his two daughters, and a woman who ran a little grocery store. Two teenage boys supported the limper, who was a broad-shouldered guy Harry knew as Derek Knochhouse. Harry had pumped Derek's stomach twice in the past six months. Both times, he had looked better than this. He could tell without touching him that Derek had a shattered pelvis.

"Thank Christ," said the schoolteacher. "Harry, you have to help us."

"What's happening?" said the grocery store owner. She was clutching her necklace, a crucifix. "Oh God, is that Beth?"

"We have to get Derek to the hospital."

"Car came out of fucking nowhere," said one of the teenage males. "Fucking *took aim*. Then it reversed over him."

"*Hnk*," said Derek.

"We've gotta get him to the hospital, Harry."

"You can't take him to the hospital," he said. "It's not safe."

"Then where? What should we do?" One of the schoolteacher's daughters tried to push Derek's hair out of his eyes. Derek coughed and spat meatily.

"Find a place you can lay him still and barricade yourself in until this is over."

"Until *what* is over?" said the girl. He could see she was looking for a reason to give in to complete hysteria, and this could be it. "Until *what*?"

"He plays footy," said one of Derek's friends. Harry didn't know what possible reason the kid had for volunteering this, then realized he was saying it was a tragedy. Derek played football and now would probably never be the same again. It was the worst thing the kid could imagine.

"He's got internal bleeding, I think," said the math teacher. "What do you think, Harry?"

"Is that *Beth*?"

"Yes," Harry said. "She's dead, and I'm sorry, Derek, but nobody can go near the hospital. They're killing people."

They began to argue with him. He looked for Emily. He was becoming increasingly nervous about where she was.

"Police!" said the girl. She broke from the group and ran down the road, waving her arms, the sleeves of her dress flapping. A cop car was sailing toward them, its lights dark, covered in dents. "Over here! Help!"

Harry called out to her and there was a hard, flat sound and the girl folded up and lay on the road. The cruiser continued toward them.

"What?" said the kid.

"Go," Harry said. "Move. Run."

The girl's father, the schoolteacher, stared at her with his lips apart. In the streetlight, tiny visible hairs all over his face stood on end. Harry had seen this reaction once before, when a fellow paramedic helped him peel open a wrecked car to find her husband inside. He'd had to wrap her in a space blanket, because she froze. She literally froze. Like she'd fallen into ice. It had been the strangest thing he'd ever seen.

"Jess?" said the kid. He wasn't calling. It was a question for the group. The cop car drew closer.

"*Run*," Harry said, and shoved the schoolteacher. He pulled the other girl, the dark-haired one, by her wrist. There was another flat retort. He was tempted to see who that was, the father or possibly Derek Knochhouse, but it made no difference. The girl screamed and twisted in his grip in a way that meant it could have been either, and then he did turn, and saw the cop with one hand on the steering wheel, the other resting his service revolver on the crook of his arm, his eyes moving between the road and the people he was shooting.

The grocery store woman trilled like a bird and sat heavily. The father was already spread out, arms folded, as if he'd carefully lain down. One of the kids had fled but the other was dragging Derek, the one who'd said *he plays footy*, and Harry shouted at him to run but of course the kid didn't. Harry tripped on the curb, which was a handy reminder to keep an eye on where the fuck he was going, losing his grip on the dark-haired girl. She began to walk back toward the cop car, her arms out, in order to accomplish what, Harry didn't know. He spat a curse and went back for her. Then he saw Emily.

She was walking down the center of the road. He couldn't see her face because the streetlight was behind her. There was an appeal in her posture, which he first thought was directed at him, then realized wasn't, because she was angling toward the police cruiser.

The dark-haired girl spun in a half circle. Harry ran by her falling body. He leaped onto the hood of the police cruiser, skid across, and hit the tarmac on the other side. He reached Emily and threw her over his shoulder. He heard the whine of the cop's power window behind him. The closest shelter was a bakery, a squat weatherboard much too far away. He jagged, to put a degree of difficulty into it for the cop.

"Put me down," said Emily.

Ten feet from the bakery door, something bit his ear. The glass door shattered. He kept going and crashed through it, tripping and sprawling onto the tiled floor, feeling bullets everywhere, losing Emily. The interior was lit by a refrigerated drinks cabinet. "Em." He crawled toward her in the corpse light. "Emily." He found her hand and got to his feet and hauled her up.

"I want to die."

"No," he said. He dragged her into the back room. His hip clipped a table; a stack of baking trays clattered to the ground. He found the rear door and discovered it was bolted in several different ways, some of which required keys. He released Emily and shook it. "Fuck," he said. He abandoned the door for a smaller, metallic one, with a horizontal handle like a refrigerator's. Chill air spilled around his ankles. He pulled Emily inside and closed the door and groped in darkness for a lock. But there wasn't one, of course. You didn't put a lock on the inside of a cool room. The door didn't even open the right way—that is, in a way he could block. He gripped the handle and planted his feet and cursed. Maybe the cop wouldn't chase them. There were plenty of other targets. He listened, straining for sound. The door was so thick, the cop could be right outside. He relaxed his muscles, for the moment when he'd need them. There was a snuffling. Emily was crying. "Em," he said. "Be quiet."

"I'm sorry."

"Quiet."

She kept crying. "I did something really bad."

"I know. Shut up." He thought he heard something outside. But it could be anything. It was incredibly cold. Too cold for a permanent hiding place.

"I should have been able to stop it."

The handle turned in his hands. He resisted. After a moment, the opposing force vanished. He waited in the dark. Something hit the door, hard and sharp. A bullet. Then two more. He held the handle with one hand and flailed in the dark with the other, trying to push Emily down. A sizzling smell reached him. Light bled through three holes in the door. He hadn't thought a steel-lined refrigerator door would be bulletproof, but the confirmation was still disappointing. He found Emily's hair and yanked it. She squawked but then he had her wrapped in one arm while he held the handle with the other, hoping the cop would please not shoot off his hand. For a while there was only their breathing. He heard the cop moving around, doing who knew what.

"Does it wear off?" he said. "The word?"

"No."

"Jesus fuck."

"Why are you trying to save me?" He ignored this because it was a stupid question. Something outside went: *fwick*. "I thought you didn't love me."

"Quiet." He saw a flicker. Only a glimmer through the holes in the door, but it was enough to recognize: The cop was setting the bakery on fire.

"I got everything wrong." In the dark, she cried brokenly.

He could see it in his mind: the cop hanging back, leaning against a door frame, gun aimed at the cool room. The second Harry popped open this door, the cop would shoot him. Maybe the fire wouldn't catch. Maybe the cop would give up and go away. Or maybe not. Because it wasn't KILL A BUNCH OF PEOPLE, was it? It wasn't KILL AS MANY AS IS CONVENIENT.

"There's something in my eye," Emily said.

He could hear crackling. The cool room was growing brighter. "Em, I need to open the door." She had her head in her hands. "*Emily.* Listen to me. Wait here until I call for you. Understand? Do not move until I call your name." Was there anything out there he could use as cover? Something he could throw? Yes. Yes, he would hurl a baking tray at the cop, and it would deflect the bullets, and dazzle him with its reflection of the flames, which of course he would have to run through, and then he would disarm the cop with his superior hand-to-hand combat training. "Are you fucking listening to me?" He resisted the urge to take her by the shoulders and shake her.

"Please just leave me, Harry."

He could feel the heat through the walls. The cop must have moved by now. Retreated to the storefront, at least, maybe right out to the street. The greatest danger now was waiting too long, until there was nowhere to go except into an inferno. He released the handle and pried Emily's hands from her face. For a moment, he thought he really did see something in her eye, but it was only the dancing reflection of flames. "Em. You are pissing me off. But I will never leave you. Ever. So stop talking. We're getting out of here." He wound his fingers into hers. "Ready?" She stared at him. "Sure you are," he said. He scooped her up. Her arms around his neck were stiff as poles. He took a breath, watching the door, the flames flickering behind it. He kissed her, because fuck it, he was probably about to die. Then he kicked open the door and the fire roared like a living thing and he ran into it.

She woke in a bed. No. Wrong. On a stretcher. Something portable. She was in a room full of stretchers and it smelled bad. Burned. Wait. That was her. She was singed. She put her hand to her hair and it felt very wrong.

The room was very bright. Beyond wide windows, sunlight leaped from the chrome of half a dozen muscular vehicles, Humvees and trucks and Jeeps. Beyond those was endless rolling earth. She was encircled by a colorful strip of paper on which were letters and numbers and puppies and dinosaurs and elephants. The walls were lined with posters about Brazil and global warming. Beneath the windows were desks, all pushed together. It was a classroom. She was burned, on a stretcher, in a classroom.

"Oh," said a woman. "You're awake."

Emily didn't know this woman. Which was odd, because Emily knew everyone in Broken Hill. Also, the woman was wearing fatigues, like a soldier. She came closer and checked Emily's tubes. Emily had tubes. They ran from the insides of her elbows to plastic bags on a trolley beside the bed.

"How do you feel?" Before she could stop her, the woman peeled up one of Emily's eyelids with her thumb. "You're in Menindee. It's a little town outside Broken Hill." A patch on her khakis said: NEILAND, J. "We're using the school as a hospital. Are you in pain?"

Her hands were wrapped in bandages. Like big mittens. There were three other stretcher beds in the room but none were occupied. She tried to sit up. She remembered fire, smoke. Harry carrying her through it. She had passed out. Then she had been flying, skimming across the earth, and bouncing, being held by Harry on a dirt bike. She had seen kangaroos fleeing flames. "Where's Harry?"

"The man who brought you in?"

"Yes," said Emily. "Yes, yes."

"He's up the hall. They're working on him."

"Is he all right?"

"Just relax," said Neiland.

She almost asked, *Are you a dog person or a cat person?* Because she really wanted to know if Neiland was telling the truth. "Who else?"

"Who else what?"

"Made it," she said. "Out." She was a little freaked out by the empty stretcher beds.

Neiland didn't answer. Emily felt ice in her heart, a thin sliver, like a stiletto. She put her face in her mitten-hands. Her eye hurt. "I'll tell them you're conscious," said Neiland. "For now, rest."

Once Neiland had left, Emily climbed off of her stretcher. There were tubes to take care of, which she did with her teeth, because her mitten-hands were useless. She was in a green smock, which flapped at her ankles and admitted a breeze at the back. Beneath this she suspected underpants and bandages. She felt padded. She peered out a glass panel on the classroom door and saw nobody so she opened it. A passing soldier pointed at her and said, "Get back inside," not slowing, and she said, "Okay," and closed the door and waited until he was gone. The hallway floor was warm. The adjoining classrooms were empty. Farther down the hall, behind a window almost completely obscured by posters, she saw soldiers wearing face masks around a gurney. On the gurney lay someone wrapped in odd gray packages and bandages. The person's face wasn't visible but she could see a forearm, blackened and blistered, and knew it as Harry's. She covered her mouth.

One of the soldiers in face mask saw her and gestured, and Neiland turned and frowned at her. Emily went to the door and tried to open it with her elbows. Neiland pushed it open. "Back to bed," Neiland said in a low, no-nonsense voice, almost poet-like, which gave Emily a small start. "Bloody hell, did you remove your drip?"

"Let me sit with him," Emily said, but without the baritone or the persuasiveness, and Neiland took her arm and marched her down the hall. "Please," Emily said. But Neiland did not engage. She took Emily back to her classroom and deposited her on the bed. "I want to sit with him."

"He'll be okay," Neiland said. "Stop worrying."

For some reason this caught Emily unawares and she began to shake. She couldn't even say thank you.

"You love him?"

"Yes," she said. "Yes, yes."

"He was half-dead when he made it to the perimeter. Hard to believe he kept going. He wanted to save you very much." Neiland gently forced her to recline. "Rest. If anything changes, I'll let you know."

She let herself be forced. "Okay."

"Everything will be fine," Neiland said, and sunlight flashed from a car outside the windows. It was a low black sedan, very different from the other vehicles, its windows tinted dark. It pulled alongside a truck and stopped.

She sat up. "How long have I been here?"

"About four hours."

"I need to see Harry." The sedan's door opened and a woman in a suit emerged, pushing back her hair. Emily had seen this woman once before, years ago. Her name was Plath. "Are you a dog person or a cat person?"

"Excuse me?"

"Dogs or cats? Which do you like more?"

"Dogs." Neiland rose. "Now sleep."

"What's your favorite color?"

"Mauve," said Neiland, one hand on the door, and there was no time for further questions. Emily had spent a grand total of about five minutes with Neiland, and there were twenty-odd segments to which she could feasibly belong, but Emily had spent time piecing together psychographics from first principles and had a strong feeling about fifty-nine.

"*Vecto brillia masog vat*," she said. "Come back here."

Neiland swiveled in mid-step. "Thank you," Emily said. "Thank you, thank you; take me to Harry."

She followed Neiland back to the other classroom and approached the gurney while Neiland invented convenient excuses for why the doctors or medics or whoever these face-masked people were to leave. Neiland had said Harry would be fine, but he was swathed in layers and layers and the only parts she could see were swollen and red. His eyes were beneath soft white circles and she wanted these off. "Wake him up," she told Neiland. "But please be careful."

She reached for his fingers, which were poking out from gauze, but of course her hands were encased as well. "Harry, can you hear me? We're going to get out of here." Neiland finished pushing fluid into

Harry's drip and Emily set her to unwrapping her mitten-hands. They looked worse than she'd expected: Her fingers were cracked and blackened, the crevices between them oozing pink fluid. She took Harry's hand and it hurt but it felt better, too. "When he's awake, help me get him to a car. We don't want anyone to see us. You have to get us out of here and not let anyone stop us, understand?"

"Yes," said Neiland.

He made a noise. She peeled one of the white circles from his eyes and then the other. His eyes moved beneath the lids. "Harry, wake up."

The door opened. She turned. In the doorway stood a soldier she hadn't seen before, a young guy with a buzz cut. His eyes were focused and intent.

"Oh, shit," she said. "*Vecto brillia masog vat*, don't let the guy near us."

The soldier ran at them and Neiland moved to intercept. They exchanged flat, wordless blows and fell to the floor and Neiland got him in a headlock and began to wind surgical tubing around his throat. Emily was surprised and impressed by Neiland's badassery. She returned her attention to Harry. He was swimming somewhere beneath consciousness like he was under glass. "Harry, please wake up. You have to wake up. I can't get you out of here by myself."

Neiland and the soldier crashed into a trolley, scattering surgical equipment. The soldier got free of Neiland and his eyes fell on Emily. She abruptly saw that this wasn't going to work, her whole escape plan; this guy was going to knock out Neiland and throttle her and Harry, or not even that—the noise alone would bring more people than she could handle, people and soldiers and Plath. She felt panic. "Kill him!" she said, because maybe Neiland wasn't going full throttle. It seemed to make a difference, because Neiland picked herself up and punched the soldier in the throat in a way that dropped him immediately. "Kill everyone who tries to stop us," Emily said, and something in her mind leaped, and she realized what she'd said.

She felt undone. She felt the realization sinking into her: that she had finally done it, found a way to screw up so badly there was no way back. She had gotten a star in her eye. There were who knew how many people dead in Broken Hill and Yeats had put instructions in her head and she had carried them out. She couldn't believe, in her core, that she wasn't responsible. She had killed people and now there was a star in her eye that wanted her to kill more.

"I'm sorry," she told Harry. She began to cry, partly for herself and partly for Harry, who had tried so hard. Neiland and the soldier grunted and gasped. Emily leaned over and kissed Harry on each eye. "I love you."

His eyes moved rapidly, as if in REM sleep. She hesitated. "Harry," she said. She saw a response, a tiny neuroelectrical spark. It reminded her of DC, when she had sought out examples of psychographic segments and tested word fragments on them. Back then she had reverse-engineered entire words.

Harry was immune. But maybe he was only immune to the words she knew about. Maybe he was nothing more than a slightly different kind of machine, a psychographic segment of one, which the organization hadn't targeted only because they didn't know about it.

"*Ko*," she said. She watched his eyelids. "*Ka. Toh.*" She knew him very well. She understood which movements were his. "*Kik.*" A muscle above his lip jumped. She almost gasped. Her mind moved with possibilities, sifting conjugations. "*Kik*," she said again, to be sure.

The soldier gargled. She glanced down and saw that his face was purple. Neiland was choking the life from him. She returned her attention to Harry, ignoring everything except the forty-eight muscles around his eyes. She fed him sounds. She built her way to an attention word and that was a good start but not enough. She didn't know how much time was passing. She focused on the words.

None of this was going to save her. She knew that. It was too late for her, and had been from the moment the door to the paramedic van had bounced open and reflected the bareword. But it was not too late for Harry.

When she was done, she touched his face. "Harry," she whispered. "*Kikkhf fkattkx hfkixu zttkcu.*"

He changed. She had seen people fall under compromise a hundred times but never him and a part of her died to see it, his face slack, his mind open and waiting for instruction, his soul reduced to machinery. She could say *run away with me* and *do everything I ever tell you* and *love me forever* and he would. She would be loved by the thing she had made him into.

"Forget all of this," she told him. "Get away from here, forget me, forget you ever lived in Broken Hill. Become someone else. *Kikkhf fkattkx hfkixu zttkcu*, forget me."

She stumbled away from the gurney. She couldn't bear to look at him. Neiland was standing there like a statue, which surprised her. The buzz-cut soldier was on the floor, not moving.

"Neiland," Emily said. "Thank you."

Neiland waited.

"Take him away," she said. "Keep him safe."

Once Neiland had put Harry into a Jeep and Emily had watched it speed away into the dust, she returned to the classroom in which she'd awoken and searched around for a marker. Classrooms always had markers. She found a drawer full of colorful ones and took a fistful and went looking for a bathroom. There were many people running around and shouting, but they were mostly outside, drawn by Neiland's departure. She did not see Plath and was concerned about that, because the worst thing that could happen right now was Plath finding her.

She found a girls' restroom with a long counter and low sinks, for children. She gripped a blue marker in her fist, like a toddler, and began to scrawl on the mirror. The first word was *vartix*. This had left her slack-jawed in her dormitory room once, but she had been a good student and done her exercises and was not seventeen anymore, so she managed to get through it, pausing between letters to blink at the ceiling and clear her mind. She completed *vartix* and kept her eyes averted from it while she wrote the second word, and the third, and fourth, and then she had to gag into the sink for a while. But she had done it. She picked up the marker again, and, keeping her head down, added: DIE.

She closed her eyes. She took two steps backward. She breathed. It would only work if she lowered her defenses. *I am cared for*, she told herself. *I am safe.* She felt her muscles loosen. She swallowed. *Open your eyes. Open your eyes.* She began to do it and squeezed them shut again. *Do it*, she said. *Do it, you bitch—you know if they find you they'll make you tell them about Harry! Do it! You deserve it!* Then she began to cry.

She groped toward the counter and found the marker. She kept her eyes away from the command words and located DIE and added a D. Before that, she wrote HARRY. Before she could change her mind, she walked away and then she looked back.

She was sitting on tiles. Bathroom tiles. Her mind felt bruised. She had the feeling that someone had just compromised her.

Menindee. Of course. Harry had brought her here. He had dragged her out of Broken Hill and saved her life. But then—

"Oh, no," she said. Harry had died. They hadn't been able to save him. She had seen him die on the gurney. A wail burst out of her and she forced it down because Plath was out there. The whole organization was probably looking for her. She closed her fist around her grief and made it anger. There would be time for grief later. The point here was that Harry had wanted her to live. She had to survive. She would flee, and hide, and live, because she was good at that. Then she would find a way to return to Yeats and make her vengeance terrible.

But first. She got to her feet and tried to think how the hell she was going to get out of here.

MEMO

8th Combat Service Support Battalion
Royal Australian Army Medical Corps
SEC: UNCLASSIFIED
ENGAGEMENT: BROKEN HILL, NEW SOUTH WALES
DEPLOYMENT + 28 HRS

Confirming as per request AWOL status of Medic First Class NEILAND, JENNIFER C. Last signed on station E04, Menindee, NSW (-32.400105, 142.411669) at 0600 13/3, no sign off, no contact for 12 hrs ongoing.

Hesitant to put this one in the system as Neiland has been a model soldier with no prior signs of dissent dissatisfaction etc. Does not appear among any of the dead and wounded but frankly feeling that is more likely than abandoned post.

Given current state of ops around Broken Hill in general and station E04 in particular recommend delaying action until we have a clearer situation report. Still highly disrupted here with orders to hold back all personnel from Broken Hill, reports of mass casualties inside town, possible toxicity, confused comm chain due to apparent complete loss of first-entry squads etc.

Appreciate concern for process but recommend stalling until improved sit rep.

WARRANT OFFICER CLASS ONE F. J. BARNES
8 CSSB, RAAMC

[IV]

I cannot live with You—
It would be Life—
And Life is over there—
Behind the Shelf

—EMILY DICKINSON

[ONE]

Wil shouldered open the emergency room doors. After the darkness, the sunlight felt like an explosion. He gasped air. He made it to the white paramedic van and leaned against it. In one hand he had the thing. It was dark inside, but he hadn't had trouble spotting it. A piece of wood, about the size of a book, with a piece of yellowed paper speared to it. He had left the paper in there. The wood was heavier than it looked and frigid to the touch, like it wanted to leech the heat from his body. There was a symbol on it that looked like nothing he had seen before, and the more he looked at it, the more something in his gut twisted, and his eyes watered, until he looked away. But it did not change him. It was true. He was immune.

He headed back to the Valiant. Then he stopped, because he couldn't show this thing to Eliot. Eliot had been very clear about that. He glanced around for something to wrap it in. The doors of the paramedic van were open. He peered inside and found a small towel and shook the sand out of it.

When he reached the car, Eliot's eyes were closed. Wil pulled open the door. Eliot's chest hitched and his eyes peeled open. "I did it," Wil said. "I got the word."

Eliot blinked.

"Right here," he said, raising the towel, but Eliot's eyes squeezed shut. "It's okay! I covered it up. It's a kind of symbol on a—" Eliot's head jerked left and right. "I'm not telling you details! I'm describing the general kind of object!"

"Ssss," said Eliot.

"I know what happened here. Why everyone died. There was something stuck to the word that—"

"Ssss!"

"Okay! I'm just saying, if you look at this thing, you won't *die*. It's not *fatal* anymore." This didn't seem to make any difference to Eliot. "You look terrible. Have you been drinking the water?" He spotted a bottle near Eliot's feet, the lid off. The mat was wet. "Jesus, you haven't." He leaned over Eliot, looking for the other bottles. The smell in the car was very bad. "Drink." He twisted the bottle's top and held it to Eliot's lips. Eliot's throat clicked. His Adam's apple bobbed. When water spilled down his chin, Wil lowered the bottle and waited until Eliot no longer seemed to be drowning. Then he said, "More," and tipped it forward again.

"Gguh," said Eliot.

"I have an idea. We drive to a hospital. A hospital with living people in it. Then I use this thing to make them help you. Right? I just word them. We tell them to help you but not tell anyone we're there." Eliot was leaking water again, so he put away the bottle. "Good plan?"

Eliot's head turned left then right.

"Oh," Wil said. "What's your plan, then? Because it's pretty obvious to me that you're dying. And we both know I don't have a hope in hell against the people who are after us all by myself, even if I do have a magic word. So it's either a hospital or I try a little amateur surgery on you myself with whatever I can find lying around. Do you want me to do that?" Eliot said nothing. "I'm not doing that. I'm getting you to a hospital." He closed the door and jogged around to the driver's seat. "Keep drinking the water."

He tucked the towel and its hidden package between the seats and turned the key. The engine clicked emptily. He blinked. He'd forgotten about the gas. He glanced at Eliot and saw Eliot looking at him with a complete lack of surprise.

"Shut up," said Wil. He studied the roadway ahead, filled with bones and rusted metal. "I can find gas. I'll be five minutes. Can you not die for five minutes?"

Eliot's chin dropped.

"Don't lie to me. If I have to, I will cut you open."

"Ff," said Eliot. "I. Fine."

Wil eyed him. But he wouldn't learn anything from Eliot's face that Eliot did not want him to know. "Sure," he said. "You're fine." He climbed out of the car.

He found a dust-coated SUV with keys in the ignition and gas in the tank. This was a much better option than trying to reintroduce life to the disintegrating piece of shit that was the Valiant, so he climbed in and steered around wrecked vehicles. The interior had an odd smell, which he tried not to think about. When he got close enough to the Valiant, he put the SUV into neutral and jumped out. Eliot seemed to have deteriorated in the meantime: His skin was papery, his eyes unfocused. "Hey!" Wil said. "I found a better car." He pulled open Eliot's door. "Throw your arm around me."

"No."

"Yes."

"You. Go. I. Stay."

"No, that's not what we're doing. You're coming with me. That's the plan. We're taking you to a hospital."

"Bad. Plan," said Eliot. "Gets you. Killed."

"You have an alternative?"

"North. Two miles. Dirt road. Then. Cross-country. Forty miles. To blacktop. Town. Kikaroo. Then. Any way. You want."

"Is there a hospital in Kikaroo? No. So we're not doing that."

"Must."

"I tell you what. Look me in the eye, tell me you believe I can do this without you, and I'll leave you here."

Eliot eyed him.

"Unconvincing," Wil said. "Put your goddamn arm around me."

"No."

"Get the fuck out of the car!"

"No."

Wil leaned in to grab him. Eliot's head pivoted to hit Wil in the nose: a small movement, but enough to knock him back, his vision flaring. "*Mother fuck!*" He turned in a circle. "You prick!" He lunged across Eliot and grabbed the towel. "I'll fucking make you!" He began to unwrap it.

"*No.*"

The intensity of Eliot's tone stopped him. "Then—"

"Never." For a moment, Wil thought Eliot was climbing out of the car. But he was only leaning. "Never. On me."

"Okay," Wil said, intimidated. "Point made, fine." But then Eliot slumped back in his seat, becoming less terrifying and more fragile, and he changed his mind. "You know what? I am going to use it." He peeled the towel from the petrified wood. It caught on a sharp protuberance and ripped. A noise came out of Eliot, something halfway between a snarl and a moan, and his head turned away. Wil had to twist him back to face the bareword, then realized Eliot's eyes were closed. "Goddammit." He tried to thumb up his eyelids while keeping a grip on the word. "Open up!" He forced open one eye. The pupil dilated and the fight drained from Eliot's body. "Okay, now," Wil said. "Get out of the car."

Eliot's hand shot out and gripped the door frame. Wil retreated a step. Eliot's other hand came out and twitched around like a spider until it found purchase. His body began to shake.

"Are you, uh, okay there?" Wil said.

"*Harrrgh,*" said Eliot. His expression was very intense. He was trying to pull himself out of the car, Wil realized. Straining, but lacking the strength to do it. Wil moved forward to help and realized that Eliot's entire body was vibrating, his muscles tight bundles of wire.

"There," Wil said. Eliot straightened. He threw out a foot in a jerky, searching motion. Wil released him. Eliot fell to the pavement. "Oh, shit! Sorry!" Eliot's hands scrabbled at the concrete. "Jesus! Eliot! Let me help you."

"*Ghee.*"

He wrapped his arms around Eliot's torso. "Come on. This way." After four steps, Eliot vomited. His eyes were wide and staring, the pupils milky. He looked dead. "Eliot, I'm sorry. But it's just a little farther." Eliot's foot slid out and Wil maneuvered it to touch the ground. "That's it." Eliot made a noise like it might become a cough one day. "Please, Eliot." Eliot was not going to make it. He was already dead, and Wil was making him walk to an SUV. "I'm so sorry. But I can't let you die."

"*Haargh.*"

"Don't die! Do not die!" He was still holding the bareword and tried to wave it in Eliot's face. Whether Eliot could even see anymore, Wil didn't know. "*Don't die.*"

Eliot's body convulsed. Flecks of spittle flew from his mouth.

"Fuck!" he said. They were inching toward the paramedic van, and Wil wondered if there was a sedative in there, something in a syringe, which he could use to knock Eliot out. Then Eliot would stop being so much like a reanimated corpse. "Come with me!"

He propped Eliot against the rear of the van and Eliot keeled over. Wil climbed inside anyway and began ransacking drawers. The sensation that he had been here before descended again, more strongly this time. He could feel memories scratching at the underside of his mind, just out of reach. But he didn't have time for that. Eliot was lying in the dust and Wil had to get him to the SUV. He should use a fireman's carry. Why had he been shuffling along, holding Eliot by the arm? That was stupid. You wanted to move someone, you put them over your shoulders. Everyone knew that. Anyone in emergency services had practiced in drills a hundred times. He looked around the van. This vehicle wasn't just familiar. It was his.

He crawled past the trolley and into the cabin, dropping into the driver's seat. He put his hands on the wheel. Eliot was bleeding to death back there. But it was calling to him. He had the feeling he was a paramedic.

He popped open the compartment between the seats and rummaged through the junk inside. Among the loose change and plastic wrappers was a yellowed newsletter. He glanced at it and almost tossed it aside before realizing the picture on the front was of him. He looked different. He was standing with a bunch of other people in front of the emergency room. Everything was clean and bright. His hair was long. He had a tan. His shoulders were broader. He was relaxed in a way that Wil couldn't ever remember feeling. He read the caption and counted the figures from left to right, to be sure. HARRY WILSON. That was him. His name had been Harry.

Behind him, Eliot coughed. Wil thought, *That guy has lost a lot of blood.* He blinked. For some reason, he hadn't attended to Eliot's gunshot wound. He was letting him bleed out, apparently. He felt bewildered. Why had he let Eliot go so long?

He climbed back through the van and manhandled Eliot into the bed. Eliot groaned. That was a positive sign. Well. It was a sign. He ransacked the shelves for a scalpel, surgical gloves, dressing, and saline, all of which were in their assigned places, rolled Eliot on his side, stuck the scalpel between his teeth, and forced Eliot's knee up and his arm over. He cut away the shirt and there it was, an exit wound, big as his hand, pink and torn and oozing blood. He was appalled at himself. Timely first aid would have saved this guy's life. All he could do now was compress and close anything that looked like it was fountaining blood.

He inserted a finger into Eliot's lower intestine and gently lifted. There was a sucking noise, a *glunk*, and a small sea of Eliot flowed onto the back of his hand, which was bad, about the worst thing he could see, because that meant Eliot had holes. To locate the source he had to force four fingers in there, and Eliot made a terrible sound. Wil did what he could. It was not much but maybe enough. He began to dress the wound.

As he did, memories burst in his head like popping corn. Tiny, irrelevant things. The look on a girl's face. The smell of earth in the morning. But they were coming. Squeezing past whatever barrier had been erected in his head. Something important came to him, and he paused.

Eliot breathed. He was unconscious. His face was gray. The problem was too much of Eliot was spread across two different vehicles. Eliot was on his shirt and his coat and on the floor of two different vehicles. He was about a hair's breadth away from hypovolemic shock and there was nothing Wil could do about that. He looked out the back of the van at the emergency room. Twenty feet from a hospital that was full of blood product, and every pack would be black and hard as stone.

He leaned forward. "Eliot." He twisted Eliot's ear. This was extremely painful, if you did it properly. "Eliot, you motherfucker."

Eliot groaned.

"Eliot." He put his lips to Eliot's ear. "Eliot."

"Uh," Eliot said.

"What's your blood type?"

Eliot opened his eyes. There was a ceiling. Tiled. A false ceiling: the kind that had pipes and wiring snaking through it. He didn't know where he was, or when.

He heard a *crack*. He tensed. His abdomen hurt. There was a lot of pain in his body. He tried to raise his head and his vision swam. He saw pale blue walls and a cracked ceiling. A corded phone implanted into one wall. Chairs, a bedside table. A bed, for that matter, in which he was lying. The air smelled of dust.

Oh, Christ, he thought. *I'm in Broken Hill.*

He explored his surroundings with his hands. Something tugged on his arm, which turned out to be a tube. He was attached to something. He levered himself up his pillow, inch by inch, and saw a hat stand, draped with tubing and three bags. One of the bags bulged with clear fluid, one had dark fluid, and one appeared to have contained dark fluid until recently but was now mostly empty. He felt bewildered, because he didn't remember any of this.

A second *crack*. This time he identified it as a gunshot. A rifle. His thoughts began to order themselves. He had driven to Broken Hill with the outlier, Wil. A farmer had shot him. When he'd realized the wound was fatal, he'd told Wil to leave him. But Wil hadn't wanted to. It had been one of those frustrating situations where Eliot had needed to convince Wil of something but couldn't, because the guy was an outlier. Also, stupidly stubborn. Eliot had passed out before this was really resolved. It seemed that in the meantime, Wil had saved his life.

He heard footsteps. He lay still until he was sure they were approaching, then began to feel around for a weapon. As Eliot saw it, there were two plausible scenarios. In one, Wil had driven away with the bareword, as Eliot had instructed, and the footsteps belonged to someone from the organization, coming to kill him. In the other, they belonged to Wil, who had been too cowardly to leave, and instead hung around hoping Eliot would wake up and tell him what to do. Either way, Eliot felt the need to shoot someone.

The deadliest object he could see was the hat stand, which could possibly serve as a club. He tugged at the covers to free his legs. He hadn't progressed very far with this when a man appeared in the doorway. The man had a rifle slung over his shoulder and for a second Eliot didn't recognize him.

"Lie down," Wil said. He crossed the room and peered out the window.

Eliot sunk into the pillow, crushed by the weight of his own bitter disappointment. He shouldn't have expected any different. Wil had done nothing Eliot asked of him from the moment they met. Eliot had been foolish to think he would start now just because everything depended on it. He plucked at the blanket. "We . . . leave. Now."

Wil ignored him. He was looking at something outside. Eliot couldn't tell what.

"Listen, you . . . fuck," said Eliot. "Woolf . . . is coming." He tried to say more, but it degenerated into coughing. When he opened his eyes, Wil was holding a cup of water. Eliot took it. There was something different about Wil's manner. The reason Eliot hadn't recognized Wil before: Wil was different somehow. Eliot had the odd, discombobulating thought: *That isn't Wil Parke.*

The Wil-person watched him drink without expression. When Eliot finished, he said, "Lie down."

"Have to—"

"You're about to pass out again," said the Wil-person. "Lie down."

He felt the truth of this but fought it anyway. "Woolf."

"You mean Emily. Emily Ruff."

Oh, God, Eliot thought.

"Don't think you mentioned that. You talked a lot about Woolf. But you never mentioned that I knew her. Knew her pretty well, as it turns out."

"I . . . can . . . explain."

"Yeah," said Wil. "You'll explain. But first, you're going to sleep." He hefted the rifle. "I need to shoot some guys."

What guys? Eliot tried to say. But unconsciousness got him first.

He fell into sleep, but not far. He remembered a phone ringing in the dark. It had been a while ago. But he had been lying down, like this, feeling Broken Hill all around him. He had opened his eyes and seen curtains. A bedside clock. *Hotel*, he'd remembered. *I'm in a bed, in a hotel, in Sydney.* The phone rang and rang but he hadn't moved in case it dissolved, revealing that he was back on that road, his face in the dirt, lying still.

He picked up the phone. "Your wake-up call, Mr. Eliot. It's four thirty."

"Thank you." He placed the receiver back on the cradle, carefully, and it did not dissolve. He rose and drew back the curtains. Beyond was the city: the famous Sydney Opera House wreathed in light; behind that, the hulking steel bridge. A few boats on the bay, lights bobbing. These things were comforting to him, the water, the steel, because they proved it was not three weeks ago, when Broken Hill had died around him.

He showered and dressed. A newspaper lay outside his hotel room door and he stepped over it. Downstairs, a limo idled for him, the bellhop already moving to open its door. The city's winding streets slid by, tinted dark, then the bay, as they crossed the bridge and navigated the zoo. On a narrow road, dark waves lapped at rocks. The limousine finally drew to a halt beside a set of steep steps and the driver indicated that Eliot should ascend them.

At the top was a colonial house. There was a terra-cotta plaza, lit by a dozen craftily concealed garden lights, with a small ornate table and chairs, and on one of these was Yeats.

"Before you come any closer," Yeats said, "take a look at the water."

He turned to look. The bay was a black mirror; he wasn't sure what he was supposed to notice. He turned back to Yeats.

"It's good to see you." Yeats had risen silently while Eliot's back was turned and was now coming at him with a hand outstretched. Eliot took it. As always, Yeats was about as readable as a wooden fence. Within the organization, there was conjecture as to whether he'd had cosmetic surgery to paralyze his face. Eliot tended to think yes, because he knew Yeats had a personal surgeon, but occasionally he saw a contracting procerus or occipitofrontalis and doubted himself. "How are you?"

"I was briefly paralyzed three weeks ago," he said. "Since then, I've been fine."

Yeats gestured to a seat. "No lingering effects?"

"Not since sunrise on the second day."

"As she instructed. Fascinating. To be honest, I remain shocked that a poet of your caliber could succumb to it."

" 'It.' " He sat. "Let's call it what it is. A bareword."

"Apparently so."

"You'll excuse me," Eliot said, "but I'm feeling somewhat put upon."

"How so?"

"You sent me to Broken Hill without telling me what I was dealing with."

"I believe I told you it was high-testing."

"There's high testing," Eliot said, "and then there's *that thing*."

There was silence. "Well," said Yeats, "obviously its efficacy took us by surprise."

A woman appeared and began to generate tea and coffee. Eliot waited. When she left, he said, "Are we going to talk plainly?"

Yeats spread his palms.

"You arrived in Broken Hill within hours. Clearly, you were nearby. Clearly, information has been kept from me. I want to know why. Because I'm having trouble understanding what I did to deserve less trust than *Plath*."

"What was it like?"

"What was what like?" he said, although he knew.

"Quick, I imagine. But you must have perceived something. A split second of vanishing awareness. A grasping at a shrinking light."

"It was like being fucked in the brain."

"I wonder if you can be more specific."

"You had this thing in DC. I'm sure you have plenty of data from those poor fucks you put through the labs."

"Some. But I wish to hear it from you."

He looked out at the black water. "Regular compromise feels like sharing the cockpit. Like there's someone else in there with you, flipping switches behind your back. This gave me no sensation of being able to regain control. None at all. It felt like being worn. By something primal."

Moments passed. "Well," said Yeats. "For that I apologize. It was not my intention to sacrifice you. Indeed, I selected you precisely because I consider you my most able colleague, and most likely to stop her. As for why I kept my whereabouts from you, I confess that was insurance against the possibility that Woolf would turn you against me. A selfish decision. But I have no wish to square off against you, Eliot. The very idea terrifies me."

He let this pass. In the distance, an animal, unidentifiable, made a very Australian sound. "So we have a bareword."

"The first in eight hundred years," Yeats said. "It's rather exciting."

"Where is it now?"

Yeats shrugged slightly. "Where she left it."

"Pardon me?"

"We haven't recovered it," Yeats said. "It's still in the hospital somewhere, apparently."

"Apparently?"

"Local authorities have sent in several teams, none of which have made it out. I presume it's the word that's killing them."

He took a moment to compose himself. "It's surprising to me that you haven't taken all necessary steps to recover it. I cannot express how surprising that is."

"Mmm," said Yeats. He gazed into the darkness awhile. "Let me ask you a question. If the word is so powerful, why did those who wielded it fall? For they did fall; the stories are united on that. In every case, the appearance of a bareword is followed by a Babel event, in which rulers are overthrown and a common tongue abandoned. In modern terms, it would be like losing English. Imagine the sum total of our organization's work, gone. Our entire lexicon wiped out. And yet apparently this has happened. Apparently it happens following each discovery of a bareword, without fail. Is that not curious?"

"All empires fall, eventually."

"But why? It's not for lack of power. In fact, it seems to be the opposite. Their power lulls them into comfort. They become undisciplined. Those who had to earn power are replaced by those who have known nothing else. Who have no comprehension of the need to rise above base desires. Power corrupts, as the saying goes, and the bareword, Eliot, is not only absolute power, but worse: It is unearned. I need do nothing to possess it other than pick it up. This troubles me. I ask myself: If I seize the bareword, do I remain as I am? Or does it corrupt me?"

"I have no idea," he said. "But I'm pretty certain we can't leave it in the fucking desert."

Yeats was silent.

He leaned forward. "Bring it back home. Seal it up. Christ, sink it in concrete. Bury it for another eight hundred years."

Yeats glanced away.

"We don't need it," Eliot said. "Unless you have an urge to build a tower."

"There is another issue. Woolf escaped."

He closed his eyes. It was unprofessional but he needed to do it. "How is that possible?"

"She's quite resourceful," Yeats said. "As I believe you know."

"The newspapers said nobody made it out alive."

"Surely you didn't trust them."

"Where is she?"

"I have no idea."

"You have no idea?"

"As I said," said Yeats, "resourceful. She managed to get someone out, too."

"Who?"

"Presumably, the man she went back for."

"Harry?"

"Yes, that name sounds familiar."

"So let me get this straight," he said. "There's a bareword in Broken Hill. The whereabouts of the poet who used it to kill three thousand people remain unknown. Am I missing anything?"

"No," said Yeats. "I believe that's everything."

"I feel I must be missing something," he said, "since this situation is insane."

Yeats was silent.

"The bareword must be recovered. Woolf must be neutralized. Surely you see that this is indisputable."

Yeats tested his tea. "Yes. You are correct, of course. It shall be done."

For some reason, Eliot didn't believe him. "I'll find Woolf."

"Actually, you will return to DC. Your flight is booked. You depart this afternoon."

He shook his head. "I want to stay."

"How are you, Eliot?"

"You already asked me."

"I ask again, because this is the second time in our conversation that you have used the word *want*. Were you a third-year student, I would be appalled."

"I'll rephrase. It's important to neutralize Woolf and I'm the best we have."

"But how are you?" Yeats's eyes held his. "She has shaken you. I see it plainly. Was it the bareword? No. Something else. You were always too close to her. You developed affection. Why, I have no idea. But it clouded your judgment then and continues to do so now. You feel betrayed. You are infected with the desire to atone for your failure to stop her in Broken Hill."

"That's how you see what happened? As my failure?"

"Of course not. I speak of how you see it." Yeats gazed across the bay, to where soft fingers of sunlight edged over forested hills. "A tragedy like this, we all blame ourselves."

Do we, Eliot thought. "I strongly believe I should stay."

"That is why you cannot." The sun bloomed along the tree line of the far hill, throwing spears into the bay. "Ah," said Yeats. "Here we are. Watch."

A menagerie of animal voices rose to greet the light, hooting and cawing. Where sunlight touched it, the water flared bright blue. It took Eliot a moment to realize that the glittering wasn't a visual effect: The waters were moving.

"Kingfish," said Yeats. "The light draws the plankton, the plankton draws smaller fish. The minnows draw the kingfish. More precisely, the kingfish are already there, waiting, since they are intelligent enough to perceive patterns and draw inferences."

Eliot didn't respond.

Yeats sighed. "Stay. Search this country for Woolf, if that is what's required to regain control of your conscience."

He turned these words over. He couldn't tell whether they were a kindness or a threat. But there was no denying how he felt. "Thank you," he said.

He sensed light. At first he thought it was the sunlight on the bay. Then he opened his eyes. The light was coming through windows. Between the windows stood Wil. Wil with a rifle. The walls were a pale hospital blue. He was in Broken Hill.

"Morning," said Wil.

"What," said Eliot. "Time. Is it." He began to extract himself from the sheets.

"You're going to want to stay in that bed."

"No. Definitely. Not." He got his legs over the side. This caused some flaring of his vision and a looseness in his head, and he took a few moments to sit quietly, eyes closed. When he opened them, Wil was pointing the rifle at something outside. Eliot remembered the noise he'd heard before: *crack*. "What are you doing?"

Wil didn't answer. He was holding that rifle very naturally, Eliot noticed. The barrel followed whatever Wil was tracking in a smooth line, like an extension of his body. Then it jerked. Wil stepped back against the wall, pulling back the rifle's bolt and reloading it with a cartridge from his jeans. "It's about six in the morning."

Eliot felt disbelief. If that were true, Woolf would be here already. The town would be flooded with proles, or EIPs, or poets, or all three. It couldn't be morning because they were still alive. "We have to leave."

"We're not going anywhere, Eliot."

"We—" he began, but Wil raised the rifle very quickly, and Eliot fell silent. Wil's body became completely still. The rifle jerked. Eliot said, "Please tell me what you think you're doing."

"Shooting guys."

"What guys?"

"Proles, I guess."

"You're shooting proles," Eliot said. "I see. When it's a guy in a chopper and I ask you to shoot him, you won't. But now you're shooting proles."

Wil moved from one window to the other.

"There isn't a limited supply," Eliot said. "If you haven't figured that out. She'll send as many as it takes."

"Who? Emily?"

Oh, yes, Eliot thought. Wil had remembered. That was why he was handling a rifle like he'd used it all his life: because he had. "What do you think you're doing, Wil?"

"Harry."

"What?"

"My name is Harry Wilson."

"Right," Eliot said. "Of course, my mistake—what the fuck are you doing, Harry?"

"Waiting."

"Waiting for . . ." His mind reeled. "For *her*?" Wil, or Harry, or whoever he was, didn't answer. But clearly yes. Clearly he had a terrible, ill-informed notion of the situation, which was going to get them both killed. It was Eliot's fault, of course. Like everything else. "She isn't who you think."

"Is she Emily Ruff?"

"Yes," Eliot said, "Woolf is Emily Ruff. But—"

"You understand why I have a problem with that. The whole thing with you wanting to kill her."

"Are you aware you're acting like a different person? As in, a completely different person?"

"I remembered."

"Okay," Eliot said, "but I regret to inform you that what you're remembering is no longer valid, because when you changed, so did she. She is no longer the girl you used to hang with in Broken Hill and share milk shakes and ride kangaroos or whatever the fuck. Now she kills people. She is coming to kill us."

"I don't believe you."

"Why would I lie about this?"

"Charlotte."

He searched for the words. "You think that's why I hate Woolf? Because of Montana?"

Harry shrugged.

"Well, fuck!" Eliot said. "You got me! Since she made me shoot the woman I loved, I've been carrying a grudge! Jesus fucking Christ!" He dragged a hand across his brow. Harry regarded him expressionlessly, and this absurdity, the stillness of the man he knew as Wil Parke while Eliot raged, was not lost on him. He'd been a poet, once. "There is the little fact that Woolf was a murderous bitch who was hunting us both even before that."

"You lied to me."

"What was I supposed to do? You're the only outlier! I didn't have the option of finding one who hadn't slept with her. Wil, I get that you're pissed. I do. But look at yourself. The instant you found out she used to be Emily, you gave up. I'm sorry I lied to you. But that doesn't change the fact that we have to stop Woolf. We have to. What can I say to convince you?"

"I don't want you to say anything. I want you to sit there and wait until she gets here."

Eliot sank into the bed. It was pointless. Every technique he knew, useless, because Harry could not be persuaded.

"What happened to her?"

"When?"

"After Broken Hill."

He looked at the ceiling. "She disappeared. I searched for months."

"Then?"

"Then," said Eliot, "she came back."

STUDY PROBES BILINGUAL PUZZLE

From: The City Examiner, Volume 144, Edition 12

. . . the electrode was applied to the brain of a French-Chinese bilingual and the patient asked to count to twenty. He began in French, but when the electrode was applied to his left inferior frontal gyrus, he involuntarily changed to Chinese. When the stimulation was removed, he reverted to French.

In another case in Dorset last year, a bilingual who suffered a traumatic brain injury in a car accident was left unable to speak English, although she remained fluent in Dutch.

The results provide further evidence that languages develop in discrete parts of the brain, explaining why bilingual speakers tend not to mix up words from different languages.

"If your brain is a computer, then bilingual speakers dual-boot," said Dr. Simone Oakes, of Oxford University's School of Medicine, referring to a machine with two operating systems installed. "They have multiple modes of operation, but only one can be active at a time."

Further research is expected to probe the effects of specific languages on the brain, such as the puzzle of why particular attitudes and beliefs appear more commonly in speakers of one language than another, regardless of cultural factors.

[TWO]

She caught the train to Blacktown and wandered the streets until she found the Army Disposals store she'd read about the previous day. It was big, almost a warehouse, its aisles packed with quasi- and wannabe-military gear, camo netting hung across the ceiling. She squeezed between bikers and bushies and young men with large, clearly defined chips on large, clearly defined shoulders, occasionally picking up a bottle or knife or pack that seemed interesting. In aisle three, a bearded man in jeans and a light T-shirt approached her and offered assistance.

"Yes," Emily said. "I'm looking for a camouflage tarpaulin that can be made into a tent."

"Desert or bush?"

"Desert," she said, pleased to have skipped the *oh-ho-and-what-do-you-need-that-for*s.

"We have tarps and we have camo netting. You can throw one over the other."

"I want a single product, if there is one."

"You'll be carrying it?"

"Yes," she said. "Exactly."

"Then may I recommend a space bag?"

"What's that?"

"A lightweight sleeping bag, foil interior, waterproof canvas exterior. Little mesh part on the face you can open for ventilation without letting in the bugs. Folds up to nothing. Very new. Hard to acquire, as they're still in service."

"How hard?"

"Two thousand dollars."

She nodded. That she could do. "It's camouflage?"

"It's not. But I tell you what, if that's what you desire, I will sew some camo onto it."

"Yes!" she said. "That would be terrific."

He led her to a counter and processed her deposit. "Call you in two days. Anything else I can help you with?" He saw her hesitation. "If you're planning to spend any time in the desert, I hope you have a water system."

"Water isn't a problem. But I have a concern about snakes."

"Rightly so."

"What can I do to keep them away?"

"The general idea is to keep away from them."

"I have good boots. But . . ." She gestured. "Is there some kind of electronic device that scares them? Like the ones that keep insects out of your house?" The man had begun to look amused, so she guessed no. "Anything?"

He scratched his beard. "You can watch where you put your feet."

"Hmm," she said.

"And take a stick," he said.

So she was not thrilled with the snake situation, but otherwise things were coming together. The space bag was the final piece in the puzzle; with that, she could begin testing. Which was tempting to skip, but she had uncovered some alarming numbers about sweat-related water loss in the desert, and this wasn't something she wanted to confirm forty miles from the nearest living human being. Nearest *benign* human being, that was, since she was working under the assumption that Broken Hill was surrounded by proles, men and women who worked in bakeries or gas stations or drove trucks or simply stood at key intersections and would, upon seeing her, become very focused and intent and proceed directly to a phone.

Hence the need for a desert crossing. A few months before, when she'd been coming for Harry, she'd done it on a dirt bike. In retrospect, it seemed wildly risky. But she'd been impatient. She had hurried for him. And it had ended so badly. She didn't want to think about that. This time there would be caution. There would be thirty miles of desert traversed by foot, and no one would see her coming because what she was doing was unimaginable.

Once she had the word, she would begin the next stage of her journey, to DC. When she got there, she would rip out Yeats's heart, just like he had torn out hers. What happened after that didn't matter.

She spent a lot of time on trains, reading dictionaries. She wore a hoodie and pulled it down, in case of cameras. She could ride all day for two dollars and never be in the same spot for more than a few minutes. The last service was around two, so then she had to find a place to sleep, but that wasn't hard. She had done that before.

Sometimes she nodded off on the train. She tried not to, because she feared waking up to poets moving through the carriage, no way out, but it was kind of unavoidable. The dictionaries were not very interesting. So when she felt her head drifting toward the glass, the factories or fields passing by outside, she let it happen.

The day after she ordered her space blanket, she drifted awake to find a man sitting opposite, watching her. She was half out of her seat, words forming on her lips, before she realized he wasn't Eliot. He wasn't anybody. She sank back into her seat. Her head was full of terror; it always was, coming out of dreams.

"Sorry," said the man. "Didn't mean to startle you."

"That's okay." She was getting her bearings. The man was about forty, nicely dressed, sweater, a good watch. She talked to such people sometimes, as a precursor to persuading them to give her money.

"That's a lot of books. Dictionaries?"

She nodded.

"Are you a student?"

"Of life," she said. People liked this kind of quippery. It caused them to open up. "I just read them for fun."

"Dictionaries?"

"Yes."

"That doesn't sound like fun. That sounds awful."

"*Awful* used to mean 'full of awe.' The same meaning as *awesome*. I learned that from a dictionary."

He blinked.

"See?" she said. "Fun."

"That is actually fascinating. What else?"

She looked at her notes. She had notes. "*Cause* has changed. The definition used to be 'to make something happen.' Now they've added, 'especially something bad.' "

"They've changed *cause*?"

"They've noticed a change. Dictionaries record common usage."

"I thought it was a panel of professors," said the man, "at a university somewhere, deciding what words mean."

She shook her head.

"So it's bad to cause something now?"

"Yes. And to join causes, probably. Because of semantic leakage."

"Well," he said. "You are the most interesting person I've met all week."

"Thanks," she said, but she was getting a bad feeling. She was regretting this conversation. "My stop is coming up." She packed her dictionaries into her bag.

"Do you have somewhere to sleep tonight?" She didn't say anything. "I'm sorry, that didn't come out right. I mean, are you okay? You don't look okay."

"I'm okay."

"I don't mean to be rude, but I'm sitting close enough to smell you." His expression looked genuine but she didn't like his eyes. There were a lot of tiny muscles there and they were not consistent with the rest of his face. "Is there any way I can help you?"

"Thanks, but no." She stood up. "This is my stop."

"Mine, too."

She sat. "My mistake."

He leaned forward. He did this slowly, like he wanted to get it right. "Do you need money?"

She hesitated, because she did need money. But not from this guy. She didn't even want to compromise him. She just needed to get away. Her eye was starting to hurt.

"Whatever trouble you're in, I can help. I'm a lawyer. I have money. No strings. I see an intelligent young woman who needs a helping hand. That's all. Say no and I won't bother you anymore."

The train stopped. The carriage was almost empty, the platform bare. She waited until she was sure the man wasn't moving, then stood and walked quickly to the doors. She got there in time, hit the button, stepped off, and kept walking. A night breeze stirred her hair. She wanted to look around but kept her head down, in case of cameras.

"Five hundred dollars," said the man, right behind her. "Look at it." She ignored him. "Are you stupid? Just take it. *Take it.*" He put a hand on her shoulder.

She turned and shoved him. He staggered backward. He really was holding a fistful of cash. Behind him, the train began to pull out.

"I'm trying to help you."

"Fuck off!" she shouted. And she went after him, for some reason, and pushed him again. "Leave me alone!" He tried to catch her arm. But she was too quick for that. Whatever else he was, he wasn't prepared for someone who fought back. She shoved him again. "*Leave me alone!*" His back hit the moving train and he rebounded a step onto the platform. Her brain was full of violence and her star was singing and another push could send him between the carriages. If she timed it right. She thought, *Yeats, Yeats, save it for Yeats.*

"Jesus," said the man. "Jesus." He got around her and ran away.

She stood there, breathing. She needed to get out of here. She had to leave before the cops arrived. She made for the exit, her hoodie pulled tight. She couldn't wait for the space bag. She would have to call and have it mailed. She had to take herself out of the cities, away from people, before someone got hurt.

A month later, she was trudging across the desert. She had a stick. It was night, because during the day you could see for twenty miles in all directions, and she assumed someone would be looking. Also snakes slept at night. She wore a fur-lined parka and loose shorts, maybe an odd combination, but the thing was the nights were cold enough to freeze exposed sweat. A twenty-eight-pound backpack was strapped around her waist and shoulders. She was loving her boots: big, brown, comfortable shit-kickers.

She made good ground on night one and stopped at the first hint of dawn. She found a depression in the dirt beside three scrubby trees, a long-dead waterhole, and spread her space bag beneath them. She sat on it awhile, cooling, watching the stars retreat and the sky lighten. Her body felt satisfyingly used. Not exhausted. She was in good shape. She ate a hard biscuit and crawled beneath the space bag and fell asleep.

She woke a few hours later in a furnace. She was swimming in sweat. She peeked out, thinking maybe she'd lost her shade. But no. It was just hot. She wriggled out, keeping flat to the ground to avoid presenting a profile, and unzipped her backpack. She pulled out four wooden stakes and used them to suspend the space bag a few feet above the ground. The idea was to remain camouflaged from above while allowing air to move around her. She stripped naked, crawled under the sheet, sucked water from her drinking tube, and tried to sleep.

The second night was harder. Her legs felt suspiciously sore, which they hadn't during her trials. She might have been pushing herself, walking faster than she needed to. She was blowing her water budget, too. She forced herself to slow down, stop for more rests, but then worried that she was falling behind on distance, which would create new water problems. The chances were excellent that she could source fresh water in Broken Hill, in which case she had no problem. But she did not want to rely on this, since if she was wrong she would die. She kept walking, her stick ready, in case of night snakes.

She made less ground than she wanted and stopped early, feeling dizzy. She drank a lot, even splashing some on her face. She ate more biscuits. She hadn't brought many of those, to avoid temptation, because digestion increased the body's demand for water. That was starting to seem like a mistake. She crawled under the space bag.

Again, she was woken by the sun baking the earth and had to convert the bag to a little tent. This time, however, she realized the trees she'd camped beneath were basically leafless, which was a serious problem, because no shade. There was no wind and the underside of the space bag radiated heat. She lay there as long as she could, watching her skin turn mottled pink then red, and crawled out and curled against the trunk of a tree. It was better but only a little. She began to seriously wonder if she would die. Two weeks ago, she had decided against bringing the long white Bedouin robes that would have made it possible to walk in the daytime without passing out, thinking they weren't worth the weight. This decision might kill her.

She drank her electrolytes. Every thirty minutes, she tipped tiny amounts of water onto her hands and wiped them across her face and neck. The water pack grew scarily thin but it was either drink or expire. In late afternoon, a light breeze began to shift the sand and she cried a little despite the fluid loss.

Finally the sun eased toward the earth. Sometime after that, she began to feel human. She got to her feet and began to pack her bag and thought about which direction to go. The smart thing was to head back. It would take two nights but she had enough water and would be able to recover and rethink how she was going to do this. But it would mean starting over. And the town was only one more night away. It would probably have water. Even if the tanks had gone bad, there would be bottles. Stores and cafés with darkened refrigerators. She ignored the part of her that asked *but what if* and started walking.

Her feet became sore, then wet-feeling, then numb. She didn't want to blame the boots but she had the feeling they were letting her down. They were like boys who at first were cool and suave and then after a couple of weeks you realized were assholes. Around midnight she began to hallucinate a little and forget important things like checking her compass. She came across a boulder and sat on it and woke up face-first in the sand. Her lips felt like a baked cake. She drank and drank and finished her water.

The town rose with the dawn. She walked toward it. She lost her stick somehow. She began to pass houses, places she recognized. She saw the first body and tried not to look but her eyes wouldn't stay still. It was a woman she knew. Cheryl. She recognized the dress. *I'm here to fix it*, she told Cheryl. *To say sorry.* But she couldn't really believe Cheryl would be pleased by that, or would forgive Emily in any way. She sucked on her water tube and remembered it was empty and turned in at a gate because it was time to search for water. She walked up the path and stopped because on the house's concrete front steps lay a brown snake, sunning itself. She stared at it. "Fuck off!" she shouted, and stamped her boots, and it wriggled away.

She pulled open cupboards and passed out in a bedroom and threw up in a toilet and wasn't sure in which order that happened. She found water and slept. When she awoke the sun was throwing shadows at forty-five degrees and she had to stare at them a long time to figure out whether it was morning or afternoon. She had slept for a day and a half. She was ravenous.

She found and devoured a box of fruit bars. Her brain liked this and she began to be able to make sense of things. Empty water bottles were everywhere. She sat at the wooden kitchen table and waited for the sun to go down. Then she strapped herself into her pack.

A strong wind was blowing, tossing stinging sand at her face. She hiked along the road. She had steeled herself for the bodies, and kept her eyes up and her mind focused, but the closer she got, the more the wild, clawing terror grew inside her, wanting to turn her around and steer her out of here. Sand stung her eye and she rubbed at it but it made no difference.

She passed the gas station, with its burned cars and trucks. She made herself machinery: legs and feet and purpose. She reached the hospital. She stepped over a snarl of cloth and leather and gleaming bone and pushed open the side door. These were things she did. She walked down the corridor. She didn't recognize anything because that part of her brain was closed. She reached the double doors for the emergency room and dropped her pack and closed her eyes. Then she went in.

The smell was very bad. Old but wrong. Her nose began to run. Her boots hit something and she shuffled around it. When anything blocked her path, she carefully stepped over it. Her fingers found the counter. She followed it along to the place where she had left the bareword.

It wasn't there. She stood awhile, breathing. She followed the counter all the way to the wall, sweeping its surfaces. Her fingers found objects, small things she could identify like a stapler and a nameplate and larger things she dropped upon ascertaining they were not what she wanted and did not think about. She reached the wall and began making a low sound, equal parts moan and hum.

She circled the counter twice. She made her way back to where the bareword had been and dropped to her hands and knees and began to feel around on the floor. Almost immediately she found cloth and hair and her hum became a shriek and she couldn't do it anymore. She couldn't grope around corpses. She got to her feet. The idea crept into her brain: *I'm lost.* She would never find her way out. She would spend the rest of her life crawling over the bodies of the people she'd let die, searching for an exit she was too afraid to open her eyes and look for. Her breaths came in hitching shrieks. She tripped twice and then her hands found the doors and she crawled through them.

She returned to the house. She could have sought out Harry's but wasn't up to facing more memories. With four walls around her, she felt safer. She scrubbed her hands in a toilet cistern. She sat on the seat and stared at nothing. She felt numb. The word should have been there.

Yeats had probably wanted to put her in exactly this position. He had probably recovered the word months ago, in secret. She had been tracked all the way in, and right now they were moving through the streets, corralling her, whispering to each other guttural words.

But this did not seem right. She did not understand Yeats well, but in her experience, people with power used it. She felt the word was there. She felt that strongly.

After a while, a thought occurred to her. She rose from the seat.

She went back to the hospital and through the corridors to the emergency room doors. She put her pack against the wall and withdrew a digital camera, which she had found at the house. She had tested its batteries already but took a photo of a fire extinguisher, just to be sure. Then she closed her eyes and pushed through the doors.

She shuffled inside a few steps and raised the camera. Her idea was that this thing really was a word. It was on petrified wood, but the wood wasn't the important part. The important part was the mark.

She pressed the shutter button and felt the flash on the inside of her eyelids. She shifted her aim and pressed again. She would accumulate photos. Most of the photos would contain unbearable things, but in one would be the word. People kept coming into this room and turning into killers, ergo the word was somewhere it could be seen. She adjusted her aim, pressed the shutter for another photo. She would keep taking them until the camera ran out of room. Then she would download the photos to a computer. She would magnify them a thousand times and inspect each picture a handful of pixels at a time. It would take forever. She would see awful things. But she would do it. Eventually, she would find the edges of something that looked like wood. She would know where in the image the bareword was located. She could magnify it a hundred times, until it was too big to see all at once. And she could copy it. The word was not a thing. It was information. It could be duplicated. She could copy it one piece at a time, carve it onto wood so it would be just the same. Maybe she'd get someone to help, so she'd never hold the whole thing in her brain. Then she'd have a hundred tiny pieces, numbered on the back, which she could reassemble. She would have to find a way to carry it safely. To keep it always close. She pressed the shutter again. She was thinking maybe a necklace.

She came out of the hospital. The air felt incredibly fresh and she gulped at it. She started walking, then running, her pack bouncing on her back. She was clutching the camera. She should stop and seal it in plastic, stash it away safely. But she couldn't stop. She ran through dead streets and a crow cawed and she shrieked back at it, an insane yodel that wouldn't stay quiet. She was supposed to be stealthy. They could be listening. She ran, hiccupping and gibbering, desperate to put distance between her and this place, to reach somewhere she could open her lungs and scream triumph like she wanted.

Yeats trotted up the mansion steps and was set upon by butlers. He'd thought he had lost them at the foot of the stairs, but there were more. One attempted to steer him through the great open double doors and another began gently inquiring if he required refreshment and a third wanted to take his coat. All this was conducted in a low-register butler octave, making Yeats feel as if he was moving through a burbling stream. He allowed himself to be de-coated. A fourth butler seized the opportunity to step forward and brazenly adjust his bow tie. The butler who wanted to infuse Yeats with refreshments positioned himself so that Yeats need only take a step forward for a champagne flute to slide effortlessly into his left hand, but Yeats didn't know this butler, and in no fucking universe did he allow strangers to insert fluids into his body.

"There's Spanish," said Eliot. He had followed Yeats up the steps and was peering into the house. Butlers navigated around Eliot as if he were a rocky prow in a seething ocean, because he was not wearing a tuxedo. He was in a brown suit and beige coat, which apparently Yeats would need to physically pry from his body if he ever wanted to see Eliot in anything else. There was a code, of course. The organization imposed a ceiling on the quality of dress a poet was permitted to enjoy, commensurate with the poet's level. The point was to address the situation whereby a newly graduated poet realized there was very little in the world denied to him and began to get about in outrageous suits and three hundred thousand dollar cars, drawing attention. And technically the code applied to Yeats. Technically, his entire ensemble should have cost roughly half the price of his current shoes. But Yeats did not follow the code, because he was not a twenty-year-old idiot who required protection from temptation. He was intelligent enough to respect the intent of the code without slavishly adhering to its letter. Eliot, however. Eliot in his last-century suit, his repulsive department store shoes, his wrinkled coat. The most important thing about Eliot was that he wouldn't break a rule to save his life.

"Are you coming in?" Yeats said. "I believe that some of the delegates have brought advisers."

"No. I'm not dressed for it," Eliot said, then realized it wasn't a real invitation.

"Then I will see you at the office."

"Russian's not coming. That's what I came to tell you."

Yeats hesitated. The butler with the champagne flute took the opportunity to slide forward and Yeats glanced at him, bestowing upon the butler the terrible shame of having drawn notice. The butler fell away, mortified. "What do you mean?"

"Russian's doing it via speakerphone."

"You must be joking."

Eliot shrugged. "It's what his people have said."

"Well," Yeats said. He prepared for these meetings carefully. He attempted to consider every eventuality. But a *speakerphone*? Was Russian that afraid of compromise? Was he not aware that employing a *speakerphone* would broadcast his fear, screaming his vulnerability to every delegate in this house? It was ridiculous.

Eliot was still hanging around, eyeing the swirling gowns and tuxedos inside the room. "Thank you," Yeats said. Eliot nodded and began to trot down the steps. Yeats felt his mood lifting with each step Eliot took, with each increment of distance added between him and those shoes. Butlers began to swarm, excited by his inattention. Yeats shrugged them off and entered the house.

Just inside the doors was von Goethe, regaling a glittering circle that included, if Yeats was not mistaken, one senator and two congressmen. Goethe was German, short and sharp-nosed with dark, slicked-back hair. He was wearing gold-rimmed spectacles, which Yeats was sure were decorative. His shoes were fine brown soles. Goethe excused himself from the group and clasped Yeats's hands in both of his. "*Guten Tag, mein Freund*," said Yeats, which caused Goethe's face to crumple in disgust. "*Wie geht es Ihnen?*"

"Rather nauseous, after that."

"I apologize," said Yeats. "I do not have the opportunity to practice my German as often as I would like."

"You are forgiven." This exchange established that Goethe didn't wish to engage Yeats in German, which was sensible, since it was easier to resist compromise in a learned language than a native one, but cowardly, for the same reason. Yeats was happy to roll with it, in the spirit of the occasion. He wasn't here to compromise anyone. Also, he sincerely doubted Goethe was capable of troubling him in English. "A fine occasion you have arranged. So worthy."

"Well," said Yeats. For the first time he took in the stage, the tables draped in white cloth, the tasteful sign by the podium that declared: A WORLD OF LITERACY. "We do what we can."

"I was speaking with one of your politicians and he informed me that your government is investing some hundreds of millions of dollars to teach children across Asia to read."

"We do what we can."

"Read *English*," said Goethe.

"Well," he said. "You can hardly expect us to teach them German." He clasped the hand of a tall, bronze-skinned woman who had met his eye across the ballroom twenty seconds ago and begun to cross it like a torpedo. "Rosalía, what a pleasure."

"William," she said. "I swear, you age backward."

"De Castro," said Goethe, casting an eye over her green gown, which was daring when she stood still and practically scandalous when she moved. De Castro offered her hand, which Goethe kissed. "Yeats and I were just discussing his latest plan to seed the world with English missionaries."

"Surely you see that a common world language would serve the organization's interests."

"I suppose," said Goethe. "But I weep at the prospect that this language would be *English*."

"It won't be," said de Castro. "It will be Spanish. English plateaued some time ago. It will take more than Yeats's missionaries to reverse that." She looked down her nose at Goethe, who stood a foot shorter. "I suppose these things are more alarming to delegates whose languages are in decline."

"Ah, it begins," said Goethe. "The traditional German pile-on."

"Honestly, I admire your spirit. It cannot be easy to watch your language slip into the footnotes of history."

"It is doing no such thing."

"Although I suppose you must be used to humiliation," said de Castro. "German being the second most popular Germanic language."

"Children, please," said Yeats.

De Castro turned to him. "Did I hear correctly? Pushkin will be joining us via speakerphone?"

"Apparently."

"I do hope we don't need another Russian delegate. They've been dropping like flies. Alexander was doing so well."

"It's the language," said Goethe. "Too many morphemes. Inherently vulnerable."

"He can't expect to save himself with a *speakerphone*. The idea is preposterous." She used a German word for "preposterous," *lächerlich*, slightly mangling the first syllable, watching Goethe as she did. So Yeats presumed that de Castro had dropped a little linguistic depth charge there. The entire meeting would be like this: delegates continually probing each other, seeking weakness. It was an inevitable by-product of the fact that the organization was a loose coalition of independent entities; no delegate outranked any other. Technically, Yeats was no more important than al-Zahawi of Arabic or Bharatendu Harishchandra of Hindi-Urdu. This was something he planned to change.

"Let us assume Pushkin has other motives," said Yeats, "and not waste our time together on speculation."

"Agreed," said de Castro. "Speaking of which, William, I was hoping you might be able to end some speculation of my own. Have you recovered your bareword?"

His phone buzzed against his thigh, which was surprising, since everyone who knew that number should have known not to call it. "Sadly, no."

"How disappointing," said de Castro, "and, simultaneously, bullshit. William, none of us believe you would allow a bareword to lie in Broken Hill unmolested for almost a year."

"The concept is extraordinary," said Goethe.

"We can discuss what you are willing to believe in the meeting," Yeats said. "Which has not yet begun."

De Castro glanced around the room. "There is a reason the other delegates have not approached you yet. I imagine it is the same reason Pushkin is not here at all." Her eyes settled on him. "Do you plan to compromise us?"

"How ridiculous," he said.

De Castro watched him. Goethe said, "There is no denying you have been making efforts to retrieve it. However, the more time that passes, the more one wonders whether one is witnessing not *efforts* so much as *charades*."

"I do not have the bareword," Yeats said. "For proof, please note the obvious fact that if I did, I would be using it to spare myself this conversation." His phone buzzed again. "Excuse me."

He turned away, plucked the phone from his pants, glanced at the screen, and repocketed it. He gazed into the distance, digesting the words: SIGHTING 3+1@95.65 IN 24 POI 665006.

The message was automated, sent by a computer whenever a person of interest—a PoI—was sniffed out by one of the vast number of surveillance systems to which he had access. Because those systems were less than perfectly reliable, possible sightings became messages only when the computer had accumulated sufficiently many of sufficient quality to pass a particular confidence level. In this case, they were informing him of three sightings in the past twenty-four hours, plus one from earlier, which were ninety-five percent likely to be Person of Interest number 665006, which, he knew from memory, was Virginia Woolf.

He returned to Goethe and de Castro. "Frankly," said de Castro, as if no time had passed at all, "I see little point sitting down to discuss digital interconnectedness and social media when such an overwhelming issue remains unresolved."

"It is resolved," he said. "I honestly don't know what else I can tell you." It struck him as remarkably suspicious that there would be a Woolf sighting at this moment, in this meeting. He wondered which delegate was responsible.

"You can tell me the current location of Virginia Woolf," said de Castro. "That troubles me, also."

"We looked. We didn't find her. It seems likely she is dead."

Goethe looked at de Castro. "He claims not to know."

"William, I hear things," said de Castro, "from people in your organization, as you no doubt hear things from people in mine. And the most disturbing tale has reached me. In it, Virginia Woolf steals the bareword and brings it to Broken Hill not out of some adolescent fit of pique, as you described, but rather at your command, as part of a test of the word's effectiveness. Clearly, given the current population of Broken Hill is now zero, this test was a resounding success. Which is alarming in itself, William, for as much as we hold you in the highest regard, we are all undermined by your possession of a kind of persuasion against which there is no defense. But the part of this tale that troubles me most is the idea that Virginia Woolf, as your agent, is out there somewhere, engaged in some activity that serves your purpose. I cannot imagine what that might be. And that makes me most uncomfortable."

Throughout this, Yeats's phone had continued to vibrate. He had developed the uncomfortable suspicion that the coincidence of Woolf's sighting during this meeting might not be due to a delegate. It might be due to Woolf.

"Confide in us," said Goethe. "We are your allies, William."

"I do not have the word," he said. "And Virginia Woolf is dead. Now, I am terribly sorry, but I will not be able to attend our meeting after all. Something unavoidable has come up."

He took a chopper cross-town and set down on the DC office helipad. This occupied thirteen minutes. In the meantime, he attempted to coordinate people via his phone. This proved difficult because every few seconds it wanted to tell him about an incoming message, which required a tap to dismiss, and by the time the building was in sight this was what Yeats was spending the majority of his time doing, tapping to return his phone to a useful state. When a computer server became so busy acknowledging incoming requests that it had no time to respond to them, it was called a Denial of Service attack, a DoS. Yeats was being DoSed. He surrendered and put his phone away.

Freed from the helicopter, he considered the elevator but opted for the flexibility of stairs. One flight later, he emerged into tastefully muted lighting. His assistant rose from her desk, mouth opening, full of messages. "Not now, thank you, Frances," he said, and closed the double doors behind him. The lights brightened in response to his presence. This month, his office was a paean to eighteenth-century feudal Japan: paper dividers, low, simple furniture. On the wall behind his desk a samurai sword hung under lights. Yeats had chosen none of this; it was periodically redecorated in a random style, to avoid betraying personal aesthetics. He planted himself behind his desk and tapped the keyboard to wake his screens.

His predecessor hadn't used a computer. They had been considered secretarial tools. Hard to imagine now. His displays filled with red boxes. Now that the computer's thresholds had triggered, it was vomiting up sightings from days ago, even weeks, made newly plausible by more recent data. A voiceprint from a hotel in Istanbul. A woman with matching facial characteristics in Vancouver. He inspected the picture: sunglasses, hat, nothing he would bet on, but the computer liked the cheekbones. A taxicab security photo, grainy and desaturated, from a route that corresponded with what the computer was figuring out about Woolf's movements. That was Seattle, yesterday. The notification boxes were a moving stream but Yeats managed to snag one with a recent time stamp. It was from the building's security system. Its confidence level was ninety-nine percent. Woolf was outside, right now.

His office had a balcony. He was mildly tempted to go out and peer over the railing, see if he could pick her out. But that would be risky. That was, possibly, what Woolf wanted him to do. There could be a sniping issue. The fact was, as much as he believed he understood Woolf, she had been missing for a year and he had no idea how she had changed.

His phone chimed. He felt rising excitement and waited until it was gone. "Yes?"

"I'm so terribly sorry. But there are so many people who wish to speak to you, and they're saying quite alarming things."

"Is one of those people Frost?" The poet responsible for building security. Yeats had spoken to him from the chopper, in between phone notifications, and asked him to execute certain important, long-planned orders. Specifically, Frost was to fill the lobby with Environmentally Isolated Personnel, men and women with black suits and guns who saw the world through a computer-filtered display and heard nothing but white-listed words. These had proved insufficient to retrieve the word from Broken Hill—the teams sent in had rather spectacularly killed each other—but that meant nothing, because he had deliberately engineered it. He was fairly confident that they could stop Woolf.

"No, I haven't heard from Frost."

"I'll speak to Frost," Yeats said. "No one else." He closed the speaker. Red boxes continued to slide down his monitors. He saw the word LOBBY. He leaned back in his chair.

So she'd entered the building. If all was proceeding as he'd instructed, Woolf would currently be on the floor, her hands bound in plastic, electrical tape being spread across her mouth. She would be lifted up and borne to a windowless cell. Then Frost would call.

He folded his hands and waited. A new red box slid up his screen. POI POSSIBLE SIGHTING: WOOLF, VIRGINIA. SECOND FLOOR. He looked at this awhile, trying to imagine circumstances in which Security might have decided to take Woolf up rather than down. He reached for the speaker. By the time he got the handset to his ear, a new notification had arrived. THIRD FLOOR. Was there a delay on these? A few seconds? It had never mattered before.

"Frances, would you mind putting the floor into lockdown?"

"Yes, sir."

"And please attempt to reach Frost."

"Right away."

His screen blanked. The lights went out. Part of the lockdown. Nothing to be concerned about. He waited. His breathing was steady. He felt no emotion. Minutes passed. The lights came on.

He pressed for the speaker. "Frances, why has the lockdown lifted?"

"I don't know. I'm finding out."

Noise in the background. Quite loud; he could almost feel its low echoes through the door. "Who else is there?"

"It's . . . how can I help you?"

A female voice spoke. Indistinct; he couldn't identify it. The phone clicked off. He slowly put it down.

He had recognized Woolf's natural aptitude for attack very early on. It would have been disappointing if she'd fallen to Frost and the soldiers. He would have missed his chance to test himself. Of course, there was the real possibility that she was about to walk in here and destroy him. That was a concern.

These were feelings. He didn't need them. He would prevail or he would not.

He steadied his breathing and began to pray. *O God, be with me and guide my hand. Let me transcend this petty flesh and become Your holy force.* Warmth spread through his body. His relationship with God was his greatest resource. It had allowed him to become who he was. So many promising colleagues had fallen to temptation. They managed their physiological needs, eating and breathing and fucking deliberately and on schedule, taking care to remain in control at all times, but their social needs—their basic human desire to love, to belong, and be loved—these were simply suppressed, because there was no safe way to indulge them. And yet they were named *needs* for a reason. The human animal craved intimacy at a biological level, relentlessly, insistent. Yeats had seen many promising careers derailed by surrenders to intimacy: men who whispered confessions to whores, women whose eyes lingered on children. On such small betrayals were psyches unraveled. He had unraveled several himself.

He had struggled in his early years. It seemed vaguely amusing now. Infantile. But he remembered the loneliness. The way his body reacted when a woman smiled at him, the surge of desire it evoked to join with her, not merely in a physical sense but beyond that, to confide and be understood. It had been almost overwhelming. Then he discovered God.

It had been terribly alarming. The very idea, a poet succumbing to religion! He was shocked at himself. But the feeling was undeniable and grew week by week. He could no longer believe he was alone. He began to see the divine in everything, from the circumvoluted fall of a leaf to the fortuitous arrival of an elevator. Occasionally, when the sterility of his job pressed close, he felt the presence of God like a figure in the room. God was with him. God loved him. It was ridiculous, but there it was.

It was a tumor, of course. Oligodendroglioma, a cancerous growth in an area associated with feelings of enlightenment. The feelings it aroused could be reproduced through electrical stimulation. It wasn't fatal, but it would need to be removed, his surgeon told him, as Yeats looked over the black-and-white scans, because it would continue to grow. Over time, there would be less and less of him and more of the tumor. His brain was being eaten by God.

He left the clinic in fine spirits. He had no intention of removing the tumor. It was the perfect solution to his dilemma: how to feed his body's desire for intimacy. He was delusional, of course. There was no higher presence filling him with love, connecting him to all things. It only felt that way. But that was fine. That was ideal. He would not have trusted a God outside his head.

The door opened and a woman stepped through. She was wearing a long white coat that reached the floor. The hem was spattered black with liquid that might have been mud or dirt or might have been Frost. She had white gloves. A necklace, something on it that twisted and hurt to look at. He closed his eyes. He reached into his diaphragm for his strongest voice. "*Vartix velkor mannik wissick! Do not move!*"

There was silence. "Ow," said Woolf. "That kind of hurt."

He groped for his desk drawer.

"Credit to you, Yeats. I spent a long time preparing for you to say those words. And I still felt them."

He got the drawer open. His fingers closed on a gun. He raised it and squeezed the trigger. He kept firing until the clip was empty. Then he dropped it to the carpet and listened.

"Still here."

There was a sword on the wall behind him. Three hundred years old, but it could cut. He had no training. But that might not matter, if she came close enough. She might think it was decorative, until too late.

"So I'm here to kill you," she said, "just in case there was any doubt."

He breathed. He required a few moments to calm himself. "Emily."

"Woolf," she said. "Woolf, now."

Interesting. Had she changed segments? It was possible. She might not have merely improved her defense but managed to alter her base personality in certain important ways. It could be done, with practice. In which case, she would be vulnerable to a different set of words. Yes. She would have rejected her previous self in order to distance herself from what she had done in Broken Hill. He needed to figure out what she had become. "How did you get here?"

"Walked, mostly."

"The lobby was supposed to contain a fairly overwhelming number of security personnel."

"The goggle guys? Yeah. They're screened somehow, right? Filtered against compromise."

"They're supposed to be."

"They are. But Frost isn't."

"Ah," he said. "So there were no goggle guys."

"Nope."

Difficult to read a person you couldn't see. The visual cues were so important. But it could be done. He could do it. The important thing was that she was still talking. "I gather you feel wronged by me?"

"You could say that."

"Well," he said. "I won't demean us both by pretending to apologize. But may I point out that killing me won't serve your interests?"

"Actually, I disagree with you there. I mean, I thought about it. Come here with the word, make you run the organization for me; that would be interesting. And I can't deny there is a real appeal in turning you into my slave for life. But that's not an option. I have a little problem, you see. I picked it up in Broken Hill, when you sent me to deploy that kill order. I kind of looked at it. I caught a reflection. It wasn't enough to compromise me. Not completely. It was backward, you know. And not very clear. But I think a piece of it got in there. I call it my star. That's what it feels like. A star in my eye. It's not very nice,

Yeats. It wants me to do bad things. But I figured out a way to control it. I just need to concentrate on killing you. When I do that, the star isn't so bad. I don't feel like I need to hurt anyone else. So you see, you dying is kind of a nonnegotiable at this point."

He was fascinated. This part he had not known. "Then what?"

"Excuse me?"

"After you murder me. What then?"

"That's not really any of your concern."

"I suppose not," he said. "Very well. We will save that for later."

"But there's not going to be a later, Yeats. Not for you."

"Mmm," he said. He had narrowed her down to a dozen or so segments. He was mildly tempted to run through words for them all, which he could do in about fifteen seconds. That was a last-resort kind of move, though. It would spark an immediate response from her, of whatever kind. He would keep that in his back pocket while he attempted to learn more. "Before we proceed, I feel I must confess something."

"Oh?" He heard her coat scuff the carpet.

"You are here because of me. There is no part of these events I have not engineered. The most difficult part of the exercise, in fact, was finding excuses as to why I left the bareword in Broken Hill for so long. To be honest, I expected you to move faster. It was becoming untenable. But here you are. Bringing the word back to me, filled with vengeance, according to plan."

"Really?" she said. "I have to tell you, from where I'm standing, that looks like a really shitty plan."

"When I came to Broken Hill in the midst of its immolation, I found myself moved. I felt desire. I realized then the danger of the bareword. It would have corrupted me. It would have been my undoing, as unearned power always is, sooner or later. And I have no intention of wasting this life on temporary greatness. What I will do with the word once I've taken it from you is leave a mark on this world that will never be erased."

"You're not making a hell of a lot of sense, Yeats."

He shrugged slightly. "Perhaps my motives are beyond your comprehension. But I wish you to know that I don't require words to make you perform my will. You are my puppet regardless. You stand here not because you willed it but because I did. Because defeating the bareword in your hands is the challenge I set myself to prove that I am ready to wield it."

"Dude, I'm going to kill you," she said. "I've walked through every defense you have. There's no doubt about that."

He rose from his chair and spread his arms. He began to increase his breathing, although she shouldn't notice that. Segment seventy-seven. He was sure of it. It was 220 with more fear and self-doubt. Often paired in families, interestingly: a 220 elder child and a seventy-seven younger sibling. It was plausible that Woolf might slide from one to the other. "Here I am," he said. "Kill me."

He heard her approach. There were two wide chairs opposite his desk, reducing the possible space she was occupying to a relatively small cuboid. Close enough to slice a sword through, if he was quick.

"You have no idea how much I want this, Yeats. I know it's bad form to say that. That I *want*. But I do. I want it so much."

He could hear her breathing. Very close now. He could probably reach across the desk and touch her. He pulled air into lungs, preparing to speak the words that would make her his.

"Hey," she said. "What's that word? When the Japanese guys did something bad they'd atone by gutting themselves? You know? Disembowel themselves? What's that called?"

He didn't answer.

"Seppuku," she said. "I think that's it."

Doubt entered his mind. She was a seventy-seven, yes?

"I've been planning this awhile, Yeats. Consider that."

He considered. "*Kinnal forset hallassin aidel!*" He turned. His hands closed on wood. He drew the blade from the scabbard. "*Scream!*" This was to locate her. To provide a signal that he had analyzed her correctly. He lunged across the desk and swept the blade horizontally. It cut nothing but air, and he overbalanced.

"Not even close," she said, from somewhere near the doorway.

He steadied himself, bringing up the blade. How foolish. He was disappointed in himself. It was that garbage about her name: *Woolf, now.* The purest bullshit, and he'd bought it. She was Emily, of course. She always would be.

He moved around the desk toward the sound of her voice, holding the blade flat, prepared for a stroke. He thought he heard something and jabbed speculatively. He turned in a slow half circle.

"This way," she said from the corridor.

He felt his way to the doorway. In the corridor were strange whisperings. The vents? He felt surrounded. She had plans for him, apparently.

"There are people here." Her voice floated ahead of him. "Just so you know."

He took two steps and stumbled over a chair. He felt the toe of his right shoe bend in a way that suggested a permanent crease and felt grief.

"So I have a proposition for you, Yeats. You can open your eyes, look at this thing I've got around my neck, and follow my instructions to disembowel yourself. This way, nobody gets killed but you. Or you can stand there swinging that oversized butter knife while I send your own people against you. What do you say?"

He ran at her. Someone grabbed his arms. He slashed the blade at his aggressor and there was a gasp and the hands fell back. He thrust the sword out again and felt it puncture something. Weight pulled at the blade and he retreated before he could lose it. Something thumped against the carpet.

"Congratulations," Woolf said. "You killed your secretary."

He swiveled toward her voice, panting. The corridor was full of people. He could sense them. They were standing silently, waiting for his approach. To reach her he would need to kill them all.

"So, no surprise," she said. "I don't know what I was expecting."

She was still a 220. She had practiced her defense. But he could find a way in. There was always something. A hidden desire or secret shame. With that, he could unravel her.

He explored air with the sword tip. "You were never going to be one of us. Eliot thought you could learn to discipline yourself. But the idea was laughable. You could never learn to discipline your excesses."

"I don't know, Yeats. You may not be giving me enough credit there."

He swiveled toward her voice. "Do you really think you can hide your mind from me?" He swung the blade. The tip glanced against something and he scrambled forward, slipping and sliding, got the blade into something, and pushed.

"Yecck," said Emily. "That was Frost."

Perhaps she was unsettled by violence. "*Vartix velkor mannik wissick! Scream!*"

There was a pause. No screaming. "So you figured out I haven't really changed. Congratulations. Not going to help you."

"I can practically feel your emotions," he said. "You radiate them. Tell me something, Emily. Why do you want me dead so much?"

"Isn't it obvious?"

"I think it's because you need to blame me. You need to believe that what you did in Broken Hill was my fault."

"It was."

"But a part of you knows the truth. That if you had tried harder, you could have stopped it."

"Goddamn it, Yeats. You're persistent. I'll give you that. But I didn't come here to listen to this. I was going to make you apologize of your own free will, but you know what, screw it. Open your fucking eyes."

"You tell yourself you had no choice but you don't believe it. That is why you desire me dead. You hope to kill a part of yourself."

"Grab him," she said, to whom, he didn't know. "Hold him down. Force open his eyes."

He raised the sword. "Who killed that boy at the Academy? Was that me? He was the first to pay for the mistake of loving you with his life. But not the last." Hands plucked at him. He flailed with the sword. "Did I make you a killer, or were you already?"

"Shut up!"

"*Vartix velkor mannik wissick!* You killed your lover! Scream!" Hands gripped him. "*Vartix velkor mannik wissick, you deserve to be punished, you deserve to die for what you did! Vartix velkor mannik wissick, scream, you evil bitch!*"

A weight of bodies bore him to the ground. Fingers groped at his face. Above this, a thin sound: a keening wail, like escaping steam.

"*Vartix velkor mannik wissick,*" he said. "*Emily, lie down and sleep!*"

His eyelids were dragged up. He saw faces he recognized, their expressions intent and focused. He knew their segments but nothing he could say would dissuade them from holding him down. He could work around that. He could convince them to release him once their duty was done. Because between the seething bodies, he saw a prone figure, sprawled on the carpet, her white coat gently rising and falling. His heart sang, because it was over, and he had won.

4 QUESTIONS TO QUICKLY KNOW SOMEONE WELL

From: http://whuffy.com/relationships/articles/8we4y93457wer.html

1. What do you do in your spare time?
2. What would you do if you had a year to live?
3. What are you most proud of?
4. What do you want?

[THREE]

Eliot went to the eighth floor, where burly men in gray uniforms were pulling up the carpet. "What the fuck?"

"Ah, Eliot," said Yeats. He had a white cloth and was mopping sweat from the back of his neck. His shirt was wet beneath the armpits. Eliot had never seen Yeats so much as breathing quickly, so this was disconcerting. "We had a little disturbance."

"The delegates have scattered. They thought you were about to bomb the place."

"Really?" said Yeats. "It's a children's charity."

Eliot backed out of the way of a man carrying carpet. The walls were lightly spattered. Fine dark droplets like mist. "I'm asking you," he said, "what the fuck?"

"Woolf came back."

He said nothing, because surely this was a joke.

"Look," Yeats said, indicating a dark patch on the carpet. "That's Frost."

"I told you she wasn't dead."

"Yes, you did."

"I asked for more time. Christ, she killed Frost?"

"Essentially," said Yeats. "A few others, too."

"How did she do that?" Yeats continued patting his neck with the cloth. There was something odd in his manner, a kind of satisfaction, which Eliot didn't understand. Maintenance workers came forward, wanting to get at the carpet on which he was standing. "Get out," Eliot said. "All of you."

The men looked questioningly at Yeats, who didn't respond. The men slunk away, leaving the aroma of cigarettes and carpet glue.

"Did she have it?"

"Yes."

"She had the word."

"Just as you predicted," Yeats said. "I should have listened to you."

"Where is she?"

Yeats said nothing.

"Did you kill her?"

"Fascinating, your priorities," said Yeats. "I tell you that the bareword has returned to us and your first question is about her."

"I have a lot of questions. They're not necessarily ordered."

"Ah, Eliot. As I have grown, you have shrunk. I offered to help you after Broken Hill. I gave you a chance to go away and find the man you are supposed to be. But no. You chose to stay. You wanted to pursue her. You actually said those words: you *wanted*. To make amends for failing to stop her, to beg forgiveness for failing to protect her, I honestly don't know. I doubt that you do. But what is plain is that she broke you. A sixteen-year-old girl and you let yourself care for her. It was clear from the beginning, but what was a weakness became nothing less than a psychological disintegration. Look at you. You are an echo of who you were."

"Well," he said. "How refreshing to have an honest opinion."

"I have faced the word and won. This is what I have done while you were falling into yourself. The day I realized the bareword could corrupt me, I began to prepare myself to face it. That is why I left the word in Broken Hill, for her to recover."

"You what?"

"I have no intention of triggering another Babel event. I have worked rather too hard for that. It was only by proving myself worthy of the word that I could trust myself to resist its temptations. And I wish to wield it for such a long time. The thing that I find disappointing about empires, Eliot, is they are so transient. On reflection, it seems that real power would be not to merely rule the world but to mark it." He shrugged. "Perhaps that's just me."

"You've become fucking incomprehensible. Woolf could have killed us all."

He shrugged. "She didn't."

"She *could have*."

"She set it into a necklace. In order to keep it close, I suppose." Yeats reached into his jacket pocket. Eliot shifted his gaze away. "I have it wrapped, Eliot."

He looked. Whatever it was lay beneath a white cloth.

"That you think I need a bareword to compromise you is adorable," Yeats said. "Eliot, in your present state, I would barely need *words*."

"Where is Woolf?"

"Downstairs. Confined. Sleeping."

"What are you going to do with her?"

"You know that. Eliot. It is time to let go of Woolf. Let me help you."

He said nothing.

"She is a murderer. She killed three thousand people. In the process of which, incidentally, she managed to inflict the word on herself. Caught a reflection in Broken Hill. An accident, I believe. But she is now under instruction to, and I quote, 'kill everyone.' How far below the surface that lurks, we can only guess. She has been attempting to resist it by channeling her thoughts toward me. But it is a part of her. It will never go away. She is irredeemable, Eliot. She always was. Accept this. And please do it quickly, because I have a job for you in Syria."

"I am not going to help you rule the world."

"Yes, you are."

"You don't know me as well as you think."

"Eliot," said Yeats, "if that were true, you wouldn't need to say it."

She woke and felt for the necklace and it was gone. The world was yellowish. It was six feet by eight. It had a padded bench seat, which she guessed doubled as a bed, and carpet she recognized. A thick gray door with a small window in it, obscured by something on the other side. She was in her underwear. Her head felt bruised. No, not her head. Something deeper than that. She sat up. She put a hand to her forehead and closed her eyes a moment, because things were very, very bad.

Time passed. She stood. She paced. She grew thirsty. She discovered a plastic bucket under the bed-seat, which she guessed was for pee. She spent some time breaking off a long, triangular shard, and tucked this into the rear waistband of her underpants. When she positioned the bucket right, you couldn't tell. It seemed to Emily that this room wasn't monitored. Maybe it was unnecessary, when you had a person in a six-by-eight cell with nothing but a bucket. But if she got out of here because the organization wasn't monitoring her, that was going to be really hilarious.

These were positive thoughts. She was not actually getting out. She was just keeping busy until Yeats turned up.

Someone did come, but not Yeats. At first, Emily didn't recognize him. He had cut his hair. It had been eight or nine years. But his eyes were the same, and she hadn't forgotten the way they had bulged in that fast food restaurant bathroom, when he'd tried to coerce her into a blow job.

She threw out some words, just in case. "Please," said Lee. The door closed. Emily caught a glimpse of people out there, who would provide obstacles to any attempted flight. She considered it anyway, but decided to save the bucket-knife. It would be a shame to waste that on Lee if she might get a chance at Yeats.

Lee went down on his haunches. It was kind of an odd pose, but it brought his eyes level with Emily's as she sat on the bench seat. Her skin puckered. She felt the urge to fold her arms, but didn't, because she didn't want to give him anything.

"We write reports, you know," Lee said. He looked odd, sickly, but that was probably the yellow lights. "When we recruit someone, we send along a little write-up, saying what we think. Yours . . . well, yours was negative, Emily. I won't lie. It was extremely negative. I know what you're thinking: I gave you a bad report because you punched me in the balls. No. I put that aside, like the professional I am. I gave you a bad report, Emily, because you were actually going to suck my cock. It was a simple test. I used weak words. Starter words. And still you were going to do it. You're fragile. You have no defense. And people like that don't last in the organization." He spread his hands. "Imagine my surprise when the Academy *accepted* you. It makes sense now. Now I know you cheated your way in. Eliot taking pity on you. Now, I understand. But at the time, I was amazed. And then they made you Woolf. . . . I took it personally. I don't mind admitting it. It felt like an insult. I mean, my report was very clear. *Candidate shows no aptitude for mental discipline nor the inclination to develop it.* Those were my words. Well, look at you now. Just like I predicted. And you know what? How it's turned out is actually pretty good for me. Now I look like a genius. It took awhile but I finally made it to DC."

He paused, as if for a response, but she didn't give him one because she hadn't figured out why he was here. He sighed and straightened, plucking at his pant creases. She wasn't thrilled with the new eyeline.

"So," Lee said, "as you might have guessed, you're going to die soon. In fact, as I understand it, the only reason you're still here is Yeats has become too busy with a new project to get around to debriefing you yet. When I say *debriefing*, I mean compromising you and getting you to dump out the contents of your brain, in case there's anything in there that might be useful to us. Now, this is going to happen. There's nothing you can do to stop it. But my idea, Emily, was to spare Yeats some trouble. You see, my being here is a very big opportunity for me. A test, you might say. And if I'm able to go back to Yeats with the information he wants, well, that would be good."

He removed his jacket and began to roll up his shirtsleeves. "Why am I telling you this, since clearly you have no interest in doing what I want? I'll tell you. It's because, Emily, I want you to understand how extremely, intensely motivated I am right now."

She said, "Uh, Lee? The idea that you can compromise me is laughable."

"Oh, I realize you're not sixteen anymore. I'm not expecting it to be that easy again. In fact, I hear you've been working on your defense pretty hard." He began to unbuckle his belt. "The thing is, Em, I think, deep down, you're just the same. I think you're fragile. You subscribed to the idea that the best defense is a good offense, and it's served you well, sure, but . . . here we are." He pulled his belt free and began to wind the strap around one hand. "I think once we test that defense, I mean, really put some pressure on it . . . we might see some cracks. I'm pretty confident about that. Because once a person is under severe physical stress, a lot of the higher brain function falls away. The critical thinking. The learned behaviors." He tapped his forehead. "What am I saying? You know all this. You were in school more recently than me. You know what I'm talking about. And you know I'm not leaving this room without getting what I want. The only question is how hard you're going to make it." He let the belt buckle dangle from his fist. "So," he said, "how are we doing this?"

Two large men came in, wearing white uniforms that Emily recognized from Labs. They approached her with their hands out like claws.

By this time, she was in a pretty crazy place, screaming and waving the bucket-knife around, spattered with blood from head to toe. Lee was lying on the floor, quietly pumping out his life through his throat. She swiped at one of the orderlies, shrieking semi-random words, but he caught her wrist and wrapped his arms around her. It felt oddly comforting. They twisted her hands and forced the bucket-knife from her fingers and held her down for what felt like hours. Some other people took Lee away. That was the last time anyone visited her who wasn't Yeats.

She picked Lee's blood off her flake by flake. It had dried hard, so this way she was able to clean herself one piece at a time. Maybe *clean* was the wrong word. It was pretty disgusting, but she kept at it, because the alternative was worse. Every flake of Lee that she removed made her feel better.

Days passed. It felt like days. She became extremely thirsty. After enough of that, she developed a tremble that wouldn't go away. Her bowels and bladder shut down. She could feel them inside her like stones. She was being tortured, she assumed. Her physical needs were being deliberately left unmet.

She thought about Eliot. About whether he knew she was here. She figured no, because if he did, he would have shown up. She just had that feeling. Of course, she had left him facedown in a ditch in Broken Hill, and it would have made complete sense if Eliot hated her with a fiery passion. But she had the idea that the kind of relationship she had with him allowed for mistakes, even big ones. And that when this door next opened, it wouldn't be Yeats but Eliot, and his eyes would be full of reproach but there would also be forgiveness and hope.

She considered removing her underwear, which were spattered with dark brown Lee spots and made her feel permanently stained. It might even be intimidating to Yeats. *Nothing here but Emily, pal.* But she didn't do it. She wasn't that badass. She made herself climb off the bed every now and again and jump on the spot, or at least bounce up and down. So she wasn't just lying there. The light never went off. She couldn't tell how much time was passing. Her thoughts went around and around. Sometimes she caught herself singing.

Eliot swung the car into the school driveway and crawled up to the house. It was late, most of the windows dark, but not Brontë's. He sat in the car for a few moments. Then he climbed out and went inside.

The corridors were empty. It had been a while since he was last here and the place felt unfamiliar, although nothing was different. He entered the East Wing and passed a boy with a white ribbon tied around his wrist and dark bruises beneath his eyes, reciting something in Latin. The boy saw Eliot and broke off, then looked pained. Eliot did not stop.

He knocked on Brontë's door. She called for him to enter in the imperious voice she adopted for students and he stepped inside. She was behind her desk, surrounded by papers, her hair pinned up but threatening escape. She set down a pen and leaned back in her chair. "What fortuitous timing. I was about to start grading papers." She gestured. "Will you sit?"

"I'm going to Syria."

"Oh," she said. "When?"

"Now. Tonight."

She nodded. "You should try to visit the museum in Damascus. They have a tablet with the world's oldest recorded linear alphabet. It's quite humbling."

"I want you to come with me."

She became very still. "I'm not sure what you mean."

He looked around the room. "Do you remember the watch I had? The digital one, to wake me so that I could get back to my room before dawn. I was terrified of it failing. Or sleeping through it."

"Eliot. Please."

"Atwood knew," he said. "She told me as much, many years later."

"Please," said Brontë.

"We thought we were being clever. Carrying on under their noses. And when . . . when we had to stop, we thought we did that in secret, too. We did it because we were terrified of being discovered. But they knew."

Her eyes glimmered. "Why are you saying these things? Are you here to compromise me?"

"No," he said. "God, no."

"Then stop talking."

"They persuaded us. Without saying a word."

"There was no alternative, Eliot."

"I don't believe that anymore. I can't. I'm sorry."

"It's the truth."

"I have this idea that it would have been a girl," he said. "I don't know why. But I've thought that for a while. I find it hard to shake."

Brontë put her face in her hands. "Stop talking."

"She'd be grown now. A young woman."

"*Stop!*"

"I'm sorry." He caught himself. "I'm sorry."

"I want you to leave."

He nodded. He hesitated, almost apologized again, then moved to the door. Before he closed it, he glanced back, in case she'd looked up from her hands. But she hadn't.

He landed in Damascus. Heat enveloped him the instant he stepped over the threshold of the airplane, a taste of Australia with a different scent. He made his way across the tarmac to the airport proper and submitted himself to the impatient eyes of various mustachioed officials. His papers were impeccable and so he was soon released into the main hall, which was large, framed with high, latticed keyhole-shaped windows, and even vaguely air-conditioned. A short man in a tight suit stood gripping a sign that read:

إلْيُوت

"I'm Eliot," he said. "You are Hossein?"

The man nodded, extending his hand in the Western manner.

"مهين ة صيريحيخاأاف الأبد," said Eliot. The man's hand dropped. His face relaxed. "My plane is delayed," Eliot said. "It is due in ten hours. You will wait here for it and that is what you will believe." He could see the exit. There was no shortage of drivers on the pavement outside. "And when Yeats asks you what happened," he said, "tell him I retired."

Someone entered the room. She squeezed shut her eyes as soon as she realized, so was left with only the briefest impression: a square man in a dark suit, silver hair.

"Hello, Emily," Yeats said.

She sat up. Her brain felt soft. Lee had been right: It was harder to marshal mental defenses while under physiological stress. She needed to think clearly but all she wanted was a sandwich.

"Lee is dead. You assumed, perhaps. But in case you were wondering about the possibility of last-minute medical heroics . . . no. He died. Another for your collection."

"I'll stop at one more."

"No," Yeats said. "You won't. I think we both understand this. You are infected with a murderous impulse. You've managed to ameliorate this so far by plotting my demise. If you actually succeeded . . . well, that would be a problem, wouldn't it? Since you would inevitably begin to, well, *kill everyone*. I think you must realize this. You must plan to kill me. But you must not do it. Quite the conundrum."

She wondered how quickly she could get off the bed and get her hands around Yeats's throat. Probably not very fast. Probably to no great effect, even if she did. She needed to be smarter. This was her chance; she would not get him alone again. She needed her head to stop pounding.

"Was this a suicide mission? I don't think so. It goes against your character. I think you came here with a plan to kill me and the vaguest hope that you would somehow be redeemed. For you are such an immediate girl. You live from opportunity to opportunity. Does that sound right?"

Maybe, she thought. She didn't know. She was hungry. She wondered where Eliot was.

"I'm founding a religion," said Yeats. "I use the term *religion* loosely. But then, so does everyone. It's rather a lot of work, even with the bareword, and once it's done, that's only the first step. So I won't waste any further time. Here's what's going to happen. You will open your eyes. You will look at the bareword. I will say, *Forever serve my interests.*" He loomed closer, a shape she couldn't quite bring into focus. "I see from your expression that this is unexpected. You thought you would be killed. A natural assumption. But what I realized, Emily, is that you have made yourself useful. You are skilled, resourceful, adaptable, and you have a kill order in your head that will be triggered in the event of my death. You are, in fact, the perfect bodyguard."

"No. I won't do that."

"Of course you will. You have no way of stopping it."

She bared her teeth, trying to rise from the bed. He was right. She was alone in a cell. She didn't even have a bucket. But there had to be something. There had always been something before.

"As many people as I've enthralled, I don't think I've ever encountered someone who hates me quite this much. Which makes this rather fascinating, Emily, since, the brain being what it is, your mind will invent a series of rationalizations to justify why you're choosing to serve me. How far will you bend in order to reach that place?

That's what raises my curiosity. I wonder whether the end result will still be able to be accurately called *you*."

"I will kill you."

"Well," he said, "you'll want to."

"Stay back." She thought she heard him approaching, and threw out her arms. "Stay back, you motherfucker!"

"I'm not going to grapple with you, Emily. You will open your eyes of your own volition. You will do this because you see there is no alternative."

"Eliot," she said. "I want to see Eliot."

"I'm afraid Eliot is in Syria. He flew out last night."

"Tell him I'm here."

"Oh, Emily," said Yeats. "He already knows."

She didn't want to believe him. But she couldn't find falsehood in his voice. *Eliot*, she thought. *Eliot, you were my last hope.*

"Open your eyes, please," Yeats said, and she began to shake very badly, because she was going to do it.

word ***(w ɑ : d)***

(noun)

1. a single distinct meaningful unit of language
2. a basic unit of data in a computer
3. something spoken or written: *a word of warning*
4. *(with negative)* the smallest amount of something spoken or written: *don't believe a word of it*
5. contentious or angry speech: *he had words with her*
6. a command, password, or signal: *she gave the word to begin*
7. one's account of the truth: *her word against his*
8. a promise or assurance: *I give you my word I'll return*

[FOUR]

"So you left her," Harry said.

Eliot rubbed his forehead. His throat was sore; he had been talking for some time. It was taxing, because he was recovering from a near-death experience and outside the window forces were gathering to kill him. "That's what you get from that story? That I left?" Harry didn't respond. "Yes. I left. There was no alternative."

"There's always an alternative."

"Well," he said. He felt tired. "It didn't feel like it."

"What then?"

"Yeats sent her after me. I had this crazy idea that I'd be left alone if I went far enough away. That I could start a new life. But she came after me and systematically murdered everyone who was in the way."

"She's probably compromised."

"You think that makes a difference?"

"Yes," said Harry, "because I can *un*-compromise her, with the bareword."

"Can't be done."

"Why not?"

"You can't erase an instruction. Not even with that. You would only create conflicting instructions."

"Which means what?"

"It's unpredictable."

"Well, that's fucking something."

"The original instruction won't go anywhere. It could reassert itself at any moment, based on situational factors, such as where she is, how she's feeling. Do you want to take that chance when one of the instructions is *kill everyone*?"

"Yes."

"Well, you fucking can't."

A low thrumming began outside. Harry peered out the window at the sky. "I love her."

He shook his head. "You're misremembering."

"I remember that."

"Listen to me carefully," Eliot said, "because over the last twelve months, I have been highly motivated to figure out exactly what happened in Broken Hill, and as a result I know for a fact that your movements diverged from hers shortly after she left me facedown in a ditch. What I pieced together from this was that when she went to you and asked you to leave with her, you said no. This is how I first began to suspect your existence as an outlier. And it's how I know you didn't love her."

"You said people are defined by what they want. That it's the most important thing about them. Yes?"

"Yes."

"Then I know who I am."

He looked out the window. "Well, terrific. That's terrific, Wil. I'm so glad you could find your emotional core, before your ex-girlfriend murders us. Imagine what would happen if she got her hands on a bareword again. Imagine that."

"I'll keep it from her."

"Okay," said Eliot, "well, now we're entering a magical fantasy land, because with all due respect to your newly regained assertiveness, you don't have a hope in hell of keeping her from anything she wants. What's that noise?"

"Choppers."

"More than one? What do they look like?"

"Why would she do anything to help this guy Yeats? She *must* be compromised. He's *making* her chase us and you say she has to die for it."

"You think I like it?"

"Yes. I do. Because of Charlotte."

He looked at the ceiling. "Well," he said. "Maybe you're right."

"So?"

"So it doesn't matter. Is it Woolf's choice? Maybe not, but she is what she is. You, right now, are shooting at people for the crime of being compromised. Why is Woolf different? Also, may I add, she wasn't made this way out of nowhere. Yeats sowed that seed in fertile ground."

Harry raised his voice over the din of the choppers. "Meaning what?"

"Meaning she wiped out Broken Hill!"

"Maybe she was compromised *then*!"

"You're choosing what you want to believe! Christ! I would love to believe that I didn't let three thousand people die because I couldn't see her for what she was. But I can't. The truth is she was always like this and I refused to see it."

"I tell you what, how about we kill *Yeats*?"

"Sure, we'll ask Woolf to stand aside for a minute. Don't look at me like that's a realistic possibility. She'll defend him to the death. And even if she could be circumvented somehow, Yeats being alive is what keeps Woolf in check. Remove him and she's left with an instruction to *kill everyone*."

Harry was watching out the window. The loudness of the choppers seemed to have leveled.

"You want a nightmare scenario? Yeats goes down, Woolf takes the bareword. Yeats cannot die. Not before Woolf." Harry didn't react. "What's happening out there?"

"Guys coming out of choppers."

"What kind of guys?"

"Military. Big black helmets with goggles. Can't see their faces."

"Ah," said Eliot. "So we are completely fucked, then."

Harry looked at him.

"Environmentally Isolated Personnel. They see the world through filters, to protect them against compromise."

"Should I shoot them?"

"Sure," he said. "Why not?"

Harry raised the rifle. A part of the window frame near his head exploded. He ducked against the wall. "Shit."

"Yes," Eliot said.

Harry moved to the other window, checked outside. "They're encircling us."

"I would imagine they're landing on the roof, too," Eliot said. "Rappelling down from the choppers, perhaps."

"What happened to Charlotte?"

"What?"

"When I met you, you had a buddy. A whole bunch of guys, on that ranch. Including Charlotte. How did they get there?"

"Who gives a shit?" Eliot said. "Honestly, Harry. At this point, who cares? You think they're going to take us alive?"

Harry rubbed his chin, a gesture Eliot hadn't seen before. "Under the mattress."

"What?"

"I got you a pistol from the armory. It's under the mattress."

Eliot stared at him.

"You want to maybe get it out?"

"I maybe want to shoot you with it, if it would make any difference."

"It's going to be all right, Eliot."

"No," said Eliot, "these guys are going to kill us while Woolf watches from a distance. Sometime later, an unimaginable number of people are going to devote their lives to shifting dirt, because Yeats has developed a hankering to dig a very deep hole in one place and pile it up in another. That's how it's going to be, you stupid asshole. Those guys on the ranch? They were the ones I could persuade to leave the organization. I thought Charlotte was one of them, but it has since become abundantly clear that she was compromised by Woolf, and feeding back information, such as your existence, what we were planning, and so on, the entire time, and then she turned Charlotte against me and I had to shoot her! I had to fucking shoot her, Wil!"

"Just get out the gun."

"Why bother?" he shouted. "Since Woolf is coming only to shower us with chocolates and kisses?"

Harry paced.

"Oh," Eliot said. "Oh, oh, are we having regrets?"

"Shut up."

"Twenty years," Eliot said. "My entire adult life, I've guarded every word that's come out of my mouth. And you know what? I'm done. I am finally, completely fucking done. So hey-o! Fuck you, Wil Parke! Harry Wilson! Whoever you are! Fuck you very much! And fuck you, Yeats! And you, Emily Woolf! Fuck you the most of all!" He threw back the blanket. He slid a hand beneath the mattress and found metal. "Let's go!" His body hurt everywhere but his mind was soaring. "Here we go, hey-o, diddle diddle!"

Emily came out of the chopper and jogged to the shelter of a falling-down building that had once sold wire, apparently. She had forgotten about stores like this. Shops, she meant. Shops that only sold one thing, which you could not conceive of wanting. You could live a lifetime in DC and never see a wire store. If you wanted wire, you would go to a warehouse-style hypermarket and it would be one shelf in aisle twelve. But here it was a whole shop. You went in and asked for some wire, because the roos had knocked down a section of your side paddock fence again, and you would have a conversation about it.

She hadn't wanted to come back to Broken Hill. She had been

operating for a while now as a compartmentalized person, putting different pieces of herself in different places, and she didn't know what Broken Hill would do to that. But she was here, because she didn't get to make choices about that kind of thing anymore, and had to do the best she could. One part of her, one of the compartments, was glad. It thought she was coming home. The rest was pretty freaked out.

"We're deploying," said Plath. Plath was running around with a headset that wouldn't stay put, talking to security guys. Emily was not very happy with Plath. She had crossed paths with Plath a few times and each time Plath was more neurotic. There was something wild and jumpy in her eyes that Emily did not trust. Also, Plath had come on board shortly after the terrible failed attempt to corner Eliot and his outlier at the Portland airport, during which the poet Raine had died, and although Plath hadn't said anything, Emily knew she viewed that incident as a shameful fuckup on Emily's part. "It's so hot." Plath began to extract herself from her jacket. Emily was not wearing a jacket, because it had been obvious in advance that the desert would be hot. "Like an *oven*."

"Yes." She watched Plath get her jacket tangled up in her headset.

"I'll call Yeats, tell him we landed."

"No."

"He asked to be kept up to—"

"Don't call Yeats," Emily said. She was still in charge. She was still the best in the organization at hunt-and-kill.

"We need a command center," said a man. His voice was machine modulated, coming out of a helmet. His name was Masters. He was in control of the soldiers. Currently, Masters had EIPs spreading through Broken Hill like a toxic spill, establishing perimeters, getting fixes, whatever else it was they did. It was to help her neutralize Eliot, but she didn't like it, being around people she couldn't compromise.

She remembered a burger place. It was a good distance from the hospital, close enough to coordinate the action but not so close that Eliot was likely to be able to sneak up and shoot her. She had eaten there, alone, sometimes, other times not. But she wasn't thinking about that. Harry was trying to surface in her brain but she was not going to let him. The point was, it was a good location. "I know somewhere."

A small squad swept the burger place while she and Plath stood outside, shielding their faces from the sun. A chopper passed overhead, whipping up hot, stinging sand. "Ugh," said Plath. "This place."

A soldier opened the rear door and gestured. She passed through a small kitchen, where a dark skillet lay under a layer of dust. Utensils dangled from overhead racks, surprisingly bright. Then she was in the serving area, passing familiar tables. There were no bodies. Maybe the soldiers had removed them. Plath hung back for some reason but Emily moved to the front of the store. There were dark shapes outside, hard to see through the dirty plate glass, and she approached with some trepidation. Outdoor tables. A ragged umbrella still over one of them. A few cars. If she put her face to the glass, she could see farther down the street. She didn't look for detail but could see the shape of the hospital. Somewhere inside were Eliot and his outlier.

Her phone rang. She pulled it out. "I hear you're in Broken Hill," said Yeats.

"Yes." She looked at Plath, the snitch.

"I find myself wondering why Eliot would go there, of all places."

"Well, my guess is to get the word," she said. "The outlier can just pick it up." There was silence. "Hello?"

"I'm sorry. I was rendered speechless a moment, just then."

"The bareword," she said. "It's in the emergency room."

"I *have* the bareword."

"You have the copy I made. The original is still there."

"How useful it would have been to have this information before this moment."

"Oh," she said. "I'm sorry." She had known that, in one of her compartments.

"You will kill Eliot," Yeats said, "and the outlier, and, for that matter, anyone else Eliot has managed to conjure up who doesn't work directly for me. You will then cordon off the hospital until I arrive. Is this clear?"

"Yes." In her head, she added: *you jerk*. She did this sometimes. It was a kind of game.

"I really am vexed by this outlier business. I have felt decidedly uncomfortable, knowing that one exists. It is a most unwelcome distraction to my work."

"I can imagine." *You jerk.*

"Call me when Eliot's dead," he said. "I won't set foot in Broken Hill until then. Oh, and Emily? At some point, you will fill me in on exactly how you managed to copy an object you can't look at."

"I will do that," she said. The phone clicked. Her jaw worked and for a moment she thought she was actually going to say it. But she only made a little grunt, *yuh*. She glanced at Plath. But no one seemed to have noticed. So that was okay.

In the beginning, she hadn't even been able to think it. Perhaps eventually she would be able to say the words to his face. *Hey, Yeats! You're a jerk!* It was a fun idea. Implausible; most likely, this was as far as it could go, a mental game. She would see. For now, the important thing was that a part of her was still her.

Eliot strode to the door, pulled it open, and disappeared. This happened much more quickly than Harry expected, because until a few moments ago, Eliot had looked very much like a guy recovering from a near-fatal gunshot wound. What had suddenly revived him, Harry did not know. "Wait," he said. But Eliot was running down the corridor; Harry could hear his footsteps.

He hefted the rifle. This was going to be especially useless for close-quarters combat. He hadn't intended to leave the room. He'd intended to stay and pick off guys until Emily got the message and came to see him. He blew air through his teeth. "Fuck," he said, and went after Eliot. He jogged down the corridor, passing two neonatal rooms that were once staffed by a woman named Helen who'd always had pink iced doughnuts, any time of day or night. Harry had never seen her eat one. She just had them. He'd visited this place often, for those doughnuts.

He reached the corner and poked his head around. Eliot was nowhere to be seen. He had just fucking disappeared. Harry debated the merits of opening his mouth to make the kind of noise that might attract armed men, then there was a quick one-two of flat gunshots in the near distance, which decided him.

He reached the stairwell and peered over the railing to see Eliot standing below him. At Eliot's feet was a man in a black suit with no helmet. The man looked dazed. His gun, a semiautomatic, lay a few feet away.

"Shoot them in the face," Eliot said. "They're armored, but it's distracting."

"What did you do?" The man in the black suit began to grope for his gun. "He's moving!" He raised the rifle.

"Don't!" said Eliot. "He's on the side of the angels now."

The man retrieved his gun and got to this feet. He looked up at Harry questioningly.

"He's cool," Eliot told the man. "Neither of you shoot the other." He began to descend the steps.

"How did you . . . ?" But Eliot had disappeared. Harry ran after him, jumping the steps three or four at a time. He caught Eliot at the top of the second floor, which was the surgical wing. "Will you fucking wait?" He went to seize Eliot by the shoulder but the black-suited man slapped his gun into his shoulder and looked down the barrel at him.

"Don't alarm my prole," Eliot said. "He wants to protect me."

"What do you think you're doing?"

"Looking for Woolf."

"She could be anywhere."

"Yes. But it's a better option than sitting in that room." Eliot looked around. His pupils were dilated. "You used to work here. What's a clever way out?"

"I don't know. Can you tell this guy to stop pointing his fucking gun at me?"

"He's finding you threatening. So am I, actually."

"You look like you're on drugs."

"I'm releasing a lot of dopamine," Eliot said. "It's a natural high. Joel! Gun down."

The soldier lowered his gun. He stared at Harry with baleful eyes.

"How about a laundry chute?"

"What?"

"A chute," Eliot said, "that we slide down to a basement or somesuch."

"No. They don't work like that. This is a hospital—we'd lose children down them."

"What, then?"

"I don't know."

"Think," Eliot said. "You must have lost a few patients. People who snuck out somehow. It's not Fort Knox."

"No one . . . okay, one time a guy broke into a storage room by climbing onto the roof of the building next door. We might be able to—"

"Yes. That." Eliot looked at the soldier. "Go cause a distraction. Shoot at nothing. Report false information. Things like that." The man nodded and began to jog down the stairs. "This storage room, then."

"How did you compromise that guy?"

"I know him. I used to work for the organization, you know. Storage room."

He led Eliot through double doors. He had never liked coming here. It was the surgeons. He'd never been completely sure they really gave a shit. They seemed to enjoy challenges more than people. "So you, what, shot him in the face, pulled off his helmet, and used words?"

"Correct," Eliot said.

He reached the storage room and tried the handle. No one had been by in the past year or so to unlock it, apparently. But he knew where the key was kept. He jogged down the corridor, pulled open the second drawer in the nurse's station, and found it among paper clips and rubber bands. When he returned, Eliot was tugging at the door. "Quick," Eliot said.

"I am being quick."

"Quicker."

He pulled open the door. He was finding the new Eliot unsettling. Somewhere in the distance was a staccato of gunfire. They waited but it wasn't repeated.

"Joel," said Eliot, fondly.

They entered the storeroom. The window had been fitted with new locks since the intruder but they wouldn't be much of an impediment from this side. He peered through the glass. A short climb down to a secluded part of the roof, then a short run and leap to the roof of the pharmacy next door. He did not see any soldiers.

"The real problem is finding Woolf," Eliot murmured in his ear. Harry flinched. He hadn't heard him approach. Eliot looked at him. "Where is she, do you think?"

"Can you take a step back?"

"I think you know." He tapped Harry's forehead.

"Don't fucking touch my head." He began to wrestle the window out of its frame.

"This place," Eliot said. "It brought you back to yourself. Maybe it's having a similar effect on her. And you know her. So tell me. Where is she?"

"That plan you had before, about getting out of Broken Hill? I'm coming around on that."

"Where," Eliot said.

He tossed the frame to the floor and climbed up the shelves. The window was narrow but he managed to work the rifle through it and drop to the rooftop six feet below. He crouched against the wall until Eliot dropped beside him.

Eliot looked around. "This was a good idea." He rose and ran to the edge of the roof, leaped across the gap, and landed on the tin roof of the pharmacy. Harry saw his head turn left, right. Then he stopped moving. Harry froze. Eliot crept back toward the edge, peered over, and dropped out of sight.

Harry ran after him. Halfway there, he heard Eliot bark out words in a strange, guttural tongue. When he reached the edge, he saw Eliot in the alley standing over another helmet-free soldier. This one was bald.

He tossed the rifle down and lowered himself over the edge. "I'm starting to feel like you don't even need me."

"Oh, I do," said Eliot. "I don't know where she is." He looked at the pharmacy.

"She's not in there. I don't remember her ever going in there. Eliot. Eliot?"

"What?"

"You're staring at nothing."

"Oh," said Eliot. "I was thinking about earplugs."

"Is that . . . that sounds like a great idea."

"It's great against verbal compromise. It's not so great for hearing someone coming up behind you with a gun. So there's a trade-off."

"Right."

"I'd rather be shot than compromised, though." He looked at Harry. "Shoot me if she manages to compromise me. Did I already say that?"

"No."

"Well, do. I'm serious."

The bald man said, "We're on the third floor. We know you're not there."

"Thank you, Max," said Eliot. "Harry. Where is she?"

"How the fuck should I know?"

"Think."

He looked around. If he were Emily, where would he go? Somewhere near the hospital. There was a café on the other side of the block, but Emily had never liked it; she said it smelled like men. They'd usually gone to the burger joint farther down. That was actually where they'd first met. Outside of her being a patient, that was. She'd been eating and Harry had walked by with some girl, whomever he was seeing at the time, and she'd called out. He remembered thinking she was a nutcase. Why had he thought that? The card. She'd sent him a card with something crazy written on it, TO MY HERO or YOU SAVED MY LIFE, something like that. But then they'd spoken and she hadn't seemed crazy. There had been something about her. Something bright, to which he'd responded.

"You thought of something," Eliot said. "I see it on your face."

He shook his head.

"Don't hold out on me." Eliot leaned closer. "Come on, now, Harry."

"You are creepy as hell right now."

"This state is temporary. I need to make the most of it. Comedown is going to be a bitch."

"I'll make you a deal."

"Oh, yes."

"I might know where she is. But if I tell you, I go in first. I get to talk to her. If it goes badly, fine. You do what you have to do. But I get five minutes."

"Deal." Eliot stuck out his hand.

He hesitated, suspicious. "You don't mean that."

"What do you want me to say?" Eliot shouted. "You're confronting the futility of your own proposition! Shoot that guy!" This part was directed to the bald soldier, who dropped to one knee and raised the semiautomatic. Harry turned in time to see a pair of dark-suited figures at the end of the alley. Eliot grabbed his arm and then they were running.

"It's the burger place," Harry panted. "Right, right, circle around the block." They rounded the corner. "Five minutes. Promise me."

"Okay, okay," Eliot said. "Fine." He stopped, eyes widening at something on Harry's gun. "Whoa, shit, fuck."

"What?" he said. He couldn't see the problem, and looked at Eliot, and Eliot's pistol butt was moving very quickly toward his face. That was all he knew.

The soldiers went in and then there was a problem. Emily could tell because at first Masters emitted updates at intervals of fifteen seconds—who was where, doing what, and for how long they were expected to do it; a nonstop cataloging of physical facts that he seemed to enjoy on a deep, sexual level—then, for no reason, a whole minute went by with no updates at all. This manifested in Plath as a series of increasingly dramatic hair corrections, and finally a question, and Masters turned his goggles toward her and said in his machine voice, "We're trying to fix target location."

"I thought you *had* target location," Plath said. Masters did not answer. "Did we not *start* with target location?"

"Eliot is slippery," Emily said.

"We are *not* having another Portland." Plath directed this at Masters, but what Masters thought of it was unknowable. Emily kind of hoped Masters would become so pissed off with Plath that he would unsnag one of what had to be five or six different weapons strapped to various parts of his body and do something unspeakable with it. *Yeats, Yeats*, she thought, as she did at times like this. *You jerk.*

She rose from the table. The front glass was very dirty but she could see through it. A chopper was hovering above the hospital, but aside from this, nothing seemed to be happening.

"We're regrouping," said Masters. "We may have a new fix."

"You get a fix," said Plath. "You get a fucking fix right this second or you'll regret it for the rest of your life." Her face was flushed. Globules of sweat formed a neat line all along her hairline. She was displaying an awful lot of emotion for a poet, which made Emily think that Plath had reason to believe the consequences for failure were particularly terrible. She kept watching the road. She needed to think like Eliot. She knew him better than most. She could imagine Eliot skulking around out there, sniffing her out. That's what he'd be thinking about. Not escape. He would be coming for her.

A black-suited soldier emerged from the crossroad and jogged toward the burger place. "Who is this guy?" she said. Nobody answered, so she tried again. "Who the fuck is this fucking guy?"

Plath came up beside her. "Speaking for myself, I don't mind adding a little manpower to this location."

Masters said, "We're redrawing our zones."

This sounded like bullshit to Emily, because if her current location had become part of Masters's operational zone, that would have been something he would have mentioned. Soldiers moving locations: That was all he talked about. She eyed the approaching guy. "Oh," she said. "That's Eliot."

"That's . . . that's impossible," said Plath. But there was uncertainty in her voice. Plath was beginning to realize what Emily had known for a while: that you could not underestimate Eliot. Every time you thought you had him figured out, you didn't. "Let's . . . let's get some security here, huh?" Plath reached across Emily to Masters, who may have been barking orders over his internal radio or may have been just standing there; it was impossible to tell. "Masters. Masters."

"Unit is not responding." Masters drew a fat pistol. "May be hostile. I advise retreat."

Plath vanished. Emily hesitated. She really did want to face Eliot and end him. But this was not the way to do it: with Eliot in heavy body armor, filtered against compromise. There was taking a risk, and there was suicide. She turned to follow Plath, then had another thought. There was always the possibility that this was another layer of sneakiness. Eliot could have deliberately sent someone who would be spotted—the outlier, perhaps, or just a soldier he'd managed to overcome—toward the burger place from the front in order to flush her out the back. That was just the kind of thing that Eliot might do. She considered. There was a side door, leading to the dumpster. She decided to be prudent.

She pushed her way outside. The brick wall of the adjoining store faced her. This was the kind of thing Emily liked: a closeted escape route. This, right here, was her element. Then she stopped, because it occurred to her that maybe this was a problem. Maybe the last thing she wanted to do in this situation was follow her instincts, since those might be predictable to someone who knew her very well. Eliot stepped around the corner.

"Shit," she said.

Little yellow plugs poked out of Eliot's ears. He was holding a pistol. His eyes were wide and there was a sheen of sweat on his face that told her he had put himself into a heightened mental state. Poets could do this, if they really wanted. She had seen them do it. They talked and moved very rapidly for about an hour, then slept for days.

"Gotcha," said Eliot.

She held up her hands. She wanted to speak, but it seemed like if she opened her mouth, he would shoot her. He would shoot her anyway, of course. That was why he was here.

They faced each other a moment. Maybe some guys would come through the door and take care of Eliot. That would be super handy.

Eliot wiggled the plugs out of his ears with his free hand. "I had to render the outlier unconscious. He couldn't be trusted."

"Okay," she said.

"I blame myself for what happened. I should have stopped it." She didn't know what to say to that. "I have to kill you."

She nodded. It had been like this for a while.

His fingers flexed on the pistol. "I'm sorry I didn't teach you better." His expression was very strange.

"Eliot," she said.

"You have to stop."

"Eliot."

There were soldiers approaching. She could feel them. This idea was distressing in a way it hadn't been a few moments ago.

"I made mistakes," he said. Around her, soldiers boiled out of the air like ants. There was a great deal of noise and Eliot could have shot her but he didn't and he fell down and died.

After this, she felt strange. People came and went, soldiers and poets, and sometimes they stopped to speak to her but she didn't hear them. When they began to package Eliot, she walked to the front of the burger place and sat at a table. Occasionally someone walked by but for the most part she was alone. She began to cry. She didn't understand why, because she had wanted Eliot dead. She had wanted that very clearly. But there was grief coming out of her anyway, spilling from her compartments, and she was reminded that not all of her wants were hers.

A shadow fell beside her. She looked up to see who was stupid enough to disturb her in this moment, and saw Yeats.

He righted a fallen chair and composed himself into it. He was wearing a beautiful dark gray suit and his hair looked fresh and bright. He was wearing sunglasses but he removed these and set them on the table, and behind them his eyes were flat.

"Oh," she said. She felt stupid. Of course Yeats was here. She should have realized that.

"Congratulations." He surveyed the line of dust-blown buildings across the road. "You see now why I wanted you, specifically, on Eliot."

She didn't reply.

"Persuasion stems from understanding. We compel others by learning who they are and turning it against them. All this, the chasing, the guns . . ." He gestured vaguely. "These are details. What Eliot could not escape was the fact that I understood him better than he understood himself." Plath hovered at the edge of Emily's senses. Yeats said, "A glass of water, please. Let's make it two."

Once Plath had gone, Yeats shrugged his jacket and passed it to Masters, who was standing like he was planted there. "I have been visiting delegates. Not all of them agree with my new direction for the organization. Some tried to move against me. Expected, of course. Futile, since I understand them. We attempt to conceal ourselves, Emily, but the truth is we do not entirely want to be concealed. We want to be found. Every poet, sooner or later, discovers this: that within perfect walls, there is nothing worth protecting. There is, in fact, nothing. And so we exchange privacy for intimacy. We gamble with it, hoping that by exposing ourselves, someone will find a way in. This is why the human animal will always be vulnerable: because it wants to be." Plath arrived with two glasses, of a kind Emily recognized from years before, and set them on the table.

"I feel bad about Eliot."

"Yes, well," said Yeats. "Some kind of suppressed emotional overflow, I would imagine."

"And I'm remembering things."

"Oh? Such as?"

"I came out of the ER. Through that door." She pointed. "I went that way. People were killing each other. Because of the word. Harry came after me. He knew what I'd done. But he saved me anyway."

"I'm not sure why you're telling me this," said Yeats. "It's irrelevant."

"I'm not talking to you."

A figure was walking toward them, coming from the direction of the hospital. In the heat haze, it could have been anyone. But she had a feeling.

"Harry," she said.

Harry peered over the edge of the roof at the street below. His head throbbed. Eliot had hit him. He had frowned at something on Harry's rifle, and Harry had looked to see what, and woken up slumped in a doorway. Now Eliot was gone and Harry was on the roof of a furniture store, trying to see what was going on.

A few minutes ago, a soldier had walked toward the burger place, then another emerged from the front door and approached with his pistol drawn. It seemed like they were going to have a confrontation, but they stopped at three feet's separation and stood there as if communicating telepathically. Then they both ran back to the burger place and plenty more soldiers appeared and there was gunfire. Eventually a young woman emerged and sat down at a table. He stared, because the woman was Emily.

He had begun to doubt that a little, because of Eliot. Whether she was still the same. But now everything was clear. He wriggled back from the rooftop. It was always this way: The more people talked, the more they obscured. You didn't need to argue for the truth. You could see it. He had almost forgotten that. He gripped the rifle and went to get Emily.

Yeats turned to look at the figure approaching them out of the heat haze. "Who?"

"The outlier, could be," said Plath, peering out from a raised hand. The figure's arms were extended from his sides. He was wearing jeans and a T-shirt. "Wil Parke. Looks unarmed."

"Well, how about we shoot him?"

"On it," said Masters. He gestured and two soldiers stepped onto the road.

"We know Parke," said Plath. "He's indecisive. Untrained with weapons. He's a carpenter."

"Emily, you appear anxious," said Yeats. "Is there something I should know?"

"Yes."

"Tell me."

"I thought Harry died. But he didn't. I just made myself believe that."

Plath said, "Who's Harry?"

"Her lover," said Yeats, "of some time ago. He's the outlier?"

She nodded.

Yeats drummed his fingers on the table. "This changes nothing."

They watched the soldiers fan out. Harry began to slow. She could see his face.

"Wait," said Yeats. "I'm missing something. Aren't I?"

She had to answer. "Yes."

"What am I missing?" He clicked his fingers at someone behind her. "You, too." A poet, Rosenberg, a young guy with longish hair, stepped onto the road, heading after the soldiers. "Emily?"

"Two things."

"Name them. I am instructing you to name them."

"I don't think you've been in love. Not recently, anyway. I'm not sure you remember what it's like. It compromises you. It takes over your body. Like a bareword. I think love is a bareword. That's the first thing." Yeats didn't react. If anything, he seemed baffled. "The second thing is I wouldn't characterize Harry as indecisive and untrained with weapons."

Plath said, "Perhaps we should move inside."

"Yes," Yeats said. "Quite." He smoothed his pants and began to rise from the table. Then he stopped, because Emily had seized him by the tie.

"Also," she said, "you are a jerk."

He walked toward the burger place until soldiers moved onto the road to intercept him. Then he changed course for the real estate office. He clambered through a space that had once held a plate glass window, collected the rifle from where he'd left it on the counter, and jogged toward the back offices. He'd been here a few times when dating Melissa, the real estate agent. Enough to know the layout, anyway. He took position in Melissa's office and waited.

A few minutes later, a soldier shuffled in. Harry waited until the second appeared, then put a bullet into his faceplate. Both men vanished like smoke. He pulled the bolt, reloading as he jogged out into the corridor. He went right instead of left, eased open the rear door, and then was in sunshine. He trotted around the side of the building to the air-con vents and peered through. The second soldier was moving away from him in a crouch. He raised the rifle and shot him in the back of the head.

When he reentered the building, he was surprised to find both guys still alive. He wouldn't have credited a helmet with being able to stop a high-powered .28. But he guessed that momentum had to go somewhere. One of the soldiers had pulled off his helmet and was vomiting down his chest. The other was crawling weakly toward the front door.

He raised the rifle. The helmet-less solder raised a hand. Harry shot him. He walked around to the other one, reloading the rifle. A man unexpectedly appeared outside the window, a young guy in a cheap suit and tie, stringing together nonsense words, and Harry shot him through the window. He looked back. The crawling soldier had stopped crawling.

He reloaded the rifle. He could hear a chopper approaching. Soldiers would be coming from both sides, he guessed. They would be jogging slowly, like these two guys, since they were encased in forty-pound armored ovens. They had been lumbering around in the noonday sun for about an hour. He couldn't really imagine what that was like. He had seen people drop dead out here, trying to do too much. They had the idea that the worst the sun could do was make them uncomfortable. They applied their sunscreen and their hats and headed out and just fell over.

He went into the bathroom and slid open the window. There was a low fence offering cover to the adjoining building, and from there he thought he could make his way unseen to pretty much anywhere he wanted. He climbed out the window and began to crawl.

Yeats's eyes widened across the table. She had never seen him look shocked before. She had never really seen him look anything.

"Release me," he said.

"You release *me*," she said, although that was just to fill time; there was only one way she could ever be free of Yeats, and she was going to have to make that happen herself. He pulled back, reaching inside his jacket for the thing that would take away her mind again. Which showed Emily that Yeats really did not get it. He thought the word had worn off, somehow; that she no longer felt compelled to obey him.

She went after him but found herself gripped from behind by Plath, of all people. Plath was thin and wiry, not the kind of person who could hold Emily for long, but she hadn't expected to be held at all, and it gave Yeats time to get out the word.

"Sit down and stop moving," he said.

"No." Disbelief spread across his face. Plath's arms were already slackening, anticipating Emily's compliance. But Yeats's hand was coming out of his jacket, and she didn't want to face what was in there, so she threw her head backward. There was a satisfying connection. She stepped forward, swiped a glass from the table, and tossed the water over Yeats's shoes.

Yeats made a frightened, high-pitched sound. This was very beautiful in Emily's ears, but the point was Yeats was not making other sounds, sounds that commanded people to kill her, so in the moment he was occupied with the horror of his softening leather, she broke the glass against the edge of the table and sliced it across his throat.

He tried to speak. Little red bubbles popped along his lips. She took the bareword from his fingers as gently as could be. He dropped to his knees, and she should have been turning to face Plath and Masters and whoever else was back there, but instead she just stood and watched him die.

Harry jogged toward the burger place. He thought there must be soldiers about, but couldn't see them. The choppers had retreated; he didn't know why. He circled around the block but saw no one so he came at it from the front. Emily was there. A few bodies lay on the ground. There was a black-suited soldier but his helmet was off and he was standing with his feet loosely apart, not holding a weapon, looking around the town like he was vacationing here.

He kept the rifle ready and began to cross the street. Emily turned to him. She had something in her hand. Her expression was strange.

"Hey," he said. "Em, it's me."

He came toward her and for a moment she didn't know who it was. She had just killed a bunch of people and compromised Masters and her head was full of bees.

But she recognized his expression. It was like the last time she'd been surrounded by death and he'd come for her. He was going to save her again, she saw. Of course he was. He was going to forgive her everything, again.

"Oh, Harry," she said. "It's so good to see you."

He smiled. She'd thought she would never see that again, his smile, and it killed her, because she knew it couldn't last. None of this could last.

"I love you," she said, "but I'm sorry, I need you to do something."

"Sure." He slung the rifle and came toward her, his hands reaching for hers. "Name it."

"*Kikkhf fkattkx hfkixu zttkcu,*" she said. "Shoot me."

BROKEN HILL TO REMAIN SEALED

The Sydney Morning Herald, Vol. 183 Issue 217 Page 14

A government body charged with reviewing the toxicity of Broken Hill—site of the 2019 disaster that killed more than three thousand people—has recommended that the town remain fenced off for an indeterminate time.

The review was triggered by photographs last summer of what appear to be two large helicopters hovering over the town. This fueled long-running local speculation that the town was not uninhabitable, with conspiracy theories proclaiming the town as home to everything from a secret mafia treasure trove to government military programs.

The review, which published a 300-page report today, should hose down such talk, with scientists finding critically high levels of methyl isocarbonate still present in the soil.

"As much as I enjoy a good story, it would be highly dangerous to start thinking it's okay to go have a look at Broken Hill," said spokesperson Henry Lawson. "The town is, unfortunately, a grim reminder of what can happen when people and businesses operate without proper oversight."

Broken Hill remains the site of one of the world's worst environmental disasters.

MEMO

Subject: Re: revisions to models post-BH

Update as per request—report not finalized, don't quote me on this, etc. etc.

Our chief finding is that what we saw in BH was a multilingual effect. Which I realize makes no sense on the face of it, since no relevant parties are/were multilingual to any known degree. But whenever we've seen rejection of this magnitude before, it's been because the recipient is fluent in more than one language. (Can be reliably reproduced in testing: e.g., while counting in Dutch, bilingual subject exhibits increased resistance to compromise in English.) We've theorized that when the brain is keyed into one language, words from another are more likely to be first-stage filtered as nonsense syllables—not actually processed as words, i.e., carriers of meaning.

So the question is, what second language? And—again, don't quote me, data to be crunched—our answer is the language of the bareword. Whatever that is. We haven't dealt with a bareword before, so our knowledge here is sketchy. But we believe a bareword belongs to a fundamental language of the human mind—the tongue in which the human animal speaks to itself at the basest level. The machine language, in essence.

We're still not clear on exactly what relationship existed between V. Woolf and the outlier Harry Wilson—some kind of love affair? But we accept that upon discovering he was alive. She shifted to a primitive, animalistic state. Mentally, she was operating in that underlying language, feeling desire as a bareword.

As we know, when a subject experiences conflict from instructions of roughly equal compulsive power, results are situationally dependent, i.e., unpredictable. That scenario, we're basically talking about free will.

(Note that when instructions conflict, they do not cancel out. Subject experiences desire to do both. Just worth bearing in mind.)

Bottom line, we see no reason to discard established models. No need to throw the baby out with the bathwater. This may sound like we're trying to cover our asses, i.e., avoid admitting flaws in past research, but it's our honest opinion.

I realize this may create something of a political issue, given the current organization restructure/bloodbath. Sorry about that. Although the bigger issue, for me, are the questions raised by this underlying lexicon. What are its words? How many are there? Can they be revealed through lab research, i.e., direct excavation from the brain? Can we learn to speak them? What does it sound like when who we are is expressed in its most fundamental form?

Something to think about.

R. Lowell

[FIVE]

He rose at four and pulled on his pants and boots and jacket. The house was cold as glass and he tried to coax life out of the remnants of the fireplace but there was nothing there. He tucked his hands into his armpits and went outside. The air was frigid, the sky an open box with no real hint of sunlight yet, and he traipsed through the near paddock to the barn. The cow, Hong, heard his approach and mooed hopefully. He led her inside, positioned the bucket, and took his place on the stool. He massaged milk from her teats, resting his forehead against her side for the warmth. He fell asleep like this sometimes, slipping into dreams of death and words. Then Hong would take a step or two away, jerking him awake.

Filling the bucket took eight minutes. It had seemed ridiculously slow at first. He'd craved greater efficiency. But it was a good lesson in reconnecting. He now enjoyed it as a chance to exist in the moment. There was no past or future when you milked a cow. You were just milking.

He carried the bucket back to the house and transferred its contents to six bottles. The cat curled around his boots, purring like a tractor, and he gave her a little, too. He built a little tepee of sticks and newspaper and lit the fire. By then the first rays were creeping along the tree line, and he paused to watch. The best thing about this house was the view. He could walk around it and see forty miles in every direction. If a car was approaching, he would know thirty minutes before it arrived. The sky was wide and empty. It was a good house.

He heard bare feet on floorboards and Emily emerged, her eyes full of sleep, her cotton nightdress running down from her shoulders.

"You should be sleeping," he said.

"You can't tell me what to do."

"No," he said. "You have that backward."

She came to him. They kissed. The fire crackled. She tucked herself against him.

"Want to watch the sun come up?"

"Sure," she said.

He grabbed two blankets from the pile and threw one over the bench seat he'd built on the veranda. He put an arm around her and threw the other blanket over them. She rested her head on his shoulder. The sun freed itself from the tree line and he felt its warmth on his face.

"I love you," she said. She nestled closer, her hand moving up the back of his neck. The wind lifted.

"Don't kill me," he said.

"I'm not going to," she said.

JOIN OUR MAILING LIST!

We hope you have enjoyed this product. For the inside scoop on hot up-coming titles, plus a chance to win prizes, simply fill in the following!

1. Name: ______________________________
2. Address: ______________________________

   ____
3. E-mail: ______________________________
4. Are you a cat person or a dog person? ______________________________
5. What is your favorite color? ______________________________
6. Please select a random number. (Circle one)

   1 2 3 4 5 6 7 8 9 10
7. Do you love your family? ______________________________
8. Why did you do it? ______________________________

____

____

____

____

____

____

____

____

____

____

____

ACKNOWLEDGMENTS

Acknowledgments used to be rare glimpses inside the author's mind when he/she wasn't trying to lie to you. Stephen King had some of the best. They were long and rambling, like you'd caught him after dinner and a few glasses of wine. I grew up in rural Australia, the nearest bookstore a town away, and Stephen King never toured there, not even on a motorcycle*. I didn't even realize authors did tours. Acknowledgments were all I had. They were blogs, before blogs were a thing.

Now blogs are a thing, and tweets, and you never need to wonder what any author thinks about anything. Which is a little sad, I feel, for Acknowledgments. They've been reduced to a parade of names. Important names, if you are the author, or one of the names. The names are the reason we have Acknowledgments. But still. I liked the rambles.

My important names begin with the usual suspects: those people who read my first drafts and then, six months later, my second drafts ("Try to pretend like you don't know what's going to happen"), and so

* In 1997, Stephen King rode across Australia on a Harley-Davidson."Until you get here you don't realize how different it is," he told the *Kalgoorlie Miner*. "[America's West] is empty but you always see a power line or a house twinkling off in the distance. Out here there's fucking nothing."

on, for far too long. You might think this doesn't sound too bad, getting a sneak peek at a book, but that's because you don't realize how terribly broken my drafts are. Imagine your favorite story, only every so often the characters do stupid things for no reason and then nothing ends like it should. It's horrible, right? It's not merely *less good*; it ruins the whole thing. I am very grateful to those people who let me ruin stories for them, especially Todd Keithley, Charles Thiesen, Kassy Humphries, Jason Laker, Jo Keron, and John Schoenfelder.

Thank you to everyone who keeps publishing me. Many people put a great deal of work into each and every book, and if they do a good job, the author gets all the credit. There are editors and marketing people, assistants and copy editors, translators and salespeople, buyers and bookstore employees, designers and techs, and plenty more. Thank you for all the times you did a little more than you had to. In particular, thanks to my U.S. and UK editors, Colin Dickerman and Ruth Tross, who steered me through the final draft with insight and precision, which is like a gift to an author.

Luke Janklow is my go-to guy, literary agent by name, guardian angel by nature. I don't know what I'd do without him, but I bet it would suck. Claire Dippel, the wind beneath Luke's wings, can do just about anything, apparently, while remaining bright and good-natured. Almost suspiciously so. Thank you, both.

Most of all, thank you, Jen, for making this possible. There isn't a single piece of this that works without you. Not the book, not the writing, not me. Definitely not me.

And, hey. You. Thanks for being the kind of person who likes to pick up a book. That's a genuinely great thing. I met a librarian recently who said she doesn't read because books are her job and when she goes home, she just wants to switch off. I think we can agree that that's as creepy as hell. Thank you for seeking out stories, the kind that take place in your brain.